# Threads of the Departed Trilogy

*Thread by thread*
*the strands will twist*
*and you will see the effect*
*as the weaving of lives*
*begins to unravel*
*leaving the fabric of life*
*frayed.*

M A Bonuso

## Threads of the Departed Trilogy

# STRANDS

M.A. Bonuso is a writer, wife, and mother of two sons based in a small town west of St. Louis, MO. After being caught in several economic downturns that forced her in and out of employment and taking a disheartening job in a call center before her family's health insurance ran out, she decided to pursue her dream to write stories that readers would enjoy. Her first novel in the Threads of the Departed Trilogy is *Strands*. She is also the author of *Unraveled* and *Frayed.*

This is a work of fiction. Names, characters, places and incidents are products of the author's imagination, used fictitiously and are not to be construed as real. Any resemblance to actual events, locales, organizations, or persons, living or dead, is entirely coincidental.

Printed by CreateSpace, An Amazon.com Company
THREADS OF THE DEPARTED – TRILOGY
STRANDS


Published by M A Bonuso, Defiance, MO



ISBN: 978-0-9963398-0-3
ASIN: B00Y1NNLOE
eBook ISBN: 978-0-9963398-1-0

Printed in the United States of America
*** Paperbacks edition / May – 2015
*** eBook edition / May – 2015

If you enjoy this book, I really hope you'll do me the favor of leaving a review. You can connect with me at:

www.mabonuso.com
www.facebook.com/mabonuso

BOOKS BY M A BONUSO

THREADS OF THE DEPARTED TRILOGY

STRANDS
UNRAVELED
FRAYED

This book is for my husband, Joseph,
our two sons, Andrew and
Joseph, and my daughter-in-law Becky

---

With all my love

# ACKNOWLEDGMENTS

The author wishes to acknowledge the
invalauable assistance to the following people.

I am sincerely grateful for your time,
your support and your friendship.

My Readers: Carole Aiello, Debbie Brazill,
Carol Sutherland, Helen Zahner, Nancy Yarmouth,
Gerry Letourneau, Candi McClanhan,
Larry Beekman, Tom Eisenbeis

My dear friends who provided priceless
knowledge and assistance to the story:
Gary Pyles, Terri Pyles, Jason Robb,
Charlie Letourneau, Lt. Jeff Lange,
James Steinlage, Kristin Wilder McCollum,
Lloyd Hekhuis, Gwen Ramsey,
Stephen Manoj Thompson
Camille Johnson and her girlfriends
(Thank you for Jerry Richards)

First Review Edits: Mitchell Gerringer, Delia Carr
Assistant Reviewer/Edits: Karen Silverberg,
Andy Aiello
Final Review Edits: Ellen Geerling

Special thanks to Chris Dickhans.
Without her assistance in helping me land a new job,
I would never have written this trilogy.

## Threads of the Departed Trilogy

Historical Fiction Action Romance Mystery

## Webster-Mirriam Definition of Weaving

**Weaving** is a method of fabric production in which two distinct sets of yarns or threads are interlaced at right angles to form a fabric or cloth. The other methods are knitting, lace making, felting, and braiding or plaiting. The longitudinal threads are called the warp and the lateral threads are the weft or filling. (*Weft* or *woof* is an old English word meaning "that which is woven".) The method in which these threads are interwoven affects the characteristics of the cloth. Cloth is usually woven on a loom, a device that holds the warp threads in place while filling threads are woven through them. A fabric band which meets this definition of cloth (warp threads with a weft thread winding between) can also be made using other methods, including tablet weaving, back-strap, or other techniques without looms.

The way the warp and filling threads interlace with each other is called the weave. The majority of woven products are created with one of three basic weaves: plain weave, satin weave, or twill. Woven cloth can be plain (in one colour or a simple pattern), or can be woven in decorative or artistic designs.

# STRANDS

# Chapter 1

**The** slow-ticking clock repeated the same tune, as time raced away with each disquieting heartbeat thumping on Carrie's eardrums. She looked at the clock again. No way could it be 2:00 a.m. on Sunday morning! Carrie had begun weaving that afternoon around three o'clock and had only taken a powder break at seven.

Getting up and stretching her stiff back, Carrie went to the kitchen to make a sandwich with hot, brown sugar-encrusted country ham. The ham dripped with juice that would make decent red-eye gravy for tomorrow morning's grits. She took a bite and washed it down with a glass of iced tea loaded with sugar. This was eastern North Carolina and all that hand wringing over an extra pound or two hadn't made it to the shoreline . . . and make no mistake, they'd shoot it down if it tried.

Even with the luscious lingering smell of ham and cornbread, reality vanished when Carrie wove, but Father Time wouldn't stop his tap dance, not even for weaving. Finally, when a broken strand took too long to fix, Carrie knew it was time to quit.

Carrie's Grandma Hattie had once been the ruling matriarch of this eighteenth-century, colonial revival-style, humble abode.

French doors swung open from Grandma Hattie's bedroom onto the balcony overlooking the attractive estate. Although the house felt terribly lonely since Grandma had passed several months ago, it looked the same as the day she died.

Grandma Hattie, a thick-skinned woman with sloping shoulders, plump waistline, bluish-gray hair, and hazel eyes, had been an avid weaver. She had two large looms and several smaller looms scattered about the house. She gave away her work as gifts to family and friends who displayed them proudly.

Even though Carrie's grandma would never have admitted it, the way her intricate detail and the adaptation of color intertwined within the weave made her a supreme artist.

Carrie's love of weaving, a gift from her grandma's soul, continued even after her death. Weaving was Carrie's peace, her reclusion, her solitary diversion.

Carrie had inherited not only her grandma's love of weaving, but also her father's blue-gray eyes and tousled auburn hair. She wove into the early morning on a beast of a loom made of heavy pine. It ate up nearly every square inch of floor space on the second floor that looked onto the wildflower-filled flatlands. One of the smaller looms would have been more manageable when she was learning at age 10, but this was the loom she begged her grandmother to teach her how to weave on and it had spoiled her for all others.

Hattie herself used to weave on this room-consuming, wooden loom, and on this loom, she taught Carrie the arts of self-discipline, patience, and perseverance that were needed when you broke a thread on the beast. It was during one of those early lessons that Carrie first heard curse words through the door and unladylike epithets that could peel paint off wood as she tiptoed down the creaky wooden floor of the hallway. After a while, she got used to the swearing and became skilled at steering clear while her grandma fixed the firmness and tension of a broken thread. When the swearing stopped, she would cautiously peek through the open door, often seeing her grandma's untidy graying hair falling limply over her right eye while she crawled on her knees using liquor bottles or fishing lures to make the broken thread's tension just right so that the loom kept the fibers stretched tight and spaced properly.

Her grandma was a natural teacher, and weaving was a constant lesson. Certain common aggravations made weavers a resourceful bunch of practical and patient problem solvers. Hattie's approach was to use whatever was in the toolbox and get on with it. Wine also helped, though Carrie knew that little trick hadn't come from her grandma. Grandma Hattie was all about the whiskey.

It was late. Tired, but not too tired, the wine she had been thinking of suddenly sounded too good to pass up. A respectable bottle of Cabernet Sauvignon sat on the countertop in the kitchen that would do just fine. Opening the creaky door to the loom room and walking down the steps, Carrie turned on the light, uncorked the bottle, and poured a glass. It was a generous pour. Corking the bottle and taking it with her, she headed back upstairs and out onto the second floor balcony overlooking the front of the house.

The clapboards were a weathered mustard color now, but the construction of the porch protected its original bright yellow. Her grandparents, Scott and Hattie, had painted the shutters a bright crimson when they bought the house from a cousin right after they married, and Carrie had no plans to change anything.

Two massive, red-brick chimneys, one on each end of the house, two stacks apiece, served four giant fireplaces that helped keep the rooms toasty during the cold, wet winters. The sturdy heart-pine framing steadied the house during the wicked storms that sometimes moved up Pamlico Sound, pushing water into the creek rising to a short distance from the side of the house. The path that ended at the crimson front door followed the creek bank from town to a circular drive elegantly announced with clipped boxwood hedges and, more recently, lampposts. Century-old crimson crepe myrtles framed the covered front porch.

Carrie sat on a yellow-flowered, cushioned wicker couch, embracing the splendor of the night sky. Tonight it was thick with stars and garnished with the brilliant upended crescent moon that appeared on the state flag of South Carolina. *No offense, Charleston, but screw you! Beaufort County's got your moon right here . . . No more wine tonight*, Carrie thought as she sat gazing at the stars thinking about her beloved grandma.

While her grandma was alive, it had been her desire that Carrie concentrate only on her studies. She had requested that Carrie not pursue finding a job, other than the occasional hours she could pick up at the yarn shop. This may have been for Grandma's own selfish reasons—to ensure that Carrie would be able to come home on the weekends and holidays.

However, Carrie was resourceful. With her small portable wooden loom in tow, she made extra money at college by selling her crafted wares to the other students.

She recalled the day her grandma passed away from a rare pulmonary disease, lymphangioleiomyomatosis, and left Carrie the house. Grandpa Scott had already been deceased for twenty-something years. Hattie laughed at the morbid irony of dying from a disease called 'LAM'. She thought it was appropriate after the many lamb sheerings she'd performed and from which she had processed the wool into the yarn she used for her artistic projects. Grandma Hattie kept her sense of humor until the day she died and probably took it with her to the grave. At 63, Carrie knew her grandma was too young to die. At 25, Carrie also knew she was too young to let go of certain deeply held emotions.

Hattie's disease was diagnosed in 1984. That was four years ago, but LAM was a slow killer. While Carrie attended the University of North Carolina in Chapel Hill, she came home often and noticed each time that her grandma had a little more trouble breathing.

Grandma Hattie had a cough for a few years prior, but always said, "It's just a tickle," and flatly refused to see her doctor. In fact, there were two reasons for her refusal. First, when it came to her health, she was a serial procrastinator with an extra helping of denial. Second, her doctor was the same doctor who failed to diagnose her husband's heart condition and treated him instead for acid reflux. As a result, he died at age 51 of a massive heart attack. In all fairness to Grandpa Scott's doctor, he did have terrible acid reflux along with a few symptoms of heart trouble.

Grandma Hattie knew this but had long considered all physicians to be either incompetent quacks or stupid expletives—depending on her mood and to whom she was talking.

Carrie was sure that her grandma had passed away with the notion affirmed in her own mind, since they initially told her she had emphysema.

Debra Jennings, Hattie's only daughter and Carrie's mother, had problems of her own. Shortly before her father, Scott, died, Debra went into a drug rehab program out of state. She had fallen on some ice during a heavy winter storm two years before and developed an addiction to Percodan that she added Quaaludes to, just to mix it up a little. Carrie was only two at the time.

Debra was a thin, dark brunette with Grandpa Scott's honey glow tan and was naïve to a fault. As her drug habit spiraled out of control, she became an egocentric, bitter human being who stole from everyone to support her habit. She also did a little dealing, but wasn't lucky in her attempts. By the time Debra was finally found guilty of felony possession with intent to distribute, her mother Hattie was angry and exhausted. She cut Debra off, and Hattie died without ever mentioning her daughter's name again.

Tom Pyles, Carrie's biological father, left them cold on a wintery day when Debra gave birth to Carrie. He was a thin, wavy, dark blonde who couldn't draw in a mustache with a paintbrush. He and Debra had been high school friends and hooked up during a high school party. They left the party early, as Tom persuaded Debra into drinking and smoking weed in his car while listening to rock and roll. Things got heavy in the back of the 1960 Corvair. Later, when Debra told Tom she was pregnant, he did the respectable thing and married her at a small ceremony with the Justice of the Peace in a nearby town. When Carrie was still of a young age, Grandma Hattie explained to her what had happened the day she was born. When Debra delivered Carrie, the nurse placed her in her mother's arms and at this moment Tom asked for a divorce. Then he disappeared.

When he left, Debra tore up every picture of Tom and neither she nor Carrie ever went looking for him.

Carrie's grandparents loved her more than their own life. With Tom in Timbuktu, and Debra doing time in a prison somewhere out of state, they became Carrie's legal guardians. This was good for all of them.

After high school, Carrie set off to UNC to earn a Bachelor of Fine Arts with a minor in business. The white-framed photograph on her dresser displayed Grandma Hattie and her at her high school graduation before the disease began to affect Hattie's physical appearance.

Hattie was a native Carolina beauty and the graying hair she wore on the long side was always tied in a ponytail at the nape of her neck. She wore a sharply tailored silk dress in the color of chicory blossoms with small, white, covered buttons and short sleeves. The hat, however, shadowed the dress. In the South, it was all about the hat, and Hattie's was a light, wide-brimmed, straw hat trimmed with a trio of silk gardenias.

By that time, Grandma Hattie's lung function was weakening, but no one would have known it. When Carrie Pyles' name was announced at the graduation ceremony, Hattie stuck two fingers in her mouth and managed a bellowing whistle that embarrassed Carrie while also making her proud.

Carrie always knew where her grandma was in the crowd and loved having her as a cheerleader. Walking off the stage, Carrie looked up to Grandma Hattie and Patty and blew them both a kiss.

Patty McMurphy was Hattie's closest friend and had driven them to the ceremony. The two women were inseparable as they smiled and beamed on Carrie like a ray of sunshine. Patty loved taking pictures, and it was this picture that Carrie now had proudly displayed on her dresser.

After Carrie's college graduation, she settled back into the pleasing, sunny bedroom that had been hers for so long. She slept with feather pillows, on a mattress that was high in the middle since she only slept on one side of it, making it look somewhat like the gopher burrows she used to see out in the countryside west of Raleigh. The elaborate and ornate crown molding was painted a warm taupe and the plastered walls a soft topaz. On one wall was mounted a pair of old portraits in simple flea-market frames. One portrait featured a sagacious girl of maybe fifteen, the other a rosy-cheeked younger brother and his greyhound. Things never changed much, really.

Carrie's reverie faded as she realized how tired she was. Finishing the glass of wine that had a crisp chill on it now, she placed it and the near-empty bottle on the hall table and flipped on the bathroom light to get ready for bed. Squinting from the glaring light, Carrie managed to complete her nightly ritual and a couple minutes later crawled into bed and closed her eyes. For the first time in many years, she sent up a short prayer.

"Thank you, Lord, for your many blessings. Please keep my Grandma Hattie and Grandpa Scott safe in your fold. Amen."

***

Waking up to the aroma of freshly brewed Carolina coffee this morning, she looked at the white alarm clock that displayed a reasonable 10:28 a.m. Entering the kitchen and pouring a cup of deep, buttery, chocolate coffee, she opened the unlocked front door and looked out at the blue sky with its thin, wispy clouds dancing by. In just an oversized T-shirt and boxer shorts, she reached underneath the hedge to fetch the newspaper. The paperboy's skill would not get him onto any professional baseball team. Carrie pushed her arm through a spider web, making her dance around foolishly. She shook her arm to free the attached web. Struggling to catch her breath, she squeamishly grasped a small stick and dragged the paper out into clearer view. She loathed spiders and webs even more than stubbing her toe in the middle of the night.

Carrie opened the newspaper and started her morning off by looking for a little humor, since the day didn't always end that way, and so, just to be safe, she read her horoscope first. The brief prediction for Sagittarius read:

"Today is full of surprises; the strands of life may become tangled."

This was not an auspicious sign for a weaver. Good thing she was not superstitious . . . at least not much, anyway. She fortified herself with a biscuit split filled with strawberry jam and washed it down with her third cup of coffee. Snarky horoscope aside, a trip to the yarn shop was today's first order of business.

The sky was an ocean blue and now full of fluffy white clouds. A slight, cool breeze uplifted the soft May afternoon. A couple of kids, not allowed in the shop with their drinks, sat on a bench outside the door picking out cloud animals, though Carrie wasn't sure *Jerkface* qualified as an animal. They, however, seemed to think it was hilarious.

The yarn store resided in a beautifully renovated, timber frame, eight-horse barn behind Patty McMurphy's house and was the first yarn shop in which Carrie ever set foot.

Carrie's fictitious aunt, Patty McMurphy, was the proprietor and occupied the house within a short walking distance from the shop. The lot rested on higher ground just a little past Sparrow

Creek, overlooking the bank of the Sound to the east. It was in close relation to the sleepy old town of Chocowinity.

The black shutters on Patty's house, set against the massively strong, tall, wooden walls, made it feel suspended in time, as if awaiting the original admiral's return home from an adventure at sea. Mysteriously, the large domicile faced inland, but there was little written history on the property and the cause for this orientation.

The store sat apart from the house to the rear and at a right angle to it, surrounded by beautifully meandering hedges of Carolina jasmine in full bloom, their perfume waxing lazily in the early morning sea breeze. The essence was irrefutably charming.

Patty McMurphy had owned the shop, called Pheasant Mill Wool and Weaving, for more than twenty years. She and Hattie had known each other since high school and had played on the women's baseball team together. Carrie often visited the shop with her grandma while she was growing up and used the opportunities to pick up yarn and listen to the conversation of a certain pair of women who were as deeply rooted to Beaufort County as the shop itself.

Hattie and Patty chatted, raised their eyebrows, and giggled a lot. The two of them were Tar Heel fans, and Carrie never knew what she might hear when they were together.

This was Carrie's first visit since her grandma's passing. With a heavy heart, she reached for the doorknob. The bright red doorbell jingled as she entered the shop.

This was fiber heaven.

The exterior of the store retained much of its former character with its cedar shake roof and slabs of unfinished cedar on a stone foundation. Obvious renovations included the outside horse doors sealed closed, a black door with a large glass window, and an aged, bronzed doorknob. Two large nine-pane, double-hung windows trimmed in black crossed the front of the shop and a large skylight filtered the sunlight. The face of the barn had been well restored, but inside was where the real magic started.

The structure had been converted to usable storage many years ago with quarter-sawn heart pine wood with longleaf southern yellow pine floors replacing the horse stalls.

Where horses once munched on hay, yarn in every imaginable color and type of fiber was stacked in bins from floor to ceiling. The cones, skeins, and balls were sorted loosely by the weight system familiar to yarn lovers—bulky, chunky, worsted, aran, dk, sport—then by brand. Large fruit baskets scattered about held Patty's own wool yarn dyed on the property, and there were sections for painted rovings for spinners and raw fleece sheared from local sheep for fiber artists interested in the sheep-to-shawl process. The tack room had been converted to a space for books, patterns, needles, notions, and fiber tools such as hand carders and wonderful hand-turned drop spindles. Above the tack room was a loft containing used spinning wheels and a couple of small looms made available by patrons offering them up for sale. In another room with new spinning wheels and several rigid heddle looms on stands, along with a multitude of tools and parts for looms commonly in use, in the center of the space were comfy chairs and a loveseat for knitters. There was a separate room to the side with weaving looms, warping boards, and a spinning wheel for the weaving students.

Patty heard the door jingle and came out of the back room, looked up over her black-framed readers, and with a warm greeting said, "Hello, Carrie dear, how y'all doin?"

Patty had felt Hattie's death deeply and called Carrie every day for the first week or so after. While Patty had never struck Carrie as the grieving kind, Carrie knew she was lonely and seemed to be searching for, not comfort exactly, but maybe a little closure or companionship anyway.

Carrie knew Patty didn't have to be alone. Patty was ageless and lovely, petite and willowy with milky skin and glossy, reddish-orange hair flecked with strands of white. Her deep mossy eyes were set in the delicate face of a wood sprite. A slightly crooked tooth added character instead of stealing beauty. With customers, she was charm itself, but outside the shop, she was unexpectedly cool and reserved with nearly everyone except Hattie.

Today, Patty appeared to be her usual self again. There had been little time to visit the shop while settling Grandma Hattie's estate, and at first, it was a bittersweet feeling to be here without her, but Carrie felt genuinely happy to see Patty and smiled back.

Two women smiled at Carrie as they left the store with their purchases and gathered up the boys outside.

"Hi, Miss Patty, I'm good. I just thought I'd drop in and see if anything new has come in."

Patty smiled back.

"I've been commissioned to make a hall runner for a house being restored over in New Bern and the design is a little different for me. Here's my initial sketch. I need to look at some yarn."

Patty shook her head and reviewed the design, knowing Carrie's routine and her need to 'always look' at some yarn.

Patty glanced at the drawing, didn't speak, but raised a finger as if to say, "Just wait a minute, I've got something for you to see." She disappeared into the storeroom behind the studio. Moving about and looking around, the fixtures in the old store were so familiar and yet Carrie noticed a subtle change in the way the room felt and smelled.

Carrie caught a noise and stood motionless.

It was an odd sound, very faint. A chill moved up Carrie's arm, as if someone had brushed past her and touched her arm with ice-cold fingers. It was a feeling she had experienced several times over the past years.

She had also heard strange sounds in the shop and felt the cold before, but only in the yarn area, not in the studio. It sounded like a clatter and then something falling. Its origin was shrouded in the unknown.

She had asked Patty about it once when she worked in the shop as a teenager.

Patty just returned a strange look and said, "Animals probably. Who knows? Maybe the barn is haunted."

Now, trying to move from that spot, Carrie felt as if both her feet were cemented to the floor. Breaking free of the feeling, she stumbled slightly. Carrie was not the most coordinated of people.

Crazy, Carrie thought.

Patty seemed to be taking a long time. Carrie wandered back to a corner of the old tack room area and turned around to look at the sley hooks on a wooden shelf when a large, black moth with white-stripe flew up from below and straight into her eye.

"Durn it," Carrie cursed. She ducked and swatted a little too fast, lost her balance and fell against a wooden shelf. A colorful tapestry backdrop collapsed sideways, pulling one of the ceiling anchors out of the wood and causing a sequential chain reaction. The shelving assembly came crashing down in slow motion, with several items missing her by a hair. The other shelves fell like dominoes, dumping small weaving utensils onto the floor in every direction.

In a panic, Patty reappeared and stood in the background looking pale and startled.

"Oh, God, I'm so sorry, Patty. A moth flew right into my eye and I lost my balance trying to swat at it. I'll pick all this mess up," Carrie said, surveying the damage.

Carrie moved toward the wall and looked to see where the tapestry had come loose. Something looked odd. The walls around the area were vertical, heart-pine boards of assorted widths like the floor, only more smoothly planed. In the section that had been hidden behind the tapestry, three or four of the fallen boards had been noticeably bashed in and a wall of dark gray metal was exposed. The opening was narrow and flush.

Removing the rest of the disarranged shelves, Carrie followed the indentation upwards and saw that it extended to the line of the ceiling and possibly beyond. There was definitely air movement along the opening and a musty smell seeped from behind. Curious, but nervous about doing further damage, she stepped back and looked at Patty.

Patty, with her back turned, was on her hands and knees, picking up the bobbins that had rolled all over the place. She was visibly shaken.

Carrie, guilty and embarrassed, went to Patty and dropped to the floor, placed her arm around Patty and assisted her to her feet.

"Leave that, Miss Patty, honestly. Let me get you some tea. You can sit over here, and I'll take care of the mess I made."

Carrie looked back toward the altered wall. Wow! While she had been talking to Patty, the gap between the boards had closed. She was sure that was not her imagination.

In the meantime, Patty had slipped into a chair and sat very still with her eyes closed. She was breathing unevenly and the pinkish color had fallen from her face.

"Miss Patty?"

Patty was apparently flustered and let out a low sigh.

"I'm all right, sugar. For sum reas'n I just felt a lil' dizzy."

"Let me go get you some tea."

"A cup of tea would be nice. Don't feel bad 'bout the shelf. I'm surprised sumthin' like that hann't happened soona'. I'm just glad you weren't hurt."

"I'm fine, but you stay here and I'll be right back with your tea."

"I'm goin' to the lavatory to put some cold wata' on my face," Patty said as she slowly stood up.

Carrie went into the kitchenette, filled the kettle with water, and turned the pilot on, dropping a tea bag into a cup. She refused to think about anything else until the tea was ready.

Patty hadn't returned yet when Carrie got back with the hot sweet tea, so she placed it on the candle stand beside the chair.

Moving the mess on the floor with her feet, Carrie returned to the gray metal wall and noticed it was hung on hinges. For a moment, she heard a slight creaking noise as she pushed it back just far enough to peek past the edge of the hidden entryway. She looked up and then down. The door seemed to be suspended on a pulley with a small metal grip attached low near the floor. Carrie grasped the handle, pushing just a little, and the whole door slid up toward the ceiling, opening a void several feet high and maybe two feet deep. A rush of air blew past her and the stench of rotten eggs hit her in the face, throwing her back and making her gag. Carrie wrapped her hand around her nose, stepped forward, and peered in a bit further. There was a thick layer of cobwebs covering the opening. Maybe this was a crawlspace of some kind, she thought, but she couldn't recall the shelf being moved—ever.

They were on the high bank side of the river, she remembered, but likely swamp water had leached in, probably snakes too—and definitely spiders. She shivered.

A dirty, damp rope dangled on the inside of the door near the bottom by the oxidized metal handle, which would allow some one to pull the door down if it moved up and out of reach. The rope was clearly disintegrating.

Fairly certain she'd glimpsed stairs of some kind, Carrie's first thought was to make sure the door didn't close on her if she entered. There was a hook on the rope, probably from an old hook-and-eye closure. That meant there would be an eye on the wall. Stepping in just enough to reach behind the planks, she felt a round metal loop screwed securely into the wood. Dropping the hook into its eye, Carrie turned and looked around the store for a flashlight.

She was more than apprehensive about what she might see at the bottom, but her curiosity won this time.

# Chapter 2

In fact, with the dull beam streaming from the flashlight, Carrie couldn't see much of anything.

As she approached the top of the steps, she was oblivious to Patty's whereabouts. Carrie surveyed the musty wooden stairs going down into the secret structure with shaky hands and jerky knees. The air surrounded her with a strange chill, pricking and biting at her.

Using the flashlight, she knocked down the sticky, sickening spider webs she despised. As she slowly went down the wooden steps into a constricted band of darkness, she stirred up specks of dust that floated in and out of the light before finally drifting down like snowflakes in a wintery storm.

Tentatively, she shifted her weight onto the first step, then another, then two more.

So far, so good.

Stooping and bending ever so slightly under the low ceiling, she reached out to take hold of an iron pin protruding from the wall. It wiggled in its hole, and there was a risk it was rusted enough to break off, but it would do for balance. Noticing several of these hooks, she used each one to make her way down the stairs. Each pin had an eye on the end aligned vertically, as if intended to hold a rope that may have provided a rudimentary railing.

Carrie lowered her head a bit more, allowing her eyes to adjust to the darkness of the underground room. She could not see more than two feet in front of her, at best.

*Maybe this is not such a good idea*, she thought when reaching the last step. Her knees bounced off one another like two clacker balls.

She glanced back up at the door—her only escape if there was a snake or something worse down in this hole.

Carrie's legs wouldn't move. Her feet were frozen to the last step. Her hand trembled uncontrollably while holding onto the last iron pin and the goosebumps on her arms were unrestrained.

Listening intently and not hearing anything moving about, she stepped down onto the dirt-crusted floor. A frozen cloud of something touched her nose and she let go with a huge sneeze. Her whole body convulsed and the flashlight flew out of her hand and landed on the floor about four feet away.

"Great!"

The light reflected dimly off the floor as it lay in the sheeting of dust and dirt. Slowly, she moved her feet, feeling like her ankles were buried in concrete. Then she noticed the floor. What had felt like hard-packed dirt, she discovered, was really a dirty and stale hardwood floor.

Carrie's sense of smell had all but shut down. As she approached the flashlight, she could see nothing of the surroundings but had a sense that it was an open area, though not a large one.

Stepping forward, she picked up the flashlight and saw that the glass had cracked.

"Shit!" she exclaimed as the light weakened. Knocking it hard against her hand several times didn't help much. The dim light vanished into the chasm of this gloomy place.

Without venturing further, she aimed the diminishing light outward and slowly scanned the area.

She saw a couple of large framed paintings leaning up against some crates and wondered if they were copies of famous artists' work.

Various-sized boxes and wooden crates were stacked up along the walls.

Wondering if she was in some type of cave, she took three steps forward and swiped at the cobwebs that hung from the ceiling.

"Durn, I hate going through cobwebs," she said aloud.

Then she froze and choked on a scream.

She was not alone.

There in the corner was a woman with red hair. The woman didn't move, but the hair on the back of Carrie's neck stood at full attention. With a flash of insight, she realized her error. It was a painting, a full-length portrait. Surrendering into full retreat toward the stairs, Carrie imagined the cold deepening with every step she took.

That's stupid, she thought, it's just a cellar for chrissake.

Embarrassed that she was a coward, she nevertheless decided next time to get someone else to come down there with her. Suddenly the cold reached around her waistline, embracing her bladder and she had to pee, badly.

At that moment, there was a loud noise from upstairs.

"Miss Patty! Oh, my God!"

She wondered how long she had been down here. Shaken out of her freezing trepidation, Carrie climbed quickly back up the steps, hoping the fading flashlight would keep her from falling on her face. Upon reaching the cramped landing, she flipped the hook out of its eye, took hold of the handle and pulled. She watched the door slide smoothly back into its berth.

"That's just wild."

Carrie dodged the fallen shelving and merchandise still scattered about on the floor and all but ran to the bathroom, kicking items out of the way, unfastening her jeans as quickly as she could. Thankful that there were no customers in the store at the time, she barely made it to the toilet.

Washing up and exiting the bathroom, she realized she hadn't seen Miss Patty and noticed her tea still on the candle stand.

Nervously Carrie called out, "Miss Patty?" She slowly walked around the shop biting on her cuticles.

Taking a glance up into the loft, there still was no sign of her. Carrie checked the studio and looked out toward Patty's house and again into the cool neutral light of the shop. Seeing spools, threads, bobbins, hooks, and shuttles strewn all over the floor from the fallen shelves, she began to panic. She made a beeline for the moving wall, thinking irrationally that she may have shut Patty inside the wall.

But she didn't get that far.

From a shadow in a corner to the left of the tack area, she saw two feet sticking out into the light, almost as if a house had fallen on the woman the feet belonged to.

"Oh, God," Carrie said fretfully as she rushed over, dropped to the ground and instinctively leaned down to Patty's face to check to see if she was still breathing. Her lips were faintly blue. There was no sign of life. Carrie shook Patty's shoulders and yelled, "*Miss Patty! — Miss Patty!* —**Holy Shit!**"

As she reached for the black, rotary-dial phone on a nearby table with trembling hands, the phone fell to the ground. She grabbed the cord, pulled it toward her and dialed 9-1-1.

"9-1-1. What's your emergency?"

Carrie's words came tumbling out faster than a racehorse out of the gate.

"I need an ambulance at Patty McMurphy's shop, Pheasant Mill Wool and Weaving. She's not breathing and her lips are turning blue. Hurry, please. I'm here by myself and I need to do something . . . CPR or something. Please help me!"

"I'm goin' to help you ma'am. My name is Janisa. What's your address, sweet pea?"

"814 Bay Ridge, in Beaufort County near the banks. We're in the barn behind the house. She's on the floor and—"

Janisa calmly intervened, "Thank you, sweet pea. The ambulance is on the way. What's your name, sugar?"

"Carrie. My name is Carrie Pyles."

"OK, Miss Carrie. The ambulance is on its way to 8-1-4 Bay Ridge, in Beaufort County. OK?"

Moving back towards Patty, the phone fell from her shoulder and bounced off the floor.

"**Shit**," Carrie said aloud and dropped to her knees to put two fingers to Patty's neck.

There was no pulse.

Placing her cheek down to Patty's nostrils, pinching her nostrils closed, Carrie lifted Patty's head and breathed deeply into her cold blue lips. Carrie slowly started CPR, nervously pumping her heart up and down with crossed hands, and repeated this several times. She could hear the siren in the distance.

Gently lifting Patty's head and chin back to open her airway, Carrie continued performing CPR when the door burst open.

Two paramedics came through the doorway with their kit and a gurney before Carrie could even straighten up.

"Back here," Carrie yelled.

The two paramedics, both men, one tall and thick, the other a small, rounder man, rushed forward as Carrie stumbled back and watched. One of them started CPR and the other began taking vitals. Patty was still lifeless and Carrie saw one of them firing up a defibrillator. In a matter of a few moments, she heard "Clear!" Whump. Check pulse. Nothing. "Clear!" Whump. Check pulse—nothing.

As the taller paramedic continued CPR, the smaller partner reported in on his radio. A salt-and-pepper-haired police officer with a full gray mustache had followed the paramedics in and gently but firmly led Carrie back a few steps and began taking information.

Carrie knew she was speaking, but was so completely tuned in to the paramedics that she couldn't hear her own voice. Suddenly, she burst into tears, but the cop was a pro and advised her to stay where she was. He grabbed a chair for her to sit on, then one for himself and continued as if nothing was going on behind them. He asked about the shelving and the mess on the floor, when Carrie realized he was inquiring to see if there had been an accident. She told him in a rush about the moth and how she'd lost her balance and knocked down several wooden shelves, which caused the mess, but said nothing about the gray metal door or what was down below. Twenty minutes or more had gone by and the paramedics, having done their work efficiently, lifted Miss Patty onto a wheeled stretcher with the gentle respect reserved for the newly dead. Carrie abruptly stood up and, before the cop could intervene, she stopped one of them by grabbing his arm.

"Please, tell me—*is she gone*?"

"We can't raise a pulse, ma'am. We are goin' to take her to the hospital. Are you a relative?"

"No, I'm her goddaughter. I'm coming with you," Carrie said.

"You can't ride in the ambulance, ma'am, but you can follow behind. Does she have any immediate family we can contact?"

Shaking her head, Carrie spoke quietly, "No, I don't think so. Where will you be taking her?"

The larger paramedic was not helpful and Carrie took an immediate dislike to his contrived demeanor. He was a thick-necked, tall man with a bulging belly, blonde messy hair and was, apparently, a jerk. His nametag read Marcus, but she had settled on *Dick-head*. He addressed her matter-of-factly as she felt her frustration rising.

"She'll be going to Memorial Hospital on Eighth Street. That's the closest hospital," Marcus advised without looking her in the eye as he wrote something down on paper.

Heading quickly for the door, the cop detained Carrie just long enough to ask if she knew who could lock up the place.

"I can," she said as she grabbed the keys from the register and saw Patty's purse. Clutching it under her arm, Carrie actually managed to get out the door, locking it behind her.

The officer handed Carrie his card as the paramedics closed the ambulance rear doors.

The last hour had been a blur. Carrie realized she had barely seen Patty since she arrived. All she really wanted was for one of these guys to confirm what was already presumed and to quit patronizing her. She touched the arm of the younger man and he flinched.

She realized then that she had seen him before, but couldn't recall where—although she knew it was recent. There was no way she'd forget a face like his, slightly long, black, straight hair, pale blue eyes, a trimmed goatee around his mouth. He was a little shorter than Dick-head. Very nice looking, but he also did not intend to answer her.

"Do you know where the hospital is, ma'am? We have to leave."

"Is she dead? Please tell me. She was my grandmother's best friend. I'm not stupid."

"Well, Miss—?"

"Carrie."

He flashed a dimpled smile at her. "Miss Carrie, they'll talk to you when we get to the hospital. Honest, that's all I can tell you."

His nametag read Travis.

Travis didn't wait for her to speak as he jumped into the passenger side of the ambulance. Marcus flipped on the lights and sped off.

The ambulance had gained considerable distance. Carrie's thoughts were a blank as she blew through yellow traffic signals ignoring the speed limit. The hospital was now in sight.

When the ambulance turned about a half mile up the street, she noticed red lights blazing and flashing in her rearview mirror. It was a traffic cop.

**"Shit!"** *I'll make this quick. He'll surely let me get on to the hospital. It's right there.*

She pulled over with Memorial Hospital in clear view.

A fine-looking man wearing dark sunglasses sauntered up to her driver's side window. Carrie was in no mood to waste precious time trying to reason with this cop but couldn't afford to antagonize him either. She spoke quickly as she rolled down her window.

"It's Mrs. McMurphy from the yarn store. The ambulance is taking her to Memorial Hospital. She wasn't breathing. I was there and—"

"Ma'am, you need to take a breath," he said with ease.

"I *need* to get to Memorial right now. Someone needs to be with her. I don't think she has any family. I just need to get to that hospital—it's right there," she said as she pointed up the street and continued on with no small amount of agitation. "You can follow me if you want, but I need to go."

"License and registration, ma'am."

"Are you kidding me? I need to get to the hospital." *This cop wants a pissing contest.*

"License and registration, please, I'm not going to ask again."

Taking the wallet from her purse, Carrie handed him her license.

The shiny badge the cop wore displayed Sgt. Lament. Flipping the console open, she snatched up the registration and handed it to him. Carrie was fuming when she saw the ambulance disappear from her sight.

Carrie watched him walk back to his police car from the rearview mirror and thought, *Screw this shit. I'll be at the hospital. Come get me.* Then she took off from the curb and headed straight for the red lights announcing the emergency room.

A parking spot was open just past the Emergency Room entrance. Carrie parked her 1983 Honda Accord and quickly leaped out of her car, slamming the door before Sergeant Lament could catch up to her.

Carrie ran into the emergency room and saw Travis leaning against the front desk talking to a young, thin, very blonde nurse.

"Hey, Travis, do you know where they took Mrs. McMurphy?"

"Hey, Miss Carrie, she's in an examination area in another part of the hospital. The doctor should be out in a bit."

She assumed Travis had spared her some angst by choosing not to use the word 'morgue'.

At that moment, Sergeant Lament blew into the emergency room like a strengthening snowstorm pulling off the Atlantic Coast. He was not smiling. He placed his hands on his waist and stared at Carrie—fuming, as if she must have lost her mind somewhere on the road. She was afraid that in two shakes he would reach for his handcuffs and take her off to jail. Carrie floated a pitiful tear toward Travis' boyishly handsome face.

*Oh, my God.* Carrie realized she had seen Travis before at a local diner.

"He's here for me, Travis. I was right behind the ambulance rushing to get here, and he pulled me over just down the street. I took off when he went back to his car to check and see if I was a serial killer or something."

Travis grinned.

With the cop an arm's length away, Travis told her to stay put as he addressed Sergeant Lament. Travis was shorter with rounded shoulders and the sergeant was tall and confident with strong muscular arms. His chiseled mouth resembled Michelangelo's David.

"Hey, Phil, did Miss Carrie do somethin' wrong?"

Phil paid no attention to Travis' attempt at conversation.

They knew each other, but of course they did. Travis was a paramedic and Lament was a cop. Their paths probably crossed all the time.

She kept her mouth shut for once, waiting anxiously to see where this conversation would go.

Sergeant Lament turned and walked toward her. Carrie swore she could feel the pounding of his steps on the concrete underneath her feet as her stomach reached up and grabbed her throat.

He's really going to arrest me, she thought, trembling.

Foolishly, Carrie opened her mouth again. It must have been the adrenaline speaking.

"I'm sorry I left you back there, but you have to understand, I needed to get here. Travis was waiting for me—to tell me what was going on with Mrs. McMurphy. I had to get here," she asserted nervously, practically shouting at the sergeant.

Travis put his hand to his mouth and coughed a little, choking back a laugh. She could see the small dimples spreading deliciously across his face. It was the sole bright spot in her day.

Sergeant Lament gave an exasperated sigh as he handed back her registration, license and a ticket for doing 55 in a 30 mile-per-hour construction zone.

He looked her square in the eyes, over his stupid sunglasses, and said, "Have a nice evening, ma'am."

Carrie exploded with unladylike words as Travis dragged her by the waist outside.

"That cop is a low-life piece of shit. What a jackass! God, I hate that bastard, son of a bitch—whistle dick." She couldn't stop herself. Travis chose to do the right thing and wait her out.

Pacing back and forth, she continued her rant. "What in hell's the matter with him? Miss Patty is dead and I had to get here. What's so hard to understand about that?"

Carrie stopped and for the second time that evening, she felt the tears rise and overflow. Travis pointed her toward a brown-painted bench and told her he'd be right back. He returned with coffee and a box of Kleenex.

*God love him*, Carrie prayed silently.

Travis sat down next to her. "Everything's goin' to be OK. Things will work out, but I need to get back to my station. Ya' gonna be alright?"

Carrie sat there wiping her eyes dry with a tissue.

"I know the timin's not the best, but 'cha can call me if ya' want." Travis scribbled his personal number on his card and handed it to her.

The look on her face told Travis she wanted him to stay. He was all sympathy, with his pale blue eyes twinkling in the bright overhead emergency room light. Travis reminded her that the hospital would need to get some personal information on Patty. He walked back to the ambulance, glancing once over his shoulder and smiling kindly back at her.

Staring down at the speeding ticket in her hand, she grew angry all over again.

What construction zone? There was no construction zone and that cop knew it.

This wasn't her first ticket, but it would be the first one she'd be going to court over. She crumpled the yellow ticket in her hand. She imagined how it would feel to run the sergeant over, but she was forced to delay that thought as a young man in blue scrubs came through the automatic doors and asked if she was there for Mrs. McMurphy.

Carrie swallowed her anger and followed the orderly back into the hospital as he directed her to the front desk. Sergeant Lament was still there talking to the front desk nurse, the young blonde.

Sergeant Lament stepped back as Carrie approached the nurse.

"I'm here for Mrs. Patty McMurphy."

"Are you a relation of Mrs. McMurphy?" she asked.

*Apparently, it's against the law to die without relatives.*

"No, I am not! I'm her goddaughter!" Carrie snapped, visibly shaking.

The orderly intervened. "Ma'am, are you alright?"

"That cop," she nodded her head toward Sergeant Lament, "just gave me a speeding ticket, so no, I'm not alright. I'm a little pissed off right now. But will someone just tell me what's happening with Mrs. McMurphy, please?" Carrie said, trying to calm down.

"I want to, but the law says we need to first contact Mrs. McMurphy's relations or someone with power of attorney for her."

"I don't know of any. She was my grandmother's best friend since high school and I've never heard her speak about any family that might be living. I brought her purse with me. Maybe I can find something that would help."

The orderly was the first to state the plain fact that Mrs. McMurphy was in the morgue, there was paperwork that needed to be signed, and the sooner they could find out, the better. He suggested that of more immediate concern was whether Mrs. McMurphy wanted to donate any of her organs and asked if Carrie would check Mrs. McMurphy's driver's license first.

"That I can do for you right now. For anything else, I'll have to go back to her place. Besides her house and shop, I wouldn't know where else to look."

"That's fine. We'll need to know if she left any instructions for her remains and which funeral home she wanted to go to, that type of thing. There needs to be some legal backin' for whoever makes those decisions if Mrs. McMurphy didn't make her wishes known."

Carrie hadn't seen Patty for several months, and when she returned for the first time since her Grandma Hattie's passing, Patty goes and dies on her like flowers in hot water.

What a mess!

Carrie figured she was probably not the person who was going to end up handling the legalities anyway, but now she really did need to find out who that person was so that she could hand over the torch.

*How sad,* Carrie thought, slightly ashamed. *I'm already moving on. Patty was like a favorite aunt and she was good to Grandma Hattie and me over the years. I should show a little more gratitude.*

"I'll do what I can," she offered. "How soon do you need to know?"

"Well, she can stay in the morgue for a day or two, but past that depends on what's happenin' with tracin' her kin. She's not a Jane Doe, so there's no reason to keep her here. The county will want her cremated if there is no next of kin found. It would be better if we knew right away if she wanted any part of her body donated, though. That really can't wait," he added hopefully.

What? The woman was in her sixties, she thought. What can you use from an old woman?

Carrie squinted at his doggedness.

"If there's anything you can use, I think Mrs. McMurphy would have found something poetic in sharing her organs, you know, like a thread woven through the lives of other people. Is there something I need to sign?" Carrie asked, hoping a little cheesy sentiment and lack of authority on behalf of the deceased would make him go away.

The orderly waved at the little fashion-doll nurse and left without speaking to Carrie again. The switchboard buzzed and the narrow-assed pixie picked up the receiver and chirped, "Emergency Room." She listened for a moment, hung up the phone, and reached behind the desk, pulling out a clipboard. She brought it over to where Carrie was standing with her arms crossed.

"Hi, I'm Dana. It's Carrie, right? Dr. Orf was Mrs. McMurphy's doctor and, by luck, he was on call tonight. He was just on the phone and said you were authorized to sign the paperwork for Mrs. McMurphy to donate her organs. He also asked me to tell you to stay right here for a moment so you can sign the death certificate."

"Fine. Thanks," Carrie said sarcastically as she took the clipboard and pen from her. People in her sphere were in danger tonight. She clicked the pen open and closed until she annoyed herself with the noise she was making. Carrie was wondering how to run over both Sergeant Lament and *Too Blonde Dana* at the same time with minimal damage to her car when something Nurse Dana said clicked in her brain—*Authorized to sign?*

In no hurry to pick up some weird kind of infection, Carrie scanned the room looking for an isolated place to sit. Not finding one, she took the clipboard outside and sat back down on the bench, hoping any germs that followed her out would disperse quickly in the early evening breeze. Looking at the paperwork and then at her hand, she noticed the crumpled, dull, yellow paper ticket was still clenched in her fist. She was frustrated, like at the start of a bad movie that she just knew would only grow worse. Now this brown clipboard that should have been passed off to some waiting, distant cousin of Patty had become her responsibility.

She looked around for Travis and Sergeant Lament, but the angel and devil had both disappeared. Now she was alone with Miss Patty's purse, a wrinkled paper ticket, clipboard, paper, and a pen.

Carrie procrastinated, as she had always been unenthusiastic about rummaging through other people's things. As a child, she was hesitant to fetch change or gum out of Grandma Hattie's purse, even when asked, and now she faced violating Patty's trust by emptying her wallet. Carrie thought about the empty shop and the metal door down to the cellar. In a few days, someone else will take possession of all that and she may never know what secrets the cellar held. It scared the daylights out of her while she was down there, but in the safety of the artificial light of a hospital emergency entrance, it took on a kind of romantic mystery. She knew that she needed to go back and at least open up the skylight so the cellar smell wouldn't permeate the yarn. It wouldn't happen tonight though. She had Patty's purse to go through, looking for clarification of how Patty saw the end of her life with donation of her organs.

She took a deep settling breath, opened the brown handbag, with everything securely in its place, and found Patty's wallet. As Carrie removed the wallet from the purse, several items dropped to the ground from the sleeve they rested in.

It was an expired driver's license from years gone by.

Carrie saw the beautiful, reddish-orange hair on the green-eyed woman. That wary, suspicious look came through the official picture as if Patty were sitting right next to her. Then she noticed the name: Camille Eden-Worth.

Patty's sister maybe?

Carrie noticed that Camille was the spitting image of Patty. Looking at the date of birth, she saw Camille was a year older than Hattie. *So the sister thing fits*, she thought.

She decided to try and find Camille tomorrow. If she wasn't the correct person to be handling Patty's estate, Carrie hoped Camille would be able to point her in the right direction.

Fishing a little further and eventually finding Patty's driver's license, she noticed Patty was born in October, four months after her grandmother.

*Well, they're together now, and Grandma Hattie will be glad to see her friend,* she thought.

Carrie only had to break the news of her grandma's death to a few friends, but all who knew her were aware that it was time. When the Good Lord decided to bring her into his fold, she was ready. Grandma Hattie battled for her life for such a long time before she drew her last breath in her own bed, a long welcoming sigh of liberation.

Carrie wondered if she should call the county police about Camille Eden-Worth and let them track her down and inform her of Patty's passing.

She noticed that Patty had signed the back of her license agreeing to organ donation. Filling out what she could on the forms, she handed them back to Nurse Dana. Her antagonism toward Nurse Dana was exhausted for the night.

"Dr. Orf will be here shortly so you can sign Mrs. McMurphy's death certificate."

Carrie waited a while when an older, thin man with receding gray hair and kind brown eyes approached her.

"Hello, I'm Dr. Orf. I'm so sorry for your loss. Mrs. McMurphy died of a massive heart attack. I'm going to need you to sign the death certificate. You can pick up copies in a few days."

Then his pager buzzed, and he excused himself.

Nurse Dana stood there watching as Carrie signed the death certificate, smiled, and handed the clipboard back to her.

It was dark outside now. Getting into her car, she placed Patty's purse on the seat and looked up. A yellow parking ticket was tucked under a windshield wiper, issued by none other than Sergeant Lament.

That son of a bitch!

Angry didn't begin to describe her mood. She was coming up in a cloud of fury. In spite of her anger, she drove home cautiously, fully expecting Lament to be waiting with his lights out on the side of the road for her as she drove by. Trying to relax, she turned on the radio. It thumped out "Radar Love."

"**Oh! Hell no!**" she said aloud and punched off the radio.

***

Tonight wasn't a normal night; she'd planned on staying in and getting lit. She slammed the door behind her and smacked her keys on the countertop as if to punish it. There was a bottle of tequila and margarita mix in the liquor cabinet with her name on it. Taking one shot of tequila and then another, she made herself a pitcher full of the tasty yellow drink, not sparing the tequila.

With the pitcher in hand, she headed upstairs.

She walked out to the second floor balcony, sat the pitcher down on a small, white wicker table, and dropped her body into the cushioned, sunflower-design couch.

Two hours later, the crickets and tree frogs were singing a sequence of forest tunes.

The moonbeam coreopsis in the garden below began to glow. As Carrie breathed in the damp smell of the spring evening, the anger and frustration of the day began to wane.

Relaxing with her head reclined against the house, legs on the rails, she heard the crunching of gravel on the driveway below. Lightheaded, remembering she hadn't eaten since morning, she slipped into Hattie's bedroom. Instinctively, she stepped to the side of the window, not wanting to be seen, and peered down at the driveway. The approach of the vehicle set off the motion sensor on the porch light, but she didn't recognize the car, a dark Ford sedan of some kind.

The driver didn't stop the engine and no one got out. The car slowly pulled away and paused at the entrance to the driveway before disappearing.

*What the hell*, Carrie thought, *maybe they had the wrong house*. Still, it left her a little unnerved.

She went downstairs, grabbed for a bag of chips, proceeded to the front door, locked it, turned on the television for a little noise, and called a college friend, Celeste Parodi, "CiCi" for short. Carrie told her about the day's events (everything but the hidden cellar), which was calming. She didn't know why but she was relieved that someone else knew—*just in case*. In case of what? At least if something else should happen, CiCi would be aware of the facts.

It was just after midnight, but Carrie decided to leave the porch light on and called it a night. Nothing else happened and she fell fast asleep when her head hit the feathered pillow.

In the morning, the tequila handed her a gift in the form of confusion and indecision. In other words — a hangover. She managed to crawl out of bed and locate the aspirins, tossing down a couple. After a tense moment or two, they thankfully stayed down. After splashing cold water on her face and drying it with a thick gray towel, she brushed the flavor of tequila road-kill out of her mouth. She wandered downstairs, after bouncing off the wall a couple times, and made some coffee.

The phone began to ring and so did her head. She was in no mood to talk to anyone, but it continued to ring.

"Shit!" She realized the recorder was turned off.

"Damn it—whoever you are, take a hint," she declared, but the phone continued to ring. Unable to stand the noise any longer, she answered.

"Hello?"

"Hello, is this Miss Carrie Pyles?" the woman on the other side chirped much too cheerfully.

"Yeah," Carrie replied rubbing her forehead.

"Miss Pyles, this is Nurse Dana at Memorial Hospital. The coroner has confirmed the death of Mrs. Patty McMurphy as a massive heart attack. Will you be makin' the arrangements for her?" Dana asked, apparently with every expectation that she would.

"What?" Carrie said with confusion. Her mental engine was not firing on all cylinders quite yet.

"Miss Carrie," she repeated, "ya'll need to make arrangements for the body. Mrs. McMurphy is still here at the hospital right now, but we'll need to transfer her out soon. If you need assistance, I can have someone from the hospital call to help you," she said as if she were talking to a child.

*What time is it?* The microwave read 11:02 a.m. *Shit! That's too early to deal with pixie Dana. But then there was never a good time to deal with Dana.*

"Dana, can I call you back? I'm not sure what the arrangements are going to be." Carrie was in no shape to do this right now.

"Sure," Dana said, "just call the main number and mention Mrs. Patty McMurphy. They'll direct you to the proper area."

*Ok, but I really have no freaking clue*, Carrie thought, but politely replied, "Thanks," as she hung up, relieved that the conversation was over.

Carrie poured some orange juice in a small mason jar and drank it in one go, grateful for the sweetness and the cold as it went down. She started to feel a little better, but needed a cup of coffee—Now! As she poured the ground coffee into the holder without a filter and hit the brew button, she looked down at the counter. There she saw the crumpled piece of yellow paper sticking out of her purse, and quickly turned her back in disgust, realizing it was one of the two tickets she'd received yesterday.

After retrieving the newspaper from under the porch, she went back in the kitchen, removed a blue ceramic bowl from the overhead cabinet, and filled it with granola and milk. Without waiting for the coffeemaker to finish, she poured herself a cup, stirred in the sugar, inhaled it deeply, took a slow sip and proceeded to the backyard with cereal in the other hand and the newspaper under her arm. She sat down at the white, wrought-iron table to eat. Wildflowers were beginning to bloom in the pasture and the view was quite wonderful, but it barely registered.

Carrie rested in the warmth of the sunshine until a bee buzzed by her ear and she remembered that she had to make Patty's funeral arrangements today. She contemplated what Patty would have wanted.

Procrastinating again, her mind wandered back to the cellar and that god-awful smell, all those cobwebs and the damp cold biting at her. Carrie remembered the portrait of the woman and the hair on her arms began to rise. She wanted to go back there, but not by herself.

Maybe Travis would go. That could be fun.

The sun started heating up like a pot on a hot stovetop. Starting to sweat, Carrie went back into the kitchen and placed her dirty dishes in the sink. She picked up Patty's leather handbag from the counter and emptied the contents onto the wooden kitchen table.

A tube of mascara and some lipsticks raced along as the Chanel eye shadow compact clonked down, followed by a few tiny mints and a wide-tooth comb that Carrie immediately threw in the garbage. She took Patty's keys and placed them in her purse.

As she opened the side pocket of Patty's purse, Carrie was delighted to find a familiar photograph of Grandma Hattie and her. She was around six years old and wearing her favorite dress. Grandma Hattie, gifted artisan that she was, had made her a frilly cotton sundress with pink flowers and a flouncy skirt that she'd proudly worn for Easter that year. Carrie remembered the thin, white, cotton bobby socks and her new black patent Mary Janes. Carrie's dark strawberry-blonde hair was shoulder length with bangs cut straight across to match Grandma Hattie's hairstyle at the time. Her grandma had on a red dress with a yellowish-brown scarf with red and blue flowers she'd woven. *That scarf is still in my closet,* Carrie thought. *The scarf brought out the hazel color in her eyes.*

Grandma Hattie was a stunning woman and Carrie, at age six, thought she was the most beautiful woman in the world. *Patty was sweet to keep this with her and carry it for so many years.* Eager to see if Patty had more pictures or other keepsakes, she kept looking in the various sections of Patty's purse in great wonderment.

Carrie worried about not having a chance to retrieve any keepsakes of her grandma from Patty's house before she tried to locate Camille Eden-Worth—whoever she was.

Camille might be a complete bitch. Maybe that's why Patty never mentioned having any family. As long as Carrie had known her, which was all her life, she'd just thought Patty was an orphan like her.

*Next time I go to Patty's house, I'll take a look around for mementoes of Camille and Grandma Hattie*, she thought as she tucked the photograph and wallet back in Patty's purse. In a small, silver, business card case, she found a card for a local attorney named Victor Abbott. Reaching for the phone, she called the number on the card.

The receptionist answered on the first ring.

"Victor Abbott's office. This is Hope speakin'. How may I help you?"

"Yes, Hope, my name is Carrie Pyles. Could I please speak to Mr. Abbott?"

"May I tell him what this is regardin', please?"

"Yes, ma'am. I'm calling about a woman named Mrs. Patricia McMurphy. I need to know if Mrs. McMurphy was a client of his."

"Sure, let me see if Mr. Abbott is available. I won't be a minute."

Within a few seconds, Victor was on the line.

"Hello, Victor Abbott."

"Mr. Abbott, my name is Carrie Pyles—"

He interrupted her. "Well, hello, Miss Pyles, I've been expectin' you. I heard about Mrs. McMurphy's passin'. If you hadn't called me soon, I was goin' to call you. I expect you have some questions."

Word gets around fast in a small town. He had her at a loss and she told him just as much.

"Mrs. McMurphy talked about you and your Grandmother Hattie all the time. I knew your grandmother, though she wasn't a client of mine. Are you aware of the terms of Mrs. McMurphy's will?"

"No, sir, I'm completely and utterly ignorant to the terms of Mrs. McMurphy's will. All I know is that I was authorized to sign some paperwork at the hospital for her yesterday and I don't have a clue about how that was possible."

"You were there when she passed?"

"Yes, I was with her at the yarn shop when she died. The coroner said she had a massive heart attack."

"I see."

"Do you know if she has any next of kin? I had to sign the death certificate and organ donation forms yesterday at the hospital. I wasn't sure if I should, but I did find her signed driver's license stating she'd consented to be an organ donor in her wallet."

Now that she was talking to Patty's attorney, she was concerned about whether she'd had any legal grounds to donate her body and wondered if they'd already started . . . dismembering Patty.

"Why, yes, you did have the authority. I drew up her estate documents and because you're directly concerned, we should set up a meetin' as soon as possible. I believe its best that we wait until that time before we get any further in discussion on this. I'm goin' to give you back to Hope to make the appointment."

The image of the gray metal cellar door came into Carrie's mind.

"Mr. Abbott, before you do that," she ventured, "I have some questions I'd like to ask. Do you know what she wanted to do with her yarn shop?"

"Mrs. McMurphy left the shop to you. I share that information now because I recognize that Mrs. McMurphy was runnin' a business that may require your attention," Victor said, "but let me give you to Hope."

"What? Patty left the shop to me?"

The attorney seemed anxious to get her off the line, but Carrie wasn't quite finished as she needed to get one last item out of the way.

"Hold on, Mr. Abbott, please. I have another question and then I'll make the appointment. The hospital wants me to tell them what to do with Miss Patty's remains. Do you happen to know what she had planned? I'd like to give them an answer today if I can," she pressed. She didn't want to have any more conversations with Nurse Dana if it be could avoided.

Carrie was aware her attitude toward Dana was uncalled for, but she couldn't help that.

"If you'd like, Miss Pyles—"

"Carrie is fine, sir."

"Ok, Miss Carrie, if you would like, I can contact the hospital and arrange to have Mrs. McMurphy's body moved to Holtz Mortuary, since they will be handlin' her service and burial."

Three questions down, only a million more to go.

"Thank you, Mr. Abbott. Yes, that helps. If you want to give me to Hope now, that would be great."

"Very good."

Hope was back on the line again almost instantly, and she was ready for her. If they couldn't make the first appointment, Carrie knew Hope had another one already picked out.

"Hello again, Miss Carrie, I'm just checkin' Mr. Abbott's calendar. Can he meet you at the store tomorrow mornin' at 10 a.m.?"

"The store? Umm—OK."

"That'll be perfect, then, Mr. Abbott will see you in the mornin', sugar."

Victor had been brisk and noncommittal, but the little he had told her had come as a major surprise. Carrie was pleased he'd offered to call the hospital and she was pretty sure she would get a bill, but it would be worth it to have that responsibility taken off her hands.

Carrie remembered how painful it was when her grandma passed only several months ago. She'd had to deal with having to call the funeral home and arranging to have her body removed from the house and then put together a memorial service too. Patty had helped her back then, but for Patty's service, Mr. Abbott had taken the first step off her hands.

*Bless his heart,* she sighed.

Since she had been able to reach out to someone who knew about Miss Patty's personal and business interests, she didn't feel the need to do anything else with the funeral rites.

The yarn shop was hers.

Tomorrow, she would go over to the store before meeting with Victor and begin the process of sorting things out to make it go as smoothly as possible. Good thing that she wasn't walking into a business that was completely foreign to her. Patty had given her a job as a teenager, but she had been going to the shop with her grandma and on her own for years before that. She already had the keys, but no energy—or courage—to face it today.

With Patty dying there just yesterday and the incident with the freaky cellar still fresh in her mind, she remembered the store and tack room area were still in disarray. Although Carrie was fully aware there was much to do, her hangover only seemed to get worse.

She contemplated why Patty had left anything to her at all. With the exception that she was the granddaughter of her closest friend, the only explanation was that her grandma's friendship must have meant a great deal to Patty.

Spotting the comic section of the newspaper on the table, Carrie opened it to read her daily horoscope as she finished her last cup of coffee.

"Today is full of surprises; the threads of life may be tangled."

Hold it—that was yesterday's horoscope!

The astrologer may have been spot on, but she did not want a repeat of yesterday under any circumstances.

That settled it. She was staying home today.

# Chapter 3

**After** a lazy day and early to bed, Carrie woke the next morning to the alarm clock sounding like a half-crazed rooster that refused to give up and she was forced to give in. It was 7:08 a.m. She lingered in bed a bit longer before getting up.

Unenthusiastically, she wandered into the bathroom, turned on the shower, climbed inside, and savored the warmth and refreshing flow of the water.

Wrapped in a towel, she went downstairs to the kitchen and poured a hot cup of coffee. As she looked out the kitchen window, several fox squirrels were jumping and chasing each other about the yard in carefree spirited play. The sunshine was beckoning her to be embraced by its warmth, but she knew she had more important things to do today.

She had a meeting with a lawyer. She suddenly became aware that this was a new day indeed—a crossroad to her future. Getting dressed, she pulled her hair back into a ponytail, applied her makeup, and placed the coffee cup on the kitchen counter.

There was a friendly, off-the-road diner just down from Patty's place, toward Chocowinity. She decided to make the detour for their tasty hot coffee and jumbo muffins—the ones with fleshy, sugary blueberries. Afterward she'd take the back way to Patty's store, following the road along the river that's eventually-ingested by the Sound.

*My store now*, she thought, confused by the remorse, excitement, anticipation, and fear that welled up inside her.

Assuming everything was in order with Victor, after learning only two days before that she had inherited a yarn shop, the whole picture was just beginning to take form in her consciousness.

She left the diner and arrived at the store earlier than anyone who knew her would have expected. Patty's shop didn't normally open until 10 a.m., but today the shop would be closed. The humidity and the age of the building made the lock stiff, or maybe the shop was merely reluctant to let her in. Carrie understood.

The sunlight that beamed through the large windows was sufficient for the shop's electricity replacement, but the other day's stench from the cellar, while not strong, was still evident in the air. She turned the copper crank and opened the skylight to allow the sweet smell of jasmine into the shop. Walking back to the tack room, she saw that the shelving looked slightly banged up, but the proud old heart pine took the fall and survived. With no plan of resetting it in its former spot any time soon, she leaned it up against the wall.

Looking toward the metal door, she was tempted to revisit the cellar, but pride of the shop took over and she methodically tidied up the disarray.

Carrie lugged a twelve-foot aluminum ladder from the storage room. With the 'S' style hook from the fallen tapestry and all the strength she could muster, she twisted and turned until it was secured in the wood ceiling. It was lucky that the heavy tapestry was still suspended by one hook, which made it easier to drape it in front of the gray metal door. Easy or not, sweat still materialized on her forehead.

A massive wooden cupboard situated between the large front windows had always seemed out of place, so she unloaded everything, pushing and pulling it on a woven rug that made it easier to slide it in front of the tapestry. When she replaced the items on its shelves, she affirmed that it at least put the gray metal door out of sight and contained the smell.

Preferring to have the large nine-paned windows open whenever possible, she struggled with the stubborn latches, sweat streaming placidly down between her breasts. She climbed several steps on the aluminum ladder, pushing her thumbs harder against the stubborn steel bolt, until the reluctant thing finally unfastened.

She lifted the window sash with force and the fresh morning air enveloped her body. A black Mercedes convertible pulled into the lot, driven by a man who seemed too tall for his car. He had silver strand hair with a matching mustache, and a red sweater accented his tan over a red-and-white checked shirt with a red-and-navy striped tie. The baggy, acid-wash jeans rode nicely on his hips as he observed Carrie from behind a pair of black Wayfarers. He carried a slim black leather briefcase stitched in white. The effect was casual but elegant. He looked like a rock star.

"Miss Carrie Pyles?"

"Yes sir."

"Hello, I'm Victor Abbott. Please call me Victor," he said as he reached out his hand to shake hers.

She returned his firm handshake with the same. Carrie was taught by her grandma how to shake hands and didn't like wetfish handshakes or people who beat around the bush, and she assumed he didn't either.

"Miss Carrie, is there a place we can sit?" Victor asked as he entered the store and looked around appraisingly.

It struck Carrie as strange that he may have never been in the shop. She wondered why he wanted to meet her here and not at his office.

"Sure, let's go back to Miss Patty's office," she said, leading the way. Soon enough she would have to get used to calling it her office, but today was not that day.

Victor followed her in as she flipped on the overhead light and took the specified place as the new owner behind the heavy, vintage oak desk. She motioned for Victor to have a seat and she spoke first.

"I appreciate you coming over, but I didn't know lawyers made house calls."

"You remind me of Mrs. McMurphy. She was always inquisitive too. As for coming by the shop, just curiosity really. I suspected you might come here first after learning the place is yours and, even though I've known Mrs. McMurphy for years, I've never been in the shop. There's nothing we were going to discuss in my office that we can't just as easily go over here."

Victor flicked open the straps on his briefcase and pulled out a thick manila folder. He removed photocopies of several documents, slid the folder across the desk to her, and kept what appeared to be the originals in front of him.

"Let's begin with Mrs. McMurphy's last will and testament. It couldn't be simpler, so I'll give you the condensed edition. Mrs. McMurphy has assigned to you, without encumbrance, all of her real property, the house, shop, all her financial assets, and a list of those are attached here along with all her personal belongin's. In short, Miss Carrie, her entire estate passes to you."

She was as confused as a gnat doing the backstroke in buttermilk.

"I can see by the expression on your face you're wondering why she would have chosen you to inherit everything. Her intention was to leave the entire estate to your grandmother, Hattie, but should she precede Patty in death, and that is exactly what happened, the estate would pass to you and you alone. That likely makes more sense to you."

It was as simple as that. Having a feeling of relief and feeling comfortable enough to ask what surely would be the next question for anyone named in a will, she took a deep breath and proceeded.

"Can you give me an idea of the value of the estate?"

"That question is better answered by an accountant, but I strongly suggest you to first pay a visit to Robert Twiford at Henderson's Bank and Trust. One of the assets you will notice on the list is a trust fund for you set up by Mrs. McMurphy when you were young. That trust fund has a present value of around two-hundred and fifty-thousand dollars, the entirety available to you as of the date Mrs. McMurphy passed away."

***Good Lord!*** *Miss Patty left me a quarter of a million dollars! What was this woman worth?*

She sat in awe, wondering why Patty would have even considered doing something like that for her.

"Last, Mrs. McMurphy left a signed power of attorney for you, executed immediately following the death of your grandmother, Mrs. Hattie Jennings. You will need to sign it, retain the original, and I recommend you put it in a safe place. You are going to need it to transact anything on behalf of the estate until all deeds and assets have been transferred into your name. I've brought the paperwork with me for you to sign to transfer title to the house and business. Just sign here, here—and here."

"I hope you understand, Mr. Abbott, I'd like to read the documents first. I don't want you to think I don't trust you, especially since Miss Patty did, but I don't put my name to anything I haven't read."

This was the truth and Victor made no protest.

"Of course, Miss Carrie, you absolutely should. In that case, we can move on and discuss Mrs. Murphy's funeral arrangements. There were some specific requests in the way of music and flowers that I have taken care of, including the pallbearers. I have notified the Rt. Reverend Bellew at St. John's Baptist Church, as he was a friend of hers and he will address the mourners. Mrs. McMurphy's body has already been transferred to Holtz Funeral Home, and she asked to be buried at Heart

Strings Cemetery on the other side of town at Laredo and Larimore. She has a plot prepared and a memorial already selected."

"Holtz Funeral Home is on Powell Street, isn't it?"

"Yes, ma'am, that's the one. You should call them as soon as we're finished here, but all of the funeral expenses have been prepaid. Also for your information, my fees are paid up through the normal conclusion of the estate. So far, everything we have reviewed thus far is covered."

"Oh, OK," Carrie nodded.

"Read the documents; sign these as soon as you can, and when you return them I'll forward to the address they should be sent to. But please, make a copy for your files first. Mrs. McMurphy requested that I retain her documents and I can start a file for you, if you'd like, but in that case, you would be responsible for any services I render you. As for the transfer documents, unless you just want me to do so, you can mail them. You will need to include a death certificate and a copy of the power of attorney, but both require a raised seal."

"Victor, I can't thank you enough for taking care of Miss Patty's affairs. I'd be grateful if you handled the transfer documents. I just went through this with my grandmother and in all honesty, I was dreading having to do it again so soon."

"You're welcome, Miss Carrie, but you know how Miss Patty was. She thought through everything."

Victor just referred to the dead woman as Miss Patty and Carrie wondered if he had slipped or if that was a deliberate display for her benefit.

"Well, Miss Carrie," he said, packing up. "That should be all we need to do right now. Call me anytime and let me know when you've completed those documents. You have my number."

They shook hands and their business was finished.

In just a flash, her life had changed completely.

She should have locked the store door right after Victor left, as not ten minutes later, the bell jingled and in shuffled a troll in a dirty blue shirt with a stubbly beard and grey teeth.

*He looks like something the dog's been keeping under the porch,* she thought.

The old man was so hunched over that she thought he could topple forward any moment, but somehow he didn't. Possibly due to his raggedy, bulging, blue sack slung across his back.

The bulge isn't moving, thank goodness, but he's as welcome as an outhouse breeze.

He looked at her with yellow, watery eyes that sent a shiver up her spine, but try as she might to discourage it, he insisted on speaking.

"Who are ya'? Where's Mrs. McMurphy?" he asked gruffly.

"I'm Carrie Pyles. I run the shop now. Who are you?" she questioned, thinking it prudent not to discuss the death of Mrs. McMurphy with this hobgoblin or anyone else before the ink was dry on the paperwork.

"I'm Walter—I deliver the mail," he snarled.

"Here," he said and slapped the stack of mail onto the counter. "Is anythin' goin' out?"

"Not today, Walter," she replied without bothering to check. There was something about Walter that made her immediately dislike him.

He hesitated for a moment before he trudged out the door.

She decided it was time to get down to business and saw the heavy, heart-pine shelving still angled against the wall. Yesterday's chaos left a large impact on the shop. She made a large handwritten sign stating that the shop was temporarily closed and attached it to the front-door glass. She returned to the office, and after an examination of the dark oak file cabinet drawers, she realized just how organized Patty had been.

Opening the drawer, she removed the register where Patty kept everything.

It was the shop's lifeline.

The register contained not only the store's inventory, vendor information, orders placed and received, but also customers' information and the shop's checkbook.

Next, she familiarized herself with the stock, and to Carrie, this was the fun part. She already knew where everything was. She tried to remember what yarn she had wished Patty had carried, as now it would be wholesale for her.

Carrie thought about her small rug business in the context of running the shop and secretly hoped her rug weaving wouldn't suffer. No matter what, there was nothing for her to complain about. She had dreamt about having her own store, but never in a million years had she thought it would happen like this.

After several hours, she realized that coffee wasn't enough to sustain her rumbling stomach and decided to lock up and go for a late lunch. A few years prior, about halfway between Patty's place and town, a truck had broken down. Rather than towing the truck away, the owner bought a smoker and opened a barbecue joint. Something was very poetic and appropriate about that.

The clouds had broken apart and the sun was casually tossing shadows. Carrie parked herself at a long picnic table by the barbecue truck with a young woman and a couple of rambunctious boys.

Picking up the laminated menu, she gave it a good look over, even though she knew it by heart. She was just about to decide on pulled smoked brisket on slaw when a tall shadow strolled by the table causing her stomach to churn.

There he was.

Sergeant Lament passed a look at the picnic table. Since the menu was no cover and Carrie hadn't learned the trick of becoming invisible, she did the next best thing—she left. She doubted that she was the first person in this town to run from a cop.

The next option down a bit further was Malphur's Diner. The diner was in an old 1940s bungalow with a cinder block addition. This was where she'd snagged the excellent muffin and coffee on the way to the shop this morning. Knowing the waitress, Charme, well enough to stop and chat on the street, she decided to go there. She approached the register and ordered a cheeseburger, fries, and a diet coke to go. She did not want to get comfortable some place and, once again, to be interrupted by that bothersome cop.

But then she noticed Travis sitting at a table with a couple of friends and told Charme that she'd had a change of mind. Charme waved an arm over the restaurant, as if parting the Red Sea, and told her to help herself. Travis was in the middle of telling a joke when he saw Carrie approach a booth and apparently decided the punch line could wait.

Lament was soon forgotten as Travis swaggered to her booth.

"Hey, Carrie, how's it goin'?"

"Well, hey, Travis. Are you working today?" she asked.

"Yep," he said with his boyish grin. "My dispatch station isn't far from here. We're just gettin' some lunch. So, been back to the shop yet?" Travis asked while he scooted in across from her.

"I went back this morning."

Her reticence with Lament did not apply to Travis in any way, shape, or form.

"Why? Who owns the shop now?"

"I do."

"Cool. Is that something you're interested in?"

"Yes," was all she could say, as one of the other paramedics called out an alert and Travis headed for the door. He winked at her just as the sun came out in full force.

"Gotta go, beautiful. Catch ya' later," he said with his Southern charm.

*Yes you will, sugar,* Carrie thought, *yes, you will.*

Charme brought the food to her table and Carrie dug in with enthusiasm.

As Carrie finished up, Charme breezed by and asked if she would like a nice slice of pie. Naturally, she wanted pie. Everyone who came here wanted Malphur's pie. Charme came back with a nice piece of pecan pie and Carrie savored the first bite before she scarfed the rest down all too easily.

Happy and gratified, she left a big tip on the table and proceeded to the register where Charme rang her up. Carrie was looking down as she placed the change in her wallet and pushed open the door with her butt and ran straight into another patron.

"Oh, my gosh, I'm so sor—," she started to say as she looked up, staring at the starched, pressed blue uniform of Sergeant Lament.

*Well, this sucks*, as she realized she was being stalked and that stalker was a cop.

"Miss Pyles," he said mildly.

"Sergeant," she snarled and skirted past him before her anger resurrected and got the best of her. She got into her car quickly and headed back to the shop.

After fumbling for the store keys in her purse, she unlocked the door, placed her purse under the register, and picked up a phone message from a yarn vendor. She took down the door sign and left the door unlocked, deciding that there was no reason to get between yarn addicts and their soft, squishy, wonderful fix. Her heart rate returned to normal for a moment as she moved about the store.

It didn't stay down for long as the bell jingled and over the threshold stepped Sergeant Lament.

Carrie stared him down in a hot mix of rage and astonishment. The sergeant stopped and stood near the door like a human barricade. She couldn't escape and began to worry in earnest that the cop was going to be a problem. She refused to let this asshole intimidate her, in her shop, no less.

"What are you doing here, Sergeant?" she snapped. "I'm beginning to feel harassed and if you don't knock it off immediately, I'm going to call *your boss.*"

"So, is this where the incident with Mrs. McMurphy took place the other day?" he asked, as if they were friends and he was merely making conversation.

"Yes, it is. You may remember that I was following the ambulance to the hospital when you pulled me over. You have no idea how pissed off I am," she said, walking around the counter. "I mean, what the hell, it wasn't bad enough that you couldn't be bothered to assist me in an actual emergency, but you had to pile it on at the hospital by writing another ticket? You're a jackass and I have no intention of letting this go, Lament."

"Yeah, about that. That's why I'm here," he said ruefully.

"What about it?" she asked, lowering her voice but not the burn level.

"Well, since you apologized, I thought I would come by and ask you for those tickets back."

"I wasn't exactly apologizing, Sergeant. I thought you were going to arrest me." *Wait—what did he just say?* Now, confused about what he was asking her for, she stood still like a deer in the headlights.

The sergeant looked at her with something akin to real remorse in his gaze and changed his tack.

"I was a little hasty, Miss Pyles, and I'd like to collect the two tickets. You're not going to be responsible for those."

"And then what?" she asked suspiciously.

"Then—*nothing.* You were driving a bit recklessly, and if you show up to court, I'll be there, but I'm offering to make this go away. I understand that you don't trust me as far as you can throw me. What would it take for you to believe me?" He relaxed his hands and laced his fingers in front of him, while leaning against the doorframe.

"Are you offering me a bribe, Sergeant?" she questioned. "That's not going to cut it. What happens if I just hand you the tickets?" She was now extremely confused.

The sergeant looked aggrieved, but Carrie wasn't aware he had laurels to uphold.

"I don't want anything from you, other than the tickets I issued you yesterday. You can check with the traffic division in the morning, or go down there if you want something showing they've been dismissed. You're not going to end up with points on your record or anything, either."

She pondered this and weighed it for a minute. Perhaps it was a trap, but she couldn't see where the harm was in handing him the tickets. She found one of the yellow slips, but then frantically searched through her handbag for the other.

*Where did I put it?* She thought and reluctantly gave up looking.

"Well, here's one of them, Sergeant. I don't know what I did with the other one. What should I do when I find it?" she said as she reached out with a shaky hand, passing the one ticket over to the sergeant. "Too much coffee," she explained.

Sergeant Lament said nothing. Instead, the cop pushed his stupid mirrored sunglasses up his nose and walked out the door.

*That was interesting,* she thought, but the fact is the cop was wrong and she was getting out of two very expensive tickets only to allow him to cover his arse. Then again, no court appearance, she realized. But she was still irritated by the issuance of the two tickets in the first place.

She dumped everything out of her purse, but the second ticket just wasn't there. It must be in the car or the house.

The phone rang. It was the funeral home, so holding the receiver to her shoulder, she made a sticky note to hunt the citation down. The director explained that they needed a burial outfit for Mrs. McMurphy.

Here was a task Victor Abbott couldn't take care of. Taping the sign back on the door glass, she picked up the documents Victor left and walked across the path through the jasmine garden to the back door of Patty's house.

Victor had been correct when he said Patty had specified what she wanted upon her demise and that document was easy enough to locate. But Patty hadn't mentioned what she wanted to spend eternity in. The least she could do was lay Patty to rest dressed in her own good taste.

Patty's elegant house was a direct reflection of the woman herself and Carrie wanted to explore it, but right now she didn't have time for that. Victor said visitation would be tomorrow night with the service the following morning. Going into Patty's bedroom and opening the double doors of the closet, she reviewed Patty's clever mix of high fashion and simple style. Dry cleaning and other storage bags protected the more expensive pieces. Carrie pulled out a few things, laid them out across Patty's carved-wood four-poster bed and considered what might be practical to put on a dead woman.

*Nothing with a lot of pattern and buttons down the front.* She also nixed anything that might bunch up, blazers, and awkward sleeve lengths. She decided that a simple dress would be best.

Carrie flipped through the hangers like pages in a book. An image of Patty with Grandma Hattie at her college graduation came to her mind. Patty had looked positively radiant in a simple cream crepe shift with a pebbly red leather belt. That's how she wanted Patty to be remembered—like a prestigious family member with a more helpful sales lady reflection. She hoped that Patty still had the dress and looked through dry cleaning bags until she finally found it.

Patty washed and pressed the cream shift dress, then slipped the red belt over the neck of the hanger. With nothing else she needed to do, she placed the ensemble on the bed. Carrie couldn't remember what shoes Patty had worn that day and realized she should have asked the funeral director if Patty actually needed shoes. She spotted two shoeboxes on the top of a two-drawer filing cabinet hidden behind her closet doors, but instead of some nice, strappy sandals, she found a bunch of receipts, check stubs, and invoices.

Disappointed, she opened the next box and found a bunch of old pictures. Remembering the photograph Patty kept in her purse of Grandma Hattie and her, curiosity got the best of her, and she pulled out the box and sat down on the floor.

The first picture was of Patty and possibly Howard, Patty's husband, standing next to a barn when they were younger. But Carrie noticed it didn't look like the barn the shop now occupied. There was another of Patty standing with a smaller girl and a larger team picture with Patty and Hattie from high school. Realizing this could take a while, she placed the box on the bed next to the dress.

The dress was lined, so a slip would be unnecessary and even a dead woman would have to be grateful for that. Hose and a clean bra and panties were easy enough to find in her lingerie drawer. Nice lingerie seemed like a waste, but Carrie could just imagine the hearse getting into an accident with the coffin sliding out the back doors, breaking wide open, and there's Patty lying on the pavement with no underwear on.

*Ok, that's just wrong*, she thought and decided to look for shoes.

Trying a closet in another bedroom, lo and behold, a golden light shone from the open closet doors and Carrie swore she could hear angels singing. In Patty's guest bedroom closet, she found the golden egg—a shoe nirvana.

The double closet had rows of shelving, floor to ceiling, running the entire gamut of the space and lined with one pair after another of amazing shoes. It even had a mirrored step stool handy so none of the spectacular pairs of silver sandals or jaunty raffia D'Orsay pumps or spotless white leather mules were out of reach. Organization reigned in Patty's shoe closet as it did everywhere else in her life. Patty had sorted her shoes by color first and then by heel height.

Carrie noted with a huge smile that Patty wore the same size shoe as she did. The temptation to try a few on was more than she could resist. Half an hour later, the evening light beamed in through the window and reflected on a pair of simple red pumps with three-inch stacked heels.

*These red shoes are lovely*, she thought, *but they won't be coming home with me.* She slipped them into a shoe bag and placed them next to the dress and the other items on the bed.

Patty loved accessorizing with jewelry and the dress needed something, but Carrie decided that a necklace wouldn't lay right.

Maybe Patty had a brooch that would help complete the outfit.

In Patty's bedroom standing next to her bed was a tall, mahogany jewelry chest with a music box attached. Carrie opened the music box and found it chimed a few notes from Schubert's *Trout Quintet.* This cheerful, pastoral piece that somehow seemed right at home in a house by the shoreline. Allowing the music to keep her company, she sat down on the bed, opened the door to the chest, and slid the top drawer out.

A collection of bracelets sparkled up from the drawer. The second drawer contained side-by-side trays of earrings, and as Carrie lifted the left tray out, she spied a pair of large charcoal-colored pearl studs. Carefully lifting the right tray out, she noticed underneath there was a very old sepia photograph plus a couple of later black and white pictures.

The pictures had faded over the years, but she could make out an image of a woman dressed in black. This figure, standing alone in front of a brick wall, looked like she belonged in a silent horror film. She was definitely creepy, whoever she was. There was no name written on the back of the picture and her face didn't mean anything to Carrie, but it must have meant something to Patty.

Gathering up the pictures, she placed them on the light tan quilted bedspread and reopened the top drawer. As she lifted up the tray, sure enough, she discovered more pictures.

Carrie eventually found a suitable brooch in the fourth drawer down. By then it was getting dark outside, so she decided it was time to run by the funeral parlor and then do something about supper.

On the way to the store to get her purse, she stopped at her car with the documents and Patty's items and placed them on her back seat. She retrieved her purse from under the store counter, slipping it over her shoulder. As she dug inside her purse for her car keys, the sticky note sank deeper. She removed the sign off the glass on the door and locked up the store before heading for Holtz Funeral Parlor.

The funeral parlor was a distance from the store. As she approached the intersection of Ashford Avenue and 3$^{rd}$ Street, about two blocks from Powell Street, she slowed down for the approaching stop sign and looked both ways.

She looked down at the clock and noticed that it was 7:42 p.m.

Holtz should still be open, she thought.

As she edged into the intersection, a dark, possibly black car, without its lights on, flew right on through, ignoring the stop sign.

Slamming on her brakes, she swerved to the right and barely avoided losing the front end of her car. Her tires screeched as her purse flew off the seat with the contents scattered everywhere.

"Damn it—you freakin' idiot!" she screamed.

The car vanished out of sight. No one was behind her, so she sat there long enough to regain her composure and make it to the funeral parlor without personally needing their services.

She pulled into the lot at the side of the building and took Patty's items inside.

"You almost didn't make it. I was just thinkin' about lockin' up," said a pale girl wearing red streaks in her dark, charcoal-black hair and sporting a diamond stud in her nose. "Whose clothes are these?"

*That girl could fall over dead and no one around here would be the wiser until she started to smell,* Carrie thought.

"Sorry for getting here so late. The clothes are for Mrs. Patricia McMurphy."

"The redhead, huh? I'll take 'em," she said without waiting for a reply. She reached out and snatched the items, then disappeared from the room.

"Yeah, thanks for your concern. Nice night to you, too, sister," Carrie said aloud, shaking her head as she reached for the doorknob to leave. Her mood was souring as the night progressed.

Although she was not usually paranoid, a chill ran up her spine as she walked to her car. She couldn't shake a genuine feeling of being watched. She picked up the pace and settled into the driver's seat. As she locked the door and looked around the lot, nothing looked unusual until she looked back at the far end of the building. She saw a troll standing in the dim light as he leaned against the white building wall, looking directly at her.

Walter.

She buckled the seatbelt, started the car's engine, and checked the rearview mirror. When she looked back, Walter had vanished.

***

The visitation the next day went as expected. There had been a small announcement in the local paper, but Patty hadn't made a lot of friends outside the shop, hence it wasn't overly crowded. No one pretended to be on intimate terms with her. Those who came by seemed to be reasonably confused about who they should console and chose instead to socialize with one another. Carrie walked restively around overhearing some older ladies in the corner ruminating nastily about the Eden-Worths.

Carrie realized, somewhat ashamed, that she didn't know anything about Patty's family.

Victor Abbott came over and introduced her to Robert Twiford, the banker. He was a short, gray-haired man with a potbelly and about the same age as Patty. Carrie advised Mr. Twiford that it was imperative she visit him as soon as possible and he agreed. Travis made it a point to stop by to console Carrie, interrupting the conversation and once again leaving on the spur of the moment when his beeper went off.

After the visitation, Carrie met privately with the priest who would be conducting Patty's memorial service, the Rt. Reverend Bellew.

He asked if there was anything anecdotal she would like to share. Carrie smiled and told him about her Grandma Hattie and Miss Patty being best friends, her working at the yarn shop, and her graduation memories. The reverend took some notes.

The priest had known Miss Patty for years and said he had talked with her often, but in confidence. He told Carrie how much Miss Patty cared for both Hattie and her and said he was glad there was someone who mattered to her that she could trust with her estate. Reverend Bellew didn't invite questions afterward and Carrie didn't ask any. When the visitation was over, she called it an early night.

***

Beep, beep, beep. . . . The alarm went off, but only once this morning. Today was Patty's funeral and Carrie could not procrastinate today. She had her coffee and biscuit on the porch. Thunder rumbled in the distance and dark clouds rapidly converged.

Well, this doesn't look good, she thought.

It was going to rain and she hoped it was over before the service started. There's nothing worse than being poured on at a cemetery in the middle of the burial.

Shaking off that gloomy thought, she headed in to get ready.

Carrie jumped around as she stretched her arms almost out of their sockets trying to zip up her only black dress. She skipped the nylons and tucked her feet into a pair of black flats. Worried about the rain, she pulled her hair into a high ponytail and applied some black mascara, pinched her cheeks and smeared on a little lip gloss.

Carrie made the trip without getting pulled over this time and walked in and greeted those she knew. The service seemed to be a hotter ticket than the visitation and the number of people pleasantly surprised her. By now in this small town, it was common knowledge among the gathering group that she had inherited Patty's estate. It was assumed she'd be the primary bereaved and she received more attention than desired, with some of it fairly meddlesome. Some of the mourners were unexpected, such as Charme and Malphur, the waitress and the owner of the diner. A number of Patty's customers were there and Carrie reassured them the shop would not be closing anytime soon. The gothic chick from last night trudged about looking dull and clueless.

Carrie walked around to the various flower arrangements displayed on their stands and reflecting the sender's sympathies. Then she moved toward the beautiful gunmetal-colored polished casket Patty had chosen for her eternal rest. Standing alone in the front row of the assembled chairs, Carrie watched a middle-aged man with salt-and-pepper hair paying his last respects.

The gentleman turned to her with a gentle smile, nodded, and walked past her without stopping, taking a seat in a back row. She felt she knew him, but she couldn't quite place the man, but she was distracted from this thought when Reverend Bellew walked in, followed by Victor.

Victor made his way into the empty real estate behind Carrie, settling in as the priest led the assembly in the prayer for peace. Carrie was not a religious person and as the Rt. Reverend Bellew was speaking, Carrie silently made a promise to Patty to make the most of her trust and generosity.

"We are gathered here today to remember Mrs. Patricia Ann Eden-Worth McMurphy, a friend to many of us—"

The priest spoke eloquently of a woman who was inexplicably private but fiercely loyal to those she cared for. Carrie reflected that truer words had never been spoken, and she found it a refreshing departure from the usual banalities doled out at funerals. The more this priest spoke, the more Carrie felt as though she could actually confide in him. She filed that thought away for future reference.

Carrie stole a glance over her left shoulder in Travis' direction and caught him looking back at her. When Travis grinned, his whole face lit up and his dimples knocked her out. The boy was cute and it was hard to ignore that no matter what the circumstance.

Reverend Bellew closed with another prayer for those left behind, meaning her, Carrie supposed. The melancholy strains of Satie's *Gymnopedie No. 1* rose, and for the first time since Patty arrived at Memorial Hospital three days ago, tears welled up in Carrie's eyes.

The mourners lined up for their final respects, squeezing Carrie's hand before they headed for their cars. Sergeant Lament, in a good, dark worsted wool suit and paisley tie, instead of that aggressively pressed dark blue uniform, was among the last. By now Carrie was no longer surprised to see him. Lament had not known Patty and his condolences sounded sincere, so Carrie thanked him and he moved on.

Travis had waited by the door to walk Carrie out to her car.

Lament stopped to say hello to Travis. Carrie wondered if that was just a ruse to speak to her again.

"Travis," nodded the sergeant.

"Hey, Phil, how's it goin'?" Travis replied, as they shook hands.

"Not bad. You?"

"I'm OK, but Carrie over there doesn't want to ride with me to the cemetery," Travis advised, smiling at her.

"The way she drives, we would all be safer if you tossed her in the back of the ambulance," replied the sergeant.

"Hmm," was all Carrie could say, as she rolled her eyes at Travis and pushed on the side door.

"Miss Pyles, did you happen to find that other ticket?" the sergeant asked.

"What? You got two tickets and the good sergeant here asked for 'em back? This might be a good day to count your blessin's girl," exclaimed Travis.

Forgetting he was at a funeral service, Travis laughed out loud, then clamped his mouth closed with his hand, looking guilty. Carrie wanted to tell him he had no idea just how many blessings she had to count right this minute, but she decided to keep that to herself.

"Yeah," Carrie replied.

Carrie spoke to Lament without sarcasm for the first time since they met and thanked him again for attending the service. With Miss Patty nearly in the ground, if the living wanted forgiveness, Carrie really wanted to believe she was up to forgiving Lament. They had gotten off on the wrong foot. While this may be a funeral, it could also be a chance to press the reset button without unwanted conversation—but Carrie still needed to find that other ticket.

"I've been a little busy, Sergeant. If it's alright, I'll bring it by the station tomorrow." *God, I only hope I find that stupid ticket by then.*

"That'll be fine," said the sergeant, "but call me Phil," he said, nodding to Travis and Carrie as he walked away toward his Chevy Cheyenne.

"I think the sergeant likes you," Travis said impishly.

"I think the sergeant's opinion of me is lower than dirt, Travis. Besides, I like *you*," she said, biting her lip too late.

Travis looked at her as if she had just made his day. He lifted Carrie's hand, brought it to his mouth, and lightly kissed it, then released it and headed for his car.

Wow, flirting at the funeral of a woman who thought enough of Grandma Hattie to leave her everything she had. Carrie tried to look solemn, but honestly, that was hard to do with Travis around.

Carrie put the orange funeral sticker inside her windshield, turned the flashers on, and took her place behind the hearse. The cemetery was in the proximity of Patty's house, and as Miss Patty was Anglican, she had chosen to have a quiet, secular service.

Sergeant Lament turned the lights on top of the car on and acted as a police escort leading everyone to the cemetery. Phil wound the funeral procession through town, and the cars snaked along like children playing a game of whip-it, where they hold hands and try to whip the last person off the snake chain.

As Carrie drove, she paraphrased a line from the priest's ceremonial speech, "We take our kindness where we can find it."

Her mind went to Sergeant Lament, whom she assumed meant to see this through. *Good. I can take it if you can. Until I find the other ticket and move on.*

When they arrived at the burial plot, the Rt. Reverend Bellew said a few words over Patty's mortal remains.

*Thank the Lord, the service was blessedly brief,* Carrie thought, she had known in advance about the bequest. There were many things she would have liked to have asked Patty in the living years.

Afterwards, an old acquaintance named Emeline Browning asked Carrie if the rumor that she had inherited the shop were true.

Carrie told her it was.

Emeline informed Carrie, "Well, Carrie, weavin' class was supposed to pick up next week, and I don't want to bother you 'bout it today because you have a lot on your plate, but I just wanted to know if the class is still on."

"What day was the class supposed to start?" Carrie inquired.

"Monday mornin' at ten."

"That's fine, Miss Emeline, I can take over the class. It shouldn't take more than a few minutes for y'all to fill me in on where the class is at. Do you know who else is in the class?"

"My sista' Adeene, Jenny Lee Jones, an' Virginia Firth have all signed up."

"I don't know Jenny Lee, but I'll get a number and call her to make sure she's OK with having me as the instructor instead of Miss Patty. Could you tell your sister, Adeene?"

Emeline nodded that she would and walked away. Carrie noticed the small crowd was beginning to disperse as it started sprinkling. Umbrellas came out and now the clouds released their tears and tossed them down on everyone remaining. Carrie stepped back under the tent to thank the Rt. Reverend Bellew, who had been speaking with Victor.

Right now, Carrie knew she owed both the priest and Victor a fair amount of gratitude.

Carrie turned around to thank Victor and was startled to see that about a half dozen yards behind Victor, standing under a tree, holding a black umbrella and wiping chewing tobacco off his mouth, was the troll.

*Good Lord, what's Walter doing here? Digging up a body probably.*

Walter saw her staring and slithered away.

Carrie continued turning and noticed one of Patty's regular customers, Mona Robson, approaching Sergeant Lament. Mona held out her hand to shake his, but Carrie noticed Mona's body language. *She's interested in shaking a lot more than his hand.*

Mona was a few years older than Phil, a tad too rounded off, but cute. In spite of herself, Carrie eavesdropped on them. Mona wanted to know what the sergeant thought of Miss Patty's service. Mona didn't seem the cop's type, but Carrie could be wrong. They chatted a moment before parting ways. Mona then turned to Carrie to express her condolences.

"She'll be restin' in peace 'n the marble orchard soon," Mona said as she stood looking at the closed casket. Then she asked Carrie, "If ya' happen to need any help wit' the store, jus' let me know."

Carrie just smiled, nodded, and watched Mona leave the burial tent with her purple umbrella in full bloom.

Things at the cemetery were winding down and after Carrie gave her thanks to the Reverend and Victor, she was finally alone. She just wanted a moment by herself with Patty.

"Rest in peace, Miss Patty, and *thank you* for everything, but if you don't mind doing me one more favor, please tell my Grandma Hattie and Grandpa Scott hello for me."

She took a yellow rose from the spray on the casket, blew Patty a kiss, and turned away from death. Carrie sat down, reached for her purse under her chair, and swiped a fallen tear from her cheek.

In the land of the living, rain was coming down now in buckets.

"Miss Pyles," a deep voice spoke.

Startled, Carrie looked up quickly, "Sergeant, I didn't realize anyone was still here."

"May I walk you to your car?" he asked politely. "It's a big umbrella."

She started warming up to Lament, though unsure of his intentions.

"Sure, why not?" She joined Lament as the rain punished the rippled grass on the uneven ground.

In a pair of slick black flats, she attempted to keep pace with the man's long stride, but on slippery grass it was just downright treacherous. Carrie's shoes filled up with water as she stepped in a three-inch chuckhole and stumbled sideways. Phil had her arm in a split second.

"Hold onto my arm, Miss Pyles. I'm not trying to be cute, but you may find that it will allow you to steady yourself better."

"Thanks, I wasn't worried. I'm woman enough to take help when I need it."

*The man has a muscular arm, I'll say that for him.* After a short silence, she needed to fill the air between them. She was a talker, and apparently, Phil was not.

"Sure is raining hard," was the only thing she could think to say.

"Yep."

They reached her car and he opened the door, held the umbrella over her until she was safely in her seat. It was a nice gesture.

"Drive safely, Miss Pyles," he said.

"Thanks. You too."

OK, he's not such a bad guy. When the tickets are taken care of, she decided, he'll be off the hook.

Kicking off her wet shoes, she placed them on the back floorboard. She started the car, debating about whether to go back to St. John the Baptist church for the post-funeral gathering or go back to the shop. She chose home, as she didn't particularly like being the center of attention. With everyone in town knowing Patty left the shop to her, she thought it best to let the townsfolk satisfy their need for incursion on someone else. It had already been a long and draining day.

The rain had only slightly begun to slow, but the clouds grew angrier as she was driving home. She planned on calling Travis later to make a date, but then her mind wandered back to Phil. He didn't know Patty well, but there was little doubt he came to the service today because of Carrie.

Phil and Travis were two very different men. Travis was boyish, relaxed, and fun. *Phil might be fun, too, under that entire cop attitude, but I don't believe he was ever a boy.* This thought was interrupted by a bolt of lightning striking a tall post on the left side of the road.

She braked abruptly, and as the car skidded, it hit the curb hard and bounced off like a marble against a wall.

"Shit!" she screamed as she straightened the car out and pulled over to the shoulder. She could feel something was wrong with the tire. Her umbrella was on the passenger side floorboard and with her wet shoes in the back, she settled on just the umbrella for the moment. Unfastening the strap, she let it slightly unfold before opening the car door. She cursed her rain-soaked flats and pushed the umbrella open. Getting out of the car and tiptoeing to the curbside to check for damage, sure enough, she saw she had a flat tire and a busted rim.

"Dammit!"

She walked around to the rear of the car, popped open the trunk, and tried to balance the umbrella between her neck and shoulder in search of the spare tire, when along came a huge furniture truck, drenching her with the gushing, dirty street water.

"Holy shit, *you mudder—*"

Then, there *he* was again. As she looked up from the soaking umbrella, she saw Phil had pulled up several car lengths behind her. No flashing lights this time.

She was glad to see him and his ridiculous sunglasses, now perched on top of his head.

"Hello again, Miss Pyles. May I help you?" he asked, using his best good-Southern-boy manners.

"Don't you have anything else to do?" she snapped, exasperated.

"Miss Pyles," he said calmly, appraising her tire and wheel, "I don't think you're going to be driving anywhere. Two of the nuts are broken off and even if we get your spare on, it's not safe to drive."

"Great, now what do I do?"

"If you will allow me, I'll call a friend of mine, Gary Pilotti, who owns the auto repair shop just down from Mrs. McMurphy's place. You've seen the place, I'm sure. With a few nice words, I bet he could get you fixed up by the end of the day. Do you know any nice words, Miss Pyles?" he slyly quipped.

*I'll be durn, Phil has a sense of humor after all*, she thought—with those being the most words Lament had ever spoken to her and the most welcome ones, indeed.

"OK," she said, relieved. "I'm not in the mood to stand out here in the rain and change a tire if I don't have to."

"As if I'd stand here and let you change your own tire. What kind of man would that make me?" Phil laughed and shook his head.

Not the kind of man I'd want, for sure.

The sergeant looked at her and nodded in the direction of her bare feet.

"Oh, yeah."

Phil walked back to his car and made the call to the auto shop.

With umbrella in hand, she opened the passenger door. She bent over, gathering the contents of her purse that had been thrown onto the floor, and as she reached under the seat for her brush, there it was—the other yellow ticket.

Relieved, she put everything back in her purse, reached into the rear seat, and grabbed her wet shoes. She intentionally put them on showing a little high thigh knowing that the sergeant would be watching.

As she walked back to where Phil was standing under his umbrella, she handed him the second ticket. He grinned and she knew right then he had already taken care of it.

*Nice*, she thought.

Phil assured her that the tow truck was on its way. He pointed to his car and asked her if she would like to sit inside while they waited. The rain had slowed, but she was still dripping wet with a slight shiver.

"Should I sit in front? I've never been in a cop car before and besides, I'm wet."

"You're not being arrested, Miss Pyles, but I can throw the cuffs on if you want," he teased in his low voice.

He opened the front passenger door, allowing her to enter.

As they sat in wait, Carrie asked him if he knew the McMurphy family.

"Can't say I do. I think the McMurphys lived on the other side of Beaufort County."

Carrie stated that even though Miss Patty was her grandmother's dearest friend and she worked at the shop when she was in high school, she realized how little she actually knew about Patty or her family.

The tow truck arrived, cutting short further conversation, and backed up in front of her car. Knowing the auto shop, as did everyone in town, she was happy to hand the young man her keys.

"Ma'am, your car should be fixed by five o'clock. Ya' might want to call the shop at that time to make shur. Would ya' like a ride somewhere or is the good sergeant takin' ya' back to your house?"

"Robbie James, I'll take Miss Pyles back to her house," Phil told him.

The tow truck made its way into traffic with them following behind. As much as she wanted to go home, she suggested the sergeant drop her off at the shop since it was a lot closer to Pilotti's Auto Repair Shop.

"Do you have someone to call that can bring you to the garage to get your car?"

"The last time I had work done, one of Mr. Pilotti's guys brought me my fixed car and I drove him back to the garage, since it's only a few minutes from the shop."

"Well, why don't I come back just before five o'clock and take you there? I've seen how you drive, and I wouldn't want to put Gary's guys at risk like that," Phil smiled.

"You're pretty transparent, Sergeant," she said, calling his bluff.

"Nonsense—to serve and protect, Miss Pyles, that's my job."

Phil pulled into the rocky parking lot at the yarn store and told her to wait while he opened her door. He escorted her to the shop entrance as she unlocked the door.

"Thank you for your help," she said as she entered the store and watched as he drove away.

*What a day*, she thought.

Still chilled and damp, she looked across the way to Patty's house, realizing it belonged to her now. She wondered if there was something dry she could put on until her car was ready.

There must be.

She walked through Patty's back door and wondered what she was going to do with the house. It was a wonderful place, perfect for a bed and breakfast. Carrie didn't have time to run one herself, but maybe someone locally would be interested in taking that on. She didn't want to sell the place as long as she owned the shop.

Soon enough there would be plenty of time to consider all of that.

Looking through the bedroom closet, she found a loose white cotton pullover and a pair of long navy cotton shorts with a string tie at the waist.

Patty was a thin-framed woman, and Carrie was just glad she had anything at all she could get into. Finding a pair of canvas boat shoes in Patty's majestic shoe closet, she put them on and they immediately warmed up her feet. Feeling better now that she was a lot dryer, she got a towel out of the bathroom and rubbed her hair until it was only damp dry. Then, looking in the mirror, she got an unpleasant shock. Her mascara apparently was not waterproof, and a terrible case of raccoon eyes stared back at her.

*Man, I got into Phil's car looking like that. Great,* she thought. Oh well, there's nothing she could do about it now but clean her face and erase the smudges.

Wrapping her wet black dress and black flats in a towel, she glanced around Patty's bedroom and set them down on a woven rug. Sitting on the bed side-saddle, she examined the old pictures still lying there. One was of a young girl, another of a fair-haired boy and girl, a third of an old man. All were black and white shots.

One picture looked familiar.

The photograph was of Grandma Hattie and Patty, maybe seventeen years old at the time, smiling, with arms around each other. The information Carrie had about Patty's early life was scant and she hoped that would change as she started to go through Patty's things and possibly make contact with Camille. That felt less urgent at the moment, but Carrie knew she shouldn't put it off.

As she continued looking at the photos, she noticed the surly storm had picked up again. The thunder clashed and it grew suddenly darker outside, as if someone had closed a heavy theater curtain.

The lights flickered twice, but remained on. *Thank goodness.* Carrie's nerves quickly convinced her on this day of all days, the day of Patty's burial, that she should not be in the unoccupied two-story house of the deceased alone in the dark. She put her wet head towel back in the bathroom and walked toward the door. She wasn't halfway there when a massive crack of thunder shook the house—and the lights went completely out. In high gear now, she double-timed it back to the store. Unsuccessfully dodging the mother-sized rain drops, her nerves were raw.

Carrie finally reached the store and caught her breath upon entering.

"BANG! . . . BANG! . . . BANG!!"

It sounded like someone was whacking the pipes beneath the floors with a wrench. The noise resonated from everywhere, growing louder each time. She couldn't locate the source or the direction. Then as suddenly as it started, it stopped. Carrie tried hard to focus, but the sudden silence was deafening. Even the storm seemed to subside and all she could hear was the pounding of her heart. Willing her heart to slow down, she listened, but the sound didn't repeat.

*Old plumbing*, she told herself, not quite believing it. Instead, images of the cellar came to mind.

Carrie walked over to the hidden cellar door. She moved the heavy wooden shelving unit slightly away from the wall, just enough to get her body behind it, then placed her ear near the gray metal door—and waited.

# Chapter 4

**As** Carrie stood at the shop's door trying to hear anything on the other side, lightning flashed like a strobe light from a bad horror show. The thunder was still rolling, pounding from directly overhead now and resounding like a woman in labor. This was going to be a bad storm. The rain was relentless, bouncing off the black flaking store sashes, painstakingly penalizing the walls of the building. Electricity was irregular, on and off, flickering, confused as to what it wanted to do.

Shit! The cellar can't be any creepier than this.

She decided to go down, but first she needed light.

Carrie had seen a glass candle on the table behind the counter where she had placed her purse. Locating and lighting the small-wick, honeycomb candle with the green-tipped, wooden matches lying next to it, she placed the matchbox in her pocket for safekeeping.

After confirming the store door was locked, she approached the mystery cellar door with the diffused light from the circular container. Now was as good as anytime to examine it further.

It was not a normal-sized door, but slender, more adapted to a willowy fitting, like someone had used this as a secret passageway.

But why?

While standing in the doorframe, which architecturally speaking had no business being in a horse barn, she observed how very basic in design it was. It was as if an amateur carpenter had tried his handiwork. As she wondered about its design and placement, the noise suddenly started again.

Thump—then another thump—then an even more resounding THUMP.

What the heck? Carrie thought. Are the pipes moving and hitting against something? What in the world could it be? Was the noise coming from down there or somewhere else?

She pressed her ear to the door again and—CRASH! The thunder scared the living hell out of her, triggering Carrie to fall onto it, causing it to move inward. Carrie faintheartedly allowed her curiosity to carry her through the metal door to the stairs. Trembling, holding the glass candle with an unsteady hand, she gradually stepped down into the vast darkness of the crypt. The stench in the air was thick. The cinnamon scent of the burning candle made it only slightly more tolerable.

A gentle gust of air joggled the flame, making it dance as if doing the rumba inside its glass cage. Carrie's neck scrunched down into her shoulders in an instinctive protective measure. She looked below and could barely see anything in front of her. The candle wasn't projecting much light and darkness still shrouded her inspection.

As Carrie stepped awkwardly onto the lower steps, almost at the bottom now, she felt coldness on her unprotected ankles. Tripping off the second-to-last step as if something had grabbed her shoe, she stumbled onto the dust-covered cellar floor but still held onto the glass candleholder. The matches flew out of her pocket.

She instinctively looked to where she had heard the wooden matchbox slide and saw the matches lying next to a wooden crate.

As she picked herself up off the floor, there was a sharp pain in her left ankle. She limped across the floor to retrieve the matches. The candle's light reflected against the side of a wood crate boldly stamped with, 'Worth Manufacturing Company.'

Worth Manufacturing Company? *Interesting.*

If she remembered correctly, Buster Mills bought this company out in the late '40s. Worth Manufacturing Company was at that time a huge textile company in North Carolina. It was now just an old derelict building.

Carrie wondered what was inside the chest-high crate. She moved the light around looking for something to help her and spied a rusty crowbar up against the wall. She placed the candle on the floor, grabbed the crowbar, and tried to pry up the nailed lid. Using as much strength as she could muster, she slowly inched the lid off the crate. Leaving the crowbar leveraged in the crate, she picked up the candle and used its low light to look inside. Then she reached in to feel the contents.

She moved moldy paper shreds and felt a hard, cold steely object and then—***Shit!***

The candle blew out. The room went pitch black.

Carrie stepped away from the crate, making a huge effort to breathe.

She swallowed hard to get her heart out of her throat as the crowbar dropped to the ground with a loud BANG reverberating off the walls and floors. Jumping, heart thumping, she reached shakily into her pocket for the wooden matches. With all the courage she could gather, Carrie tried steadying her hand as she struck a match to relight the candle.

Six '*Dammits*' later, she manufactured a good flame with a glow that illuminated the portrait.

The possession of the crate forgotten, she was now drawn to the unknown portrait. She apprehensively approached the area when she felt something on the back of her neck like the feathery light breeze from the wings of a bat.

**"Oooh shittt!"** she screamed.

She brushed the thing away as fast as she could, and then realized it was a string swinging back and forth from the ceiling attached to a light bulb. She caught the swatted strand and pulled it. There was a popping sound and then a shallow light illuminated the room.

Oh, thank God! The electricity must be back on.

The light from the small bulb was not great, but a lot better than the sparse light the candle provided.

She placed the candle down on the top of a crate and walked precariously toward the area of the reflection. Swiping at the cobwebs dangling in her path with disgust, she slowly approached the object.

A monstrous thunderclap erupted overhead and then the lights went out—and stayed off.

Carrie was absolutely terrified. The hair on her neck and arms stood straight out in hysteria.

She lumbered on her sore ankle, reaching out her arm to retrieve the candle off the crate top too quickly and the wick was snuffed out. Trying to relight the wick, as soon as she struck the match, another breeze would blow it out. She lit another one and again it was blown out. Now, as if she was playing a game with a child, she covered the opening so that no breeze would blow the candle out. It was as if the cellar spirits were telling her to leave and stop invading their solitude.

Finally, she got the wick to light.

Knock! Knock! Knock! Carrie nearly jumped out of skin. It took her a moment to realize that in the real world above her, someone was knocking at the store door.

The breeze rushed behind her and pushed her toward the stairs.

*This is too freakin' weird*, Carrie said to herself, as she spun too quickly and once again became painfully aware of her sore ankle.

Gingerly climbing back up the steps, she pressed forward. Trying to throw off the spirits as if shaking snow off her good foot, she climbed as quickly as she could to the top.

Carrie closed the door behind her, pushing the wooden unit back to the wall as if to trap the cellar spirits in their own habitat.

Though the electricity had gone out again, with its large windows, the store was not as dark as the cellar. The lightning flashes illuminated a silhouette at the store door. It was the profile of a small man, an old man—it was Walter.

***Holy shit!*** Even his silhouette frightened her.

An overly drenched Walter entered as Carrie unlocked the door. He looked worse than on a normal day.

"Here," he said coarsely forcing the mail into her hands, while he puddled the floor under his feet.

"Thanks."

Walter stood and looked around the store.

*What does he want?*

Walter then turned and walked out of the store.

"That is one strange old troll," she exclaimed aloud, shaking her head.

Carrie looked around for something to clean up the wet floor where Walter had stood. She found an old rag and as she unraveled it, she read the imprint on the corner, 'Worth Textiles'.

She was in a yarn store and Worth Manufacturing Company was a textile manufacturer so she thought nothing more of it.

After cleaning up Walter's mess, Carrie took the towel to a back room, wrung it out, and draped it on the side of the slop sink. As she returned from the sink, she saw a car pulled up outside.

Gary Pilotti, Phil's friend, pulled on the door handle causing the bell to jingle.

Carrie reappeared from the back room.

"Hi, I'm Gary Pilotti," he said as he reached his wet hand out to shake hers.

"Hi, I'm Carrie Pyles," Carrie said, shaking Gary's hand firmly.

Gary was a small person, with a teddy bear belly, graying mustache, and gentle amber eyes.

"Well, ma'am," he drawled as he took off his dripping baseball cap and straightened his graying hair backwards with his hand, "I had to give ya' a wheel alignment. Ya' hit that curb pretty hard . . . an' um . . . I had to give ya' a new rim an' tire too. Nothin' much I could do 'bout 'em neither," he said.

"OK, thanks, Mr. Pilotti. How much do I owe you?" she asked while gingerly walking behind the counter to get her purse.

"No, ma'am, ya' don't have to worry 'bout it," he said. "Phil told me he'd take care of the expense."

"What?"

"Now, don't be gettin' mad at me or anythin'," Gary reacted. "Phil told me to sen' him the bill."

As if on cue, the sergeant opened the door and stood on the threshold holding a dripping umbrella outside.

"Sergeant," Carrie said in a gritty manner clearly indicating that her short fuse was lit.

"Hey, Gary, ready to go back to the garage?" Phil asked without looking towards Carrie.

"Yeah, shur," Gary said, rather confused by the whole situation.

"Oh, *NO* you don't!" Carrie said to the sergeant. "You're *NOT* just going to walk out that door —"

Gary hurriedly laid Carrie's car keys on top of the counter and quickly followed the sergeant out the door. Carrie moved to the closing door as quick as she could on her aching ankle, but it was too late. As she tried to push the door open, the rain came pounding down on the door in a fierce show of madness. Reluctantly, she gave up and went to find another rag to clean up the water that they'd both let in.

*How could he do this? Phil had no right to pay Gary for working on her car. This wasn't over,* Carrie fumed, while dropping the dry rag and using her good foot to wipe up the floor.

It was early evening when she suddenly realized she was extremely hungry. Carrie tried to avoid the overfilled puddles and went back over to Patty's house to find something to cover up with, she looked at herself in the bedroom mirror.

*Great, just great*, she thought. *I look like the classic old woman wearing Patty's clothing. Phil and Gary must think I'm a half-wit. That's probably why Phil felt sympathetic and paid for the car repairs.*

Turning away from the mirror, Carrie gave up sucker stroking—feeling sorry for herself. She viewed the old pictures still scattered on the bed and pulled a few more out of the box. In the background of a white-framed vintage photo, barely legible, was a building with a faded stencil sign 'Worth Manufacturing Company'. It was an old brick and mortar building, with several people leaning against it, as though they were on a break or holiday from work. *Perhaps it was taken after hours or something*, Carrie thought.

In another pile of pictures, she saw one of a teenage girl with light hair—not black or blonde, but perhaps light brunette or red hair. She couldn't be sure, looking at the faded black-and-white photo.

The storm seemed to be settling a little and Carrie could hear the thunder rolling away in the distance. Looking at the time, her stomach growled like wind in an empty barrel.

Going into Patty's meticulous closet, she took out a tan, double-breasted, trench coat with a sheepskin liner that could be worn together on colder days. She couldn't help to notice the snug fit against her voluptuous chest.

Going downstairs she took her wet clothes and noticed the car was parked perfectly parallel to the curb. Inside there was a white paper mat on the floor with large, dirty footprints.

Carrie drove to Ponticelli's Pizza. When she pulled on the shop's door handle, it played a cheerful tune. There were several families with small children sitting and eating together. Laughter and talking floated all about the place.

The TV behind the bar was a stitch too loud for her, but comfortable for three older guys who sat there drinking their brews and watching the baseball game.

"May I help you?" A young girl, who couldn't be more than sixteen years old, asked Carrie.

"Well, I think I'd like a booth, if one is open."

"Can ya' give me a minute while I clean one up for ya'?"

"Sure."

The young girl took an empty tray to the table, removed the dirty dishes and utensils, and used a blue cotton towel to clean it. She waved to Carrie to come over and handed her a folded menu. Carrie immersed herself in the booth.

After seating other patrons, the young lady returned with a glass of ice water and asked Carrie if she was ready to order.

"Yes, I would like a small grilled chicken with bacon pizza and a cold beer."

"OK," said the girl, goose-necking when she heard a glass break from a reckless child three tables away. She left in a flurry to clean it up.

Carrie looked around at the old pictures on the wall while she waited. There were colored pictures of the place when it opened and some black and whites of older people. Thinking about the pictures she had seen in Patty's room, she wondered if she would recognize anyone in them. She was staring at one in particular on the wall, too engrossed to notice when the door chimed again. In walked Travis and Marcus.

Travis walked up to the young girl, asked to be seated, and as he waited, started talking about the game to a guy sitting at the bar. Travis' boyish laugh caught Carrie's attention and she turned to see who it belonged to.

Travis turned at the same time.

"Hey, Carrie," he said loudly.

Marcus sat down on the black leather barstool next to the older guy that Travis was talking to.

"Hey, Marcus, I'm goin' to visit Carrie over there," he said.

Marcus nodded.

"Hey, can I join you?" Travis asked Carrie as he sat down.

"Um, go ahead. Take a seat," Carrie said, buttoning up the trench coat to conceal Patty's clothes.

After a few minutes, the young waitress came and asked Travis if he wanted to order something. Travis knew what he wanted and ordered a large pepperoni pizza and a beer.

"Can you drink on duty?" Carrie asked.

"Oh, I'm off work. I'm not on duty all the time," he said with his cute boyish chuckle.

*What a charming laugh he has*, Carrie thought.

"Hey, Carrie, a couple of the guys are goin' down to the pool hall to shoot some pool later on. Ya' interested? Would ya' like to join us?" he asked.

"Um, I don't know," but she thought that she hadn't done anything fun in such a long time. It was tempting.

"Oh, come on, what else ya' doin' tonight?" he asked.

"Nothing really."

"Well, then it's a date."

"I have to go home and change first," Carrie said, distractedly holding onto the pockets of the trench coat.

"Well, we're plannin' on meetin' up around 8:30. Do you want me to pick you up?" Travis said rather persistently.

"Um—*OK*. Do you know where 5286 Highway N is?" she said without thinking.

Travis started laughing endearingly and said, "I'm sure I can find it."

"It's been a long day, Travis, with Patty's funeral today and everything," realizing what she had just committed to.

"Hey, I won't keep you out too late tonight, I promise," Travis said, smiling as he displayed the strong, deep dents in his cheeks.

That cute dimpled smile won her over.

"Fine, what time?"

"I'll pick you up around 8:15, OK?"

"Fine, OK."

On the TV, a baseball player hit a homerun and Marcus turned to Travis and said, "Hey, Travis did you see that homer? He went yard."

"Cool," yelled Travis across the room.

"We have a fantasy baseball club and that's one of my team's players," Travis said, inching his head to the side to the see the TV behind the bar.

Carrie rolled her eyes and shook her head. *Boys will be boys.*

"Hey, Travis," she said, trying to regain his attention. "Do you know who those people are in the black and white picture on the wall over there?"

"No idea," Travis said, but Carrie knew well enough that he wasn't listening with both ears.

An older waitress brought them their beers and Carrie's pizza as Travis sat there looking.

"What's that?" he asked.

"Chicken and bacon."

"Chicken? On a pizza?"

"Yeah, and it's all mine," she said as she grabbed a slice and bit into it a little too hastily, burning the top of her mouth. Carrie spat the burning pizza out into a white paper napkin.

Travis belly-laughed loud, hard and buoyant.

She had to laugh, too, as she quickly picked up her beer bottle and swallowed the ice cold drink to soothe the burning sensation.

Supper continued with Travis' wit and charm, teasing Carrie as he secretly watched the baseball game on the TV when he thought she wasn't looking.

"Do you want another beer?" he asked her.

"No thanks, I'm driving."

"And we know how you drive," he said, laughing that cute laugh again.

Carrie rolled her eyes as the young waitress brought their individual checks. Travis grabbed both before she could take it from the waitress.

"I got this one," he said.

"No. Don't you do that," she said, giving him a very stern look. She was unwilling to have another man pay a bill for her today. "If you pay for my supper, I won't go with you to the pool hall," she stated firmly.

"Oh, well then," Travis said as he promptly handed her back the bill. "If that's how you want to be," he said laughing.

Travis asked for her phone number.

Carrie wrote it down on a white paper napkin and handed it to him.

Travis got up and said, "OK, I'll pick you up around 8:15. It's a date."

As Travis waited for her to stand up, he opened his wallet and placed a $2 tip on the table.

Carrie reached into her purse and noticed nothing smaller than a $10 dollar bill in her wallet, so she placed that on the table. She realized she had to go to an ATM before going out tonight.

"Hey, big spender," he said, noticing what she'd done.

Retreating from the table, with her trench coat buttoned up tight, they both continued to the counter to pay.

"OK, I guess I'll see you in a little while," Carrie said, opening the door to leave.

Marcus and the older men sitting at the bar started making a hullabaloo about the ballgame. Travis turned his attention to the TV as Carrie walked on out. Luckily, there was a bank a little way down the road and she pulled up to the ATM.

Driving home, she saw a police car with blue strobe lights streaming that had pulled a car over on the side of the road. She looked as she drove by to see who the officer was, but it wasn't Phil.

*Not surprised. He's only around when I do something wrong*, she thought.

Arriving home, she undressed on the run and took a shower. Time was running out and before too long Travis would be there to pick her up. After drying her hair, she teased it and applied some hairspray. She put a little perfume on her cleavage, wrist, and behind her ears. Going into her closet, she realized she was a little nervous about tonight. She moved hangers back and forth, panicky, looking for the perfect outfit. She grabbed a pair of her favorite blue jeans and a sparkly little red-button top, a blue jean jacket, and her light tan cowboy boots.

Seeing it was now 8:07, she realized Travis would be there any moment. She straightened up the kitchen counter, putting the dishes into the dishwasher. Carrie saw Travis' truck lights as he pulled up the drive and then discovered her clothes and shoes were still strewn across the floor. She hurriedly threw them into the hallway closet and answered the door. "Hi, Travis, come on in."

Travis entered, looked around, and said, "Nice house, ya' ready to go?"

"Thanks, yeah, give me a minute to get my purse."

Travis walked a little further into the house and saw her black lacy bra lying on the ground—something Carrie missed when rushing around.

"Hey, looky here," he said, laughing as he picked up her bra, stretching it out against his broad chest.

"Oh, shit—give that to me," she said as the blood rushed to her cheeks.

Carrie took it from him and swiftly opened the hallway closet door and threw it in when Travis turned away.

"Are you ready?" she inquired.

"Sure—are you?" Travis replied.

"Yeah, let's go before I change my mind."

"Yes, ma'am, don't wan'cha changin' your mind now," he said, laughing that cute little chuckle of his.

Travis opened the front door as a gentleman would and allowed Carrie to exit before him.

Accustomed to leaving houses unlocked in the country, Travis just shut the door and followed Carrie to his truck. At the last moment, Travis jumped ahead to open the passenger door of his four-door, black Chevy truck for Carrie to climb in. She noticed it was immaculate. The truck shone on the outside from the porch light and was also spotless on the inside.

"Nice truck."

"Thanks. This is my baby," he said proudly and proceeded to tell her the deal that he got on it, how long he had it, and everything that was loaded in it.

*Man talk*, she declared to herself. *Bless his heart.*

"What do you do for fun, Carrie?" Travis asked suddenly.

"I like to weave. My Grandma Hattie has a huge loom and when I want to escape, I go on the loom and get lost for hours."

This must have bored him as he turned on the radio to the ballgame while she was talking.

"Oh, I'm sorry, was I boring you?" Carrie questioned.

"No. Sorry. I just don't unnerstand what the weavin' thing is all 'bout," he said. "Have ya" been to the textile factory upstate?"

"No, but one of these days I plan on going."

"My granny used to work at one," and he paused, thinking. "A lot of other folks' parents an' grandparents used to work at them too. Guess it was the thing to do back then," Travis said.

"Really? That's interesting. I wonder if your granny would know some of the people in some old pictures I found in Miss Patty's house. I would love to know who they are."

"Well, Granny has seen better days, I'm afraid," said Travis, "but who knows, maybe."

Driving through town, passing some old boarded-up stores where graffiti artists displayed their work proudly, Carrie looked at the lighted marquee over the movie theater. They passed an ice cream parlor where several local kids were hanging out and an old, white-steepled Lutheran church surrounded by a white picket fence. Finally, they reached the pool hall, an old, whitewashed, wood-framed, black-roofed building that looked like something horse-drawn buggies used to tie up to. It was surrounded by rocks and potholes overfilled with mud puddles.

Travis came around, opened her door, and extended his hand to assist her out of the truck.

"Thanks," she replied.

"No—thank you, ma'am," and bowing his head in a cute manner. He reached out his arm to escort her through the pool hall door.

Accepting his arm, Carrie walked into the smoke-filled pool hall feeling a little shy, as everyone looked at thc both of them when they entered. Carrie noticed the pool hall was mostly full of 20- to 30-year-old guys dressed in their blue jeans and T-shirts. The girls were trying out their Daisy May shorts with striped shirts tied at the waist and cleavage showing from their push-up bras. Almost all wore cowboy boots, smoked cigarettes, and drank beer. There were people throwing darts while several TVs played different sport games throughout the pool hall. The guys stood around watching and talking.

"Hey, you want a beer?" Travis asked.

"Let me buy the first one, since you drove."

"Sure, go for it," he said as a scrawny, thin-haired guy walked up and shook Travis' hand.

"I'll be right back."

There were several gals with big hair and guys in their cowboy hats in front of her at the bar counter. While waiting, she viewed the various neons strung about the place. There was a bright green bar sign, a yellow cigar sign blinking on and off as if it had an electrical short, and other mirrored advertising signs throughout. Then she noticed some old pictures framed on the wall.

"Well, looky here, a Scooby snack. Wha' can I getcha, sugar?" said the bartender with tattoos colorfully decorated on both arms and licking his chops as he checked Carrie out.

Carrie looked around, "Who me? Two beers, please."

"I see ya' came 'n wit' Travis ova' there," he said as he placed the two beers on the counter.

"Yeah. Thanks," she said, trying to hand him a ten-dollar bill.

He said the first one was on him.

*What is it with this town? I can pay,* she thought. "Thanks."

Gary Pilotti approached her as she was putting the money back into her purse.

"Hey, Carrie, I thought that was you. How's your car runnin'?"

"Great," she said. "It's running better than it has in a long time. I don't remember the last time I had a wheel alignment."

"Well, it was my pleasure, ma'am," Gary said politely as Travis approached.

"Hey, Gary, how's it goin'?" Travis reached out his hand to shake Gary's.

"Fine, just talkin' to this pretty lady 'bout fixin' her car today," said Gary.

"What? Somethin' happen to your car?" Travis asked.

"Oh, nothing much, I don't want to bore you with small details," she said to Travis while stealing a smile at Gary.

"Hey, Travis."

"Hey, y'all. Mona—Miss Marla, how are ya' fine ladies doin' tonight?" Travis replied.

They all walked over to where Mona and Marla were seated.

"Hey, Carrie, wha'cha doin' here? Did ya' come wit' Travis?" Mona asked.

"Yeah, I ran into him at Ponticelli's and he wouldn't let me say *No* to come out to shoot some pool tonight."

Gary pulled the chair out for Carrie, allowing her to sit down.

*Holy cow*, Carrie thought, not sure she liked this kind of attention. She had been used to doing things for herself. Not having a man around for years, she'd grown quite independent.

While listening to the loud country music playing, Carrie saw a dartboard open up.

Travis was having a long conversation with Mona and Marla about this and that, that didn't pertain to Carrie.

When some more guys approached the table and started talking baseball, Carrie asked Gary, "Do you throw darts?"

"Shur."

"Do you want to throw some?"

"OK—*Ya' throw darts?"* Gary questioned.

Apparently, the regular ladies only play pool or sit at the table drinking.

"Yeah, I threw some when I was in college," Carrie said.

Gary was an older guy, not too tall, and round like a teddy bear.

"Ya' went to college?" Gary asked as he approached the dartboard.

"Yeah, my Grandma Hattie made sure I went to college, wouldn't have had it any other way."

"What did ya' learn? I mean, take up? Did ya' graduate?" he asked almost stuttering.

Smiling at Gary, "I graduated as magna cum laude with a business degree," Carrie said proudly.

"Magna cum *wha*?" he asked.

"Never mind," she said laughing. "What color do you want?"

Gary called for black and she took the red darts.

They played a friendly game of trash and Carrie beat Gary with ease.

"Hey, Gary, can I buy you a beer?" Carrie asked.

"Shur, but I should be buyin' since ya' won."

"No worries," Carrie said. She was enjoying herself now and feeling a bit more confident.

"Hey, Gary—you have lived here all your life, right?"

"Um, yeah. Why ya' askin'?" he wondered.

"Well, would you know any of the older town folks here?"

"Well, I sup'ose I've worked on just 'bout ev'ry person's car 'n this an' surroundin' towns," Gary said.

"Do you happen to know the people in that picture over there?" Carrie asked, testing him.

"Oh *shur*—that one ova' there is Billy an' Tilly Sykes an' the one ova' there is Ermita an' Paulie Henderson. Why ya' wanna know?" he asked as they walked off towards the bar.

"Well, I found some old pictures in Miss Patty's place and can't help to wonder who the people could be. Wouldn't mind you taking a look or two to see if you could recognize any of them."

"Be my pleasure, ma'am, but my gramma prob'bly be the betta' one to ask," Gary advised.

"Well, I'll call you and we'll plan on getting together sometime soon—OK?"

"Yes, ma'am."

As Carrie and Gary reached the bar, Travis yelled out, "Hey, Carrie, shoot some pool?"

Carrie looked back at Travis holding two light tan cue sticks.

"Sure, do you need a beer?"

"Yes."

Ordering the three beers, she paid the bartender the ten dollars and left.

Gary told her that it was ladies' night and the ladies drink free.

*Oh, sure, that's why I got the free beer the first time around*, Carrie thought. *Oh well, no worries.* She was having fun and felt relief at having found someone who might shed some light on Patty's pictures.

Carrie met Travis at the pool table and after beating him three games to none, she asked Travis if he would take her home.

"Sure," he said a little beaten up from the shame Carrie rendered on him.

"*Hey, Travieee,*" yelled a drunk girl.

Carrie looked around to see who it was. It was Dana, the skinny blonde-haired nurse from the emergency room at the hospital.

"*Youuu arrren'tt leavin', are you, Travie?*" she said, a little too drunk and staggering up to Travis.

"*Oh, Travis, you haven't talked to me all night long,*" Dana said, appending her hands to his bicep.

"Oh, hi, Dana," Travis said and then he looked at Carrie.

"Go ahead and talk to her, I'll be over here." Carrie turned, walked away, and sat down at the table closest to the door. She waited for Travis to settle Dana down and see if she was alright to drive. By the look on his face, it was evident that he didn't want to take Dana home, probably because he was afraid she would get sick in his truck.

Dana had whispered something to Travis while she rubbed up and down on his arm. Travis took Dana's arm and walked her to a table, pulled out a chair, sat her down, and then went off to get some coffee to sober her up. Carrie just sat there at the table, looking around at the pictures, when in walked the sergeant.

"Miss Pyles," he said.

*You again?* Carrie thought, trying to maintain her composure, not wanting to make a scene like Dana, knowing she wouldn't even if she was that drunk.

"What are you doing here, Sergeant? Are you following me again?" Carrie asked.

The sergeant wasn't dressed in his uniform. He was wearing a very nice pair of pressed blue jeans, cowboy boots, black shirt, and a black jacket. Without a doubt, Carrie thought that he was the finest looking man in the whole place.

She tried not to stare, while trying consciously to hold the drool back from her salivating tongue.

"Miss Pyles, what a surprise," he said with a snicker.

"Sure, I guess you couldn't find anyone pulled over on the side of the road with a flat tire, so you just decided to stop in here?" Carrie said a little too sarcastically with her hands on her hips and her shirt pulling a little at the top, showing her cleavage.

"Miss Pyles, I just came in for a drink. I didn't expect to see you here," the sergeant replied.

"Looking for damsels in distress, are you now?"

"Sure," he said sardonically.

Dana was causing a commotion and Travis looked over at the both of them.

"Hey, Phil, can I ask for a favor," Travis said.

*Oh, no, you don't! YOU WOULDN'T!* she thought, as her blood pressure started rising and her cheeks blowing up like red balloons.

"Can ya' take Carrie home for me? I kinda got my hands full with Dana here."

Carrie threw a death stare back at Travis, but he didn't see it. Travis had turned back to Dana who was still being loud and causing a hubbub as Travis tried to settle her down.

"Ready, Miss Pyles?" the sergeant asked.

"But you just got here and wanted to get a drink."

"It can wait."

"Sure, I'm ready."

# Chapter 5

**The** sergeant, being a polite and reliable man and perhaps a model for Michelangelo's David, walked Carrie to his silver Ford truck. Opening the truck door, he allowed her to enter, then politely closed it.

Carrie was dreading this. She was alone with the man who paid her car repair bill earlier today. She had not forgotten. She looked at him as he crossed in front of the truck and deeply admired his good looks.

*No*, she told herself, convincing herself that she was still pissed at the sergeant's transgressions.

The sergeant got in, buckled up, and started the engine. He looked over at Carrie to make sure she was in safely. Yes, Carrie had buckled up.

Carrie saw him look at her and said, "What? I always wear my seatbelt."

"That's good to know."

"Hmmm. . . ."

"Hmmm—what?" the sergeant asked.

"I'm so spitting mad at you," she said in her most exasperating voice. "Why in the world did you take it upon yourself to think that I couldn't pay my car's repair bill today? Why were you there when I hit the curb? Why did you show up at the pool hall? Why are you always—there?" Carrie grew more frustrated as she loosened her seat belt awkwardly, trying to sit side-saddle. She ran her hands through her hair as if pulling at every follicle in her head.

The sergeant just kept driving until Carrie settled down. "Miss Pyles, if I may speak."

Carrie settled back against the headrest and said, "Oh, please do."

"Miss Pyles, I was instructed to work Mrs. McMurphy's funeral today. That is why I was at the funeral and drove the procession to the cemetery. If you remember, I walked you to your car in the rain after you left the burial tent and watched as you drove off. I was a ways back, when I saw the lightning strike the pole on the side of the road. That's when I saw your car hit the curb and you hit it hard. I thought it was the right thing to do to assist you in your time of need, that's why I slowed and pulled over. Then, when you were standing at your trunk and the furniture truck drove by, I saw it splash you pretty good. Nothing I could do about that, but—" he paused and laughed in a clearing-throat manner.

"I thought I could provide you some assistance. That is when I went up to you and offered my help. When you went into your car to get your things, I called my friend, Gary Pilotti, and told him what happened. You were fortunate that Gary had just finished up with a car and was able to send someone straight away, and because it was *me* calling, he would get it done by the end of the day. I concluded that you already had a rough day and took the responsibility to bring Gary back to the shop after he dropped off your car. Gary's a good man and a darn good mechanic. I do not let anyone else work on my car, and he's a trusted friend. Yes, I took the liberty of paying the repair bill. Pay me back then if that will make you happy. I was just trying to make your day easier."

Before the sergeant allowed Carrie to speak, he continued, "and as for tonight, this isn't the first time that I have visited the pool hall for a drink, but I believe it was yours. Now, if I may ask, how did you meet up with Travis tonight?"

Carrie tried to absorb everything and determined the narrative the sergeant had just given her was, in fact, the actual truth.

"Well, Miss Pyles, I believe it's your turn," the sergeant advised.

"Huh, oh yeah," Carrie said. "You know Ponticelli's pizza parlor; well, I went there for some supper and Travis ended up there with Marcus. He invited himself to join me at my table and talked me into going out tonight. He called it a date," she said hesitantly.

"Oh, I see," the sergeant said.

"Then Dana, the ER girl from the hospital, was there. Do you know her?"

"Yes, I know Dana Foster," he replied.

"Is or was there something between Travis and her?" Carrie inquired.

"I think they may have dated, but you may want to ask Travis next time you see him to get the full story; I'm not the one to ask."

As the sergeant reached Carrie's house, she asked, "Did I tell you where I lived? How did you know?"

"Hmmm," he said, clearing his throat, "if you remember, I wrote you a ticket."

"And you remember everyone's addresses that you write tickets for?" Carrie questioned.

"No, I can't say I remember everyones'," he said with a gleaming white smile, crescent-shaped chin dimple deeply affixed to his tanned face.

Carrie started feeling a little more brazen as the sergeant stopped the truck by her front door. It was his chiseled smile that made her feel at ease. Carrie took the sergeant's hand as he assisted her out of his truck, looked into the sergeant's eyes, and saw by the porch lights that he had deep brown eyes. She just realized this was the first time she had seen his eyes because he wasn't wearing his stupid sunglasses. She was too distraught before to have noticed.

"Sergeant Lament, I would like to invite you in so I can write you a check to pay you back for the car repairs. I'll even offer you a beer, if you still want one."

"It's getting late," he said.

But before he could say another word, Carrie insisted he accept her invitation.

"OK, fine," he relented.

The sergeant opened the door and allowed Carrie to enter. Carrie walked into the house and headed straight for her checkbook on the kitchen counter. The sergeant stood at the front door, deciding if it was best to leave or stay.

He decided to stay and walked over to the brown leather couch. Unbuttoning his black jacket before he sat down, Carrie yelled, "Hey, Sarge, you want a beer, a scotch, whiskey? I think I might have some gin, but I know I'm out of vodka. I have some red wine too, if you're a wine man." Carrie came around the corner with her purple leather checkbook in hand and said, "Go ahead and sit down."

"I'll take a beer, thanks," Sarge said as he sat down and crossed his left ankle over his right knee. He stretched his right arm the length of the brown leather couch, waiting for Carrie to return with the beer.

She returned shortly with chips in a small glass bowl and two beer bottles held to her chest by her arm, and sat on the opposite end of the couch.

She handed him a beer and took the checkbook out of her back pocket with a pen attached. She started writing a check. Dating the check she looked up and asked, "What is your name, Phil, Phillip, Felipe?"

"'Phil' is fine."

"Do I spell your last name l-a-m-o-n-t?"

"No, it's Lament," and he spelled it out.

"So, your name is Phil Lament," she giggled.

"What?" he questioned.

"You know, filament, like a thin fiber," and giggled again. "I'm a weaver and it's a yarn term." She giggled a little louder now.

"Oh, and you're name is Carrie Pyles. I bet no one ever made fun of that," he smiled playfully.

"What?"

"Yeah, Carrie Pyles full of—" and he laughed a gorgeous deep-throated chortle.

Never seeing this playful side of him, Carrie liked it, even though she was the one being made fun of. He had the most beautiful dark brown eyes and bright white teeth, with an absolutely gorgeous thin-lip smile. Carrie couldn't take her eyes off him and wanted to kiss that mouth on that bronze face of his. Recovering from the lust she was feeling, she signed the check and tore it out of her checkbook. She never wrote in an amount, and without thinking, she handed him a signed blank check.

After chatting awhile longer she asked him, "Would you like another beer?"

"Sure, one more if you're having one."

While Carrie was away, the sergeant looked at the blue paper check, folded it, and placed it in his wallet. He smiled and grabbed some chips to eat.

When Carrie returned with the cold beers, she saw he wasn't wearing a wedding ring and asked, "Tell me, Sarge, if you don't mind me asking, why aren't you married?"

"I was married," he replied, taking a big gulp of beer to hide the pain saddening his eyes.

"Oh, really?"

"No, it's nothing like that." He sighed, "My wife died two years after we were married when she was upcountry visiting her parents. There was a bad snowstorm. She lost control of the car and went off the road and rolled down a mountainside, hitting a tree. We didn't find the car for three days. The roads were that bad."

"Oh, I'm so sorry; I didn't mean to pry." She tried to hide the tears forming in her eyes.

The sergeant finished his beer before hers was half-gone.

"Look, it's getting late," he said as he stood up.

"Yeah, it is. I'm sorry I didn't mean to keep you out this late, you probably have to get to work early tomorrow." She started rambling on rather nervously and moving about the room.

"No, it's OK. I'm actually off tomorrow," he said.

"So, you won't be hanging around dark corners trying to catch me speeding then?"

"Don't speed and you won't have to worry about anyone hanging around dark corners catching you speeding," he said logically.

"Yeah, OK, point made," she said and rolled her eyes.

As the sergeant walked to the door, he turned back to Carrie, "Thanks for the beer."

"You're welcome, any time. And thank you for helping me out today," she said, watching him leave. "Be safe," Carrie said as she watched him walk to his truck. She shut the door rather quickly and missed seeing him turn to look back.

*Wow, what a day this has been,* she thought, cleaning up the beer bottles and placing the uneaten chips back in the bag after snacking on a few. *What a handsome man Sarge is without his sunglasses. His face was faultless. His body perfect and those blue jeans he was wearing were mighty fine. Yes, indeed,* she thought as she finished cleaning up the room.

She remembered the wet clothes in the foyer closet, and in her approach, she saw that her bra strap was sticking out beneath the door.

*Oh, shit, I hope the sergeant didn't see this.* Taking the wet clothes from the closet, she placed them in a laundry basket next to the washer.

Back upstairs, she washed her face and got ready for bed.

Tomorrow's another day, she thought.

***

Carrie scrunched her pillow tight and dreamed she was wearing an oversized raincoat going down a long alleyway, when the phone rang.

Rolling over, she covered her head with the pink top sheet and allowed the call to go to the recorder. The clock said 9:23 a.m. *Oh, I might as well get up.* She couldn't convince herself to fall back asleep.

Getting up and 'using the lavatory', as her grandma used to say, Carrie washed her face and proceeded downstairs. She was glad that she'd set up the coffee machine the night before. It had just finished brewing by the time she reached for the pot. Sipping on coffee, she went to get the newspaper off the front yard, but of course, it was under the porch. She retrieved it and went back inside. As she always did by habit, she opened the paper, quickly scanned the headlines, then went straight for the horoscope section. It read:

"Today will be full of unexplained connections; others may be more forthcoming."

Out of the corner of her eye, she saw the blinking recorder on the counter displaying two messages. She pushed the play button.

"Hey, Carrie, Travis here. Are ya' up? I want to talk to ya'. Call me when you're up."

The next message was, "Carrie, I really want to talk, let me know when you're up, please! This is Travis."

*How could Travis have asked Sarge to take her home? Wasn't last night supposed to be a date? Why didn't Travis ask Sarge to bring Dana home instead?*

Carrie ignored his messages. She was still upset with Travis, even though the night ended up nicely and she got to know Sarge a little better.

Eating a biscuit split with jam, Carrie finished her coffee when the phone rang again. Reluctantly, she reached for the phone.

"Hello."

"Hello, Miss Pyles? Victor Abbott here, I need to meet up with you to sign a few more papers and give you a few things that Miss Patty left in my possession."

"Hello, Victor. Good morning," she replied. "What?"

"Miss Carrie, I didn't want to overwhelm you when we met up the first time, but I have more papers about the trust for you to sign and a few more items of Miss Patty's to give you. Can we meet up around 1:30? I can meet you at your house or the store if you prefer."

"The store will be fine," Carrie replied quickly.

"OK, then I'll see you at 1:30," Victor said and hung up as if distracted by something in his office.

Remembering when Grandma Hattie passed, it seemed like mountains of papers needed her signature too and she thought nothing more of it. She continued to clean up, got dressed in a pair of blue jeans, black T-shirt, and a chambray shirt with sleeves rolled up to her elbows. She put her hair in a ponytail, applied some makeup, and a found a pair of flip-flops to wear.

Arriving at the shop about half an hour early, Carrie had no sooner put down her purse behind the counter when the store's phone started to ring.

"Hello," Carrie said.

"Hi, this is Virginia Firth. I'm sorry to hear 'bout Miss Patty's passin'," she said, "but would you know anythin' 'bout next week's weavin' lessons Miss Patty was havin'? Some of the girls are wonderin' if it was still goin' to take place."

"Well, Virginia, I don't know yet. Can I get your phone number and call you back as soon as I understand what's going on?"

"Shur, but some of the girls are goin' to the county fair ova' the weekend. I can tell them so you won't have to. My phone numba' is—"

"Thank you, Virginia. As soon as I find Patty's scheduling book, to see what she had planned, I'll give you a call."

She hung up the phone but had not let go of it when it rang again.

"Hello, this is Adeene Woode, sorry to hear about Miss Patty's passin'," she said, "but would you know anythin' 'bout next week's weavin' class?"

"Hi, Adeene, I just talked with Virginia Firth and told her that as soon as I find Patty's scheduling book, I'd call and let her know what's going on. I have your phone number, and I'll call you back as soon as I figure things out." She had no sooner said goodbye and hung up when it rang again.

"Screw it," she said and decided to let it go to the recorder. She saw that there were six other messages displayed.

Carrie looked around for the black leather scheduling book that Patty kept and recorded everything in. It was Patty's lifeline for the store. She kept the inventory, orders, bills, check register, weaving class schedules—everything—in this methodically organized book. She remembered Patty telling her she'd be lost without it. She looked on the table behind the counter, then went back into Patty's office in search of it when she heard the door jingle.

Victor entered the store and stood with his black leather attaché in hand.

"Hello, Miss Pyles," Victor said.

"Hi, Victor."

"May we go into the office?" he asked. "I need you to sign some more papers."

"Sure, but I'm going to lock the door so we won't be disturbed," Carrie advised.

Upon reaching the office, Victor opened the attaché and took out a manila folder, leaving the black attaché open.

"These are just the trust papers for the bank, so your trust will be relinquished to you. You should be able to draw from it in a couple of days," he said, moving the papers in front of her to sign. They were marked with little yellow stickies directing to the section that her signature and date were required. She signed more papers regarding the mortgage title and the power of attorney to take over Patty's banking account—paperwork putting everything in Carrie's name. The phone rang several different times during this process but she let the calls go to the recorder.

When she completed the task of signing everything, Victor reached into the black attaché and handed her a small envelope that held Miss Patty's safe-deposit box keys at the bank. She noticed the bank was on the other side of town.

"I noticed that Miss Patty used two different banks?"

Victor replied, "Miss Patty used the one down the street for the business and personal expenses and this one for the safe-deposit box."

"Oh, OK." Carrie tried to understand the concept behind this. *Perhaps the small bank down the street wasn't big enough to house safe-deposit boxes.*

As Victor closed up his attaché, he said, "Well, Miss Carrie, I think this concludes our business today."

"OK, thanks," Carrie said.

"Do you know when you will be opening the store again to customers?" he asked while they walked out of the office.

"I have to find Miss Patty's scheduler to know what she had planned before I know what to do. Mr. Abbott, I mean Victor, can I start writing checks from Miss Patty's account to pay bills now?"

"Sure, just sign it with your name. I'll get the paperwork to the banks on my way to the office, so they will know you will be signing checks on the account."

Carrie unlocked the front door, as Victor reached out his hand and said, "Miss Pyles, if you need anything, do not hesitate to call."

Shaking his hand, she said, "Thanks, I will."

Victor exited and Carrie retreated into Patty's office, gathering the duplicates of the papers she had just signed. As she looked around, she found the black leather scheduling book. She must have unknowingly moved it when meeting Victor the first time after learning that Patty had left everything to her.

Sitting down at the desk, Carrie opened it up to see if she could comprehend what was going on with the store.

Carrie learned from the scheduling section that Patty did have weaving classes starting up on Monday. Four people had signed up, Virginia Firth, Emeline Browning, Adeene Woode and Jenny Lee Jones, with everyone but Virginia paying up front. Phone numbers were all next to their names.

*Good*, Carrie thought, she'd give them all a call to let them know that it'll start up on Monday. Being a passionate weaver herself, she looked forward to the upcoming weaving classes, a type of normalcy for her.

Continuing to look through the book, she viewed what inventory had been ordered and who the orders were for. Turning to the check register section, she briefly glanced at the total Patty had in the account: $20,350.

Distracted by the sheer persistence of the phone ringing yet again, Carrie gave up looking through the scheduler. Knowing it was best not to put the recorder messages off any longer, she pressed the button to listen and started writing down names and phone numbers.

The third message was from Travis. Knowing she couldn't put off returning Travis' call, she picked up the phone and dialed.

Her back was facing the door when she heard it open and just as the phone started ringing on the other end, in walked the old troll, Walter.

Disconnecting the call before Travis could answer, she addressed Walter.

"Hey, Walter," she said coolly. He really did give her the creeps.

"Hey," he said in his gravelly voice. "Anythin' goin' out?"

"Not today."

From his worn blue satchel, Walter passed her a package wrapped in brown paper held together by strings with a few other envelopes sitting on top.

Carrie placed the package behind the counter and saw a letter from a bank and an electric bill for the store.

Walter stood in the store and looked around again, as if he was looking for something in particular.

"Can I help you with anything else?"

He just turned and walked out, mumbling something under his breath.

Opening the white bank envelope first, Carrie noted that it was a renewal notice for the safe-deposit box.

*What timing*, she thought.

She made a mental note to do that tomorrow and returned to listening to the rest of the recorded messages before spinning in the numbers on the black rotary phone. Talking to some in long-winded conversations and leaving messages for others, Carrie marked in the black leather scheduler that all had been contacted.

Writing a check for the safe-deposit box, she wrote in the check number, the amount of the bill, and saw that the total account balance was not, in fact, $20,350—it was $203,560!

"**Holy shit**," Carrie said aloud. "How can that be?"

Sitting upright and trying to comprehend this enormous sum, she heard the door jingle as in walked Travis with a lovely bouquet of flowers in hand.

"Oh, hey, Travis," she said despondently.

"Hey, I saw you called but you hung up before I could answer," he said rather serenely.

"Yeah, someone walked in just when I tried calling you."

"That's OK," he said, "I just wanted to make sure that you were alright. I got these flowers for you—here," Travis said as he handed her the assortment of daisies, carnations, and pink roses.

"I really want to 'pologize for last night. Dana was too drunk to be left 'n that state," Travis said, trying to explain.

"Yeah, OK, but I didn't appreciate being pawned off on Sergeant Lament," she said sternly. "Thanks for the flowers." She smirked as she turned away looking for a vase.

"I know an' I'm sorry. I really am. It's just that—Dana an' I have a lil' history together. We're not seein' each other anymore, so when I saw ya' talkin' to Phil, I dinn't know what else I could do." He tried justifying the situation. "I only asked Phil because I knew," he paused, "that I could ask him to take ya' home."

"It's OK, Travis."

"No, Carrie, I really wanna make it up to ya'. I really had a good time wit'cha. There's the Beaufort County fair this weekend. Go wit' me an' let me make it up to ya'," he pleaded.

"Travis, that's OK," Carrie said, trying to shake him off.

"Sweet cheeks, I won't take 'No' for an answer; I owe ya' this. Please, give me one more chance."

Carrie looked at him with his puppy dog eyes as Travis endeared himself as much as he could, his head slightly tilted to the side.

Trying to be nice, Carrie replied, "I'll think about it."

"Can I call ya' tomorra'?" he asked politely.

"Sure," she said as his beeper once again interrupted them.

"Dammit, I have to go. Carrie I'm callin' ya' tomorrow. I'm not gonna let ya' say 'No,'" he said as he opened the door and left before she could answer.

Finding a thick-necked blue vase under the counter, Carrie got water from the slop sink in the backroom and set the flowers in it. She placed the vase on the wooden table behind the counter.

Kylie Lewis came in with her Aunt Vita to purchase yarn, stayed, and talked in long-winded conversation, reminiscing about Miss Patty.

North Carolina reflects a wide variety of dialects and wherever there is language with such a vast diversity, the spoken word can be confusing, yet humorous. Kylie and Vita were from the banks on the way down toward Ocracoke and spoke a different dialect than Carrie did altogether. Vita was discussing the sideglogging on her rug and couldn't figure out if it was the threads or just her eyesight. Kylie apparently teased Vita and said it was her mind that was a sidegloggle and they both laughed heartily. Carrie only caught a few words of their conversation, but smiled, nodded, and listened politely. Vita advised Carrie that it wasn't necessary to paper poke the threads she bought and placed the coils of worsted yarn in her oversized carpet bag. Kylie opened the store door and told Vita to put on her shawl as it was airish outside. Carrie looked out and saw branches slightly swaying in the breeze.

***

Carrie drove home slowly, contemplating and planning what she was going to do for the training session on Monday, what items she might need to order, and then it hit her like a ton of bricks, she marveled at the *large* amount of money in Patty's account.

*How can that be? It's just a yarn store,* she thought.

Upon reaching the house, Carrie took a beer out of the icebox and microwaved some leftover pizza. Finding a pen and some paper, she proceeded to make a checklist of items that needed to be accomplished before the re-opening on Monday.

There would be no grand parade, no high-power sky searchlights visible for miles to tell the North Carolinians that Carrie was open for business. She did allow herself to briefly fantasize about being driven in a Pontiac Firebird Trans-Am convertible while she smiled and waved to people as they cheered in anxious anticipation, and then she unlocked the doors and welcomed them all into her store. She came out of her trance when Walter entered the store with his shabby blue mail sack weighing heavily on his hunched, drooping posture. Shaking herself back into reality, she took the blue ink pen and lined paper and began to write.

TO DO LIST

- Look at training session and see who has what from previous sessions on the separate looms? Understand what each person is doing or trying to accomplish and find a way to help
- What does Patty have on order? Estimate time of arrival of the items and look to see what the pay terms are
- Review who ordered what for the customers who were calling about their orders
- Look at Patty's bills and see what is due to be paid

Sitting back, drinking her beer while eating her now cooled pizza, she wondered what else she needed to do and wrote one more item:

- Go to bank and get into the safe-deposit box

After completing the list, Carrie decided to do some weaving and when a strand broke, she fixed it with the weight of a wine bottle, tightened up the row, and called it a night.

***

The morning was hopeful, with a cloudless sky and a wispy warm breeze exhaling like angels blowing bubbles. Doing her morning routine, she read her horoscope for the day:

"Fibers of life may unravel today, understanding will be unknown."

Trying to absorb what this message meant, she sat back and sipped on her coffee. She thought about her weaving last night and secretly hoped nothing went wrong with her project.

Putting her blue, ceramic coffee cup in the sink, she thought about everything that needed to be accomplished today.

Looking around for the list she made, she re-examined it and decided she'd better get started if she was to accomplish anything today.

Making her way to the Henderson's Bank and Trust on the other side of town, she arrived at the light brown brick building. There were a few people standing in line.

*It's Friday*, Carrie thought as she looked at her silver watch.

Grandma Hattie didn't have a safe-deposit box, so Carrie wasn't sure what she had to do and took a place in line. When she approached the young male bank teller and told him she would like to get into Patty McMurphy's safe-deposit box, the bank teller told her that she would have to talk to Andy.

"Hey, Andy, this young lady wants to get into a box. Can ya' help her?" he yelled across the room.

A thick-framed man wearing wire-rimmed glasses approached her, "Hi, I'm Andy. How may I help you today?"

"Um, well, I would like to get into Mrs. Patty McMurphy's safe-deposit box; I have the key," Carrie said not knowing the protocol.

"You want to get into Patty McMurphy's safe-deposit box?" he questioned as if she was a lunatic.

"Yes sir, see Mrs. McMurphy passed away and I have a Power of Attorney letter and her lawyer, Victor Abbott, gave me the key, so I thought I would come by. I also received the renewal bill in the mail yesterday, and I would like to pay it while I'm here," she said rather nervously.

"Can you give me a minute?" he asked.

"Sure."

Andy left her standing there while he walked away to talk to a well-dressed man in a suit with his back turned to her. Andy had taken the papers from Carrie and showed them to this gentleman. After a few minutes in discussion, the nicely dressed older man approached her.

"Hello, Miss Pyles, my name is Robert Twiford. We met briefly if you remember." He reached out to shake her hand. She obliged and shook with a firm handshake.

"Yes, nice to see you again," Carrie replied.

"Ma'am, it was only yesterday that Victor Abbott came by with the death certificate and Power of Attorney papers that you signed. I see you have your copies with you. May I escort you over here," he said and walked her to a room off of the lobby.

"Would you like something to drink?" Robert asked as he pointed for Carrie to take a seat.

"No thanks."

"If you wouldn't mind, I need a minute to get a few things."

"OK, that's fine," Carrie replied, still not fully understanding what was going on.

Robert left her alone in the room and Carrie was sure that he was confirming that she wasn't there to steal anything of Patty's. Sitting in the quiet, she pondered going with Travis to the fair when the door reopened.

"Miss Pyles, I just need you to put in your information and sign here on the contract," and he pointed. "The bank can then put the safe-deposit box in your name and remove Mrs. McMurphy from it," Robert said as he sat down. "It's just the formalities to make the change over," he said and handed her a pen.

Carrie obliged as requested.

"If you wouldn't mind following me, I'll take you to the safe-deposit box now," he said as he stood up.

She followed him into another room that had all these little bronze doors with numbers on them and looked around in amazement. Patty's number was 285 and she searched with her eyes to find it. Mr. Twiford escorted her to a larger area, not the normal little bronze boxes but to the larger-sized ones. He went directly to the box.

Carrie saw there were two key holes on each box. Mr. Twiford put his key into the left side and took her key, put it into the right side, turned both keys, and pulled the box out towards him. It was an elongated box. She could tell it was heavy when he placed it on the table with a *thunk*!

"I'll leave you in private now to view the contents and I'll lock the door from the inside latch so you will not be disturbed. Take all the time you need, Miss Pyles. When you're done, you can leave the box on the table and I'll put it away for you, if you wish."

Carrie watched as he locked the door, then she slowly opened the lid and lifted it up and over on its hinge. She saw several small wooden boxes, gold bars, jewelry, and gems in clear boxes. She started removing items one at a time.

There was a diamond necklace, like what a queen would have worn, green gems in several of the boxes, beautifully displayed and of good size. They looked like emeralds. In another large box, she found what looked like a tiara embedded with rubies, diamonds, and sapphires.

It was all so spectacular.

Removing the gold and silver bars, she noticed how heavy they were. Having never felt anything like that, she was in awe. As she continued taking the items out of the box, in utter amazement, she reached the papers in the bottom. There were stock certificates from old textile mills in the area.

Going through the papers briefly, she saw near the bottom an old folded paper where the ink had faded and was barely legible. It looked like a faded birth certificate. Putting it up to her nose to gain a better perspective, she viewed washed-out pressed letters . . . aril . . . E.

What the heck?

Putting it aside, she found a newspaper article on the imprisonment of Mr. Howard McMurphy.

**Holy shit!**

Then, underneath more papers in the box, she saw a small black envelope containing more pictures of unknown people.

Carrie's head swirled with questions.

What in Sam's hell is going on? What did Howard McMurphy do to get put in jail? She began to question everything. What does an 'aril . . . E' have to do with anything? What had she been hiding all these years? And who in this world was Patty?

# Chapter 6

**The** door clicked as Carrie exited the bronze-colored room. She addressed Mr. Twiford, who entered and took the closed safe-deposit box, placed it back into its large sleeve, and handed her back the key.

She left the bank after placing several pictures and a few papers into her purse. She had too much to do today to focus on them right now.

Driving back to the store, she couldn't help envisioning all the glittering jewelry, and she tried to comprehend where in the world it came from and why Patty would have all that in her possession.

Perhaps Patty had a history of royalty in her family that Grandma Hattie never knew of. *I'm sure Grandma Hattie would have told me if she knew,* she thought.

Reminiscing about the various times when the two ladies were deep in conversation, it was obvious they did not want her as a participant because they immediately stopped the moment she came close.

Disgruntled, she turned her thoughts to the old birth certificate she acquired and quickly decided to take a better look with a magnifying glass tonight.

Carrie changed thoughts with every passing roadside marker and convinced herself that Grandma Hattie would not have kept secrets from her as she almost drove past the store's entrance.

As she placed her purse on the table behind the counter, she noticed the brown paper-wrapped package Walter had delivered the day before and she looked for scissors to cut the strings. That's when she noticed there was no return address on it.

*How strange*, she thought.

Before she could open the package, she was distracted by Virginia Firth walking in.

"Hey, y'all, how's it goin'," Virginia called out rather enthusiastically.

"Just fine, Virginia."

"Can I pay ya' now fer the trainin' class on Monday? You're still havin' it, right?" Virginia asked, knowing full well that she had been informed of this only the other day.

"Yes, ma'am, we're still on," she said as she placed the wrapped package back under the counter and entered Virginia's information. Carrie took the payment and handed Virginia a receipt for the class.

Everyone in this town and the next three over knew that Virginia was the town gossip. Her mouth flapped like a barn door in a windstorm.

Virginia stood around talking about this and that a little too long. As Carrie politely listened, she tried to plan out what she was going to do with the shop, training classes, and everything she had inherited. When Virginia finally left, Carrie let out a sigh.

"Thank you, Lord."

Walking back behind the counter, she quickly cut the strings and unwrapped the package.

Then the door jingled and in walked the old troll.

"Got anythin' for me?" Walter said in his gravelly tone.

"No," Carrie replied, half listening.

"Here." Walter jammed the mail into her hands and turned around, but stood there looking, and said, "Ya' changed the room."

"Yes, I did."

"Why?"

"Because *I can.*"

Walter looked toward the tack room, stood and stared, then reached for the door handle and left.

Carrie was getting used to Walter's strange behavior, so she thought nothing of it now. Returning to the counter, she finally opened the package and found a sley hook used to pull fiber through heddles and reed on a loom.

I could use one of these, she thought. Perhaps it was ordered for the training session on Monday.

She searched in the scheduler to see who Patty had ordered it for.

Carrie saw that Gladys Persilver ordered it. She marked that it was received and made a call to Gladys to let her know her item had arrived.

Pressing the recorder, she heard Travis, who had left two messages.

"Hey, sweet thing, are we still on fer tomorra'? Call me," and pressing the next message, "Hey, sugar, how 'bout if I pick ya' up at seven on Saturday at your place?" Travis was relentless, trying hard to make up for the other night.

Taking out her *to do* list, Carrie considered the next thing she needed to accomplish, instead of focusing on Travis. She explored the scheduler to re-acclimate herself to how Patty had structured the working of the shop as she twirled her auburn hair around her finger.

Carrie had worked here temporarily before she left for college and she realized now that Patty hadn't diverted from how she ran it back then.

Upon her walkabout of the training area, with projects on their respective looms in an assortment of development stages, she speculated who was on what loom, then checked off the first item, completed.

Finding a highlighter in the cup on the counter, she assessed what Patty had on order and marked the outstanding items in yellow. The columns in the scheduler displayed who ordered what, dates, cost, and vendor information.

In the brown wooden desk tray, Carrie removed the stack of bills and sorted them by due dates. She wrote checks for the ones currently due, checked off the other items on her list, and felt satisfied at her accomplishments.

The store phone rang again.

"Hello."

"Hey, sweetness, are we still on fer tomorra'?"

"Hey, Travis, I don't know."

"Come *ON*, Carrie, let me take ya' to the fair, *puullleeeease*," he said in a childish demeanor.

Travis was very charming.

Carrie used to go to the fair every year with Grandma Hattie and Patty for years. So she made this one exception in forgiving Travis.

"OK, *I'll meet you* at the fair at seven tomorrow night."

"Great! Let's meet at the ticket booth."

"OK, see you then," and Carrie hung up.

*Cool*, she thought. If things didn't go well, she could drive herself home.

Walking around the store to make sure things were properly in their place, she dusted, swept the floors, and took out the trash. Going up to the cellar door, she sniffed to make sure that no unpleasant odors were coming up and was thankful she couldn't smell anything behind the tapestry.

Carrie stood with folded arms, looking at the wood cupboard, secretly hoping that no one would notice, other than Walter, that things had been rearranged and look behind it.

Touching the wall behind the tapestry, as if to feel the cool presence of the cellar spirits, Carrie said, "Behave down there," half joking, but it felt eerie, like something might answer her.

She shivered.

Not wishing to focus on the 'cellar' at this time, Carrie wanted to get home to review the papers and pictures she had taken from Patty's safe-deposit box earlier.

With only a few customers all day, she locked up the store early and drove through a fast-food hamburger joint before driving home.

Reaching home, she put the food on the table and proceeded to take the papers and pictures out of her purse. Sitting there eating over the waxed paper wrapping with the papers to the side, she tried to make sense of it all.

Carefully and selectively, she unfolded the aged, deteriorating, and faded paper that resembled a birth certificate. The corners crumbled in dust and small pieces upon the table.

The ink was so washed out that it was difficult to comprehend whatever was once written upon it. Examining the pressed key strikes embossed upon the paper, she tried to make out the person's name, date of birth, and city of birth, but everything was indecipherable.

Carrie was driving herself crazy trying to do whatever was possible to view this information. Finding a magnifying glass in a cabinet drawer and holding it this way and that was of no use.

Giving up, she removed the sepia photographs from a black envelope. One was of a tall, good-looking, thin man dressed in a dark suit and tie with a beautiful French-looking woman in a dark, flowing dress, holding a baby and standing in front of a white-framed house on dry dirt. There was another picture of a little girl sitting down at the side of a general store, and she could only read 'Belle . . .' before the store name waned and faded into the background. Pulling out the newspaper article on Mr. McMurphy's imprisonment, she read:

**Mr. Howard McMurphy was arrested for the kidnapping of a child while driving a truck back from the gas station in Bellefontaine County. The little girl went missing from the house while she was playing outside. Before Mr. McMurphy had reached his destination, he was pulled over and arrested when the little girl ran away from the truck screaming and crying. His lawyer, Victor Abbott, just fresh out of graduate school, will defend him in his first case. McMurphy is being detained in the Bellefontaine County jail until his arraignment.**

Wow, he was caught red-handed. No wonder he was never around. Carrie thought Howard had died as Patty never talked about him.

She sat back, amazed that a young attorney, Victor Abbott, represented him. She had assumed that Patty just employed him only for her legal matters.

Getting up from the table, she poured herself a big glass of cabernet. Taking it into the loom room, she continued working on the large multi-colored rug until late in the evening, thinking and wondering.

Saturday came along way too early. After straightening up her house, Carrie decided to go to Patty's place. While driving there, she knew she had to make a decision on what to do with Patty's personal items and effects. *Do I rent the place out? Do I make the store bigger?*

Walking around the two-story dwelling, she hung her purse on a brass coat hook. She never really visited Patty's house, even when she worked part-time at the store. The shop was self-sufficient and contained everything needed, like a bathroom, kitchenette, microwave, and table. She did what she was told to do and at the end of the day Grandma Hattie picked her up or she drove herself when she became of age.

Patty was a private person and Carrie respected that.

After coming to the shop for a dozen or more years, she finally took in the exquisiteness of the place. Carrie perceived it would be large enough for a growing family, but she would have to do something with Patty's excellent taste in classical Italian Baroque, carved-wood furniture. The grand and impressive sofa as well as the matching chairs were finely crafted and looked as if they belonged in a royal cottage. Patty had impeccable taste.

Carrie couldn't stop wondering who Patty really was and what her life was all about as she picked up the pictures she left on her carved-wood, floral four-poster bed.

Sitting down on the bed and thinking how well she thought she knew Patty, Carrie recalled various times that Grandma Hattie, Patty, and she had been together, whether they were in the kitchen cooking, going on small trips upstate, or just to the fair together. Grandma Hattie entered the baking contest eight years in a row without losing to anyone, and Patty was proud of every win.

Patty loved taking pictures of Grandma Hattie and Carrie with their blue ribbons and at graduation, birthdays, and various events, but for some reason she disliked having her own picture taken. Patty was somewhat shy and tended to avoid the limelight. When Carrie started working at the store, she recollected that Patty spoke only once of her husband, Howard McMurphy. All Patty told her was that Howard had passed away rather suddenly, and then she dismissed the conversation.

While Patty walked on this beautiful land, she was quite protective of personal information, and the only conversations that were had were about cooking, travel, or yarn—and Patty could talk for hours about weaving. Grandma Hattie and Patty were extreme artists and shared many moments in the large loom room in Hattie's house, behind closed doors, producing exquisite woven items.

Hoping to gain some insight into Patty's background, Carrie wondered if Gary Pilotti or his gramma could identify someone in one of these pictures.

Poking about the box, she pulled out several pictures and placed them in her purse, turned off the lights, locked up, and left for home.

After all, she did agree to meet Travis tonight at the fair.

***

Upon reaching the fair at 6:45 p.m., Carrie followed a row of cars into the parking lot. She looked around and saw older people holding hands walking toward the entrance, families with rambunctious children, and young boys and girls running around just as excited as if it was Christmas in May. She noticed that everyone seemed to be in a fun, festive, fair-going mood.

This was a big deal.

It was the biggest fair by far in all the surrounding counties and everyone came out for it.

It was a nice night with a featherlike breeze and the thick smell of popcorn in the air. The sun was courteous in its approach towards the horizon. *It's a good night to go to a fair*, she thought, *and to forget about all that had happened this past week.*

Travis was already there talking to a congregation of guys, but he spotted Carrie right away, "Hey, Carrie," he said as he approached her, leaving the others in mid-sentence of his conversation.

"Hey, Travis."

"Ya' ready to go in?" he asked.

"Sure, have you been here long?"

"No, actually, I just got here an' saw some guys I knew. How ya' doin'?" he asked.

"I'm fine."

"Hey, do ya' like goin' on rides? I got us some ride tickets," he said rambunctiously, wanting to have some childish fun.

"Um, well, I actually don't care for the rides."

"Oh, yeah?" He sounded a little disappointed.

"Hey, Gary," Carrie said when she spotted him standing on the grass by the dunking booth.

"Hey," Gary said surprised, "Carrie Pyles, this is my wife, Sadie."

"Nice to meet you, Sadie," Carrie said and reached out her hand.

Sadie took her hand and said, "You're Carrie? Gary told me 'bout ya' an' how Phil called him 'bout your car. I hear you're takin' ova' Mrs. McMurphy's yarn shop, right?"

"Yeah, for some reason Patty left it to me."

Carrie and Sadie continued to walk and talk as they approached the tents of food on one side and rides on the other. Gary and Travis followed quietly behind.

"Hey, you like rides?" Sadie asked.

"No, I'm afraid I'm not a good ride goer," Carrie said. "You?"

"Oh, I love goin' on 'em rides. Reminds me of my younga' years an' Gary ova' there is an old fogey. He doesn't like goin' on rides eitha'."

"Travis, would you mind going on some rides with Sadie?" Carrie asked. "Travis loves the rides too—don't you, Travis?"

"Um—*sure*, Sadie, you wanna' ride a couple?" Travis asked.

"Shur, why not. Should I get sum' ride tickets?" Sadie responded.

"No, I bought sum' before Carrie got here."

"I'll just be over there talking with Gary," Carrie said, and she pointed to the nearest bench.

"Hey, Gary, got a minute?"

"Got two now," he said smiling, and sat down after Carrie did.

"I found some really interesting pictures in Patty's house. Do you think I could show your gramma? Could she take a look sometime?" Carrie reached in her purse and showed one to Gary.

Gary shrugged his shoulders. He had no clue of who the people were, but said, "I suppose it wouldn't hurt to ask. Gramma's been 'round fer a long time. I'd reckon she'd know most everyone that lived 'n this town at one time 'r anotha'."

"Do you know how I could meet up with her to take a look?" Carrie asked rather shyly.

"Hey, I know, I'm seein' her tomorra' fer Sunday brunch afta' church. Why don't ya' come by the place?" Gary asked very politely.

"Thanks, but I don't want to interrupt your brunch," Carrie said honestly.

"My gramma loves meetin' new people. She won't mind one bit."

Carrie and Gary just sat and talked a bit until two teenage boys started pushing and shoving in front of them. They were making a commotion and started to throw punches. Gary jumped up faster than all get-out and grabbed one of the boy's arms and twisted it around the boy's back. Carrie jumped up and before she could yell, "Hey," —there *he* was.

Appearing from around the corner, Phil took the other boy by the arm, distancing the two.

Phil said to Gary, "Gary, take the boy and sit him down over there—OK?"

Gary nodded. "Shur Boss."

Carrie watched as Phil, with his stupid sunglasses on his face, lectured the adolescent about proper, fair conduct. As Phil asked him something, the boy looked up with somber eyes and said, "No, sir."

"Yes, that's correct. I wouldn't think you'd like me to call your momma. Now, you go on and behave yourself. If I see any more of this, I *will* call your momma, understand?" Phil said.

"Yes sir," and the boy got up and took off quickly.

Phil walked over to where Gary stood and basically had the same conversation with the other teenage boy.

"Now, get on and behave yourself or I'll be calling your momma too."

The boy got up and, without another word, went in the opposite direction from the other boy he had been fighting.

Phil approached Gary with Carrie standing close by.

"Miss Carrie," Phil nodded.

"Thanks for the assistance, Gary. The young boys nowadays just don't know the proper etiquette or the privilege of going to a county fair."

"Guess not, Boss," Gary said. "But I'm shur ya' set 'em straight," he said, half laughing.

Phil looked and smirked at Gary. You could tell they were good friends.

"Miss Carrie," Phil said, "I didn't think I would see you here."

"And yet, here I am."

"Yes, you are. Are you having a good time?"

"I really just got here. I met up with Travis, but I'm not much of a ride goer, so Sadie went with Travis on a few. Gary and I were just sitting and chatting over there on the bench when the two boys started their ruckus," Carrie said as they started walking.

"It's a nice evening," Carrie said when the conversation went silent. The sky was now displaying brilliant colors of red, orange, pink, and purple as the sun set to end its day and allow the stars to gain control of the evening.

"Yes, ma'am, it sure is," Phil replied.

"Hey, Phil, are ya' comin' to brunch tomorra' 'r do ya' have to work?" Gary asked.

"Oh, I'll be there, wouldn't want to miss Gramma's fried chicken. You know it's food for the gods," Phil replied uncharacteristically.

*Oh my.* Carrie wasn't aware Phil was that friendly with Gary, but secretly she was elated. She really had enjoyed his company the other night when he stayed for two beers.

"Well, I 'nvited Carrie to come tomorra' too. Maybe she could use a ride?" Gary suggested.

"Oh—that's OK," Carrie replied without thinking, looking over at Phil's expression, her blue-gray eyes wide open to the size of half-dollars.

"Miss Carrie, it would be my honor to escort you tomorrow. Plus, I would be doing the city a kind service by keeping you off the road."

"What?" she rolled her eyes at him, causing Gary to burst out a hearty belly laugh. She believed Phil was teasing and flirting with her.

"Sure, that would be nice." She really did want to meet up with Gary's gramma and getting to spend time with Phil was like winning the lottery.

Turning the corner, Carrie stopped short of the baking competition area. She stood there just looking and remembering herself as a little girl running around, pilfering a finger lick of her grandma's famous chocolate icing, and then being chased off by Grandma Hattie swatting a woven napkin at her. She giggled at the thought.

This was the location of some of Patty's proudest moments, too, with Grandma Hattie winning the baking competition year after year and her capturing it every time on film. Strange how memories of Patty always found her wearing a bulky hat and oversized sunglasses, but Carrie knew that her skin wasn't just fair, it was white as fresh whipped cream.

Shortly thereafter, Travis and Sadie walked up, laughing about the rides they'd just been on, as if they were two little kids in middle school.

"Hey, Carrie, ya' thirsty?" Travis asked.

"Yeah, I really am," Carrie said to Travis while looking at Phil.

She was toying with him.

She was attracted to Phil's quality of confidence, stability, and handsomeness, but that conflicted with being drawn in to Travis' playfulness.

*Oh, well,* she thought, I'm not engaged to anyone. *Why can't I be attracted to two people at one time? What harm can it do?*

"Hey, Phil, how ya' doin'?" Travis asked.

"Good, Travis. You?"

"Fine—now," he said, smiling as he extended his arm and leading Carrie away, leaving Sadie, Gary, and Phil behind.

Travis, the endearing man that he was, made fun of Carrie's name and Carrie played back, making fun of his name, "Travis Hicks."

They walked, talked, laughed, and Carrie enjoyed his simple company very much.

Carrie let loose, remembering what it was like to be cheery. They walked around the entire fair drinking beer from plastic red cups and playing the carnival games. Travis tried showing off his skills, but it was Carrie who scored the big white teddy bear by bursting three white balloons with darts—and the teasing continued.

Carrie didn't see Phil the rest of the night, although she secretly looked around for him.

Travis was well mannered, in high spirits, and there was no drunken Dana around to ruin the night. When the fair was over, Travis and Carrie stopped at his truck. He let down the tailgate as Carrie put the big white teddy bear in the back, and they sat down on it. They enjoyed the smells of the fair, laughing as they continued their playful conversation.

It was a stunning, starry night sky and warm as a buttered muffin. Travis took out two beers from an orange cooler in the back, one for each of them.

Enjoying the moment, Travis leaned in to give Carrie a kiss. Carrie allowed Travis' tongue to reach hers. It was warm, wet, and she was ready. Carrie grabbed Travis' shoulder-length black hair, tugging, pulling, and taking him all in.

Carrie's mind went to Phil. He was smiling with those bright whites and wearing those stupid sunglasses. She wanted it to be Phil's mouth that she was kissing.

Travis took the back of Carrie's neck and ran his hand up her hair, tugging and pushing himself closer to Carrie.

Fair-goers were walking to their vehicles and saw that Travis was with someone. They laughed, and yelled, "Hey, Travis, get a room!"

Travis and Carrie separated for a few minutes, trying to gain composure and at that time, just when it started getting a little too hot for such sexual candidness in a fair parking lot, Phil appeared. Travis had his arm around Carrie, but Carrie wasn't sure what, if anything, Phil had seen.

"Hey, Travis, I have your pager. Someone turned it in—*Here*."

"What the—? Phil, buddy, ya' couldn't—" and the beeper went off unexpectedly. Travis saw that he had to go.

"Carrie, I have to go. Marcus was first on the call list tonight. I didn't think anythin' would happen," he said sincerely. "Can I call ya' sumtime?" he asked softly, as if trying not to allow Phil to hear.

"Sure," Carrie said, not looking at Travis, as she was staring at Phil.

Carrie reached in the back of the truck and took out the big, white teddy bear as Phil pushed up the gate and Travis got into his truck and drove off.

"So, Travis and you are an item?" asked Phil.

"No, I'm not *dating* anyone. Travis and I are just friends," Carrie replied sarcastically, hoping she hit a nerve when he caught them together.

Carrie turned and carried her big, white teddy bear back to her car with shoulders hung low.

At least she was taking something home.

The moon was not in attendance tonight and the stars looked as close as an eight-foot ceiling.

While driving home alone on a dark two-lane road in her dark gray Honda, an older, overly oxidized car full of kids came up on her fast. Driving wild like hogs at feeding time, they passed her in the oncoming lane hooting and hollering.

Just down the road, there were several large arrow signs for an upcoming hairpin turn and as Carrie approached, she noticed that a dust cloud had discharged like an imploding building.

The unruly car had missed the turn and run off the road.

The air was still infiltrated with debris like morning fog hanging over the creek as she pulled onto the curb, releasing her seatbelt and breathlessly exiting the car.

*God, I hope they are alright*, she thought as she swiftly approached the car several yards off the road. They barely missed several large junipers.

"Is everyone OK?" she yelled towards the car's occupants.

"No—Sandi hit her head and it's bleedin'," someone yelled back.

As she reached the car, the driver door was open, and the overhead light shone on a curly-haired girl leaning her head against the seat back, with what appeared to be a large bleeding gash on her forehead.

Everyone else seemed okay, with the exception of the front passenger who had strawberry ice cream dripping from the back of his hair.

Carrie turned to go get help but before she stepped twenty feet away, Phil Lament was already there with lights on. He had received a call stating that two cars were involved in an accident.

Assessing the situation, the sergeant called for an ambulance.

Another police car arrived and a policewoman got out of the car and went up to Phil. Having her talk to the young kids to get their statements and license of the driver, Phil approached Carrie.

"Miss Carrie, are you alright?" he asked.

"I'm fine, nothing happened to me," Carrie said.

"Can you explain what you saw?" he asked.

She gave him an account of the situation and Phil looked relieved when she was finished.

"If that's all Carrie, I need to get back. I'm glad you're OK."

"I'm taking off then, if that's OK? What time will I see you tomorrow?"

"I'll pick you up at 12:30," Phil replied and then walked toward the policewoman.

*I wonder if he was worried about me* she thought walking back to her car.

The sound of his voice and the concern he displayed for her was very comforting. Thinking about his kindness—and his body—she yearned for him again.

***

Reading her horoscope the next morning sitting at the kitchen table, it read:

"Make a point to experience something new today."

*Well, OK then*, she thought, realizing that it would indeed be a new experience to have a day out with Phil.

Carrie got dressed in a pink-with-yellow-flowers oxford shirt and a pair of white jeans, small light blue jean vest, and white sandals. She teased, sprayed, fluffed up her hair, and dabbed some Chanel behind her ears, in between her breasts, and on her wrist.

She walked around the house wound tighter than a new girdle waiting on Phil's arrival.

She heard a strong knock on the door and saw Phil through the side window as he stood at the door.

She glanced in the wood-carved mirror over the foyer console and checked out how she looked.

There was a knock again.

She took a deep breath as her heart cannonballed along, and she opened the door.

"Hi, come on in."

"Thank you." And in walked the most gorgeous man Carrie had ever seen.

Her heart was sprinting like a thoroughbred at the starting gate.

Phil was wearing tight jeans that fit at his hips, a firm chest-fitting, brown t-shirt, dark brown boots, and a large-buckle brown belt that attracted Carrie's eyes.

"Um, would you like a drink or anything?"

"No, ma'am, but are you ready to go?"

"Yeah, let me get my purse," Carrie said as she went into the kitchen, placed her hands on the counter to collect herself, and told herself, *Stop it, Girl.*

"Ready?" she asked brightly as she returned to the room.

"Yes, ma'am," he replied and opened the door.

Driving to Gary's gramma's place, Carrie asked, "How did it go last night with those kids that went off the road? What happened to the injured girl?"

"Do you always ask two questions at one time?" He looked at her, smiling that bright white smile with his dimpled chin, and Carrie started zoning out, imagining that mouth on hers.

"Um, huh?" she answered. So he asked the question again.

"Oh, sorry, yeah I guess I do sometimes," she said.

Phil started recounting what happened after she'd left. "The ambulance was called and . . ." he went on.

However, Carrie could only think of his mouth and again drifted off into a daydream.

They arrived at Gramma's place at the same time Gary and Sadie did. Sadie was bringing in a yellow covered dish, and Gary was carrying in some chairs. Phil got a bag out of the truck before opening Carrie's door. As they approached the house, he held the door open for Sadie and Gary, then allowed Carrie to walk through before him.

Such a classy gentleman, Carrie thought.

Gramma came up and told Gary to put the chairs in the backyard. Sadie went into the kitchen to put her dish in a warm oven.

Phil bent over, giving Gramma a big kiss on her cheek.

"How are ya', handsome?" she asked Phil, "an' who's this pretty sweet thin'?"

"I'm good, Gramma. This is Carrie. Gary and Sadie invited her," he said. "They met up at the fair last night . . ."

Before he could get anything else out, she approached Carrie.

"Well, now aren'cha a sight fer sore eyes. Wha'sur name?" she asked, although Phil had already told her.

"Carrie, ma'am," she said.

"I heard that, but wha'cha family name?" she asked.

"Oh, I'm sorry. It's Carrie Pyles, ma'am," she said.

"Well, Carrie Pyles, where ya' stayin' at?" she asked.

"Oh, I reside at my Grandma Hattie's place off Lakeview on Highway N," she said.

"Hattie and Scott Jennin's place?"

"Yes, that's right. Did you know my grandma and grandpa?"

"Hey, handsome," Gramma said, looking at Phil. "Wha'cha' got there?"

"I brought you a bottle of red wine," he said politely and took the bottle out of the sack, showing her the brand.

"Well, handsome, ya' knows where it goes." Then Gramma took Carrie by the arm and escorted her through the kitchen and outside where brunch was going to be.

There were a few ladies in the kitchen who all smiled as Carrie and Gramma walked through, but they were busily putting together the brunch.

The delicious smell of garlic, onions, kidney beans in oil, and everything else made Carrie's stomach about to swallow her tongue.

"I knew of 'em, but they's quiet folks. Kept to themselves. Not makin' much noise 'n town. Scott Jennin's sheared sheep, dinn't he?" she asked.

"Yes, that's right."

"Your grandmotha', Hattie, was a weava', wann't she? Dinn't she have a special kinship wit' Camille Eden-Worth?"

*Gramma must have gotten the girls' names confused*, she thought. "Well, Miss Patty really." Carrie replied in awe, amazed at her level of comprehension. "They were best friends from high school."

A voice from the kitchen interrupted their conversation.

"Hey, Gramma—there's sumthin' smokin' 'n here. Wha'cha want me ta' do?"

"Carrie, my dear, I best get to gettin'," and she walked hurriedly towards the kitchen door.

Phil was talking with Gary and Sadie when he came over, sat next to Carrie, and placed his arm around the back of her chair.

"So, I see you met Gramma. She must like you," he said, taking a swig of beer.

"What a nice lady. I can see she's smitten with you, *handsome*."

"Yeah, not quite sure she's ever called me by my first name. Been coming here for a while now. I recommend her fried chicken. It's mighty good and worth trying."

Carrie smiled at Phil as Gary walked over and sat across the table from them.

"Miss Carrie, when thin's settle down I'll introduce ya' to everyone. Phil, I could see Gramma was impressed that ya' brought Carrie wit'cha," Gary said with conviction.

"Yeah, kinda thought that, too," Phil said with a smile and took another drink of beer.

"The Sarge here hann't brought a date 'n a long while, so this is a big 'casion fer Gramma," Gary said laughing.

Carrie smiled at learning that Phil must not have dated anyone in a while, she assumed, ever since his wife passed away in that accident.

"Carrie, can I get you something to drink?" Phil asked.

"Sure, I'll take some ice tea, if there is any."

"Oh, she has ice tea, lemonade, beer, and wine. Your choice."

"Ice tea will be fine, thanks."

While Phil was getting her some sweet ice tea, she asked Gary, "So—your family and friends get together every Sunday?"

"Well, fer the most part, yeah. Sometimes we have it at Sadie 'n my home."

"Has Phil ever brought his wife here?" she asked.

"Yeah, Gramma knew his wife Jodine real well. She was pretty tore up when she got news of the accident. Sarge hann't come 'round fer 'while afta' that. I guess he's been comin' back 'round now fer 'bout a year or more."

"You set this up, didn't you?" Carrie said smiling.

"Well, ya' wanted to meet Gramma din'cha? And Sarge usually comes by hisself, so it seemed to be a good idea," Gary said. "Are ya' datin' Travis or sumthin'?" he asked.

"No, Travis and I are just friends. We only met up at the fair because he was pestering me." She tried to say it without disowning Travis.

"Yeah, Sarge told me 'bout Travis an' Dana's 'ncident at the pool hall afta' I left an' Travis asked him to give ya' a ride home."

"So, he talked about me, huh?"

Gary got a little nervous as if saying too much.

"Um, yeah, jus' that though," he said nervously. "I . . . I think . . . I need to help Sadie wit' sumthin'," he stammered as he maneuvered his chair back from the table and scooted off as fast as he could.

Carrie was ecstatic. Her heart started rolling like a water wheel producing corn meal.

She got up from the table and stood there by herself for only a few short seconds. Then Phil walked up with a big glass of sweet ice tea and a cold beer for himself.

"You OK?"

"Yes, I am. It's a beautiful day," she said, smiling as she thanked the angels in the sky.

"Hey, Sarge, how ya' doin'?" said a big-haired lady with a thin waist and big bust, as she gave him a hug.

"Hi, Christy, I'm good. Let me introduce you to Miss Carrie Pyles."

"Miss Carrie, this is Christy, she's Gary's cousin and married to Tony Storr."

Christy smiled at Carrie, "It's real nice to meet'cha, darlin'."

"You as well."

"Where is Tony at?" Phil asked.

"Oh, he'll be here sumtime soon. I came early to help Gramma set up. Dinn't know ya' were bringin' anyone wit'cha," she said in a peachy pink lipstick smile at Phil.

"Gary and Sadie invited her to come," he said, "and then asked if I would bring her—"

Before he could finish Christy asked, "So, how did ya' two meet up?" Sadie took a seat next to Carrie.

"Our first get together was when he wrote me up for two tickets," Carrie said laughing.

"What? Ya' wrote this purty thing up fer two tickets?" Christy said, slapping Phil on his arm.

"Yeah, I was just doing my job."

"Well, aren'cha one sonofabitch!"

"That's what I thought too—with maybe a few more selective words," Carrie said giggling.

Carrie and the Sarge proceeded to tell the captivating story as brunch was brought out.

"Hey, let me help," Carrie asked and went into the kitchen to assist.

When all the food was on table, from collard greens to piles of fried chicken, Gramma came up to Carrie and said, "Carrie dear, why don'cha sit ova' here by me, an' 'handsome' ya' sit right next to her there," and pointed to where Phil was to take a seat.

"Yes, ma'am," he replied to Gramma, after pulling out her chair at the head of the table.

Everyone passed the food around the table, and when the plates were full of food, they all held hands as Gramma proceeded with the prayer.

"Lord, thank ya' fer bringin' family an' their friends togetha' today an' fer the food that we have to share. Keep us safe an' protect us from all harm 'n the days to come." But before the prayer was finished, she added, "an' thank ya' fer findin' sum'one fer *handsome* to brin' here to us today."

All said, "Amen."

Carrie blushed and Phil smiled.

Gary proceeded with introductions of everyone: Brody, Mercedie, Luddy, Ellis, Aleta, Bunky, Ruby, Homer, Jesse, Posey, Gabbe, Rhonda, and Melba. He went on with a few more names that Carrie would never remember and she was hoping not to be tested either.

After the introduction, Christy started the discussion about Carrie's two tickets and the chatter and laughter began.

Tony, a tall, burly man who resembled a professor at the university Carrie had attended, had arrived right before the start of the conversation. Taking the chair next to Christy, he chimed in.

"So, Sarge," continuing with the fun, "What's next, handcuffs to the bedpost?"

Everyone laughed and the commotion carried on for a while. As the food was dished out and plates were filled like abstract paintings, various conversations continued. Everything was wonderful, especially Gramma's fried chicken.

As some of the family got up from the table and gathered the dirty dishes, Carrie got up to assist and brought in several dishes to the kitchen sink. She turned on the sink faucet and started to wash the dishes.

The guys outside stood around talking and chattering about sports and car problems, and the girls placed the leftover items in storage containers and got out dessert dishes.

There was peach pie, berry cobbler, chocolate cake, and homemade ice cream. Coffee was brewing, and the people were asked which pie they wanted.

Carrie looked out the kitchen window, moved a strand of hair from her eyelash, and caught Phil looking at her as he took a swig of beer.

Her pulse galloped like a deer dancing in the valley, but she acted nonchalant and continued washing the dishes. She heard Phil say he wanted a little piece of peach pie and ice cream. Carrie brought it out to him and had herself a small piece of chocolate cake.

She remembered how Grandma Hattie had made chocolate cake for her birthdays—her absolute favorite dessert. She got chocolate icing on her face, and when Sarge was talking to her, he took his white linen napkin and sweetly removed it from her face.

Carrie blushed and smiled, wiped her face nervously with her napkin, and said, "Thanks."

Gramma was talking to Gary and Sadie, and they must have said something to her about Carrie's pictures because Gramma walked over and took a seat next to her.

"Carrie, Gary said ya' brought me sum' pictures to look at."

"Yes, ma'am, but if you're busy, we can do it some other time."

"Nonsense, no time like the present. Neva' know wha' the next two minutes will brin'," she said.

Gramma was curious, Carrie could tell.

"Well, Gary said you lived in this town for a while," Carrie said as she reached for her purse under her chair.

Gramma said, "Hey, handsome, why don'cha' op'n that bottle of wine ya' brought an' pour me a fill."

"Sure, yes, ma'am," and got up respectfully to do as asked.

"Carrie, would you like some too?"

"Um, sure. Thanks."

Carrie reached into her purse and pulled out the black envelope, removed a picture of a group of men, and handed it to Gramma. Carrie scooted her chair closer.

"Hmm." Gramma sat back and focused on the picture through her brown, tortoise-rimmed glasses. Gramma was a little lady with short, gray hair, wearing a short-sleeved dress. She had big, brown eyes, and a crease above her nose that deepened as she focused on the picture.

"Well, that looks like Abraham Twiford an' Joseph Holtz, but I cain't put my finga' on the two youngins' 'n the picture." She pointed to the two older men she knew, showing Carrie who they were.

"I think the youngin' right there's Walter Holtz, wit' his head turned sideways, but I cain't recollect who that one is." She concentrated but couldn't bring it to mind.

"Wha' else ya' got?" she asked. "I need to come back to this one," she said and left it in front of her.

Carrie showed her the next picture.

"Well, that looks like Lulu Roosevelt standin' next to Karyn Reeves, but where 'r they? An' why would Karyn be wit' her?" Looking more intensely at the photo's surroundings, she said, "Linda Louise Roosevelt. Everyone called her Lulu. Not the prettiest of girls, looked like she was rode hard an' put up wet.

The boys used to make fun of her 'cause she was flat as a flitter but empty as a winter rain barrel."

Carrie listened intensely, *Lulu Roosevelt*, she tried to lock it in her brain, but when the barn door is open—the wind blows straight through her head. She knew herself well enough to know better, and decided it was best to take out a pen and wrote on the back of a receipt *Linda Louise—Lulu—Roosevelt.*

Then Gramma handed the picture back and continued.

"Time shur has passed since I seen the likes of Lulu," Gramma said as she moved her glasses back up her nose. "Last time I recollect seein' her, she's grayin' like an ol' mare, hair all strun' out, not fixin' to find a man. I declare she's the laziest thin' that walked this green earth. I rememba' goin' to Tomboy's, a lil' groc'r down yonda', where she worked. It's boarded up real tight now. She was as useful as a milk bucket unner a bull. She used to make the people poke their own groc'ries. Why one time, lil' old Miss Vanderbelt, who had bad bones an' was all humped ova' like one of those camels, asked Lulu to help her wit' the groc'ries. Lulu grunted an' groaned a dozen or so times, when puttin' sever'l items 'n a poke an' loadin' up her buggy. Laziest thin' I ev'r knew. Old Vanderbelt was madda' than a wet hen. Dunno' wha' happened to Lulu afta' that, but she dis'peared. Miss Vanderbelt had a word or two wit' the man'ger, I sup'ose. Miss Vanderbelt passed since then, *Bless her heart*, but Lulu—" she pondered. "Wha' else ya' got?" she asked.

Carrie handed her a picture of a woman with three girls. One of the girls in the photo had hair hanging down in her face and she was looking down at the ground.

Gramma took it and said, "Why that's Theodosia Eden-Worth wit' Patty, Camille and—" she mused with her finger on the picture.

"Theodosia was a strong-willed, red-haired lady wit' a bad tempa'," she continued. "Her oldest dawta' was crazy as a loon. I think she had dark red hair—dinn't they all have red hair? Wha's her name? In all my born days—" she thought for a minute. "Lydia. Lydia it was. She was really protective ova' the youngin' Patty an' kept to her like a motha' hen. Ya' dinn't see too much of Lydia, a real embarrassment to the family, I sup'ose."

"So, Patty had a family? Her mother was Theodosia and her sisters were Camille and Lydia?" Carrie reconfirmed.

"Yea', that's right." Gramma put the picture down on the red-and-white checkered tablecloth and picked up the picture of the group of men. Calling up, "Papa—D . . . Dan. Yes, I think that there's Papa Dan Henderson. He owned the local bank. Started out small an' when the textiles bus'ness was doin' well, he was doin' well, but when it sank, he had to sell the bus'ness. Papa Dan moved out of town when I was a teenage girl. He had two sons who were so dumb one coulnn't pour piss out of a boot while the otha' one's readin' d'rections on the bottom. They almost burnt down the town back 'n the day," she said, shaking her head in disgust.

"How did they almost burn the town down?" Carrie asked.

"Stupid boys lit a rag to a bottle of hooch an' threw it through an open door at a temp'rance meetin'. Took all day to put the durn fire out."

"Really?"

"But that there's Joseph Holtz," as she pointed to where he was in the picture. "His son Walta' an' I were good friends 'n school, ev'n courted 'while. He was a looka' back then," she remembered. "Walta' is the mailman fer a piece of town. Oh, ya' must know that," Gramma said, looking at Carrie. "I knows he deliva's mail to the yarn shop," she said.

Carrie nodded.

"He dumped me fer Cora Bergerson, a pop'lar, pretty thin' 'n school she was. Married her an' left town fer 'while when he caught wind of Blackbeard's gold 'n Bath county an' moved searchin' out the rumors wit' none of 'em true. Walta' took to moonshine an' rum-runnin' an' end up comin' back to work at his fatha's bus'nes befo' becomin' a mailman. I still see Walta' walkin' 'round town when Gary or the girls brin's me 'n. Not much of a looka' anymore," she said smiling, and handed Carrie the picture back.

"Gramma, did you know my Grandpa Scott Jennings?" Carrie asked. "I didn't get much time with him. He died when I was a little girl."

"From wha' I rememba' 'bout the Jennin's, his family was 'nto farmin' an' he was a sheep herda' an' sheared his sheep, makin' a livin' by sellin' the wool to the mills. He was a lil' younga' than my sista' an' I was 'n school. He was a quiet type an' kep' to hisself. If I rememba', he was sev'ral years olda' than Hattie though. Now, 'ur Grandma Hattie, she was a darlin'. She made the prettiest an' best choc'late cake fer the fair. Always won first place, dinn't she?"

"It was good, wasn't it," Carrie confirmed.

"She neva' gave up her recipe though, but it was mighty tasty. Would love to know her secret," Gramma said, hinting to Carrie. "You say 'ur granny an' *Patty* were best friends? Do you happen to know where they'd went to school at? I don't rememba' those two goin' to the schools 'round here. Jus' wonderin' how they'd met up," she asked.

Something didn't click. *Why would Gramma ask me that question?* Carrie thought her grandma and Patty grew up here.

Phil walked up to Carrie and Gramma, "Are you two young ladies finished talking yet?"

Gramma stood up. "Ya' get 'nough to eat, handsome?"

"Yes, ma'am, I'm full as a tick."

"Ya' take care of her an' brin' her 'round sum more, ya' hear. I 'spect to see her here next Sunday." She gave Sarge a big hug and said something in his ear that Carrie couldn't hear.

He just smiled at her and kissed her cheek, returning the hug.

"Sugar pie, ya' come back next Sunday, ya' hear. Brin' me more pictures if ya' have sum'," she said as she held Carrie's hands.

"Thank you for everything," Carrie said smiling.

Then Gramma walked over to Gary and Sadie.

Phil turned to Carrie, "Well, are you about ready to leave?"

"Sure, let me go to the bathroom. I won't be a minute."

"OK, go through the kitchen; it's down the hall, second room on the right," Phil advised.

Carrie nodded OK.

They left shortly thereafter and upon arriving back at Carrie's place, she asked, "If you don't have anything to do, would you like to come in for a beer? It's still early."

"Sure," he said as he parked the truck, got out, and opened Carrie's door. As they were walking to the front door, Carrie said, "Thank you for bringing me today. I really had a good time. Gramma is such a sweetheart and she sure does like you—*handsome*."

"Yeah, if she was just a little younger," he laughed.

Carrie couldn't help but laugh; his raw, pure chuckle got to her. She walked up, and on the top step to the porch, she turned and bravely gave Phil a big kiss.

# Chapter 7

**God,** the man smelled like Obsession, Rem oil, wood smoke, and sex. He touched her chin with the tip of his finger and lifted her face to his, but he didn't kiss her again. Instead, he let his finger trail down her throat to the tight slit between her breasts and let it pause, then tugged a little at her shirt. The heat of his fingertip caused her desire to deepen, and she knew right then they had to get off the porch. Slipping one hand in his, taking three steps backwards toward the front door, their eyes locked, and she pushed open the door with her behind. Phil never took his finger off her shirt as he gently walked her back through the open door and into the house.

It wasn't hot in the room, but her nipples were on fire. She shuddered a little because she couldn't stop it and he grinned. With both hands, Phil ripped open the snaps on her shirt and that was it. Her vest and shirt went flying as she kicked off her shoes. He was trying to loosen his boots as she pulled his fit, brown T-shirt away from his pants and they tumbled against the wall, kissing hungrily. Phil had his big hands on her small waist and she swore he could have closed them around it.

*Mmmm. Big hands*, she thought.

Seeing the look on his face as she lifted his T-shirt over his head, her hands sliding against his chest and mimicking her movement, he slid his hands along her sides and found her breasts. He squeezed them roughly and pressed his groin against her, pinning her to the wall.

He was a strong man.

He released her breasts and reached under her tight thighs and lifted them, using the wall for leverage; she wrapped her legs around him like a Christmas present. It was then she really felt his manhood.

His warm embracing tongue was still in her throat when he let her legs slide toward the floor, steadying her until she could stand. He urged her toward the stairs. She would have taken him right there on the floor, but Phil seemed to have a different idea.

She directed him toward the stairs, and with his hand cupped on her derriere, he followed her up the staircase.

They stepped over the threshold into her bedroom and he was instantly squeezing her breasts and feeding on her mouth. Phil was good with that delicious mouth, and he bent down and began to play with her nipples with the tip of his tongue. Then he bit her. Just a little, barely enough to leave a mark that wouldn't be there in an hour, but it caught her breath.

Unwilling to give it up so easily even if her lady parts gave her away as a liar, she snapped a wicked little grin right back into his dark eyes, planted a hand on his chest, and took a step back.

She underestimated him. Michelangelo's David would only wish to be fashioned after such a fine, manly specimen.

Instantly, he grabbed her right wrist and pushed her hand into the small of her back with every part of her touching him full frontal.

He knew exactly what he was doing, and she bucked a little with both need and an intense desire to give him whatever would keep him in her bed.

That told him everything he needed to know.

Her breasts were heaving under him, and he knew she wouldn't last much longer but he was willing to torture her for just a few more minutes.

She was greedy for it, as her lady parts felt like a river in hell from the omission.

Phil turned his attention back to her mouth. He kissed her with such passion it would make innocent angels blush. Carrie knew he was going to stay tonight if she had to duct tape him to the bedpost . . . and he would have her again.

Lying there, she realized she hadn't really taken in the sight of his nakedness. *How does a man come to look like him?* His skin ran to an olive color, but it had that ruddiness of a man who spent time outdoors in the sun and on the water. He was lean the same way.

She liked it.

His shoulders were broad and his arms muscular. He had lifted her against the wall like she was air.

His hair was cropped close, but not in that kind-of-intimidating shaved, jarhead thing cops seemed to have gone to, and it had a little wave to it. His lips were curved like a bow and his smile, when he decided to let it come out and play on his serious face, was a little mocking. Sexy stuff.

Those dark brown eyes held her to the ground every time he turned them her way. He had a frank way of looking at her, very direct.

As a rule, Carrie had always been a little guarded, but she had no defense against him. Her heart had nowhere to run, and, long before her brain got there, her body had already decided resistance was impossible.

He had stretched out to the side of her as her fingers were toying with his dark curls, one hand tenderly stroking her breast, his head propped on the other. The little bite mark had already disappeared. She missed it. It was a reminder that his mouth had been there.

Phil was watching her, searching her face for a sign that he had given her what she wanted. He'd wanted to please her and she loved him for that.

Oh, shit, no, no, no. Not that word—not yet. Carrie let the idea pass.

"God, you're so beautiful. You are even more beautiful after making love. I haven't wanted anyone that bad in a long time, sugar."

"Well, that makes two of us. You know I'm going to wake up in the morning and want you again."

He smiled, clearly happy to hear it. "Sold to the lady with the big blue-gray eyes."

She decided not to think about where this might be headed. She simply wanted to treasure this moment.

The next morning, Phil was out the door early, before breakfast but after a second cup of coffee, and she suspected he might typically be an early riser.

Her newspaper was placed on the kitchen table and her blue ceramic coffee cup was already on the counter next to the still-hot pot. She was not a morning person and was even less an early riser, but today was the first day her weaving class would meet and she needed to get the shop opened up and the studio ready.

This was the first day that she would actually be a business owner, blessed by Patty's generosity . . . or disillusions.

Carrie was an experienced weaving teacher and was not particularly worried about how the class might go. She would adjust or wing it to the best of her abilities.

She arrived at the shop, but in truth, there wasn't much to be done. Six 36" Macombers. Wonderful, heavy-duty Gabe looms built to take the abuse dished out by both new students and long-time weavers not afraid to slam the beater against the woven fiber to pack it in like they meant it to stay.

Four of them had work in progress and she wouldn't interrupt the completion of any one of those projects for a million dollars, but the fact was those looms belonged to her now.

The studio, the shop, the business, and the fervent hope for its continuation had been left to her by Patty McMurphy. *God love her,* she thought, *for the faith she placed in me. I will do my best to live up to your wishes, Patty.*

Three of the weavings were weft-faced and seriously impressive, like a Navajo rug—a tapestry weave. The yarn is woven so that only the weft, the horizontal strands that the artist will use to create the pattern, is seen and the warp, the vertical strands that are threaded through the loom, is completely hidden.

Carrie smiled to herself and thought, That's the way life is, isn't it? You can look at a book and see its cover, but the warped (hidden) thread is what really holds the story together.

This wasn't Carrie's first dance in teaching.

She might be young in age but had taught her fair share of new weavers and guided even more experienced ones. Given the choice, she would say she loved the company of seasoned artisans. With them, she learned as much as she taught, and in the case of Patty's class, she had been handed a fair deal.

The shop bell jingled, and she found herself holding out a welcome to her customers more naturally as owner with less guilt than she had been feeling. It had been a rough few days before this moment and she had survived. The first weaver through the door was Emeline Browning.

Carrie knew Emeline, with her elegant Scottish bones and breeding. She was a straight shooter, sharp, but without a spiteful bone in her whole body. Emeline's mirror, her sister, Adeene Woode, trailed in behind her. The two of them were Gary Pilotti's cousins, a bit older than Gary, and Gramma was their maternal aunt.

Emeline and Adeene's father, Gibby Ewest had run the local newspaper, *The Post,* as Editor in Chief and Head Reporter, for several years but had since retired. Carrie hadn't thought much about that until just then. *They may know some of the people in the pictures, but that's probably a long shot.*

In a short minute, Jenny Lee Jones poked her head in before gathering herself up and stepping into the shop. Carrie had heard

Jenny Lee was a close relation of Phil Lament's late wife and, as word had apparently gotten round that the sergeant had driven her home from the bar and maybe not left right away, Carrie wondered if she would show.

Carrie was going to see that man and his very fine ass again, and she supposed now was as good a time as any to very civilly stake her ground. *If that doesn't work, there's enough of Grandma Hattie in me to stake it out firmly and not so politely.*

As it turned out, Jenny Lee was as good-natured as she could be. She was a rational woman approaching her thirties and Carrie decided she liked her immediately.

The remaining weaver in this session was Virginia Firth. Virginia, who does not go by Ginny or any other shortening of her name, was the talker in the town and yet surprisingly, her friends and neighbors were always willing to share information with her that might be better left lying in the dark. Most of the time it is not.

Virginia was only a few years older than Carrie and her family connections and education made it seem unlikely that she would continue in a small town such as Pheasant Mill. Her family had been assayers from the first settling of Carolina right up through the Great Depression, when they turned to shrimping. They put the gold money to good use in building a huge commercial fleet of shrimp boats, and if Virginia wanted to be somewhere else, she most certainly could be, but she was apparently determined to keep the deep family roots planted where they were.

*Virginia was not beautiful in the usual way,* Carrie thought, *but it was impossible not to be attracted to her. And I'll say this for the woman, she pays her own way.*

The ladies took their places at their looms. Carrie was anxious to see who was producing which piece.

She expected Virginia's to be the fourth work, a lovely shawl in Swedish lace worked in pale blue and cream silk, but that turned out to be Adeene's.

Adeene located her place in the draft she was using, shuttles were loaded, and the weavers settled in to treadle as artfully as dancers.

Evidently, assistance from Carrie was scarcely needed at the moment, so Carrie thought she might take a chance and ask whether or not anyone knew a little of Patty's family history. Fortunately, Emeline did that for her.

"We're happy to see you pick up the class, Carrie. With Miss Patty's passin' sudden like that, we just dinn't know."

"The whole situation was definitely kind of sudden, but I've been a weaver all of my life," Carrie declared, as if to prove her worthiness.

"Do you know what you're plannin' on doin' with the business?" Adeene inquired.

"I haven't made any decision yet with regard to the shop and right now I mean to run it until I know whether or not it's really what I want to do. Speaking of Miss Patty, Miss Emeline, can I ask you something? Who is Camille? I came across that name in some of Patty's papers, and I can't make a connection."

The two older women cast a glance at one another and Carrie couldn't read it.

Emeline spoke first. "Camille is Patty's sister, but the story goin' 'round is that she's only a half-sister."

"What happened to her?" Carrie asked, trying to disguise her intense curiosity, but not sure she was making a fair job of it.

Adeene spoke up first. "No one really knows. The two girls left town for a while, but Miss Patty was the only one that came back. Camille was a bitch. Pardon my language, sweetie, but there's no other way to put that. Miss Patty left because of her husband Howard's disgrace when he was put in jail. She needed to work and there was nothin' goin' on 'round here. Camille left town right after she graduated from school, and no one's seen her since that I know of. Her momma despised her for no reasons known to man. The story of Camille's life has already been passed into legend."

"Rumor has it that workers at the mill made the girls' life tough and it didn't matter that these were Mr. Wes' girls. You know how it is in a small town and everyone knows your business. Miss Patty's husband left his taint on her, but she still needed to eat," Virginia of all people chimed in.

"Miss Theodosia, that was her mama, but I think you know that. She couldn't or wouldn't help her. That woman had problems of her own. Eventually Miss Patty came back right when her momma died. She had some money in her pocket, a lot of it ev'dently, and opened this here yarn shop."

"I found an article on Howard McMurphy kidnapping a little girl. He was put in prison. Did he die in prison?" Carrie questioned.

"A few years before Miss Patty came home, her husband was released from jail, on good behavior or sumthin', and was shot within walkin' distance from the jail isself. He died that very same day," Adeene said.

"Did they get the killer?" Carrie inquired.

"Ya' know they never did. Guess it's one of those cold cases," Adeene replied.

"Talk 'bout Howard bein' a man wit' no luck. Satan was waitin' for him wit' open arms when he left that prison," Emeline replied.

"Mmm-hmm," the four weavers agreed in harmony.

"So, Camille was Patty's sister with Wesley Worth and Theodosia Eden-Worth as her parents. Just trying to understand," Carrie confirmed.

"Folks 'round town had moved on since then and afta' her momma's passin', Miss Patty built a nice little bus'ness right here on this side of town. Then she and your grandma became *real good* friends. Which was funny to some, because tale is that when they were youngins', Camille and your grandma were thick as thieves," Virginia advised.

Emeline continued, "But no one eva' asked 'bout Camille again. Both Miss Patty and your grandma seemed not to want to talk 'bout her, and those two could be pretty tight-lipped when there's bus'ness that's nobody's but their own. That's a respectable quality 'n a person." She looked directly at Virginia, who pretended not to notice. "So, that's the end of it."

It was Virginia's turn. "I'll tell ya' one thin', though; somethin' about your grandma an' Miss Patty that maybe ya' hann't heard. It's not pretty, but maybe ya' oughta know. *Maybe ya' know already.*"

Jenny Lee spoke up. "I don't think we need to go into that, Virginia. That's just gossip."

"I know it's a little betta' than gossip." Virginia could be like a dog with a good bone.

"It's OK, Jenny Lee," Carrie interjected. "I don't know as much as I feel like I should, even though my grandma raised me, but I'm a big girl now, thanks."

Virginia went on, sitting up straight at her bench like a grade school tattletale ready to spill to the teacher. "Well, my cousin and Miss Patty were headed ova' to see your grandma one day. Ya' may rememba' Miss Patty was there all the time afta' your grandpa died, but ya' know your manners, Carrie, ya' call first. This time they dinn't. Not shur where ya' could've been, but Miss Hattie answered the door nekked as a jaybird. Actually stepped out onto the porch like that. But then she saw Patty wasn't alone; she ran back inside. Miss Hattie wann't a young thin' at that point, but ya' can take from that wha'cha like."

Frankly, there was nothing she wanted to take away from that. Although another thought crossed her mind.

"What about Miss Patty's momma, Miss Theodosia? What was her deal?"

Adeene looked at her and said, "Town whore."

"There's some nice talk from a good Southern Baptist," Jenny Lee stated.

They'd all seemed to have dropped any sense of decency. Virginia picked up where Adeene left off.

"Miss Theodosia Eden married Mr. Wesley Worth fer his position 'n society and, her dignity of bein' an Eden, she hyphenated the Worth name when they got married. She was *SO* proud and he was so dull. He couldn't cut butta' with a hot knife. That's why it was easy fer her to turn out her own dawta fer sins that were a lot less than she'd done."

"So, Theodosia was married to Wesley Worth. What was his position in society?" Carrie asked.

"His family owned several textile mills an' durin' the Great Depression, Wesley started shuttin' them down one by one," Emeline advised.

"Why do you think Theodosia was such a whore?"

Adeene chimed back in, "There was stories of Miss Theodosia wit' Abraham Twiford, the Holtz brotha's, Joe an' Buck Holtz—all the while she was married to Wesley Worth wit' little ones runnin' 'round. That man was completely unner her thumb."

"Or in denial," Jenny Lee added.

Adeene replied, "But Wesley was a squirrel of a man wit' no nuts."

"That was Miss Patty's momma an' papa. Miss Patty was a lovely, small woman raised by a trashy bitch that'd been passed 'round more times than coleslaw," Virginia continued.

"Wow, thanks for the image Virginia. Got it. Actually, I have some pictures. If I brought them, could anyone tell me who was who?"

Emeline advised, "The better person to ask is my Aunt Lillie. That's Gary Pilotti's gramma. You could ask Papa, but Aunt Lillie is the betta'person to see 'bout puttin' names to faces. Papa's old an' he cain't rememba' his own Christian name, but I reckon Aunt Lillie knows the name of ev'ry person who's come an' gone 'n the last seventy years."

Carrie let the matter drop, but made a mental note of the information shared—Patty's parents were Wesley Worth and Theodosia Eden-Worth; Patty had two sisters, Lydia and one named Camille who left town after graduation; and Patty's husband Howard McMurphy was shot when released from prison.

As the women wove, shuttles were being thrown through the open sheds as warps were dropped and lifted in the ancient rhythm of African djembe drums. The familiar whack of beaters being strongly pulled against the weft to hide the warp and the underpinning holding the picture together slowly transformed each masterpiece into a great work of art.

There's beauty in that, Carrie thought.

Everyone but Adeene worked with only a drawing laid over a grid. They didn't need a weaving draft, the tiny boxes and numbers arranged in horizontal and vertical grids that, when lined up perpendicular to one another, guided the threading of the heddles and the order of the treadling like eloquence and architecture for their esthetic visual aspect.

These were the only instructions a weaver worked with. Plain weave was as old as the craft itself and they all could do it in their sleep. Adeene's more complex weave structure required a more detailed path to follow and set Carrie to wondering.

Adeene, seeing Carrie eying her drawing, spoke up and said, "Ya' know, Carrie, Miss Patty kep' a bottle of bourbon an' a little branch water fer her class."

"That sounds like a splendid idea, Adeene. After all, it's already 11:00 in the morning. Any idea where she kept it at?" Carrie asked the question with maybe a little too much enthusiasm.

This prompted Jenny Lee, who didn't really look like a bourbon drinker, to grin and say, "Actually, we all know where it's at. It sits on the top shelf wit' the cones of perle cotton, right behind the thread. There are glasses on the top shelf of the bookcase an' ice 'n the box. Hope ya' dinn't think that icebox was fer your lunch or sumthin'."

*Wow, silly me for not knowing that.* Carrie walked to the front of the shop to fetch the bourbon, unconsciously moving past the strange door that led to the mysterious cellar.

She stopped suddenly.

A very faint sound came from behind the door and found its way to her ear. Carrie swore it sounded like metal against metal.

She could feel the back of her neck tighten up and her breathing become very shallow. Clearly, the others hadn't heard it. She listened for a moment longer, but no more clatter came from behind the door.

Carrie wanted to have a look down there with a better light—and perhaps another person—before she would allow her imagination to run away . . . but right now, she really needed that drink.

"OK, ladies. Here's the morning's libation. It sounds like a sweatshop in here."

Virginia said wryly, "Yep. Sum thin's neva' change."

After class, the little group did what they did every week, they took a look around the shop, found yarn they couldn't live without, had another shot of bourbon, chatted for a while longer, and went on about the rest of their day.

Carrie broomed the dust bunnies that had evidently been fornicating and smiled because everything reminded her of Phil and their lovemaking.

She liked it.

But Carrie had learned a lot from the weaving group today and needed to think. She decided to close up for lunch and head over to Patty's house.

Patty had obviously been a meticulous housekeeper, but nothing had been done since she died. That now fell to Carrie.

She found a rag and some wood polish in the laundry room and noted there was some laundry that needed to be washed up.

*No hurry with that*, Carrie thought to herself. Patty by no means would need any of those things now, but soon she would have to decide what to keep and what could be sent off to some worthy charity.

Carrie started in the living room with dusting Patty's shelves. There were no family pictures, but she stumbled upon another photograph in an ornate, wood-scrolled frame of herself and Grandma Hattie that Patty had taken at the Beaufort county fair.

They all went together to the county fair for years when she was growing up, but that one was notable because it was the first time Carrie had entered a rug in the weaving contest and had won a blue ribbon at the young age of thirteen.

Carrie tried to think back about how Grandma Hattie and Patty had seemed, but nothing really stood out except that they were proud.

She moved to the coffee table. The table itself was lovely, with an acanthus leaf decoration and a lower shelf made of a circle of brown marble.

A Bible rested on the lower shelf.

The Bible appeared to be an old one that had been a very fine book when it was printed. The shimmery fabric cover was worn, but the gold embossing was still readable and the name inscribed in the lower right corner was one she didn't recognize. It was probably purchased during a time when the family Bible record was at least a reliable source for births, marriages, and deaths as the official county record. Given how little Patty had held onto her family history, she was curious.

Carrie sat down on the floral upholstery divan that rested on short cabriole legs with scroll feet. It was a sophisticated piece. Opening the very old and threadbare Bible, Carrie carefully turned the frail pages and found a loose and extracted 'Overleaf

Page, End Of Apocrypha,' from another Good Book, this one appearing to be from Theodosia's side of the family.

Theodosia's marriage to Wesley Worth was listed and her maiden name was given as Eden.

Listed was Theodosia's family:

- Matthew Eden (presumably her brother)
- Mother Charlotte and Father Jameson Eden
- Clay and Constance Eden were Jameson's parents
- Samuel and Orpha Worth were Wesley's parents
- Wesley's grandparents were Frederick and Cythiana

Theodosia wasn't much of a historian and her children's births were not recorded. Scripted within the page of the overleaf, the pen and ink penmanship was written by someone with excellent cursive writing as the lettering was still legible, but the ink splotches had blemished the yellowing paper. Viewing the testimony displayed:

Howard McMurphy's family:

- Henry McMurphy—father
- Rosie, neé Hicks—mother
- Leonard McMurphy—grandfather, Carabello, neé Dawson—grandmother
- Rosie's Sister—Jakayla Hicks married Beau Walker

What was Travis' last name? Then Carrie remembered: Hicks. Why Patty kept this Bible on the coffee table shelf was an enigma to her. Perhaps she had looked at it often, or perhaps it was a bequest. Nevertheless it was another mystery.

Flipping through the pages, it was clear that Theodosia's family had never actually had a look at the contents of this Bible and not likely of any other. However, stuck between the pages, somewhere in the neighborhood of the Song of Solomon, there was a photograph. Another of Grandma Hattie and Patty, only this was a close-up.

They were smiling and sitting on the bed. They're naked, at least from the top up. The room looked familiar and with a shock she recognized it as her grandma's bedroom. Something about the pose caught her eye and she needed to get a closer look.

In Patty's office she found a magnifying glass and scanned the picture, seeing plainly what had caused her to take a second look.

What the heck?

Hattie had her right arm over her breasts and her left arm around Patty, with her hand touching Patty's breast.

Oh, Grandma. This is a surprise.

It looked like Patty held the camera and snapped the picture.

The meaning of Virginia's nasty little bit of gossip from this morning's weaving class was now clear as a bell. Hattie had answered the door naked for Patty and it probably wasn't the first time.

Then something more unsettling occurred to her. Was she living there while any of this was going on? She felt that she would have known—*should have known.*

There were many times when Miss Patty would visit and they'd go into Hattie's room to *talk about things*. She knew during those times she needed to make herself scarce. That the two women might be making love would have shocked her then as it dumbfounded her now. Looking back, there were times when odd noises came from Hattie's room during Hattie's normal naptime, when the house was otherwise as quiet as a mid-afternoon field. She never imagined.

Never.

Grandma Hattie had sent Carrie to an all-girls school in a different county and drove her to school every day. If there had been rumors, she wouldn't have heard. When she left for college, it wasn't too far to where she could drive back home in less than two hours, and she had no real friends among Hattie's neighbors living in a rural part of town. Miss Patty had been around, as she had been often during her childhood, but there was no reason to suspect she and Grandma had formed a relationship that would never have been acceptable in North Carolina at the time—and is only marginally acceptable now.

She flipped through a few more pages of the Bible and found another newspaper article on Howard McMurphy's incarceration. The newspaper article stated that Howard McMurphy had proclaimed his innocence right up to the time of his death soon after he got out of prison.

*They all do.*

He was shot. It was a short article, but one that Miss Patty kept.

*Wow, this is messed up.*

Carrie stopped cleaning and walked through the dwelling into Patty's bedroom. She was on the hunt for pictures or anything that could clear this up for her, one way or another.

Looking through drawers, she found a picture of Grandma Hattie and Patty's ball team. Perhaps Gary's gramma could identify the school they'd attended. Sifting through Patty's belongings was not going to tell her the whole story.

Who were Camille and Lydia? How could a mother refuse to acknowledge her own daughters? What did Patty tell Hattie? Did Hattie know things about Patty that she kept secret?

Carrie pondered these thoughts and decided that the time to go through Hattie's room and boxes of things was long overdue.

She put the pictures in her purse and locked up the house.

At her house, going into the kitchen and finding a large crystal wine glass, she poured a towering glass of cabernet. If she was to go through Hattie's things looking for evidence of a relationship with Patty, she was going to need liquid courage. Going through Grandma's room was something she would have been reluctant to do when she was alive. Even now with Hattie dead and knowing there were questions that needed to be resolved in her own mind, she was still as tentative as ever.

Walking slowly, unsure, up the stairs to Hattie's room, she still pondered the possibilities, not liking most of them.

She turned the doorknob, took a big breath, and then a big gulp of wine. She really needed fortitude to do this.

Setting the wine glass on top of the dresser, Carrie decided the logical place to start was the closet.

*That's where it started with Patty,* she thought; *so that is where I'll begin.*

Seeing Grandma's clothes and thinking about the last time she wore some of them slowed things down a little. Most of the memories these clothes stirred up were lovely and she wanted to keep them that way. Looking in the bottom of the closet Carrie found only shoeboxes that contained—shoes.

Looking up on the top shelves she found a few old photo albums and took them down, blowing the dust off them. These she placed on the dresser. She took a few more sips of wine and opened the first.

One of the last times she had looked at this album was right after Grandpa's passing when she was just a small girl; in fact, that was one of her earliest memories.

As a little girl, Carrie sat on the bed with Hattie, who had brought up chocolate milk and some cookies, and they ate and drank as her grandma told stories about each of them.

Finding herself tearing up at those memories, Carrie reached for her wine, bumped the glass and knocked it off the dresser.

The wine splattered all about, with the broken crystal scattering like a dropped jigsaw puzzle. Was it an omen, as if a warning in protest of her being there or to delay her from finding anything else?

**"Shit!"** she screamed.

Putting the photo album on top of the other ones, she tiptoed into the bathroom closet to get some rags to clean up the mess. Starting at the point closest to her, she meticulously, slowly moved one of the rags to capture the glass shards and the other to soak up the wine.

There was glass everywhere.

Looking underneath the dresser for more glass fragments, Carrie came across a metal box.

As she mopped up the wine under the dresser, she pulled out the box. It was heavy, so she moved it out and put it to the side. She could not do anything with it right then. She had a mess to clean up.

The wine was soaking into an old-world style rug that her grandma had hand-woven in dense wool pile, a work rich in detail and textures. She had to react quickly. Soaking a sponge in some dish soap with hydrogen peroxide, she scrubbed hard to remove the evidence of her blunder. Onc thing Carrie learned in this life was how to clean up wine from a wool rug. Looking underneath Grandma's bed, she moved dusty boxes to a clean side and polished them off with a dry towel.

After the minor disaster was cleaned up, she took the albums along with the metal box downstairs to the kitchen.

It depressed Carrie to be so skeptical of Grandma Hattie, and she took the spilled wine as a warning. As she left the room, she slowly and gently closed the door so as not to wake the spirits. Maybe it was Grandma Hattie's way of telling Carrie her secrets were her own.

Opening another bottle of wine, she poured an oversize glass, though not quite as full as the last one and sat down at the kitchen table. Beginning again from the first page, she looked through the photo album and could hear once again in Grandma's soft-spoken but firm way the stories she had shared of her earlier life.

Pouring glass number three, she decided unenthusiastically to open the catch of the box, but it was locked. She hadn't noticed the small keyhole on the catch and honestly had no patience at this point to try and locate the key. Carrie resolved to pick the lock.

She was over-curious, as the wine and she were close friends now.

Finding a paperclip in a kitchen drawer, straightening it out, she inserted it into the lock. After a few moments of twisting and turning, the lock clicked. Slowly lifting the lid revealed pictures and folded papers, and at the bottom of the box, a small school pin. Setting the pictures to the side, she took out the first stack of letters and untied the baker's twine that held them together.

Carrie began to read and the letters were written in the same hand that she knew to be Patty's.

There were batches of letters, almost as if Grandma Hattie were keeping a diary. A few were from when Patty and her grandma had been in school together, but most dated from the time Patty left town and returned after Patty's mother's death to start a life different than the one she left.

There was no mention of Camille, Lydia, or Theodosia. Under the circumstances, that was not much of a surprise, except that Carrie would have expected her grandma to have at least asked once or twice about Camille. But there was nothing in the letters from Patty in that respect.

Some letters fell on the more intimate side of the fence, and at first she was much less than comfortable reading those, but that feeling ran off as she discovered she was suddenly aching to know about her grandma, Camille, Patty, and the perplexed past these three women left behind.

Sifting through, she was startled to see a letter Patty had written to her grandmother immediately after her grandpa died. It read:

*My Hattie of the Heavenly Halo,*

*I know it's been a ridiculous and sorry amount of time since I wrote—a whole week, but my mama brought me up with the notion that if you can't say something nice, well . . . you know her, you just say it anyway. But Scott was never a terrible husband to you. Nothing like it. The fact that the man slept in the only place on the face of the earth I would move God from his golden seat to sleep in doesn't mean I intend to be unkind. After all, he never knew, never needed to know and Carrie needed you both, even though it pains me as it does to say it. So we leave this as it is and I'll try very hard to behave. I'm attending the service if you allow me to. I'll bring my black faille dress and put it on and pretend to mourn, then when the minister drops a handful of dirt on top of old Scott, you can take it off and I can stop pretending.*

*Whether you want my presence at the service or not, I return in a week and no matter what, I must see you before I see or talk to anyone else. It must be the moment I arrive. I simply cannot stress the importance of this, so, please, Angel, keep my return to yourself and I'll explain all.*

*Love in due time,*
*A Woman in Copper*

She kept this letter to the side. Something important had happened here. Carrie hadn't realized Patty had returned right at her grandpa's death. She was only six years old at that time, but the reason was obvious enough. There were more letters, and they became increasingly bold in what Patty was willing to put down in black and white. On the whole, they continued as before—Patty talking about business, gossip, just life in general, always with the affection of a lover. One mentioned Carrie by name and she felt warm and light. Another was simply a slip of pretty paper with a single line apparently left when she had been physically present and was leaving the house.

*My dearest, beautiful Hattie,*

*The light here is so clear and a little yellow. Remember when we used to sketch by the river? That seems like a million years ago. I'll be back Tuesday—so long from now. Be ready for me. I can barely stand the separation.*

*Love, of course,*
*Red*

---------------------

*Hattie, Sweetest of All,*

*How is Carrie? I miss the sound of her voice and the pleasure of watching her at the loom. She's so much like you and I thank God, well, maybe not the God that looks down his nose at us, but some god, anyway, that you have her.*

*There's a bountiful supply of lovely yarn here. You would be in heaven. I've decided to carry some hand-dyed wool from a small coop in the Hebrides. We may live in the sticks, but I'll say this, my customers have an eye when it comes to yarn and I won't disappoint them. Is there anything I can bring you? You know what I want when I get back? Take a guess. The show ends tomorrow and there are a few suppliers I still have to see and then I come straight back to you.*

*Kisses,*
*Your charmed molten copper*

---------------------

*My, my, my. Leaving this in your panty drawer so you think of me and skip the lingerie*

Then there was something that hinted at a dark time involving Carrie's mother. Her skin crawled a bit and for a moment, it was possible that Patty's letter was going to end up with a match taken to it. But this was a burden Grandma Hattie faced constantly in order to keep her safe and she read on:

*Sugar,*

*I thought for a minute I wanted you to tell me what the caller said, but I don't need to know. I know what this is about. But please, please, PLEASE don't be afraid. People are hateful, Honey. I promise you that everything will be fine and I'm certain of it myself, but do what you must to feel safe. Put my shotgun where you can reach it, if that will help. I don't really mean for you to shoot Debra, I know that sounds horrible, but you can't be sure what that girl's mind is like right now. I'm glad though, that I didn't see her. I might have said some things myself you would never have forgiven me for.*

*I don't doubt that there's going to be some talk. Just ignore it. What Debra does isn't on you. These miserable bitches aren't going to say anything to your face when there's fun to be had by doing it behind your back, but the shame is on them.*

*There were other things I wanted to tell you and I hate that it's been interrupted! Maine is just beautiful and you'd love it. There's no way I can bring back every skein of yarn I fall in love with. The problem is trying to narrow it down. There's lace-weight wool I really love in the colors of the coastline here and I think Vita would have to have it instantly. I want to knit a shawl in it myself and I intend to stock four or five colors. Is there anything you'd like? I want you to make the trip with me the next time I go. Don't argue with me. By that time, this stupid shit will have blown over—I'm starting to sound like that foul-mouthed child of Ava Baucom's! Nice Southern Baptists there. Good Lord. When Carrie is old enough to be a few nights on her own, love that girl as I do, I'd like to have you alone for a while. We don't get the chance much.*

*I intend to be back next Wednesday. Take care, darlin' and if you need to call me, that's fine. I want you to. But please, seriously, don't worry.*

*So much love,*

*Your Precious Chest Nut*

And sometime later, as if whatever the incident was, it was banished from memory:

*Hey, sugar!*

*Here's my Grandma Worth's recipe for her crawdad boil. It's better than Markita's momma's, if you can believe that.*

Carrie's hand shook a little at the way Patty had written about her mother. It caught her off guard in the middle of everything else. She knew Debra had drug problems but Carrie never thought she'd actually threaten Grandma.

No one really talked about Debra in front of her and Carrie never asked.

Never cared.

Debra wasn't there for Carrie, ever.

Carrie didn't even care what her biological mom had done that made Patty so pissed off. Debra was as absent from her life as having tea in Shanghai and Carrie didn't miss that, either.

Carrie read a few more letters without really learning anything else, but still having some trouble—still trying to get her mind wrapped around Patty and her grandmother. She didn't have a problem with a woman being in love with another woman. When she was in college, she knew a couple of lesbians and stupidly thought she was cool because she believed they were cool. That's what small-minded people who want to pretend they're not do.

But crap, does anyone really want to think about their grandparents having sex? Now Carrie was thinking about how her grandparents probably weren't and that's as far as she wanted to go. Carrie loved Grandma Hattie and was already getting used to the idea of her grandma having a relationship with Patty after her grandfather passed. Carrie just hoped that Grandma had been happy. Whatever had happened with Debra didn't matter to her, but Grandma Hattie mattered and Carrie was deathly curious. She knew she shouldn't, but she wanted to talk to someone about it and she wondered if anyone knew.

As she sat there, she realized how little she'd thought about her Grandpa Scott in recent days. This was the house he'd shared with her grandma, evidently more as friends who respected one another, with love on his side, at least, if not on hers. Grandma Hattie wasn't a cold woman, and part of Carrie believed, even now, that her grandma had felt some small amount of true affection for him.

Grandpa Scott was a natural businessman with a feel for the earth underneath him. He'd farmed tobacco, corn, cotton, and sorghum profitably. He had raised some sheep for Grandma Hattie while he courted her and continued to tend the small flock after their wedding. But her reasons for accepting him now seemed sad and it weighed on Carrie's heart.

Grandpa Scott had been a gentleman with easy, familiar manners—handsome to an adoring granddaughter. But from what she'd heard, he had looks that guaranteed an easy self-assurance no matter how unassuming he'd been. He was polite to a fault and helpful to his neighbors in the face of happy occasions, natural disaster, financial ruin, and the occasional lost dog, barn-raising, and wrench-turning.

The time she had with him, growing up as a child—a child whose father had recoiled from her birth and vanished to parts unknown promptly afterward and whose mother abandoned her to a lust for painkillers—was idyllic. Looking back, Carrie understood he'd dealt with Debra by sending her subsistence amounts of money and refusing to see her.

Grandpa Scott had been different with her, as she remembered her grandma and him singing old gospel hymns and old mountain tunes together as he played the piano and hammered dulcimer. They fished in the river and on the open sea. Carrie rode on the tractor with her grandpa wrapping his warm jacket around her when it was too cold. Grandma Hattie brought them both chocolate chip cookies and fried peach pies with a tray of milk out on the porch. Grandma Hattie had read to her the story of the Velveteen Rabbit, but Grandpa Scott was having none of that. He read Eugene Field to her before bed and Robert Louis Stevenson after supper.

Carrie felt a tear fall on her cheek and decided it was time to put the letters away—for now.

# Chapter 8

At the bottom of the metal box, there were folded deteriorating yellow newspaper articles about Patty's husband, Howard McMurphy. Carrie got up from the table, grabbed a bag of chips, and sat on the couch to read the first article:

Bellefontaine, N.C. – A Sparrow Mills man was arrested with attempted kidnapping of a five-year-old child after Sgt. Edward Eschammer of the Bellefontaine PD said he pulled over Howard McMurphy in his 1934 Chevrolet Pickup for reckless driving on November 22.

The victim, a five-year-old black girl was seen jumping out and running away from McMurphy's pickup truck.

The suspect's careless driving came to the attention of Sgt. Eschammer approximately two miles past the gas station on Hwy DD. When Eschammer pulled over the pickup, he witnessed the victim screaming and crying and finally jumping out of the pickup. As her parents were driving by, they stopped, grabbed the child, and identified the suspect as the man who had taken their child.

The parents said that their little girl went missing from the house while she was playing outside. Police handcuffed the alleged kidnapper, who vehemently denied the allegations.

McMurphy said the little girl was outside the gas station crying and there was no one there. Howard McMurphy advised he was the only person at the gas station. He went into the gas station and told Tommy Reeves, a young man of age 19, about the little girl outside alone. McMurphy advised Reeves to call the police, but Reeves stated that the station phone was out of order and advised McMurphy that the police station was right down the road off Maple and Bernthal.

"The little girl's parents both said that he was lying and insisted on his arrest," said Sgt. Eschammer.

McMurphy is being held without bond for attempted kidnapping according to Bellefontaine County Jail records.

Carrie sat back in wonder and utter amazement. *What did Patty do when this happened?* Carrie continued going through the metal box and pulled out another newspaper article on Howard.

Bellefontaine, N.C. — The Bellefontaine County Court affirmed Thursday the conviction and prison sentence of a Sparrow Mills man. Howard Henry McMurphy, 20, was convicted July 11, 1940, of First Degree kidnapping of Linda Louise Roosevelt. He was sentenced that same afternoon to twenty-three years in prison.

Howard McMurphy's lawyer, Victor Abbott, Criminal Defense Attorney, fresh out of college and having recently passed his bar exam, was hired by Theodosia Eden-Worth to defend her son-in-law who is married to her daughter Patty McMurphy née Eden-Worth. Howard McMurphy repeatedly stated in court that he was innocent.

**Patty McMurphy was not available for comments and her momma, Miss Theodosia, would not allow the press to address her. Victor Abbott, Criminal Defense Attorney, declined to comment after the verdict.**

Well, that was short and sweet, thought Carrie.

She looked for a piece of paper and a pen. Carrie wanted to write down some of the things she read.

- Why would Theodosia pay for Howard's defense attorney?
- Was it for Patty?
- Victor Abbott was the defense attorney
- What was the reason behind that? She was rich enough to pay for the best lawyer in town. Why would she settle on someone fresh out of college?
- Patty had no comment?
- Why not? Was she so embarrassed or did her momma not allow it.
- Lulu Roosevelt was the little five-year-old girl.
- Why did Howard pick her up? The paper said the little girl was outside a gas station and the momma went to the restroom while her daddy was buying the little girl some candy.
- The young clerk, Tommy Reeves, said he didn't see the little girl outside.
- The court case was held in Bellefontaine County Court.
- Was it a trial by jury?

Why was this not adding up? Carrie thought.

She sat perplexed at the table and looked at the newspaper articles over and over again, then continued looking at her scribbling on the paper.

Something wasn't right.

It was getting late and Carrie thought when she had more time she would revisit this and put the items back into the metal box.

***

As Carrie laid in bed thinking about the day's events and how the weaving ladies had said Camille was a 'bitch,' Theodosia, her momma, was the 'town whore' and how Grandma Hattie had come running naked out of the house to meet up with Patty. How the pictures and letters of Patty and her grandma had proved that they indeed were more than friends—*they were lovers.*

Carrie's first thought of Grandma Hattie was that she was lonely. *Why would she have married Grandpa if she was a lesbian? Did Grandpa know? Did she and Patty have a relationship in school?* Maybe Gary's gramma could identify someone in the school picture still in the living that Carrie could talk to and gain more insight.

*Gotta start somewhere*, as she rolled over and closed her eyes.

***

Carrie put the list of questions in her purse and drove a bit out of the way to the shop.

Pulling onto a small rural road that was gravelly but filled with potholes from the spring rains that washed most of the rock away and driving to a Sinclair gas station on Highway DD, she stopped her car and went inside.

Behind the counter was a greasy old man with gray hair in a ponytail and tattoos up and down his arms chewing on a toothpick.

Carrie picked up a pack of gum and approached the counter.

"Hey," he said with a salty voice, "Ya' need gas or is that all ya' be gettin'?"

"Um, yeah, this is all I need, thanks," and she paused. "Hey, would you know anything about what happened here years ago with a little girl named Lulu Roosevelt being abducted by Howard McMurphy?"

"Why ya' askin'?"

"I found some old newspaper articles about the kidnapping. It happened here, right?"

"Nah, dun't rememb'r nuttin' hap'nin' way back then," he said.

He seemed nervous.

"Well, would you happen to know who owned this place back then?"

"This place *bin* 'n my family fer ova' fitty years," he said, "but I dun'no nuttin'. Do ya' need sumtin' else?" he asked as if trying to end the conversation. He turned his back to Carrie and started moving items hastily on the shelves behind him.

"No, I guess I don't. Thanks," Carrie said as she left, looking at the back of the old man.

When she opened the door to leave, in walked another man who said, "Hey, Tommy, did'cha get any—" and Carrie walked out.

Well, Tommy was of no help. Perhaps I'll have to ask Sarge for help.

Yeah, that's what she would do. Sarge could get her some information on this.

When she arrived at the store, she called the police station right away.

"Sergeant Lament, please," she asked the person on the receiving end.

"Hey, Lament—phone call," yelled the person, "line 4."

"Sergeant Lament."

"Hey, Sarge, it's Carrie."

"Miss Carrie, how can I help you?"

"When you're not busy, can you come by the store when you get a chance? I need to ask you for a favor and I don't want to do it on the phone."

"Sure, Miss Carrie," he said in trepidation. "I'll be by shortly."

"Thanks," said Carrie. "See you soon."

As Carrie turned to put the phone back on the hook her mind went to the vision of Sarge in her bed, lying there naked, stroking her breast.

"God, you're so beautiful. You're even more beautiful after making love. I haven't wanted anyone that bad in a long time, sugar," she remembered him saying.

Carrie put her left hand behind her neck as she stretched it out, and then brought her hand slowly down to her breast, remembering his touch—*his bite mark.*

She was smitten with him.

As Carrie began to straighten up the store and review the schedule, the noises in the cellar started up again. Carrie was thankful that she was the only one in the store. She heard it yesterday too, but the looms were going and the ladies were talking. *Those ladies have been looming here for years*, she thought. *They surely would have heard these noises before, but maybe they're used to it.*

She wasn't sure how long it would take Sarge to reach the store, so she locked the front door. Carrie remembered she needed a light bulb and found a flashlight to take downstairs. Prepared to go down the steps, she slowly moved the wooden cupboard just enough to squeeze behind and press open the door. Feeling the cold breeze and inhaling the unpleasant odor when she opened the door, she stepped back. Taking one last breath of good air, she fortified herself and descended down the steps.

Shining the flashlight up on the ceiling, she found the string for the light. Carrie moved a box to step up on, put the flashlight under her chin, and replaced the bad bulb with a good one. She pulled on the vulgar string.

The light was only good for the small area beneath it. The effect was much like having an umbrella of light spotlighting a criminal who was being interrogated by a detective in a black and white TV show.

As she walked around, she felt a cool breeze brooding in the area. Carrie shivered as if a cow had just run over her grave. She moved toward the reflection on the painting, eradicating more cobwebs as she approached it. Shining the flashlight on the area, she saw the full-size portrait. The question remained, *Who was it?* It was an oversized oil painting of a red-haired lady who didn't look much older than Carrie was now. She wore a strand of pearls around her neck that hung over a very elegant red dress with yellow buttons and a scalloped collar. She had green eyes, no smile, and a very unyielding, uncompromising demeanor. Carrie wasn't aware who it was but thought, *perhaps it was a portrait of Theodosia.*

Carrie leaned in closer for a better view and jumped back when she heard a sudden hard knock at the door upstairs.

*Shit, hopefully, they won't be looking in the store and see the cupboard moved about.* Carrie climbed the stairs as stealthily as she could. Upon reaching the cupboard, she snuck a look around and could see Sarge through the window with his back towards the door. Carrie reacted quickly but cautiously, closing the door and moving the tapestry and cupboard back into position. She began to wonder if she should tell him about the cellar, but didn't want to appear overly needy as she wanted his help in finding out more information on Howard.

Unlocking the door, she said, "Hey, Sarge, come on in," as her heart rate jumped into a sprint.

He came in and asked, "Were you busy?" He stood tall in his uniform with those stupid mirror sunglasses over his beautiful eyes.

"Oh, I was just in the other room. Hey, I was wondering if I could ask you for a favor."

"Sure, what's up, Miss Carrie?"

Carrie explained that she found some newspaper articles on Howard McMurphy that just didn't make sense to her and proceeded to tell him about what she had read.

She asked, "Sarge, do you know anyone at the Bellefontaine police department that could get me some information on Howard McMurphy? Things just aren't adding up."

"Why do you want to get involved in a closed case?"

"Well, I'm trying to find out why Patty left me everything and piece things together. I guess I'm just interested in Patty's life. I didn't even know about her family. All I knew was that she was my grandma's best friend, but there are a few things that just don't make sense to me," she said without giving away too much information.

Perhaps Sarge had heard the rumors of her grandma and Patty's relationship, but he didn't let on that he had.

"Miss Carrie, it may take me a day or two but I'll see what I can do. I have your phone number. I'll give you a call when I have more information."

"Hey, Sarge, would you like to come over for supper on Friday?"

Carrie wanted to see him again and maybe have a repeat performance of Sunday. He just looked too delicious to miss an opportunity to have him again—over to her house.

"I'll call you and let you know," he said grinning. "I have a few things that I have to do today. Is that all you need, Miss Carrie?"

"Yeah," she said slowly, still desiring him.

"Then, Miss Carrie, I wish you a good day," he said, exiting the store.

Carrie tried to regain her self-control and stared out the door watching Sarge walk to his car. He looked back and saw her watching him. Carrie knew she had been caught and panicked. She turned quickly, bumped into the nearby counter, hitting the crazy bone on her right knee.

*"Oh, shit,"* she said as she bent over and rubbed her knee, realizing how strongly that man had a hold on her.

Carrie thought about going through the metal box. *I wish I'd never found it.* She remembered one of the strange letters from Patty. Patty had mentioned how her momma, Theodosia, hated her and treated her worse than an abandoned dog you might throw crumbs to. Now why would Patty say something like that? Why did Theodosia hate Patty so much? This made no sense.

Carrie had to get more information on Theodosia. She didn't know her at all, but knew she held many secrets. Perhaps she needed to call Victor Abbott to find out some things about Theodosia, especially since she had hired him to defend Mr. McMurphy.

Calling Victor Abbott's office, Hope answered. "I'm sorry, Miss Carrie, but Victor just stepped out of the office." Hope took a message and advised Carrie that she would have Victor call her upon his return.

"Well, bummer," Carrie spoke out loud to no one. She put her hands on her face, leaned against the counter top, and then, in walked Walter.

"Hello, Walter."

"Huh, hey," he grunted in his less-than-charming way.

Carrie thought, Oh, what can it hurt?

"Hey, Walter, can I ask you something?"

"Wha'?" he mumbled and stood there hunched over and smelling with the stench of three-day-old tobacco.

"Well, I found some old newspaper articles on Miss Patty's husband, Howard McMurphy. Did you happen to know him?"

"Why ya' wanna know?" he snorted.

"Just interested, that's all. I didn't know the man," Carrie replied nervously.

"Howard's no yaller, jus' a plucked duck tha's tarred an' feathered."

"Why would you say that?"

Walter stood there looking around the store not saying anything.

"Why did you say that? What does a plucked duck have to do with anything?" Carrie persisted.

"Jus' a bunch of baloney. Time gone now," he mumbled.

"But, what? Walter—I don't understand."

"Howard dinn't do 'no good for hisself' bein' as nervous as a cow wit' a bucktooth calf 'n tha' trial, denyin' up 'til the day he died. Jury were hotter'n a goat's butt 'n a hot peppa' patch. Jus' wanna' quick fixin' to shew 'way the town's black cloud."

"You knew Theodosia, didn't you? What role did she play in all this?" Carrie was really trying to press the point.

"Yeah, I knows Theo. Wha' 'bout her?"

"Walter, what role did she play in Mr. McMurphy's trial?"

"She pay *fer it.* She done it fer her dawta'. But, she dinn't take to him. Eva'one knows that."

"Can you tell me about Patty's momma, Miss Theodosia? What was she like?"

"Why ya' wanna know fer?" he said, hiding something.

"I'm just curious. I didn't know the lady."

"Well, all that needs to be said 'bout Miss Theo is she shamed 'Lucifer' as his sist'r playin' on the souls of many men 'n t'is town an' the next." Then he turned and walked out the door.

*What the heck?* Carrie thought. She remembered the rumors and that Miss Theodosia was the town *whore* and Walter's family was part of her favored men, but was there more to this story?

*Shit, I can't solve one problem before another one pops up*, Her head was starting to spin with all the mess Patty had left her.

Maybe she should give everything up and just run the store, never go back into Grandma Hattie's room, and leave well enough alone. But she couldn't. She was too deep in this heap of crap.

**'Bang, Bang, BANG'**, the cellar noises instigated Carrie's nerves to riot in protest.

"I give up!" she screamed at the noise and stomped her feet. *I have too much to think about right now to mess with you.*

Carrie had to get out of the store before she pitched a conniption fit. She locked the door and went down to SamiJo's diner. It was best for her to get away and think in some other setting. She couldn't think in the shop.

***

Carrie sat herself near the window, distraught. The waitress, Thelma, an older, full-busted, dark-haired lady with a short waist, approached her and asked, "Hey, darlin', you alright? Can I get'cha sumthin'?"

"Yeah, I'll have some sweet tea, please."

Thelma left Carrie a menu and said, "I'll be right back with that tea."

Carrie stared at the menu, not reading it. In her mind's eye, she saw visions of Lulu running away from Howard McMurphy's truck screaming and crying when the police showed up, and at that exact time, when the police were apprehending Mr. McMurphy, the Roosevelts drove by.

*Coincidence, maybe—really? You might see that in a movie or something but in Bellefontaine County? Really? Why does this not make any sense? Like it was staged or planned,* Carrie thought.

Continuing to wonder what happened to the Roosevelts, Carrie remembered Gary's gramma had mentioned that she hadn't seen Lulu around for quite some time.

Carrie needed to investigate whether anyone knew what happened to Lulu or her family. *Maybe it would lead to some answers.*

"Hey, sweetie," Thelma said as she approached Carrie from behind, startling her.

"Oh, I'm sorry, sweetie, dinn't see you were 'n such deep thought. Would ya' like me to come back 'round 'n a few minutes or have ya' decided on wha'cha want?" she asked gingerly.

"Um—oh, yeah, um, I'll take some peach pie. Thanks," and the waitress turned to leave, but she looked back at Carrie.

"Are ya' shur you're a'right, honey? Ya' look as pale as a picket fence."

"Yeah, I'm fine. Hey, Miss Thelma, can I ask you something? Do you know who Lulu Roosevelt is?"

"Well, she's from these parts, ya' know, but cain't say I've seen neitha' hide nor hair of her 'n quite 'while. Why ya' askin' 'bout her, sugar?"

"Oh, just wondering if Lulu or her parents were still alive."

"Well, her parents live in the next town over, on the other side of Heart Strings Cemetery, near the river. Cain't say I've seen them in a real long time. They did pretty well for themselves. Live in a big house I hear."

"What? I thought they were poor?"

"Never had a pot to pee 'n at one time, I heard, but they mus'ave found sum' money sumwhere. Struck it rich an' moved from a shanty 'while ago."

"Was it a shanty by a gas station in Bellefontaine County?" Carrie just threw it out to the wind.

"Not shur if it's still there, but ya', it's sumwhere near there, I hear folks talk 'bout it," she said.

As Thelma looked around the diner, "Sugar, if ya' don't mind, I have to 'tend to sum otha' customers. I'll get ya' that peach pie ya' wanted. Be right back."

"OK. Thanks."

*OK, another piece to the puzzle but I don't know where it fits,* Carrie thought. *Theodosia, one of the richest women in the area, was the puppet master here.*

Carrie had to find out more. She had to talk to Victor Abbott and Walter again.

After drinking several fills of sweet tea and slowly eating a heavenly, delectable piece of peach pie, Thelma brought her the bill.

"That was the best peach pie I have ever eaten," she told Thelma as she paid the bill before leaving the diner.

Carrie walked back toward her car thinking about Lulu and her parents and noticed Victor Abbott and Walter talking between some parked cars. She couldn't hear the conversation, but she instinctively walked toward both men.

"Excuse me, gentlemen. But Mr. Abbott, did your secretary, Hope, tell you that I called?"

They both jackrabbited and stopped talking. The lawyer was the first to recover. "Pardon me, Walter," Mr. Abbott said and turned to Carrie.

"Hello, Miss Carrie, no, I haven't touched base with Hope yet, is there something that you need?"

"When you have a few minutes, can you meet me at the store?" Carrie said without giving too much away.

"Miss Carrie, I would love to, but I have several more meetings that I need to tend to today. Is there any way I could put you on my calendar? I can have my secretary make the arrangements," Victor replied.

"Yeah, that will be fine, Mr. Abbott. Sorry for the interruption. Good day, gentlemen."

*Something was odd there*, she thought, *but why shouldn't Victor and Walter be talking together?* She dismissed it from her mind and drove back to the store. The store phone was blinking and she was secretly hoping it was Sarge accepting her supper invitation.

"Hey, Carrie, it's me, Travis, just wondering if you're available Friday night. How about supper and a movie? Call me."

Carrie did like Travis' cute little tickle of a laugh and his playfulness. He made her feel carefree and energetic, but she had already invited Sarge over and had no intention of changing that plan.

There were a couple more messages from customers regarding this yarn or a different product and she returned those calls promptly but left Travis for last.

Carrie wasn't sure what to say to Travis when she returned his call. Should I tell him about Sarge coming over for supper Friday night? Or should I just tell him I'm busy? She knew Travis would know otherwise. She grasped the nettle and dialed Travis.

"Hey, Travis. It's Carrie."

"Hey, Carrie, how ya' doin'?"

"Fine," she said.

"Hey, I left you a message. Ya' busy Friday night? I was thinkin' 'bout supper and a movie. Ya' innerested?"

"Well, Travis, I made other plans for Friday night with Phil," Carrie said honestly.

"Phil? Oh, OK. Maybe some other time, huh?"

"Sure, Travis. Hey, I did have a good time at the fair."

"Yeah, well, so did I," he said as if still trying to comprehend the meaning of *"other plans with Phil."*

"Can I call ya' again, sum' time?" Travis questioned.

"Sure, Travis, you can call me again," Carrie said and they talked for a little while longer but made no future plans of meeting up.

When the conversation was over, Carrie decided to call it a day. Her head was spinning. She needed a drink and some downtime.

*Why did Patty leave everything to me? It just doesn't add up.*

***

Early the following morning, Carrie decided to drive by the larger county library to use the resources there for old newspaper articles. Research was a favorite school activity and she knew how to find articles via microfiche for college papers. She researched Howard McMurphy, Lulu Roosevelt, and Theodosia Eden-Worth. She printed out the articles that she found and decided to read them later. By late morning she believed she had enough information to get started, and if she needed more, she could always come back. She put the papers in her dark green backpack and left.

Going into the office, Carrie pulled out the black and white printed papers, separating them in respective piles for Howard, Lulu, and Theodosia, but before she could finish, the door jingled.

She was pleasantly surprised. "Hello, Mr. Abbott."

"Hello, Miss Carrie, did you get Hope's message of the meeting?"

"What meeting?" And then she looked at the blinking recorder, "Sorry, she must have left a message on the recorder."

"Miss Carrie, was there something that you needed to talk to me about?" Victor asked.

"Yes, please, come into my office."

"Yeah, um, go ahead and take a seat, please." Carrie sat behind the desk.

"I was just wondering why Patty left me everything. It just doesn't make sense, and I was hoping you could shed some light on some things for me."

"What is it that you want to know?"

"Let's start with what can you tell me about Patty and her decision to leave me everything."

"Well, Miss Carrie, Patty actually left everything to your Grandmother Hattie first, but when your grandmother died before she did, the clause in her will to account for that, stated, in that circumstance only, it all went to you. Why are you questioning this?"

*It just doesn't make sense,* Carrie thought. *Why would it all go to me?*

"OK, I'll accept that," Carrie said in disbelief. "Mr. Abbott, can I ask you about Howard McMurphy?"

"What about Mr. McMurphy?" he asked, as if this line of questioning was a bolt out of the blue.

"You defended him, didn't you? Wasn't it your first case out of law school?"

"Yes," Victor said. He seemed taken aback by her questioning.

"How did Miss Patty's momma, Miss Theodosia, find you to defend him, if you don't mind me asking?"

"Miss Theodosia was a big contributor to the college I attended, and seeing that I graduated top of my class, she sought me out," he said.

"Did you know her before then?"

"I had heard of her and I knew she was a wealthy woman. I thought that if I took the case, it would launch the start of my career."

"As I'm sure it did."

"Miss Carrie, may I ask you what you're getting at?"

"It just doesn't make sense. Did you investigate the accusations against Howard McMurphy?"

"I can assure you, Miss Carrie, I investigated the gas station, the police report, the Roosevelts' story, and I put together the best defense I could," he said rather defensively.

"Didn't it seem a little disturbing to you that Howard always declared his innocence?"

"Miss Carrie, I couldn't find anything that led to his innocence. I did the best I could with the information that I had. The prosecutor had the gas station employee stating he never saw Lulu or the Roosevelts in the store. Gibby Ewert, the reporter, stated the phone was in working order and testified that he used it to report the kidnapping story to the paper. Then, with the Roosevelts driving by just when Howard was pulled over and Lulu running away from Howard's truck, everything worked against Mr. McMurphy. I can assure you that I did my best, but I lost the case. Why are you bringing this up now?"

"Mr. Abbott, I don't mean to be an annoyance, but I found some old newspaper articles and pulled some more off the microfiche at the library that I still need to read. What can you tell me about Theodosia and Howard's relationship?"

Distracted by the jingle of the door, Carrie said, "Can you excuse me for a moment?" She got up to see who had entered. It was a customer who wanted to buy some yarn. After providing assistance, Carrie re-entered her office. Seeing that Victor had changed seats and was sitting behind the desk, she was perplexed.

*Perhaps he was looking through the microfiche papers that she was starting to sort through*, but she thought nothing more of it.

Sitting down, she continued. "As I was saying, what do you know about Mr. McMurphy and Miss Theodosia's relationship?"

"Miss Carrie, I have some other appointments that I need to attend to. All I can say is that Miss Theodosia wasn't particularly taken to Howard's surprise marriage to her youngest daughter, particularly at Patty's young age of seventeen. And with Howard coming from a Tar Heel family, he wasn't of good enough quality for Miss Theodosia's daughter. Is there anything else? I really need to depart now," he said, standing and looking at his gold watch.

"Oh. OK—yeah, um, thanks for stopping by. If I come up with other concerns, may I call you?"

"Yes, Miss Carrie, any time you need anything, but I really have to leave now. Just call the office and Hope can arrange a meeting." He got up and Carrie saw him out.

Perhaps Victor had done the best he could, as everything seemed set up against Howard. Sure did appear that the prosecutors had everything going in their favor, but it still didn't add up. Carrie had a gut feeling that Howard's conviction was just too convenient. Theodosia's fingerprints were all over this.

Walking back into the office, her intuition told her the papers on the desk had been examined. Well, she was gone for a while. Perhaps Victor looked through them out of curiosity or boredom.

Carrie sat, started reviewing what she had printed off, and continued to put the papers into separated piles. When she finished, she picked up Howard's pile and started reading the articles.

She had many disruptions as customers came in for bobbins, yarn, and unscheduled tête-à-têtes about Miss Patty. The day went by like a high-speed train. Carrie took all the papers from the desk and deposited them back inside her backpack. She could do more uninterrupted reading when she reached home.

Carrie put her purse down on the kitchen counter while looking at the mail. Distracted by the phone ringing, Carrie answered, placing the phone on her shoulder.

"Hello," Carrie said while opening up an envelope.

"Miss Carrie, Sergeant Lament."

Carrie nearly dropped the phone onto the counter.

"Hey, Sarge, how are you doing?" she said rather despondently.

"What's wrong?" he could hear it in her voice.

"Oh, *nothing*—by the way, did you happen to find anything out?"

"Yes, ma'am, I have some information that may interest you. I have a copy of the police file and court papers from Bellefontaine County. I even talked with Sgt. Edward Eschammer who's retired since then."

"*Really?*" she said, and her mood lightened significantly

"I can bring them by on Friday, if your invitation for supper is still open," he said with a smile in his voice.

"So, *you are* taking me up on my supper invitation then. Good. How about seven-ish?"

"Yes, ma'am, if you'll still have me."

*Oh, yes,* Carrie thought, *I will have you alright!*

Clearing her throat and trying to ease her yearning for him, she asked if she could trouble him to bring the papers by the house or the store prior to Friday. She didn't want to wait until Friday before she would see him again.

"Miss Carrie, I'm on duty tonight, I could try to come by the store tomorrow if you'd like."

"Tomorrow will be fine," she said, missing him and thanking him for going out of his way to do this for her.

"No worries, ma'am, I'm here to help."

# Chapter 9

**Carrie** laid out all the papers from her backpack on the kitchen table in respective piles for Howard, the Roosevelts, and—the biggest one—Theodosia. Carrie had to tackle these, but could only do one thing at a time. Taking out the list that she had made the other day, she decided to make changes to it:

Theodosia

- Was a major contributor to Victor's college
- Theo didn't like Howard marrying Patty at age 17
- Thought Howard's family of Tar Heels were beneath them
- Theo did pay Victor to defend Howard—Was it at Patty's request?

Victor Abbott

- He was fresh out of college and Howard McMurphy's defense attorney
- Confirmed by Victor, he was a top student in college and Theodosia sought him out

Patty

- Patty had no comment about her husband's kidnapping charges

Lulu Roosevelt

- Lulu was the kidnapped little girl
- Parents were poor, but came into money

- Parents moved down by the river across town, on the other side of Heart Strings Cemetery
- The parents told the reporter that the mother went to the restroom and the father went inside to pay for gas and buy some candy for their little girl
- The little girl was playing outside. When they came back to the car, they discovered their little girl was gone

Gas Station

- Tommy Reeves, the gas station clerk, said he did not see Lulu or the Roosevelts that day and that the station phone was working

Gibby Ewert

- Was the reporter that called on the gas station phone and reported the kidnapping

Howard McMurphy

- The little black girl had been seen jumping out and running away from McMurphy's pickup truck on November 22
- McMurphy said the little girl was outside crying alone, and Tommy Reeves and he were the only other people at the gas station
- Howard went into the gas station and told Tommy Reeves, a young man of 19, about the little girl crying outside
- Howard advised Tommy to call the police but was told the station phone was out of order
- Tommy told Howard that the police station was right down the road

Items Still to Check Out

- Review police file—Sarge bringing over
- Bellefontaine County Court Decision—Sarge bringing over
- Who was Howard McMurphy? What was his character?

- Understand Theodosia—Why would Theo pay for Howard's defense attorney if she disliked him?
- Was this a trial by jury?

*What did Walter say?* She tried remembering his statement. "The jury were hotter'n a goat's butt in a hot pepper patch. Just wanna' quick fixin' to shew away the town's black cloud."

Carrie's mind was spinning like a hamster wheel. There were so many things streaming that she had to sit back and think, particularly about the portrait in the cellar. Why was it in the cellar? What was Patty and Grandma Hattie's relationship in school? What about the letters Carrie found in the box—*ugh, I don't want to revisit those right now*, she thought as she glanced at the metal box resting on the counter.

Carrie stood up and looked at her checkbook and thought about Patty's yarn store and the money in Patty's register.

*Where was Camille, Patty's older sister? Was she involved in the inheritance after Theodosia passed?* If Carrie could find Camille, maybe Camille could help answer some of these questions.

But the question that stumped Carrie most of all was why Patty left this freaking mess to her?

Sitting back in her chair, re-reading what she wrote, she couldn't get a grip on it all. There were too many puzzle pieces missing, but she was confident that Theodosia held most of them. Perhaps she should start with Theodosia's pile.

Picking up the printouts from the library, she read that Miss Theodosia Eden-Worth was nineteen years old when she met Wesley Worth of the prominent Worth family. The Worth family owned Worth Textiles and Manufacturing Company and operated three mills on three different rivers. They were married just short of one year after courting. It was stated that Miss Theodosia Eden-Worth was heir to Eden Tobacco Manufacturing and affiliated to the Blackbeard origin in Bath County through the first Governor of North Carolina, Charles

Eden. The article continued by stating that her red hair was only an indication of her odious behavior and disposition. In appearance, Theodosia was a lovely lady to behold. Her slight build, green eyes and fashionable dress for the day made her a desirable woman—from a distance. Close up, within her grasp, she was scarier than a striped haint.

Carrie gathered while reading that Mr. Wesley Worth was not much of a socialite and stayed out of the limelight. He was often regarded as a '*social retard*' by the rest of society. He had the knowledge to run the textile company, but not much of a personality, and it appeared that Miss Theodosia would be the real spokesperson for the family. The reporters didn't seem to care to talk to Mr. Wesley but didn't favor Miss Theodosia either.

Perhaps that is why Mr. Wesley married Miss Theodosia—she was strong-willed, beautifully dressed, and well-spoken, allowing Wesley to stay in the background, Carrie surmised.

The next article was headlined:

**Birth Announcements**
**Theodosia Eden-Worth and Wesley Worth of Beaufort County are the parents of daughter Lydia Grace Eden-Worth born on June 27. Mrs. Theodosia Eden-Worth is the daughter of Jameson and Charlotte Eden, an heir to the Eden Tobacco Company. Paternal grandparents are Samuel James Worth and Orpha Tilby Worth of the Worth Textiles and Manufacturing Company.**

Carrie picked up and examined the picture of Wesley and Theodosia with Patty in her arms. With their mind-numbing and lackluster frontage in the picture, it reminded her of the American Gothic painting and made her have an involuntary response—she yawned.

While scrutinizing the picture, she tried to figure out if Theodosia was the young woman in the portrait in the mysterious cellar. It was the only picture of Theodosia from the microfiche copies she made.

There were other articles on Theodosia talking about the success of the family mills, her big house, and her well-fashioned dresses. It seemed that Theodosia was as proud as the ladies had proclaimed she was. She was there for the county bank inauguration with Abraham Twiford and for the opening of new mills. She was there riding in open cars for parades and at new business ribbon cuttings. There was only a slight mention of the house nanny, Agnes Weeden, who was not allowed to talk to the press unless given permission by Miss Theodosia. It seemed to Carrie that there was something missing from her pile. She thought there was another article she had printed out. *I remember looking at several articles and—maybe I'm wrong—but wasn't there an article about a car incident that the girls were in when being driven to school?* Carrie also thought she had printed more articles out on Theodosia. *I must be mistaken.*

Starting on the pile of articles about Howard McMurphy, Carrie began with a small article where Patty and Howard were married by a Justice of the Peace in a different township, with her sister Lydia standing as her Maid of Honor. Miss Theodosia Eden-Worth and Wesley Worth were not present at their wedding.

Thinking about how Gramma stated that Lydia provided special protection for Patty and Patty for her. After reading that Patty had made Lydia her Maid of Honor and not Camille, Carrie thought that perhaps she needed to do more research on Lydia.

But really, why did everyone think Camille was a bitch? Why did Camille deserve to be labeled that? What did she do? But most important, where is she now and does she know her little sister passed away? Carrie sat back and chewed it over.

Other articles about Howard told of how he was from a humble family of Tar Heel workers. Henry McMurphy was Howard's father, Rosie was his mother, and they lived in a modest part of town. Carrie figured that he wasn't good enough to work for the prominent Worth Textiles and Manufacturing Company. Perhaps being a Tar Heel worker was not good enough for Miss Theodosia, but it seemed that Howard always worked and could provide for Miss Patty, albeit at a lower standard than Patty was accustomed to.

Another article seemed to strike on Carrie's nerves. It was an article that showed loving parents, Henry and Rosie, holding a little baby boy, Howard. She could see their smiles and they genuinely looked like the happiest people in the world. They were both around the age of Miss Theodosia. *How could this family do anyone any wrong?* Carrie thought.

Carrie understood this. Her Grandma Hattie and Grandpa Scott were not wealthy by any means, but they were self-sufficient and happy. Money doesn't make a family. Love and kindness is all that a real family needs. Now with the monetary means that Patty had left her, Carrie knew deep down that no one would ever take the poor out of her and she was happy with how things were before Miss Patty's passing. The money wouldn't change her.

Looking again at the one picture of Theodosia with baby Patty in her arms, Theodosia showed just a hint of a smile through her pursed lips. Carrie took that to mean she was happy. She reached for her purse and took out the one picture Gramma said was of Theodosia, Lydia, Camille, and Patty. Trying to compare the pictures, like apples to oranges, Carrie decided that the portrait in the cellar had to be that of Miss Theodosia. Still—something didn't click.

***

The morning arrived in fine fashion, the sun was warm, the birds were chirping and three white-tailed deer were down along the creek taking a refreshing morning sip. With coffee in her hand, she left the piles of information still on the kitchen table paper-clipped together. She decided to just sit out back and enjoy the moment before the next crazy thing came along. She pulled the white, wrought-iron chair with a blue-flowered cushion out from underneath the table and set the newspaper down on the tabletop. The huge whispering willow tree branches embraced her presence. After opening the paper to read the comics and her horoscope, a bird flew out and took a dump right on it.

*Oh, great*, she thought, hoping this was no indication as to how her day was going to go. Folding the paper up, she enjoyed the warmth of the breeze and the svelte sun's rays and closed her eyes for just a moment.

Oh, that Sarge, tall, muscular, sexy—a perfect male specimen. Carrie daydreamed of their night together and at the thought of him, lying in her bed, when her fantasy was interrupted by a car honking in the distance.

Perceiving all she had to do today, she got off her bum to get the day started.

To get answers on Theodosia she would have to talk to Walter, Victor Abbott, or Gramma. Since she had planned on seeing Gramma on Sunday, she took her out of the equation. She thought that Walter and Victor Abbott were somewhat evasive when she last talked to them and she wasn't sure how to get more information. Perhaps she would know more when Sarge brought her his reports.

She quickly got ready, then drove to the yarn store, and when she pulled up in front of the store, Sarge was already there. Oh, how her heart pounded. Her Grandma Hattie would agree that he was finer than frog's hair.

"Good morning, Sarge."

"Miss Carrie, I see you decided to sleep in today," he said with a smile.

His smile, even with those stupid sunglasses on, made her heart leap three beats at once. As she walked past him, she could feel the electricity dancing between them. Unlocking the door, Phil followed Carrie into the store and checked her out from the back, secretly, from behind his mirrored glasses.

Carrie could see he was geared up per their conversation last night.

Accompanying her into the back office, Phil opened his black briefcase and took out a manila folder. Handing it to Carrie, he told her, "This is the Bellefontaine Police Department records, mug shot, and everything on Howard McMurphy." He reached in and took out a green folder and said, "This is the Bellefontaine County Court record that I had pulled for you." Proud as punch, Phil pulled out a tape recorder of an interview with Sgt. Edward Eschammer discussing his findings in the case. Sarge was definitely well prepared and displayed great satisfaction with his accomplishment.

Astounded by the quick turnaround time, Carrie said with wide, appreciative eyes, "Wow, thanks for doing all this. I see you went above and beyond the call of duty. I hope it wasn't any trouble."

"It was no trouble at all. I just made a few calls. I had a buddy pull the police files, and the city clerk I've known for a while, she pulled the court information for me."

*She—who is this 'she'?* Carrie thought, and how well does she know my Sarge?

He continued discussing the tape recording with Eschammer, but Carrie wasn't paying attention, she was fantasizing about an evening with Sarge.

"Carrie, are you listening to me?"

*Oh, shit, why does he do that to me?*

"Yeah, Sarge, and I don't know how to thank you. I'm glad you'll be coming over for supper. Perhaps we can discuss it more at that time," she replied, trying to get out of her unhinged thoughts.

Sarge just stood there, distracted, as he was thinking about how he would let Carrie thank him. He stopped the thought and concluded that this would be a good time to hit the road.

The afternoon came and went with customers and two vendors who stopped by, unscheduled. One of the vendors had advised that Mrs. McMurphy was late in paying an invoice. He stood and waited as Carrie looked in the scheduler and found that it had been paid two months ago. Carrie showed him the carbon copy of the check that Patty had signed. He advised that he would revisit this at the office and took down the information. Carrie thought perhaps she would have to go through old bank statements to see if the check cleared, so when the store was vacant, she locked it up and went over to Patty's dwelling.

Moving the closet door, she opened the filing cabinet and knelt on the floor, sitting on her heels. Patty had everything in separate monthly manila folders.

Looking back two months, Carrie found many interactions with the bank. Patty had a copy of a certified check from a bank attached to a transaction invoice regarding their handling of marketing some gems. The check was for a huge amount of money.

*What the heck? The bank sold gems for Patty? What in the world is this about?* She knew that she had to go back to the bank to ask some more questions.

Carrie dug a little deeper and found the cancelled check for the vendor. She took it out and placed it to the side.

She'd deal with that tomorrow.

She continued to go through years of folders, wondering what the heck Patty had been up to.

***

Carrie took the copies of the certified checks and transaction invoices to the bank the next day. She had deposits to make, so it was perfect timing.

Upon reaching the teller window, she made her deposits and asked, "Is Mr. Twiford in today?" She needed to know about the money.

Patty hadn't just left Pheasant Mills at a young age and come back an outrageously rich woman with no explanation for it, and it occurred to Carrie that maybe Robert Twiford could help.

Mr. Twiford's assistant showed her into his office. Twiford stepped in cheerfully and shook her hand stating, "It's a pleasure to see you again so soon, Miss Pyles."

Carrie handed him the transaction records she had brought along and declared, "I know that Mrs. McMurphy had lived away for a while, but when she returned she came back a helluva lot better off than when she left. Pardon my French. That money has now passed to me, and I'd like a little history, if possible. And please, allow me to ask you about these transactions."

"Naturally, it's an interesting story, Miss Pyles. I suspected there might be some questions as time went along and if I can help you, I will. My father took care of Mrs. McMurphy's earlier affairs upon her return, but I was here at the bank and have comprehensive knowledge of what was transacted on her behalf. Miss Patty's father, Wesley Worth, as you may know, owned several mills. It provided a comfortable income, but not enough for her momma, Miss Theodosia. If you'll excuse my saying so, there could never be enough for Miss Theodosia. I assume you know who Miss Theodosoia Eden-Worth is."

Carrie nodded.

"She had some rather expensive tastes. However, it wasn't really the mills that provided the resources to supply Theodosia with what she needed. Miss Theodosia's family, the Eden side, had some very exquisite gems and jewelry pieces, some old coins, and a fair amount of gold and silver bullion. The bank, that is to say, my father, was not privy to the source of this largesse and it didn't matter. Miss Theodosia exchanged some jewels and gold and sent a few coins to auction. She did this with a fair amount of discretion. Wealth was provided for Miss Theodosia in this manner until her passing, apparently."

"So, how was Patty involved?" Carrie asked.

"As for Miss Patty, upon her mother's death, she inherited everything. That much has already been made clear to you, I believe. Miss Patty had very little of her own at the time of the scandal involving her husband, Howard McMurphy, and left town shamed shortly thereafter. Her sister, Camille, had been disinherited by the family and her oldest sister, Lydia, had since passed, so Patty was the only child present at their momma's funeral."

"And Miss Patty returned to town when she got news that her momma was dying?" asked Carrie.

"True, Miss Patty returned when she got news of her momma's last days and examined, among other things, the contents of the safe-deposit box, just as you did. Almost immediately, Miss Patty selected a few items and asked that I send them to auction for her. This was the first time we had been allowed to see anything from the box and my father was quite taken aback. The jewelry appeared to be more in the category of artifacts, really, quite old with some apparent history."

"Could these items be from buried treasure?" Carrie asked.

"There was a rumor going around these parts about pirate treasure, a pretty romantic tale, but rumor is all that's ever been produced. We suggested that it might be wise to make a few private inquiries about their origin before going public. Miss Patty didn't care for the idea and was absolutely set against it and instead, said that perhaps she would simply remove and sell the stones, which were lovely—emeralds, red stones that may have been rubies or spinels, some small, old rose-cut diamonds—and exchange the gold separately."

"Was that the only time?"

"No. There were other times, too, which might surprise you, or perhaps not, that your grandmother was present at this discussion. Miss Harriet was more openhearted than Patty and was horrified at the idea, and rightly so, of breaking apart some of the exquisite pieces. Miss Harriet strongly urged Miss Patty to rethink this course of action. Your grandmother was always a woman who felt strongly about history and tradition. To this day, I believe Miss Harriet was always a little heartbroken at what Patty did with the jewelry, which was precisely what she had proposed. Frankly, it broke my father's heart, as well."

"So, my grandmother came with Patty to the bank?" Carrie asked softly in disbelief.

"Miss Patty initially wanted us to handle the removal of the stones and the meltdown of the separate parts. We're a family bank and quite cautious. So, although Miss Patty had not wanted us to proceed with verifying the origin of the jewelry, we did make some private inquiries anyway for our own protection. Our agents found nothing to dispute the ownership after some exhaustive research and not inconsiderable expense. But in the end, my father could not bring himself to break apart some of those wonderful pieces—one of which was a very large, elaborate necklace and two pairs of ear cuffs—after Miss Patty left it to our discretion. Miss Patty was more concerned with the value she would receive and deposited the capital with us, which we turned into a considerably larger amount."

"So, Patty cashed in on the gems and scrapped the gold or silver enclosures?"

"Yes, and that is the transaction on the receipt you're asking about. I can leave you with one other small detail, as well. Miss Patty had removed two rings. One was an emerald and diamond piece, not excessively large, but quite exquisite and this she gave to your grandmother. The other had a small, center brilliant-cut diamond with two coral stones set on the side and it was a delicate little thing. I thought it a very charming piece indeed. I told her it would be lovely with her coloring and she said she hadn't intended to wear it herself, but said nothing more about it."

Carrie was familiar with that ring. Patty had given it to her on her eighteenth birthday.

Satisfied with what Robert Twiford had told her, Carrie drove back to the yarn store. She had other important items to attend to like planning supper for Sarge tonight.

# Chapter 10

**Carrie** wanted supper to be perfect tonight and decided on spaghetti pomodoro, with some nice fried green tomatoes, garlic bread, and a bottle of wine for supper. Finding a pen and paper, she made a grocery list.

As she finished the list, more and more customers came through the door, talking and buying. *I can't just send them away*, she thought. The day couldn't end fast enough, though. Even the noises in the cellar didn't disrupt her this day.

Carrie drove to the grocery store closest to home. It was a small store, with five or six aisles of everyday items, a fresh produce section along the right corner, and several large sliding-window deep freezers placed against the back wall. There was no fresh-baked bread, basil, tomatoes, or garlic, so she bought what she could. As time was not slowing down and it was getting uncomfortably closer to Sarge's arrival, Carrie drove to another store that only had tomatoes and garlic.

*Why is this happening?* She was getting more frustrated by the second. She drove past the street she should have turned on to go home and tried one last attempt at a larger supermarket in the area. Finding only fresh basil and day old bread, she thought, *Screw it.*

The line was three people deep in the checkout express lane and had a limit of twelve items. The person in front of her had gone over the limit, and the cashier had to call for the price of an avocado that the sticker had fallen off of. When it was finally her turn, she took ten dollars from her wallet, paid for the items, and rushed home, keeping an eye on her speedometer and the clock.

Time was now of the essence.

Carrie arrived in the kitchen, washed the produce quickly, reached for a pot, placed it in the sink, and turned on the faucet. She found a skillet and opened the cooking oil, poured half a cup into the pan, and skinned the garlic with the backside of a black-handled butcher knife, and turned the stove on low. Carrie placed the minced garlic in the pan and proceeded to cut the green tomatoes into slices, placing them on some wax paper. Taking down the metal tin of flour, she removed the cornmeal from the sack. This wouldn't take too long to mix together, so thinking that she had time to wash up a little, she hotfooted up the stairs taking two at a time, to wash her face, throw on a low-cut blouse, and don her tightest, best fitting jeans. She took her hair down from the ponytail and teased it quickly. Expeditiously she freshened up her makeup and applied a dab of perfume when she heard the doorbell ring.

"Durn," she exclaimed, *Sarge can't be here now.*

Checking herself just one more time in the mirror, she took off like Moody's goose down the steps to answer the door with her heart rate cannonballing along.

There he was, Mr. Handsome, standing there with a bottle of red wine in one hand and flowers in the other. He was early.

"Hi, Carrie, if I'm too early, I can come back."

"No, you don't! Come on in," Carrie said. She wasn't going to let this fine, sharply dressed man, with his snapped-front, navy blue shirt and tight, *meaning*, mighty fine blue jeans snugging those thighs and round buttocks and—"Hells bells, the skillet!"

Carrie rushed to the kitchen, as the skillet was aflame a foot high and the garlic was burned to a black charcoal. Smoke billowed throughout the kitchen.

Sarge moved faster than all get out. Using a nearby towel he picked up a skillet lid, covered the pan slowly and moved it off the stovetop as Carrie stood there watching.

"You might want to open some windows and doors to let the smoke out," he advised.

Carrie started opening everything in sight, jumpy as a long-tailed cat in a room full of rockin' chairs. Luckily, most of the smoke damage was contained within the kitchen and caught early enough. Carrie found some candles and lit them to remove the burned garlic smell from the house.

"I'm so sorry. I was just running a little late and tried to do too many things at once. I thought I could get ready—and then you were early," she said disheartened.

"Hey, sugar, I have an idea," he said once things got under control and went out to his truck.

*No, don't leave*, Carrie thought to herself. She wouldn't blame him if he did.

Walking back in with a pizza box holding a half-eaten chicken and bacon extra-large pizza, Carrie's favorite, he put it on the countertop. Carrie continued wiping down the cabinetry to get rid of the soot and smell.

Finding a bowl in the glass-door cupboard, Phil took the green tomatoes and chopped them along with the fresh basil. mixing them together. He opened the icebox to gather strawberries, a nectarine, and poppy-seed dressing.

"Got any pecans?" he asked.

"Um, sure."

Every good house in North Carolina should have some type of goober pea.

As Sarge continued mixing this and that together, he said, "Hey, Carrie, why don't you open the wine and let it breathe for a minute or two?"

She obliged, feeling helpless as she watched him cook dinner.

Retrieving the special china from the maple china cabinet, Carrie placed the utensils on Grandma Hattie's favorite weaved tablemats.

Carrie proceeded to slice the day-old bread with a bread knife, but sliced her finger instead when looking back at Sarge.

"Shit," she said as she placed her bleeding left index finger in her mouth.

Sarge looked back toward her, smiled, found the paper towels and wrapped one around her finger.

"Are you alright?"

"It's just a nick."

"You might want to go and find a bandage, I'll finish up in here. Get on now."

Retreating to the back bathroom, she looked in the mirror to see black smudges on her face.

*Oh shit, I don't even want to think what else could happen,* she thought.

After cleaning herself up, she arrived back in the kitchen and found Sarge had the table perfectly set, wine poured, and even bread toasted with an oil and herb mixture for dipping. The pizza was warmed in the microwave and displayed meticulously on their plates, with salad in blue ceramic bowls, fried green tomatoes on a platter, flowers in a vase, and a candle lit on the table.

To her surprise, it was quite well done.

"Wow, nice job. I'm sorry about supper," Carrie said rather dismayed, "but everything looks beautiful. Thank you for doing all this."

"Aw, it was nuttin'," he said, rather Travis-like, with the most gorgeous boyish grin she had ever seen.

She was falling in love.

This gorgeous hunk of man was proud, polite, and pulled out her chair. As Carrie sat down, Phil bent over and softly asked, "Are you hungry?"

How could she say "Yes" when all she really wanted was to take him up to her room and do to him what any red-blooded woman would do with such a sharp-looking man? But she knew they had too much to discuss before they could go into the bedroom.

She needed information.

While sitting down and eating, she turned and asked, "Hey, Sarge, can you tell me again about how you got all that information on Howard McMurphy?"

"Well, sugar, I have a friend at Bellefontaine County Police Department that I keep in contact with. When he needs something, I try to help. So I asked him to find me the file on Howard McMurphy. When he got it all together, we met for lunch. He asked me why I wanted information on a closed case. I told him I had a friend who was inquiring about it and left it at that. He gave me the information on the whereabouts of Sgt. Eschammer too."

"Really? Wasn't that nice of him."

"And the lady at the courthouse, Fern, she worked as a dispatcher at the police station when I was a rookie. She's an older woman, but her husband ran into some trouble a while back, so I helped him out. Fern was more than happy to pull the court reports and made the copies that you have now."

Carrie breathed a sigh of relief as Phil spoke of the "older woman."

"So what about Mr. Eschammer? You actually talked to him?"

"It was a little bit harder to talk with Eschammer. He's been retired for a few years. I called him to ask if we could meet up. He wanted to know why," Sarge took a drink of wine, "but he remembered me from my rookie years and when I told him I wanted to talk about the old Howard McMurphy case, he hesitated, but agreed to talk. I had a small tape recorder, do you still have it?" Sarge asked her.

"Yes," she retrieved it and handed it over to him.

Sarge turned it on and pressed play and it started with Phil asking if it was all right to record.

"Easier than taking notes," he said as they both listened and Sarge stopped it at one point.

"See, this is where I started to get confused," Sarge said to Carrie. "Listen to this part."

Eschammer was saying, "Lulu just came out of the truck an' was runnin' 'round like a crazy girl, cryin' an' screamin' an' ev'rythin'. And right then, her parents' car pulled up an' the motha' got out and ran to her child an' held 'er tightly sayin', it's alright, Momma's here now, but the fatha' stayed back at the car."

Eschammer then said, "I looked back at the parents' car an' the fatha' stayed in the car. It wann't 'til the momma started yellin' at Howard, accusin' him of kidnappin' her lil' girl, did the fatha' get out an' get involved." Sarge paused the recording.

"Now, if the parents were looking for the child, why wouldn't they both be wrought with worry? Why did Mrs. Roosevelt react and Mr. Roosevelt just stay at the car? Doesn't add up, does it?" he said.

"You know, nothing adds up. It's too coincidental. Like it was a planned event. I heard the Roosevelts didn't have a pot to pee in, but Thelma at SamiJo's Diner said she heard they live on the other side of Heart Strings Cemetery near the river in a nice house now."

"Can't say I know the Roosevelts," Sarge said.

"Did you know Theodosia Eden-Worth?"

"Can't say I did, but there are a lot of stories about her and that's all I can say about that," he said.

Carrie didn't know Sarge well enough to understand his moral scruples about not indulging in gossip.

"It is what it is," was all he would say.

Carrie stood up and gathered the dishes to put in the sink while Sarge poured them both another glass of wine.

"Thank you for getting me all this information. I haven't had the chance to review everything yet, but I'm going to find out why Miss Patty decided to leave everything to me when she still had a sister alive."

"Sarge," Carrie continued, "did the police department look for Camille when Theodosia died? I heard that Patty was the only daughter that attended her momma's funeral."

"Well, it's no mystery that Miss Theodosia favored Miss Patty over all the others. I don't know about the other girls, perhaps I can ask the guys at the department and see what they might know. Miss Theodosia died when I was in grade school. She made the papers and I remember there were a lot of men who attended. I'm afraid Miss Theodosia was not favored by too many town women. The captain may know more about it. I'll see what I can find out."

"I do appreciate anything you can find out on Miss Theodosia, but I don't want you to go to any trouble."

Sarge got up from the table and wrapped his arms around Carrie's small waist and said, "Just let me know how I can assist. I can see that you need help. In driving and cooking and—" he teased her as he bent over to kiss her neck.

Carrie took the dish sprayer in hand, turned on the water, and started spraying him down, soaking his face and shirt. Sarge reached swiftly for Carrie's hand and grabbed it, turned it on her, soaking Carrie's shirt and pants.

They giggled, laughed, and started kissing, then engaged in some ass grabbing and pulled off their soaked shirts. The heat in the kitchen was nothing more than sheer passion.

They bounced off the walls, heading for the stairs, rebounding off the railing as they climbed higher towards the second floor with their bodies entangled, tongues lashed against the other. As Sarge reached for the first doorknob he came to, he picked her up and placed her on the bed as he kicked off his boots and socks and dropped his pants as fast as he could. Carrie stripped down to her bra and panties and didn't notice what room they were in. She wanted him and wanted him now.

Their lovemaking was as beautiful as a newfound sunrise.

After immeasurable bliss, Sarge got up and just as his bare foot touched the floor. Carrie heard him exclaim, "Oh, shit!"

"What's wrong?"

"I think I got a piece of glass in my foot." He sat down on the bed, moving his foot to his knee.

Carrie reached around to the bedside table and turned on a Tiffany reading lamp, realizing only then that they were in her grandma's bedroom. Moving to him as fast as she could and seeing in the reflection of the light a sliver of glass that she must have missed the other day, she got up to get a bandage and a cold, wet cloth to stop the bleeding.

"I'm so sorry," she said.

"It's nothing. Just a cut."

Carrie advanced to dislodge the glass, but like the baby that men are, Sarge said, "No, don't touch it. I'll get it out."

He removed the glass from the ball of his foot and Carrie took it and threw it away. She returned and proceeded to wipe the small amount of blood coming from the cut and looked up to see his manhood. She tried to pay attention to what she was doing, but she was too cognizant of his gorgeous physique.

It wasn't hard to see: she had fallen—and fallen *hard*—for this stunning man.

***

To her surprise, Sarge was there in bed when she woke up. He had called into work earlier that morning, stating that he would be in late, fully aware that she would be going to the yarn store by mid-morning.

Carrie rolled over and opened her blue-gray eyes, and Sarge was lying there enjoying the beauty of the moment.

"Morning," she said with a smile in her voice.

"Good morning, sugar."

Sarge got out of bed and Carrie asked what he was doing.

"I need to take a shower before I go to work."

"So do I."

Luckily her grandma's bathroom was the largest in the house. It had a double sink, large mirror, and a huge two- if not a three-person shower.

"Would you like some coffee first?" she asked.

"Yes, please. I already made some this morning."

"Aw, bless your heart."

Putting on a robe, she proceeded down to the kitchen.

There on the table were plates set on placemats, flowers in the center, fresh fruit cut up in bowls, and pancakes already made and kept warm by two plates enveloping them. Butter and maple syrup sat close by. Everything was displayed beautifully. She stood in awe with her hands on her hips looking at the table and thinking, *Well, if that don't take the cake.*

Sarge appeared behind her and said, "I hope you're hungry."

"What? —When? —How?" was all she could say, stunned as she was.

"I know you like to sleep in. So, when I got up to call in to work to tell them I would be in late, I did a little shopping and thought I would make you some of my famous flatcakes."

"Everything looks absolutely wonderful!" Carrie exclaimed as she took a couple blueberries from her bowl and moved towards Sarge in his white boxers. She inserted one in his mouth and one in hers, kissing his lips afterwards. "Thank you."

"Thank you for your hospitality. It's the least I could do," he said, pulling her close. "And if you notice, they're not burnt either," he said laughing.

Rolling her eyes at Sarge, she proceeded to pour them both a cup of coffee. She noticed that the paper had been removed from its sleeve and opened on the counter. Taking the paper to the table and removing the comic section, she said, "Sit down and eat some breakfast." They were naturally comfortable with each other.

"Carrie, I have to work late tonight; would you be interested in going with me to Gramma's tomorrow?"

"Yes, I have some more pictures to show her. You want to take a look and see if you recognize anything?" She got up and took them out of her purse, handing them to Sarge.

"Well, that one looks like a lady with three kids and that one looks like a school-team picture and that looks like a mill with workers standing outside getting their picture taken."

"Now, aren't you a genius. Why don't you tell me something *I don't know already*," and she rolled her eyes at him, giggling.

He shrugged his shoulders, handed them back to her and asked, "Then, may I pick you up at 12:30 tomorrow?"

"Yes, you may," she said, replying with a smile. She was on tenterhooks anticipating a repeat performance of last night's passion.

After finishing breakfast, they cleaned up and took a shower together. She washed his back and he washed hers. Putting his head under the shower, he opened his dewy eyes.

What a beautiful sight this man is. She was seriously thinking of not going in to work, but instead just staying in this moment with her Sarge.

Disrupting her thoughts, "Sugar, I have to get going, I said I would be in late that means sometime this morning."

"Oh, yeah, me too. I just don't want this moment to end."

"Me neither, sugar, but I have a job and it is my duty to serve and protect, even if I have you safe in the shower and not in the kitchen or on the road," he teased.

Carrie just smiled and went for a jab of her elbow in his ribcage. They proceeded to get dressed and she walked him to the door, kissing him in a way that would carry him through the day. At least until they would see one another tomorrow.

Later at the store, she was busy. *If things get any better, I might have to hire someone to help me enjoy it*, she smirked to herself. Customers came and went, but there were slow times where she could actually get some cleaning done. By late afternoon, her stomach was growling as if it was going to wake the neighbors. She drove down to Ponticelli's for a salad and was seated by a window. Looking out and daydreaming about last night with Sarge, she bathed in the warm, bright, sunny, picture perfect-sky, but—*What the heck*?

There he was in uniform, walking down the sidewalk toward the grill across the street, meeting up with a woman out front. She looked younger than Carrie—brunette and cute. She was wearing a saucy little pink sundress with sandals and carried a matching pink purse. When they met, Carrie saw Sarge give her a kiss and a big hug and after a few words, he opened the door, and the gentleman that he is, let her walk in first.

*That egg-sucking, piece of*—, Carrie thought, with her butt on her shoulders. She was fighting back the floodgates with both hands, when she heard: "Hey, Carrie."

As she slowly wiped her eyes, she turned to see Travis.

"Hey, Carrie, what's wrong?" he asked.

"Nothing, just got a reflection in my eyes. How ya' doing, Travis?" Carrie tried unconvincingly to remedy the situation.

"I'm fine." Travis sat down across from her with his back to the window, showing real concern for how she was feeling.

"Hey, Travis," she said, trying to recover. "Did you happen to have a relative named Jakayla Hicks?"

"Yeah, she's some type of great-aunt or somethin'. Why?"

"Well, I found Miss Patty's old Bible and it had a family tree in it where it mentioned Jakayla Hicks. I just wondered if she was related to you or not." Carrie ruminated and then asked, "Would you like to go to Miss Patty's place and take a look?"

"Sure, it's my day off and I don't have anythin' else to do."

They sat and talked for a bit, as Carrie ate her salad rather slowly while watching out the window for any movement. Travis sat there goose-necking towards the bar, watching whatever game was on TV. Carrie was almost done with her salad when Sarge and the brunette in the all-too-cute pink dress walked out of the grill, stood in front talking, then hugged and walked off separately. Carrie watched as they separated and left her sight. Still talking to Travis, she saw the police car drive past Ponticelli's in the same direction the brunette had gone.

The waitress came by and gave Carrie her bill. Carrie got up, paid the bill, and asked Travis if he was ready to go.

"Sure," he said, and they left to meet up at Patty's place.

# Chapter 11

**Carrie** was as mad as a mule chewing on bumblebees on the drive back to Patty's place. Unlocking the door, she showed Travis in. He said some cute things, but she wasn't in the mood to enjoy them. A fake smile now and then was as much as she could render.

"Hey, Travis, would you like something to drink?" she said in a blasé manner.

"Sure, watcha got?"

"I don't know. I think I saw wine in the kitchen cabinet."

Carrie left and went into the kitchen. She leaned against the cabinets trying to regain some strength and collect her thoughts. She started looking for something to drink. She wanted something strong.

Finding a bottle of red wine, bourbon, and some Southern Comfort, she came back armed with bottles and ice-filled glasses.

Putting everything down on the table, Travis and Carrie started with the Southern Comfort.

Retrieving the Bible, she opened it to the family tree on Howard McMurphy's side. Moving closer to Travis on the sofa, she showed him the pictorial.

"Howard's family tree doesn't have many branches," she observed, reviewing Henry McMurphy, Howard's father, and Rosie McMurphy, his mother. Carrie pointed to Jakayla Hicks, née Eden, who was an aunt to Howard.

Travis seemed to remember that they were old relatives, but only remembered Aunt Jakayla (Jackie) and Uncle Beau. Travis mentioned several stories about them when he was just a young boy.

"Why are ya' innerested in this?" Travis asked.

"I just want to learn more about Miss Patty and her family relations. But even more so, why she left me everything and not her sister Camille who is still alive—somewhere."

"Maybe my Aunt Jackie could shed some light on 'em. She's related to Miss Patty's momma, Theodosia. See, her maiden name's Eden, just like Theodosia Eden-Worth. My aunt is older than dirt and lives down in Charlotte. Maybe I could set up a meetin' or somethin'. Do you want to try for tomorrow?"

"No, I can't tomorrow. I already have plans."

"Oh, OK, some other time then," Travis said as he poured them another drink.

They laughed and talked, as Travis did his best to help her forget about what she saw this afternoon, and the drink started to get to her head.

They started kissing slowly, then fully embracing, and it led to straight vanilla sex—nothing exciting. She felt like a snake in snowshoes.

Travis didn't stay much longer after that, and Carrie's stomach responded as if it had been jerked through a knot, coming up like a bad cloud. Fortunately, Carrie made it into the bathroom in time.

Washing her mouth out and drinking several cupped handfuls of water, she looked at herself in the mirror feeling quite despondent.

***

Carrying her shoes back to the store and placing them next to the phone, she took the mail off the counter and opened up the envelopes with a silver letter opener. There was junk mail, invoices, and an letter from a bank for a safe-deposit box renewal.

What the heck? I just paid this the other day.

Carrie turned the envelope over and saw that it was from a different bank. Victor Abbott hadn't given her keys to this one.

*Why would anyone have more than one safe-deposit box?*

Reactively she went back to the house and started looking around. Searching in Patty's music box and in the bedside table drawers, she found nothing. Then she opened the jewelry armoire.

*Where did Patty get all of this jewelry from? With her husband being incarcerated, how could she come to possess all these magnificent pieces?*

Carrie took out a few individual pieces and examined each one. They were truly awe-inspiring.

She spotted a small drawer that pulled out by a brass, parrot-shaped knob. She pulled it open and discovered inside several different colored envelopes with bank names and numbers on the keys themselves. They all looked like safe-deposit box keys.

*What the devil was this all about?*

Putting them back into the small drawer, Carrie decided she'd deal with them some other time. She was still feeling sick to her stomach and decided to go back to the shop when she heard car tires crunching on the rock driveway.

Later, driving home slower than cream rising on last year's buttermilk, she knew she had to take a shower to wash Travis off her.

When Carrie thought of Sarge, the floodgates opened and poured down bullfrogs.

Screaming, "Why would Sarge do that to me, after such an amazing night and morning?" She couldn't find a reason, so she went into her room to lie down, slamming the door.

She was as lost as last year's Easter egg.

Needless to say, Carrie wasn't in a very responsive mood when Sarge came to pick her up for Gramma's. Walking out of the house, colder than a frogs' behind, she rather abruptly got into the truck and slammed the door.

"Hey, Carrie, is something wrong?"

"No, I just woke up with a headache."

"We don't have to go to Gramma's today if you're not feeling well."

"No, I'm fine. Let's just get on now."

Phil kept taking glances at her while he was driving and asked again, "Sugar, are you sure you're alright? Is something bothering you?"

"Well, yeah," she said, gathering up her nerve.

She reminded herself of something that her Grandma Hattie would tell her when she needed advice:

'Courage is what it takes to stand up and speak; courage is also what it takes to sit down and listen.' ~Winston Churchill.

After taking a long breath, she said, "I saw you yesterday going into the grill across from Ponticelli's with a cute little brunette, who was wearing a pink dress. What was that about?" she asked despairingly.

Sarge laughed, "Oh, that—she's my wife's cousin, Denise. Denise was the maid of honor at our wedding and I hadn't seen her since Jodine's passing. She was only driving through town on her way to the wedding of a friend and asked if we could meet up for a late lunch. It was nothing, Carrie, really."

"Oh, really? Your wife's cousin," she said, green as a gourd.

*Oh shit, what did I do?* She put her hand through her hair and her head back on the headrest. Of course—Sarge is too decent to have screwed her over.

*I'm such a whore!*

"Are you alright?" Phil asked.

"Yeah, I'm good."

Upon reaching Gramma's house, they saw Gary and Sadie's car already parked in the street along with several others. Gramma met them in the kitchen, hugging Carrie and giving

Sarge a kiss on his cheek while embracing him. Sarge tried to hand Gramma a bottle of wine and she told him to put it in the kitchen.

"You'd think after all these years of bringin' me a bottle of wine ev'ry Sunday, he'd know where to put the dang thin' when he gets here," Gramma said, laughing and taking Carrie by the arm.

"You feelin' alright, darlin'? You look a little peaked."

"I'm good," Carrie faked a smile in reply.

"Did ya' happen to bring me anythin' new to look at today?" Gramma asked.

"Yes, ma'am, I have a few things for you, when you have the time," Carrie replied.

"There's no time like the present," she declared and escorted Carrie outside to the tables and chairs set up for brunch. Sitting down, Gramma said, "Come on now, get it goin'. Show me wha'cha brought."

Carrie reached in her purse and took out the pictures.

With the brown, tortoise shell-framed glasses on her face and nose wrinkled, Gramma studied the first picture of the lady with the three girls.

"Well, that's not Theodosia. Why I do believe that to be her nanny, Agnes Weeden. She worked for Theodosia as the governess since the girls were babies."

"So, Miss Theodosia had a nanny named Agnes Weeden; I think I read her name in a newspaper article," Carrie advised.

"If ya' need to know anythin' 'bout the girls, that would be a good place to start. I knew Agnes afta' she left Theodosia's employment an' started workin' for my good friend, Josie Magowne. If St. Peter left the Pearly Gate to go to the lavatory, Agnes would be his replacement. She'd neva' predisposed a secret. I'd tried askin' her 'bout her employment wit' Theodosia a couple of times, but she neva' spilt a drop. I do believe Agnes is still alive an' livin' wit' her sista' 'n Scuppernong County. She's ova' eighty, though, so I dunno wha' she would rememba'."

Gramma picked up the next picture with the people outside the textile mill.

"This one looks like it was takin' outside at one of 'em Worth's textile mills." She studied the picture, moving it closer to her eyes. "That one 'n the background is Mr. Wesley Worth, an' him, there, is Abraham Twiford, the bank owna'."

Gramma pointed to other men in the pictures, naming several as Carrie concentrated on Agnes Weeden in the previous picture.

"Now, ya' know the Worth's family had three mills. Two of 'em were textile an' one was a manufacturin' ova' near Alamance County. They all went unner afta' runnin' high an' mighty fer sever'l years. Theodosia was as proud as she could be when they were all 'n their finest moments. Wha' else ya' got?" Gramma asked.

Carrie took the last picture of the girl's baseball team and passed it over to Gramma.

"Hmm—wha's this? Looks like a school picture of Camille an' your Grandma Hattie 'n their baseball yun'forms."

Carrie had always thought it to be Patty and her Grandma Hattie, but it didn't seem appropriate to correct Gramma.

"Do you recognize the school?"

Still studying the picture, Gramma went on. "That looks like my husband's cuzin's dawta', Ferbee Pangburn. Don't know fer shur. We dinn't see much of his family, except at weddin's an' fun'rals. They live upcountry. I rememba' her as a purty thin', though, an' I shur would bet that's her. Cain't say I rememba' the school's name—it gets 'way from me. Maybe I could call sum of the cuzins to see if any of them rememba'."

"Gramma, does this look familiar to you?" Carrie took the pin she had found and handed the small, diamond-shaped, red-colored pin with 'RS' displayed in silver in the middle.

Taking it in her hands, Gramma studied it. "Rougemont—Russell—Rocky? It was an all-girls school, right? Maybe Red Springs. I think that was a real small, private, girls school back 'n the day. Sorry, darlin', I just don't rec'nize it."

The ladies started bringing out the fried chicken, cornbread, collard greens, and Sadie's famous red-eye gravy. They placed it on the newspaper-covered table along with Gramma's crab boil. The stockpot was upended in the center of the table and the potatoes, kielbasa, shrimp, corn on the cob, and, of course, crabs were spread out.

Sarge asked, "Hey, Carrie, can I get you a drink?"

"Sure, a beer, thanks."

Gary and Tony had gone out crabbing the day before and had plenty of crabs for dinner. Their stories were quite humorous when Gary got pinched not once or twice but a few more times as Tony would tell it.

When supper was over, Carrie helped with washing the dishes and cleaning up the place. As she looked out the kitchen window she caught Sarge talking with Gary and Sadie and grew more depressed. He didn't screw her over, but she had screwed him over—literally.

*Why did I react that way? I'm going to have tell him about Travis,* she told herself.

Carrie brought out Sarge's peach cobbler, still warm with melting homemade vanilla ice cream on top. Before handing it to him, he reached for her waist, pulled her in close and gave her a very public kiss. Gramma came walking up behind them and said, "I think that pie needs sum' more sugar," she giggled and walked on.

They left shortly thereafter and on the drive home, Sarge asked, "Hey, Carrie, would you like to go to a movie? I know there is an action flick showing. It starts around six and we could stop at the pool hall to get a drink before, if you feel up to it."

"Sure, that sounds good," Carrie said rather softly.

"Carrie, you've been quiet all day. Are you sure you're feeling alright?"

"Yeah, I'm just a little tired."

Carrie was not only tired, she loathed herself. She knew she was going to hell in a handbasket and quicker than Lucifer could make the decision.

It wasn't long before they reached the pool hall, when Sarge opened her door and as Carrie got out, he wrapped his arms around her body, kissing her passionately.

"I missed you yesterday, after I left," he said, whispering in her ear.

"Me too," she replied.

Entering the pool hall, there were a few people in there, but a pool table was open.

"Do you want to shoot a game of pool?" she asked.

"Sure, let me go get two beers. You get the table."

Going over to where the sticks were and finding the right weight one for her, she proceeded to rack up the balls on the table, when in walked Travis.

"Hey, Carrie," Travis said loudly.

"Hey," she said back as she promptly looked to see where Sarge was and noticed he was talking to a man sitting at the counter with the two beers in his hand.

Travis came within an inch of her, leaning in to give her a kiss. Carrie backed away quickly as she saw Sarge walking towards them.

"Hey, how are ya' feelin' afta' last night? I had a buzz still goin' this mornin'. I don't think I should have driven home last night," Travis said, still not seeing Sarge standing now about five feet behind him.

"Hey, Travis, I'm here with the Sarge, can we talk later?" She tried saying nicely but she wanted him to tie a knot in it and go away.

Travis threw a look toward Sarge.

"Hey, Phil," Travis said rather nasty-like.

"Travis," Sarge said. "So you were with Carrie yesterday?"

*Oh, Lordie Lord*, Carrie said to herself, turning her back on Sarge, unsure of what the next thing coming out of Travis' mouth would be.

"Yeah, she invited me to Miss Patty's place to look at Howard's family tree insert from one of Miss Patty's Bibles. Seems the Hicks are related to Howard McMurphy's and Miss Theodosia's side. Who knew?"

"Yeah, who knew, indeed," was all Sarge said, looking callously at Travis.

Taking the clue, Travis said, "Hey, Carrie, see you 'round," and left without saying anything more to Phil.

Sarge handed Carrie her beer, wrapped his arms around her, gave a very public kiss, and looked in the direction of Travis to make sure that he saw it. Seemed like Sarge was establishing his territory and his testosterone level was running high.

They played two games of pool. He was quite a challenging competitor. He won the first game by sinking the eight ball in the right corner pocket with two of her solid-colored balls left on the table. But the last game, they both had a shot at the eight ball and missed. Carrie sank it with an unbelievable bank that she had only completed once or twice before. Sarge pulled her in real close, gave her a very congratulatory kiss, and said "Good shot!"

He made her heart melt faster than ocean water sinking into the sand.

Carrie only wanted this man and she knew it. But she was aware of her screw up and would have to tell him—eventually.

The movie was indeed an action-packed thriller. As they sat there holding hands, Carrie tried to forget yesterday, but it haunted her nevertheless.

When it was over, Sarge had his arm around her waist and escorted her proudly to his truck.

Upon arriving at Grandma Hattie's house, Carrie asked him to come in for a drink. She needed to talk to him.

He sat on the couch as Carrie got two beers out of the icebox. Sitting opposite from him in a chair, she handed him the beer.

"This must be serious," he said as he took a swift mouthful of beer.

"Sarge, I'm just going to be honest with you. Yesterday, when I was at Ponticelli's, I saw you with your wife's cousin. I didn't know who she was. You have to understand. I saw you meet up, give her a kiss and a big hug before you entered the grill. She was pretty and I was jealous. I didn't know how you could do that to me after the night and morning we had. *It didn't make sense to me.* I thought you were a player and you were just playing me for a fool. So when Travis came into Ponticelli's, we started talking, and when I saw you exit the grill, hug and kiss her again, and then I saw you drive off in the same direction she had gone, I assumed you were following her. So I invited Travis to Patty's place. I did show him the family tree, Travis told the truth about that. But what he didn't say was that we started drinking, heavily, and then we kissed, and . . . eventually had sex. I'm so sorry. I didn't mean to hurt you, but I was so beside myself with jealousy."

"So, that's why Travis asked how you were feeling this morning?" he said crestfallen.

"Yeah, and I truly hate myself for how I reacted. I'm so sorry," she couldn't emphasize any more than that and started tearing up.

Sarge proceeded to finish his beer in one more gulp and stood up.

"Well, Carrie, thank you for being honest. No harm done. We're not connected at the hip or anything. You're a young, beautiful woman who can make her own decisions. As it seems you have." Sarge stood up, reached into his pocket and pulled out his keys.

"I think it's best if I go now," he said and proceeded toward the door. His spirit was broken like a dozen cracked eggs messing all over the place.

"Sarge, you don't have to leave. *I don't want you to leave*," she pleaded as she followed him to the door with tears flowing down and a black cloud forming in her mind.

"Carrie . . . I'll call you some time . . . OK?" He reached over, grabbed Carrie's chin, and kissed her lightly as if saying good-bye. She tried taking hold of his arms, but he moved away, opened the door, and left.

Carrie sat on the front porch and watched as he walked to his truck and drove off.

Sarge didn't look back. He just left.

After a while, Carrie walked back into the kitchen, grief-stricken, and looked around for something strong to drink. On the counter, next to the opened bottle of cabernet, was the pile of paper-clipped papers. Carrie picked up Patty's pile and read in an article:

> **Miss Theodosia had sent Patty and her sisters to some out-of-town girl school.**

There was no mention of the name, as Miss Theodosia only wanted the press to focus on her prominence and kept the girls out of the papers. The article stated Theodosia had a very strong will and the press never sought to upset this pretentious lady.

Gramma had mentioned some school names.

*Shit! What were they? They started with the letter 'R'—'Ridgemont? Russell? Rocky Springs?" Why can't I remember?*

Carrie read more articles about Theodosia and thinking that she, herself, was no better than the *town whore*, only grew more disheartened.

She took out a piece of paper and wrote down Ridgemont, Russell, and Rocky Springs. She tried to focus, but that was the best she could do for the mood she was in.

Finding a short article that mentioned Agnes Weeden, she read on and it stated Agnes was driving the girls somewhere but didn't mention any location. Agnes had gotten the car stuck in high floodwaters caused by a hurricane. She was a ways from home and had to have the car towed.

Leaving everything on the table, Carrie left the kitchen and went to weave. She had to do something to get her mind off Sarge.

# Chapter 12

**The** members of the weaving class reassembled at their respective looms and, as before, Adeene sat at the loom with the lovely shawl in pale blue and cream silk. It was progressing rather nicely. Jenny Lee brought the drink of the day. It was a nice bottle of white wine, so as the ladies continued their weaving, they also drank.

As the shuttles were loaded and the ladies made headway into the magic of their creation, Carrie took the liberty to ask, "Did anyone know anything about Patty's nanny, Agnes Weeden?"

Adeene and Emeline looked at each other and Emeline said, "Why are ya' bringin' her name up?"

"Well, I read in an article that Miss Agnes had a car incident during a storm and got stuck in high waters with the girls in the car."

"My daddy wrote that article," Adeene said proudly. "Momma used to keep sum of Daddy's articles an' I rememba' askin' Daddy what Agnes was like. Was she pretty? Miss Theodosia would not allow anyone to eva' talk to Agnes or the girls, it was forbidden. Daddy told me that Agnes was pretty tight lipped an' got the infermation fer the article only from the tow truck driva' hisself."

"Would you happen to remember the tow truck company name?"

"Aw, Carrie, that was an awful long time ago," said Adeene, "but it was sumthin' like Crossroads Towin'. Do ya' rememba', Emeline?"

"Sumthin' like that," Emeline replied while still working on her loom as a thread broke.

"May I ask something else? What have you heard about Howard McMurphy kidnapping Lulu Roosevelt?"

"Well, all I rememba' was that Mr. McMurphy kidnapped Lulu from a gas station an' when Lulu's parents drove off lookin' fer her that's when the police had Howard pulled ova'. They jus' hap'n to drive by when Lulu was runnin' 'round cryin' an' screamin'. But ya' know sumthin' just dinn't make sense 'bout that," Emeline said, as she looked for a weight to fix the broken thread.

"What's that?" Carrie asked.

"Well, Tommy was the young boy tendin' the gas station that his parents owned an' he said to the police that he dinn't see the little girl. My daddy told the same story 'bout this ev'ry time, which is why I rememba' this. Daddy said he'd stopped at the gas station when the police car was pullin' 'way wit' Howard 'n custody an' used the phone that Howard said wann't workin'. See my daddy was the reporta' fer the local paper at that time an' called 'n on that very store phone to report the story. Now why would Tommy tell Mr. McMurphy that the phone wann't workin', when jus' a lil' while afta'ward, my daddy made a phone call on it? That just neva' made sense to him?" Adeene said.

"And Daddy said he revisited Tommy Reeves afta' 'nterviewin' Mr. McMurphy 'n jail 'bout the 'ncident, an' Daddy said that Tommy neva' talked to Mr. McMurphy at all. Tommy ev'n upheld that story 'n court too. Just seemed strange, because right afta' Mr. McMurphy was put 'n jail fer the kidnappin', Tommy seemed to be a big spenda' an' had money 'n both pockets, if ya' know wha' I mean. He told folks that he got an 'nheritance from a dead aunt. A coincidence—maybe," Emeline said with an unspoken question.

"Tommy ended up buyin' the gas station from his parents when he turned twenny-one. Guess he got a big 'nheritance," Adeene said.

Virginia continued, "Ya' know the olda' town folks really liked Howard too. They say he was good, honest, an' had a nice-guy reputation. Woulnn't cause no one any harm, they say."

"Ya' know it was well-known that Miss Theodosia dinn't take to Howard marryin' Miss Patty at such a young age. She dinn't 'prove of his Tar Heel upbringin' an' his lack of potential fer her lil' girl. No one was good 'nough fer her lil' Patty. A lot of the olda' folk knew of Theo's dislike fer the man," Adeene said.

"Mmm-hmm, that's right," they all agreed, nodding their heads.

"It jus' neva' made much sense that Miss Theodosia would pay fer Howard's defense attorney. If ya' loathe sumone why would ya' spen' the money to d'fend him? It neva' made sense to anyone," Emeline said as she found an empty wine bottle to help fix the thread tautness.

"The folks took from it that Miss Patty had begged her momma fer 'sistance since she had the resources. I heard that people of the jury thought they saw Miss Theodosia smirk when the judge came down wit' the sentencin'," Jenny Lee said.

"Guess it was a win/win for Miss Theodosia. She pleased Miss Patty wit' providin' fer her husband's defense an' she got her way wit' Howard McMurphy bein' 'ncarcerated. Why are ya' so innerested 'n sumthin' that hap'n such a long time ago, Carrie?" Virginia asked.

"I just found some old newspaper articles about Howard McMurphy," Carrie said.

"Oh, my daddy wrote those too," Emeline said respectfully. "It was sum that he was most proud of."

"Is your daddy still with us?" Carrie asked.

"Daddy's in a nursin' home now. He's been ill. Momma's been passed fer 'while now, an' Daddy needs spec'l 'sistance an' daily med'cation that we jus't cain't provide," Adeene said as if trying to give everyone a reason for the decision to put him in a home.

"Oh, Lordie be, I'm not here to judge anyone, Adeene. I'm just interested in Mr. McMurphy's incarceration. He always claimed he was innocent," Carrie said comfortingly. "I didn't know him. I was just curious, that's all. I do appreciate your memory of this. It really does help me try to piece some things together."

"Hey, Carrie, there's one otha' thin' that always threw me fer a loop. Lulu's parents, Miss Stacy an' Mr. Percy, they were down on their luck. Her daddy coulnn't keep a job an' her momma moved from job to job. They had no money. I jus' always thought that to be strange that sumhow Miss Stacy got 'nough money to go to nursin' school. I reckon we'll neva' know. You'd think if they had two nickels to rub togetha', they would've bought food fer themselves an' lived 'n a betta' place," Virginia said.

"Well, y'all know Thelma down at SamiJo's Grill. She told me she heard the Roosevelts used to live in a shanty down by the gas station, but now they live down by the river in a nice house on the other side of Heart Strings cemetery," Carrie told them all.

"Yeah, that's true. I don't think the shanty is there any longa' tho'. I think it was demolished when they brought 'n the new highway," Jenny Lee said.

"I heard it was struck by lightnin' an' burnt down," Adeene said.

"I heard it's still there an' haunted," Emeline said jokingly and everyone laughed.

*I guess no one really knows what happened to it. Sarge would know, but he's not around to ask any more,* Carrie thought sadly to herself.

Jenny Lee said something off the wall though. She said that Phil Lament's momma worked at the nursing home with Lulu's momma.

"What? Phil's momma works with Stacy Roosevelt?" Carrie was surprised he hadn't told her.

Lingering about the room, Carrie tried to summarize everything that had been said. Pieces of the puzzle were there, she just had to put them together to understand what had really happened and she was not convinced she had the whole story.

When Carrie arrived back home, she reviewed Howard McMurphy's articles and remembered what Virginia had said about the Roosevelts:

"Carrie they were poor. If they had two nickels to rub together why wouldn't they have bought food for themselves and lived in a better house?"

Continuing to read up on Howard McMurphy, Carrie saw there were repeated articles that never strayed from Mr. McMurphy's denial of his guilt. From the first day to his last on this green earth, he always declared his innocence. Even in one of the articles, written by Gibby Ewert, Howard stated he believed that Miss Patty's mother, Miss Theodosia, staged the whole thing. He didn't know how she did it, but he told the story over again and how he saw her smile when the jury verdict came down.

There must be a connection to Theodosia somewhere, and Carrie was determined to get to the bottom of it. Somehow, somewhere, there had to be somebody still alive who knew more about Theodosia than they were telling, and Carrie was going to figure this out. . . for Patty.

What Carrie knew about Howard McMurphy is that he belonged to a loving family of Tar Heel workers. He lived in the modest part of town, but the picture of his mother and father proved that they were a happy family. He had married Patty without her momma knowing, and shortly after the marriage, he was sentenced for the kidnapping of Lulu Roosevelt.

*If Howard was a nice, well-liked, honorable man, why would he kidnap Lulu?* Carrie sat there looking at Howard's pile of information and realized she hadn't really studied the court case records that the Sarge brought over. Finding the file, she read that the Honorable Judge Lloyd Hekhuis had presided over the hearing. There were twelve jurors assigned to the trial, all were from various counties nearby. Carrie recognized one person's name, Cora Holtz.

Getting up from the table to get a drink, she knocked the papers onto the floor by accident. As she bent down to pick up the papers, Carrie saw an article she hadn't read yet.

***GUNSHOTS*** heard at Fundraiser for Robert Gregg Cronkright

Future Gov. Robert Gregg Cronkright came to Pheasant Mill, June 27, as the star attraction at Mrs. Theodosia Eden-Worth and husband Wesley Worth's residence.

The fundraiser was attended by local business leaders, dignitaries, judges, and friends. McLean Hawkins had intended to bring the governor's comments, quotes from Cronkright's supporters, and an idea of who was attending the evening gathering at the home of Mrs. Theodosia Eden-Worth and Wesley Worth, president and CEO of the Worth Textiles and Manufacturing. Alas, Theodosia Eden-Worth and her aides barred us at the door . . . again.

Since we have received numerous invitations to this affair and since fundraisers given by the opponent Pamela Drummert are always open to the press, we told Theodosia Eden-Worth that we would attend. Campaign manager Allison Stacks* sent a terse note saying this was a private gathering and we would not be allowed in.

McLean Hawkins met Braxon at the front door and she invited us in. Miss Theodosia immediately nixed that gracious invitation. Candidates can run their campaigns as they choose and Miss Theodosia has chosen not to divulge her support until she has to list them in the campaign finance reports. Ticket prices ranged from $250 to $5,000 for this event.

During the brusque expulsion for the press, a single gunshot was heard. Members of the press were pushed farther back outside and we were escorted to our cars by the governor's special services. We were watched as we drove off and upon reaching an out of sight area, McLean Hawkins got out of the car and watched the residence from afar. Mclean saw that it was Miss Theodosia's eldest daughter, Lydia, chasing Walter Holtz outside with a gun in hand before being yanked to the ground by several of the governor's bodyguards. It was observed that Walter Holtz drove off the property at a high rate of speed.

More details to follow. Now we have to get out of the rain.

*As stated previously, campaign manager Allison Stacks and her staff threw us out of another fundraising party headlined by the governor last September. They escorted us off the property at that time, as well.

Carrie was puzzled. *Why in the Good Lord's name did Lydia go off the deep end and try to shoot Walter?*

She could understand why Miss Theodosia would not allow the press into her residence, but what was this shooting all about? Carrie knew the only way to get information on this would be to go to Gramma's, as she'd be the only one who would know what really happened.

Taking some articles and other information, Carrie decided to drive to Lillie Eborn. It was a rash decision and improper not to call first, but Carrie needed information and felt Gramma was the only one she could ask.

As Carrie drove up, a dark-colored car was driving slowly by the front of Gramma's house. The driver was goosenecking as if checking out the place. When the driver finally spotted a car coming up from behind, the dark car sped off quickly.

Walking up to the front of the house in late afternoon, Carrie saw Gramma out back hanging up wash on the line.

"Hey, Gramma," she said loudly approaching her.

"Oh, sugar, ya' scared my mule. Wha'cha here fer, darlin'?"

Putting her purse on the table nearby, Carrie reached for Gramma's basket and said, "I'm sorry if I startled you. I know it's proper to call first, but I didn't have your phone number. I need you to help me understand a few things. If you don't have the time, I can come back later," and Carrie continued to help her with hanging sheets, towels, and unmentionables. When they finished, she pointed to the table and told Carrie to take a seat.

Taking out a pen and paper to write down whatever information she could collect, Carrie asked, "Gramma, I found this article about Miss Theodosia and Mr. Wesley Worth having a fundraiser for the governor at their place, and I see that Lydia took a shot at Walter Holtz. Do you know anything about this?"

"Well, I was there that night at that governa's fundraisa'. Miss Theodosia always did thin's to get 'tention, ya' know, an' if she kept the men of the town, or state, fer that matta', 'n her back pocket, then the more powa' she figured she had. There were lots of impor'ant, prom'nent people attendin' it, from in-state an' upcountry."

"What about Lydia? Why did she take a shot at Walter?"

"Lydia's loony. I saw her make a gran' entrance 'n one of Theodosia's dresses. She gave the 'mpression to resemble her momma 'n hair, makeup, an' ev'n talked like her. She wen' up to sev'ral men an' when they took her hand as a greetin', she put it down 'nto the front of the dress havin' them touchin' an' rubbin' at her breasts. I do da'clare it was the most bizarre behav'r. Then when the door was op'n as otha' guests were arrivin', she caught sight of Walta's car pullin' up. He had to wait 'n line fer the otha' cars wit' guests that a'rived befo' him. As they got out, allowin' the youngin's to park the cars, that allowed Lydia 'nough time to go 'nto the drawin' room an' pull out a pistol from a table drawer. She rushed back to the door, 'bout knockin' me ova', takin' a shot at Walta' an' missin'. The governa's security guards were there lickety split an' tackled her to the ground, disarmin' her. Miss Theodosia was 'n a back room minglin' when she heard the shot. She had Lydia escorted to her bedroom, where one of the bodyguards stayed on watch the rest of the evenin'. Needless to say, Miss Theodosia raised a lot of money fer the governa' that night."

"But why would Lydia have taken a shot at Walter in the first place?" Carrie asked.

"Well, I wann't standin' far from the door when it all happened. I saw Lydia reach 'round Agnes, raisin' the pistol 'n the direction of Walta's car. I was close 'nough to hear her mumble to herself, 'Ya' sonofabitch, I'm not goin' to let ya' get 'way wit' it.' I have no idea why she said that. Ya' know, Theodosia had Lydia put 'nto a state hospital 'instead of havin' it go to trial."

"Really? Do you know where?"

"Upstate, I heard, but neva' knew where. Ya' know ruma's get started, an' it could've been 'n Morganton, cain't honestly say."

"Gramma, Sarge brought me the court report for Howard McMurphy's trial, and I see that Cora Holtz was one of the jurors. What do you know about the trial?"

"Wha'cha wanna know? Howard was convicted fer kidnappin' Lulu, an' it dinn't take the jury long to convict him," she said matter-of-factly.

"What do you think about the verdict? Do you really think that Howard could have done it?"

"Honestly, darlin', Howard was one of the most respected men of the town. Him an' his family were Tar Heel worka's but that made no diff'rence. They were church-goin', 'onorable people. I knew that Theodosia dinn't like his lack of breedin' an' wanted her dawta' Patty to marry someone more outstandin' 'n the state. I think she had her sights on Patty datin' a lawya' or a docta', but Patty was tak'n to Howard. Heard he treated her like a queen, made her laugh, an' courted her ba'hind her momma's back. I thought he was a good lookin' man too. A real 'catch' if ya' asked me, not like handsome tho'. An' since you're askin' me, wha' 'bout 'ur thin' wit' handsome. How's that goin'?" Gramma turned the table on her.

*Oh, shit, what do I say?*

"Um, well, we're taking a break right now," was all Carrie could render as her voice cracked.

"What? Ya' know he's a real find. Haven't seen him this happy wit' anyone since his wife Jodine's passin'."

"Yeah, I know," was all Carrie would deliver.

Trying to recapture their conversation, she asked, "Do you think Howard was innocent?"

"Well, darlin', that d'cision wann't up to me. It was the jurors that d'cided he was guilty. But since you're askin' fer my 'pinion, yes, I dinn't believe Howard had the behav'r to do it. I can see him helpin' out, as he said, by takin' Lulu to the police station. That would've been 'n his characta', he was a very thoughtful an' kind person. Just always seemed too well thought-out, if ya' ask me. But wha' do I know? Ya' cain't tell a book by its cova'."

"I couldn't agree with you more," Carrie said. "The setting is too coincidental and too calculated. I guess it could have happened that way, but my gut is telling me something different."

"Why are ya' concerned 'bout Howard? Ya' cain't do too much 'bout it now. He died from a gunshot when he was released from prison an' ya' cain't raise the dead," Gramma said. "Neva' did find his killa' though, did they? Hann't thought 'bout that 'n 'while. Guess it got pass me, one of 'em unsolved crimes."

"Yeah, I know. I just want to find out why Miss Patty left everything to me—and not her sister Camille," Carrie said. "What about Miss Camille? Why did Miss Patty and the family disown her? What did she do to cause that?"

"Well, Camille was just a rotten, woolgatherin', lil' brat. Middle-child syndrome maybe, but she was dis'spectful 'n public an' her momma hated that. It took 'way from her public image 'n town. Theodosia always showed Miss Patty as 'er most precious possession, an' I think that drove Camille to hate Patty. Camille dinn't come 'round town much, but when she did, she would tell diff'rent folk how she found her momma 'n bed wit' various men while married to her daddy an' she told her daddy 'bout it too. It was no secret that Theodosia disowned her an' did everythin' to keep Camille . . . well, all the girls, really, 'way from the house by sendin' them to a private school. Afta' the girls had graduated an' they were grown, Lydia an' Patty stayed at the house but Camille left town. No one's really shur where she went, but ruma's had it she wen' to one of the Worth's mills."

"So, the three girls did graduate from school?"

"Well, Lydia had prob'ems wit' school. She dinn't go to the end an' folks thought she got kicked out, but maybe she was smart an' got out early, no one really knows. But yea' I think

Camille an' Patty did graduate. It was right afta' Camille's graduation that she left town an' hann't been seen since."

"And it was after that Governor's party when Lydia took a shot at Walter and got herself put into a state home?"

"Sum'where 'round then. Patty was still 'n school, I think, but she was at the fundraisa' when the 'ncident happened. Patty had stayed 'n the room wit' Lydia 'til the party was ova', 'cause I saw her walkin' wit' Lydia 'n arm an' the bodyguard escortin' them away. I dinn't rememba' seein' her the rest of the evenin'."

"Well, what was Mr. Wesley doing during all this?"

"Wesley Worth should've been name Wesley Worthless. He's the type of person ya' dinn't converse wit'. Talkin' to a rock would be more ennertainin'. He saw wha' happen' an' just walked 'way, disappearin' 'nto an office or sumthin'. He was such a pathetic coward. But one day, sev'ral years lata', Wesley Worth came home from the mill early, unbeknownst to Theo, who was 'n their bed wit' Abraham Twiford. That's when Wesley took a shot at Abraham—missin' him. But Abraham had his gun close 'nough that he took a shot at Wesley, killin' him. It was 'n self-defense they say an' wit' Abraham bein' a prom'nent man of society an' wit' Theo concurrin' wit' his story, there was neva' a trial."

"So Wesley Worth grew some balls? Oh sorry, I don't mean to be disrespectful," Carrie said.

"Yeah, a lil' too late, an' they were small balls," Gramma said snickering.

"So then what happened to Theodosia after he died?"

"Well, Theo continued on wit' her high an' mighty livin' style an' came down ill years befo' she ended up passin' 'way. It was sev'ral years afta' Wesley bein' shot that Theo wann't 'n the limelight anymore. They said she died of some sexual disease, syphilis or sumthin'. Sumhow Lydia caught wind of her momma's illness an' escaped from wherev'r she was at. She appeared down by the riva' an' had 'nother face-off wit' Walta'."

"Really?"

"As Walta' told it, he was deliverin' mail 'n the area an' saw a lady comin' up by the wata'. He went down to help 'cause she looked confused an' dirty. When he 'proached her an' saw that it was Lydia, she tried attackin' him wit' a knife. He turned it on her an' she ended gettin' stabbed an' dyin'. Walta' did call the police an' report the story. Ya' dinn't find that 'n 'ur search?" Gramma asked.

"No, I was looking for information on Theodosia, Howard and Patty. I didn't know about Lydia's issues at that time. Let me guess, it didn't go to court either because it was self-defense, right?"

"Right—from Walta's scratches an' torn clothin' where Lydia tried stabbin' him, the police said that they dinn't have anythin' to charge him wit' as he did report it. I reckon everythin' seemed legit."

"What about Cora Holtz? She was one of the jurors on Howard's case, I saw. She was married to Walter, right?" Going back to that subject and showing Gramma the court report papers, Carrie could tell that Gramma was not fond of Cora, as she frowned when Cora's name was mentioned.

"Well, yea', Cora Holtz was a juror on Howard's case, but I cain't say I shared talk wit' her," Gramma said aloof. "She's still 'live, ya' know; maybe ya' could talk wit' her 'bout the case. Think she comes from Scuppernong County now. Heard she got remarried to a farma' an' raises hogs. Her last name may be somethin' like, Whitewall, Wishall, sumthin' like that, I heard otha' people say. I don't try to keep track of everyone, ya' know." Waving her hands in the air like swatting at cantseeums.

Carrie could see that she was testing Gramma's nerves now and didn't press on about Cora.

"Gramma, if you don't mind me asking you one more thing, the ladies in the weaving class had said that Lulu's parents were poor, but I heard that they now live in a nice house on the other side of Heart Strings cemetery, down by the river. How would something like that happen?"

"Well, I know Stacy Roosevelt wen' to a nursin' school afta' her dawta's kidnappin' when Howard was convicted. Maybe she saved her money an' bawt' the house? I dinn't rememba' when they moved from the shanty, it's been 'while. Why ya' innerested in the Roosevelts?"

"From what I gather, the Roosevelts came into money after Howard's conviction and so did Tommy, the gas station clerk. I heard he even bought the gas station from his parents. Just doesn't make sense how these two very different people who were both involved in Howard's case would suddenly come into money, enough to change their lives," she said, shaking her head. "Gramma, you had said that Agnes worked for your friend, Josie Magowne, and that Agnes was still alive and living with her sister in Scuppernong County."

"Well, I knows she's Cora's old'r sister. Don't really know if she's still 'live or not. Hann't lived 'n town fer years," Gramma replied.

"What?"

"Agnes Weeden kept to herself. Cora was six years young'r, an' Agnes was very protective of her lil' sista' in an' out of school. They were both real tight an' came from a good family in town. Maybe Cora could share sum' infermation 'bout Agnes an' Miss Theodosia's bus'ness relationship. But, darlin', I really have to get to gettin'. Is there anythin' else ya' needs to know 'bout?"

"No, ma'am. Thank you for taking time out of your day to talk with me. Again, I do apologize for not calling first."

Gramma took the pen and paper from Carrie and wrote down her phone number and said, "Anytime ya' wanna' talk, ya' give me a call. If I've got the time, ya' more than welcome to stop 'n, an' I do hope that y'all come by Sunday wit' 'handsome' on 'ur arm."

"I do too," Carrie said respectfully, but she knew that this was highly improbable. Carrie gave Gramma a huge hug and thanked her again.

Arriving back at the store, she saw that there were messages on the recorder. Pressing the play button and scrolling through them, Carrie wrote down the information from the various callers until she heard, "Hey Carrie, Sergeant Lament. I have some interesting information that you asked me to find out about the police search for Camille after her momma's passing. Give me a call when you get a chance." Then he left her his phone number.

# Chapter 13

**Her** heart went racing like a red-tailed hawk swooping down for a kill. Her breath came fast and she knew she would have to calm down before returning Sarge's call. Carrie was pacing back and forth like a duck in a shooting arcade, when in walked Mona asking about the newest yarns.

Showing her to the shelf where the newest yarns Patty had ordered were stored, Carrie pointed out the alpaca, bamboo, cashmere and the exotic fibers such as buffalo gold earth, Debbie bliss winter, and others that she had just received shipments of. Carrie had knowledge of some, but needed more understanding on the others. Mona asked questions and they talked about the weight and care. She was there a long time—too long for Carrie's comfort.

Then, out of the blue, Mona asked, "How are ya' an' Sergeant Lament doin'? Are ya' two datin', or are ya' datin' Travis now?"

"Why are you interested in my relationships, Mona?" Carrie asked.

"Oh, no worries, darlin'. I saw Phil an' you leavin' the pool hall togetha', an' the girls had said that Sadie Pilotti had told them he brought you to Lillie Eborn's the last two Sundays. I was just wonderin' if he was tak'n off the market."

Now, Mona was not the loveliest of the town girls, a little too short, too round and square in the face. She was no match for Sarge.

"Well, I was about to call him back when you walked in. He left me a phone message," she said honestly, even though she knew this was misleading.

"But, dinn't I see you at the fair wit' Travis?"

"Yes, Travis and I are just friends. We're not dating, Mona. Can I help you with anything else?"

"No thanks, but I think I'll just take this," Mona chirped, and she picked up some common cotton yarn. They went to the counter, she paid for her spool, and left not quite soon enough.

*Well, the nerve. Yeah—like she'd have a chance with Sarge. Huh.* Then she remembered, she had sex with Travis and told Sarge about it. Maybe Sarge would be better off dating Mona.

She grew more and more heartsick about the whole dilemma she had put the relationship in. It was going so well until she mucked it all up. As Carrie continued wallowing, the phone rang.

She jumped.

"Hello."

"Hey, sweet pea, it's Travis."

Carrie placed her hand over the mouthpiece. *Oh shit*, she said to herself.

"Hey, Travis, how ya' doin'?"

"I'm fine. I was wonderin' if I could come 'round to see ya'. I'd like to talk 'bout what's goin' on wit' us."

"Travis, I hate that I had misled you with what happened between us the other night." She was screwed, but had to be honest no matter how it hurt. "I just don't think it's a good idea that we get together again. I'm really interested in Phil and want to try to make that work."

"Oh, OK, so it was jus' a mistake? You'd ratha' date Phil than me, huh?" Travis said rather curtly.

"Travis, I had fun with you, but I really want to work things out with Phil. I'm sorry if I hurt you."

"Yeah, no worries, Carrie. See ya' 'round town then," and he hung up rather abruptly.

Feeling sorry as a two-dollar watch, she decided to return Sarge's call. She dialed his number, not sure how this conversation was going to end up.

"Hello, Sergeant Lament."

"Hey, Sarge, it's Carrie. You called?"

"Hi, Carrie. Yeah, the other day you asked if I could find information on the police search for Camille after her momma's passing."

"Yeah," Carried replied, sounding enthusiastic. "Did you find something out?"

"I talked with some of the older guys in the department and they said that the captain took it upon himself to do the search for Camille. However, when I tried to talk to the captain and asked him about it, he seemed a little unresponsive. Where are you at now?" he asked.

"I'm at the store," she said rather unbelieving that he asked her that question.

"May I come by to discuss this with you?" he asked.

"Yes, please, I'll be here."

"OK, I should be there shortly."

*OH, MY LORD, he's coming to the store.* Carrie was flabbergasted.

It wasn't long before the Sarge walked through the store door. He was dressed in uniform with those stupid sunglasses hanging on his nose, but stood tall, strong, and firm.

"Carrie," he said.

"Um, yeah," Carrie came back to reality.

"Carrie, what I was saying on the phone earlier, I talked with the captain, and I asked him about the search for Camille Eden-Worth after Theodosia's death and who he put in charge of the investigation. He seemed unresponsive and asked why I was interested in a closed case. I asked if they ever found Camille. He said, 'No.' So I asked, 'How can it be a closed case, then?' He came back and said that since Miss Theodosia washed her hands of her, he didn't want to use up resources to find Camille."

"What? The captain gave up the search for Camille because her momma washed her hands of her? He didn't want to spend the funds to find her, either? How does that make sense? Isn't that part of his job? Why would he let that be the decision behind not looking for Camille? Therefore, Camille is still out there somewhere. I don't care if she was a bitch. She's the only family Patty has left." Carrie said resolutely, "I'm going to find her. She has a right to know."

"Yeah, I have to say I agree with you. So what are you planning on doing?"

"I don't know. I don't even know where to start looking for her. I went and talked with Gramma today."

Right when those words exited her mouth, the noise in the cellar started, loud then soft. *Clang*, *clang*, banging pipe sounds.

"What's that?" Sarge started walking around listening.

"You know old places like this have many old sounds and smells connected to them. It's nothing."

"So, you visited Gramma today? What was that about?"

"For information, and she gave me loads," Carrie replied, and recounted to Sarge for over an hour the contents of her discussion with Gramma.

Sarge was responsive and listened politely to what Carrie had said. However, he was still on the clock and had to leave. "Carrie, I'm sorry, but I have to go back to the office. I have to clock out."

"Does that mean you're off work now?"

"When I clock out I will be."

"Sarge, can I take you out to supper? I just want to thank you for your help."

"Um, I'm not so sure that's a good idea," he said, looking uncomfortable.

"Please Sarge, it won't be anything more than supper." Carrie bit her bottom lip as she awaited his response.

"OK, I'll meet you at SamiJo's—say in thirty minutes."

"Thanks, I'll meet you there." She watched him exit the store.

Carrie was elated, *Thank you, Dear Lord Jesus.* She wondered if there was a way for Sarge to forgive her.

Right now, she had to take the moment by its tail and get him involved in the case. At least if Sarge knew she needed his help, he was still willing to assist and she would take that for all it's worth.

After about ten minutes, she locked up the store and drove to SamiJo's. Carrie wasn't paying attention to the speed limit, and by the time she looked down, she saw red and blue streaming lights behind her. Secretly wondering if it was Sarge, she looked in the mirror to make sure she looked okay, and then rolled down her window smiling, but it wasn't him. It was an older man.

"Ma'am, do you know why I pulled you over?"

"I'm sorry, Officer, but I'm meeting Sergeant Lament at SamiJo's and I was running late," she tried to explain.

"Ma'am, may I get your license and registration."

"What? Really? Did you not hear me when I said that I was meeting Sergeant Phil Lament at SamiJo's?" she said, a little too assertively. Reaching into her purse, she retrieved her license and registration. He took them and proceeded back to the patrol car. It wasn't too long before he returned, handing back her license, registration, and a speeding ticket.

"Drive safely," he said as he turned around and walked back to his car.

She would not allow herself to react as she had done when she first met Sarge. Carrie was going to meet Sarge now and she wasn't going to get all disgruntled on him. Carrie wanted to be on her best behavior. Therefore, she decided she would take the ticket with a grain of salt.

Walking up to the diner's door, Carrie took a deep breath and pulled the door open.

Sarge was already there, leaning against the bar.

Carrie smiled as she approached him. "Hey Sarge, sorry to make you wait," and showed him the speeding ticket she'd just received.

"So, Miss Carrie, again, not watching your speed?" he said as he looked at the ticket. "Oh, I see that it was the captain that gave you the ticket. *How strange*," Phil said with a crinkled brow. "Not sure when was the last time he wrote a ticket in this county. If you want, I'll take it to see what I can do about it."

"Oh, I don't want you to get into a fuss with your captain. Although I did tell him that I was meeting you at SamiJo's, but I guess that didn't matter."

"No worries," he replied as he pocketed the ticket.

"Please, follow me," the waitress said as she showed them to their table.

Sarge pulled out her chair, allowing her to sit down first. Some people you just can't take their raisin' away.

"Thank you for allowing me to take you to supper, Sarge."

"You're welcome, sugar." Possibly not thinking of what he had just said as he picked up the menu.

"Sarge, was it normal practice for the police department to not to look for Camille, regardless if she was forsaken or not?"

"I really can't say. It's a strange situation."

"Yes, it is. Do you know who Cora Holtz is?"

"Wasn't she the one married to Walter Holtz?"

The waitress approached them for their order of drinks and food. They put in their order and continued their discussion when the waitress walked away.

"Yeah, she was. Gramma seemed to think that she lives in Scuppernong County and is remarried to a hog farmer with last name," she said, taking out her notes, "Whitewall, Wishall—something like that."

"Well, there are a few hog farmers in that area. It shouldn't be hard to find her. You know Gramma could be wrong. She's not quite a spring chicken anymore."

"But it's a place to start," Carrie replied.

"So why do we need to find Cora Holtz?"

"She's Agnes Weeden's little sister. You know Miss Theodosia hired Agnes as a nanny for the girls. Maybe she could shed some light on where the girls went to school. Wouldn't you think that if Camille had friends from the private school she attended, that she may have gone back to that area or kept up with them?"

"Well, it could be a good place to start."

"Miss Agnes may have told something to her sister in confidence. I have to start somewhere and that seems like a logical place."

"I agree, when do you want to go visit Miss Cora?" he offered.

"What? Oh Sarge, you don't have to do any more if you don't want to. I appreciate you getting me this far."

"Carrie, you got me curious as well. I'll just finish what the captain didn't want to do."

"Thank you," she said, surprised as all get out.

"So where is Scuppernong County?" Carrie asked.

"How about we start with a telephone book," Sarge said with a smile and turned to the waitress and asked her to bring him a telephone book.

When the waitress returned, Carrie scooted her chair closer to Sarge. She took in his smells of Obsession and Rem oil and started craving his body again with the explosion of electricity between them.

"Well, Carrie, you said Wishall, right? Let's start there."

He turned pages to the 'wh' section. "Well, there are a few Whiteheads, a lot of Whites, and nothing at all on Wishall." Sarge sat back and thought for a moment. "Scuppernong County is not far from here. It wouldn't take any time to drive there." He turned to the back of the book where the business section was located and looked up farms, specifically searching out hog farmers. There he found White Hall's Hog Farm. "I'll be damn, Gramma was right. Look—see here, White Hall's Hog Farm. It's not far from here. I know the approximate location. When would you like to go?"

The server interrupted the conversation again as she delivered two beers. "Your suppa' should be here right quick," she said, displaying a dingy, crooked-toothed smile.

"What? You want to go with me?" Carrie questioned.

"I'm off tomorrow, you want to go then?"

"Um, OK. I'll post a note on the store door and we can make a day out of it. Are you sure you want to do this? You don't have to, you know."

"Well, you got me involved in your quest for finding out about Patty. Why the captain did not pursue finding Camille is strange. I don't care for the reason he gave me. You'd think there'd still be a need to find her." He took a drink.

"I agree."

"OK. What time do you want to get started tomorrow?"

"How about 10 a.m.?"

"That sounds good. I will pick you up at the house. I don't want you to get another ticket," he laughed.

Just then, Travis walked through the door.

"Hey y'all," he said as he approached their table.

"Hey, Travis," Carrie said suddenly demoralized.

"Travis," replied Phil harshly.

"Hey, Phil, ya' take good care of our Carrie now. For whateva' reason, she chose you ova' me," Travis said, dampening the spirit of the evening.

However, those words seemed to brighten Sarge up. Carrie spotted a smirk on his face when Travis brought that to his attention, and that tiny smirk gave him away and made her heart flip.

Travis turned around, picked up his carryout at the counter, and left. She could see that he was hurting, but she was not about to go chasing after him.

Sarge sat back and took a big swallow of beer, studying her as he did.

"What?"

"Do you want to go after Travis?"

"NO! Travis was a mistake," Carrie said in a panic.

She looked out the window, remembering how she had seen Sarge and Denise hugging and her shoulders once again sank down low meeting her butt.

The server brought their hot food and they proceeded to eat their supper.

"Well, you didn't eat much on your plate. Why don't you eat? I'll get us two more beers." He got up and went to the bar.

Carrie had lost her appetite. She only ate a few more bites of food while the Sarge was gone. He handed her a cold beer when he came back, as she continued to move food about the plate. She felt horrible, not just for Travis, but for doing what she did to Sarge. Carrie knew the jealousy devil had gotten the best of her, there was no doubt about it. She used Travis as a rebound, messed up big, and was feeling sorry for herself.

"Hey, you want to shoot some pool?" he said, interrupting her wallowing.

"Sure," she said, surprised that he was interested in continuing the evening.

Sarge motioned to the waitress to bring a box for her food and the bill.

As the waitress brought the small white Styrofoam box to the table, she handed the bill to him.

"Oh, no you don't, I invited you to supper—*remember*?"

The Sarge laughed that handsome, deep, throaty, full-hearted laugh as he handed her the bill.

Her eyes watered, an indicator of relief, happiness, and amnesty. Carrie fought off the tears as she reached within her purse and paid the waitress handsomely.

Sarge stood up and pulled out her chair, "Ready?"

"Yes, thanks."

They drove separately to the pool hall. Very few people were there at this hour.

"I'll get the first round of beers," Carrie said with a smile.

Sarge went to get a table and choose his pool stick. Playing two games, it was tied one to one. While playing the third game, Carrie saw Travis walk in with Dana.

Yeah, Dana that skinny nurse from the hospital, but it didn't matter. Carrie was with Sarge. Moreover, he invited her here. Sarge was close to an absolution, she could feel it.

As Carrie was bending over to take a shot on the black ball, aiming and getting set, she felt Sarge's warm gentle breath. He touched her back and said, "Are you going to call it?"

"What? Oh, yeah, in the right corner pocket."

Sure, trying to concentrate now, with this hunk of man's breath in her ear, she was certain to miss. Taking aim, she hit the ivory cue ball slowly at the black ball toward the corner pocket. As if by the breath of an angel, it fell in. The cue ball remained unwavering on the edge of the pocket.

Carrie turned and smiled and let out a big, "Ha ha!"

Travis turned and walked their way. "What, Phil, you can't beat a girl?"

"Well, Travis, as you can tell, Carrie is a very skilled pool player."

"Hey, Travis, didn't I beat you three games to none before?" she retorted, remembering the only games they had played together.

Sarge just chuckled as he took a drink of beer.

Travis just looked at Carrie, tipped his baseball cap, and returned to Dana.

It was time to call it a night. Phil and Carrie left in separate cars. *But tomorrow was another day*, thought Carrie, *and it would start at 10 a.m.*

# Chapter 14

**Carrie** was already up and in the powder room when the alarm made its presence known. However, if she got two winks of sleep last night, it went fast. With a white toothbrush in her mouth, she turned off the alarm. After finishing with a shower, shaving her arms, legs and other body parts, she looked for the perfect outfit.

Trying on various tops and bottoms, she thought about the drive to Scuppernong, so she needed to be comfortable and able to climb in and out of Sarge's truck. She found a blue flowery skirt with a white-eyelet, button-down top and cute blue sandals. She twirled and with a little grin thought, *I can be sexy, comfortable and with the wind blowing in the right direction, I can give Sarge a show.*

Carrie finished getting ready and pulled her hair back in a ponytail, dabbed some perfume behind her ears, on her cleavage . . . down there between her thighs and she was ready.

Prompt as ever, Sarge was there ten minutes early and wearing those stupid sunglasses. Opening the door she squirmed . . . *durn' if that ain't one fine licking . . . I mean, looking man.*

"Come on in," she said salivating. "Would you like some hot coffee?"

"No, thanks. Are you ready to go?"

"Give me a minute." She turned, feeling her skirt move to and fro, and she swaggered going into the kitchen to get her purse.

"OK, ready."

She could feel that his eyes didn't leave her for one second when she turned away from him, and they were still on her when she opened the door to leave.

He did the proper thing, opening the truck door for her, and as she had planned, the wind came blowing. She grabbed her ass fast, not certain what he had seen, but pretty sure he liked it.

She watched him walk in front of the truck, put this hand to his mouth and cough. She was confident this was going to be a good day.

Driving along NC-264, the sun was shining and light, and feathery clouds leisurely floated by.

"What a gorgeous day. Have you driven up to Scuppernong before?" she asked.

"Well, when Jodine and I were first married, we would go up to Scuppernong and visit some wineries in that area and make a picnic out of it."

"Scuppernong is a grape, isn't it? Does Scuppernong make good wine?"

"Well, Jodine liked the white wines. If the truth be told, I prefer beer myself. The white wine was a little too sweet for me. They did have some red wines that weren't too bad."

"I haven't been to a winery up there. Maybe I'll get there sometime. So what else is there to do in Scuppernong?"

"There are several different hiking trails that we went on," and he stopped for several minutes, as if Carrie had brought something back—that didn't feel right.

"Are your parents still alive?" Carrie asked, trying to change the conversation to something other than his deceased wife.

"Yeah, my mom, Della is her name, is a nurse at a nursing home and my dad, Gabe, is an electrician."

"What nursing home does your mom work at?"

"Well, come to think about it, she works at the same one that Stacy Roosevelt runs."

"Really? You just remembered that now?" Carrie said, kicking off her shoes, moving to sit on her left leg. Carrie leaned against the passenger side door and moved her skirt to be a little more ladylike.

Sarge took a quick look and continued driving. "Yeah, I'm not sure why that just occurred to me."

"So how long has your momma been working at the nursing home?"

"She's been there a long time. She used to work at the hospital in town. When the local nursing home was about to go under, Miss Roosevelt bought it. It started out small, and then when it started getting bigger with more of the older folks, she hired my mother on."

"I think Jenny Lee told me that your momma worked with Miss Stacy. You said your dad is an electrician. I may have some work for him." Carrie thought about the only light in the cellar.

Sarge looked at her and smiled, then looked down, following the edge of her skirt.

With her skirt a little high on the thigh, she could tell it was affecting him. As Sarge turned his head to look in the driver's side mirror, he wiped his brow with the backside of his hand.

"Thank you for taking me to visit Miss Cora. You didn't have to do this, you know."

"My pleasure, Carrie," he said in that seductive voice of his.

She turned her head to look out the window and dreamed about those words—*My pleasure, Carrie.* Then, she sat upright with both legs on the ground and regained her composure, although she left the side of her skirt a little high on the thigh.

They chit-chatted awhile longer discussing what type of things were happening at the police station, when Phil said, "Carrie, we're getting closer now. You might want to keep an eye out. I am not one hundred percent sure where it is. We might have to go into town and ask."

"What? A man that actually pulls over and asks for directions?" she asked laughing.

"Do you want to find Cora Holtz or Hall—or whatever her name is—or not?" Smiling back at her.

"Yes sir, whatever it takes."

Not but a minute later, they both spotted a billboard on the side of the road: White Hall's Hog Farm, exit at Hwy 94 N.

"Wow, talk about timing," Carrie said.

Sarge followed the direction on the sign, exiting at 94 North. While looking around, nothing but flat land was all they could see.

They drove for a bit, maybe fifteen to twenty minutes longer, and then on the left, was a small, corral-style entrance that read, "White Hall's Hogs and Farm."

If they had not been looking for it, they could easily have passed it, since there was nothing but cropland on this patch of roadway.

They pulled onto the rocky road entrance and drove along a long path, passing silos and a large metal barn, until they reached a house. It was noticeably located on the upwind side of the hogs. Smart move, since it looked like they had hundreds of them.

Sarge opened Carrie's door as she gracefully climbed out, holding her skirt to her butt.

As they walked toward the porch, an older man with thick, white, bushy eyebrows, wearing blue jean overalls and a white T-shirt came around the backside of the house.

"Hey, *kin'* I help ya' wit' sumthin'?"

They both walked up to him. "Hi, my name's Carrie Pyles and this is my friend, Phil Lament."

He reached out his hand, shook the both of theirs, and nodded.

"Would you happen to know a lady that used to be known as Cora Holtz?"

"Who's askin'?"

"We mean no harm. A friend of mine, Miss Patty McMurphy, passed away, and I heard that Miss Cora is a sister of Miss Agnes Weeden. Miss Agnes used to be employed by Miss Theodosia Eden-Worth as Miss Patty's nanny. Miss Patty had left me things in her will, and I'm just researching to get some answers."

"Wha' kin' of thin's?" he asked suspiciously.

Phil stepped in and asked, "Do you know Miss Cora or not?"

Carrie looked at Phil and then to the old man to see his response.

"Yeah, she's my wife. She's inside. I'll go get 'er." He turned, spit on the ground, and went inside the house.

"Now, why did you act like that?" Carrie asked.

"He seemed like he was fishing to see if you had money. Hog farmers aren't doing well nowadays, and it wouldn't surprise me that he is after something."

"So you're suspicious of his actions?"

"Sugar, you can't take everyone as they appear. Be it nice or not, don't trust everyone at first sight."

"But he seemed innocent enough."

"Don't be naïve. People will take advantage of whatever they can get away with. You already gave away too much information when you told him about getting part of Patty's will and that she is the daughter of Miss Theodosia. Do not forget, she was well known in this state and people believed her to be one of the richest. Don't give away more information than you have to," he said firmly.

Carrie reasoned that Sarge was way over-thinking this, as he seemed like a nice old man with no intentions of doing any harm. They were standing there facing one another when Cora came out of the house in a blue shirtdress with a white apron on.

Cora was an older lady with black-gray hair, big bust, and enough wrinkles to hold an eight-day can of rain.

"Hey, y'all, Ossie says y'all lookin' fer me?"

Reaching out her hand and shaking Miss Cora's, it was a cold, wet-fish shake. Carrie introduced herself and Phil.

Phil took her hand, placed his other hand on top, and said, "What a nice farm you have here, and we hope we're not interrupting your day."

*What a suck-up*, Carrie thought.

Seeing Cora smiling at Sarge and taken by his act of kindness, Phil proceeded to ask Miss Cora if she was Miss Agnes Weeden's relation.

"Well, yeah, she's my old'r sister, but why ya' askin'?" Cora asked with beaten brow.

"Well, I'm a member of the Pheasant Mills Police Department, and I noticed that after Miss Theodosia Eden-Worth passed, the police never found her daughter Miss Camille to notify her of her momma's death. Miss Carrie here is interested in finding the next of kin since Miss Patty's recent passin'."

"Oh my, where's my manna's. Please come up an' take a sit on the porch. Let me get ya' two sumthin' cold to drink," Cora said as she turned and pointed to the porch swing. "I'll be right back wit' 'em drinks," and she entered through the creaking, torn at the seam, screened-in front porch door. It slammed shut behind her.

"Wow, you're good."

"Shhh," Sarge nodded his head toward the open window.

Carrie leaned slightly forward and looked. He was right; the windows were wide open and Carrie was certain if they were to continue conversing, Cora and Ossie would be listening inside.

Carrie looked back at Sarge. It appeared as if he was looking around the property, but she assumed he was concentrating on hearing something being said inside the old, worn, in-need-of-fresh-paint, mid-size farmhouse.

*What a cop. He really is good at this*, she thought. Carrie admired his doggedness.

Phil heard footsteps walking towards the door. He reacted quickly, as he jumped up from the porch swing, which moved back and forth hastily as he went to open the porch door for Cora. Grabbing the chain's metal rings, Carrie planted her feet on the porch to stop the swing's erratic movement.

Cora came out holding two large glasses full of iced sweet tea and handed them to Carrie and Phil. Carrie took a complimentary sip and tried not to grimace over the taste of the old well water Cora had used to make it. "Thank you, Miss Cora, very refreshing," Carrie said pleasantly.

Phil did not take a drink when Cora handed it to him. He just put it down on the wood-barrel table to the side of the porch swing.

Cora took a seat in an old wooden rocking chair on the porch. Ossie eventually came out through the front door and moved his worn cushioned rocking chair in the direction of Carrie and Phil in order to make better eye contact.

"So, yur' a cop, huh?" Ossie inquired.

"Yes," Phil replied.

"And yur' lookin' fer this Camille person."

"Yes," Phil replied.

"Why ya' wanna' know 'bout Aggie fer?" Ossie inquired.

"We think she may be able to tell us where Camille went to school, which could help us to locate her."

"And ya' wanna know 'cause Miss Theodosia Ed'n-Worth pass' 'way an' so, did her youngest dawta' Miss Patty."

"I wasn't aware that anyone said that Miss Patty was her youngest daughter," Phil replied.

"Well, inn't she?" Ossie retorted, taking a spit off the porch.

"Yes, she is," Phil replied.

Taking advantage of a quiet moment, Carrie finally chimed in, "Miss Cora, where is your sister now? Did your sister ever say anything about when she worked for Miss Theodosia?"

"We was pretty close growin' up an' all, but Aggie was pretty tight lipped 'bout her 'xperience when she worked fer the Worths," she paused. "My sista' resides 'n a nursin' home down state now."

"Did she ever say where the Worth's girls may have gone to school?"

"That's such a long time ago, darlin'. Aggie may have, but I'm not shur I rememba'."

"Excuse me, Miss Cora? You're not sure you remember?" Carrie looked at Phil, cocking her head.

"Ma'am, it sure would be nice if you could remember," Phil said politely.

Cora looked at Ossie as if to find out what she should say.

"How about if we just start with what you do remember with your sister's—Miss Agnes' employment at the Worth's and go from there," Phil said properly.

"Well, Aggie wen' to work at the Worth's right afta' school an' got hired on when Miss Theodosia an' Mr. Wesley's was pregga's wit' their first baby girl. My sista' wann't the loveliest of girls, so I reckon it dinn't threat'n Miss Theodosia. Aggie was like the fifth girl that Miss Theodosia hired an' fired befo' settlin' on Aggie. I rememba' Aggie comin' home sayin' that she had to sign a legal form, a nondisclosure sumthin' where she coulnn't say anythin' 'bout the family to anyone or she would be fired an' neva' able to get 'nother job 'n this town."

Phil spoke up, "Do you know if she kept a copy of the non-disclosure agreement?"

"I'm shur she did. She's real org'nized. That was one of her special traits. She kept a box of thin's," and Cora stopped short with a startled look on her face and turned to Ossie as if she'd said too much.

"Do you think we could see the box?" Phil said directly to Cora.

"Not shur that's of any impor'nance to ya'," Ossie replied.

"Well, I go could talk to the captain of the Scuppernong police department and see if I could convince him of a warrant. However, that is up to you. All I'm interested in is finishing up police business by finding Miss Patty's next of kin," Phil said unwaveringly.

Ossie looked at Cora, turned his head and spit off the porch. He nodded his head in the direction of the house, giving her permission to get the box.

Cora went inside the house and allowed the porch screen door to spank its frame behind her.

"Ya' knows we's thinkin' 'bout writin' a book on Miss Theodosia Ed'n-Worth. Maybe ev'n sen' it to one of 'em show produca' people an' see wha' they'd give us fer it. I hears they pay pretty han'some fer good infermation like this," and he spit off the porch again.

"Oh, yeah? And, where would you have heard that from?" Phil retorted.

Ossie just sat up and took an old graying handkerchief out of his pocket, wiping his forehead dry.

*Sarge was right all along. They were after money. I have money and I don't care. I'll pay whatever they want for the information.* Carrie thought without deliberation.

Cora returned with a rather large wooden box.

As Cora took off the lid, Carrie could see school pictures, papers, and several journals as Cora rummaged around in the box determined to find the non-disclosure agreement that Phil had asked for.

Carrie looked at Sarge in shock with her big blue-gray eyes bulging, but he did not give anything away.

He stayed straight-faced.

Cora eventually found the folded non-disclosure paper near the bottom of the box. She opened it up to make sure and then handed it over to Phil.

Sarge reviewed it and it was legal, signed by Miss Theodosia Eden-Worth and Miss Agnes Weeden. He handed it over to Carrie to review.

"What else do you have?" Phil inquired. He was testing her to see how much information he could gather.

Ossie sat up again, spat off the porch and said, "D'pends on watyuh wanna pay fer it."

Cora looked at Ossie, to Carrie, and then to the Phil, revealing that she was ill at ease with what Ossie had just asked.

Phil replied, "How much are you looking for?" speaking directly to Ossie now.

"I hear 'em sho' people pay lots of money fer this type of thin'."

*Yeah, you already said that*, Phil thought, but continued, "How much are you looking for to give us this box?"

"Well, ya' know, as the missus jus' said, her sista's 'n a nursin' home an' that costs a lot of money," Ossie stated.

"Ossie, I'm asking how much it is going to cost to take this box of information off your hands," Phil asked uncaringly this time.

"Well, um, neva' gave it much thought."

Sarge and Carrie looked at each other, both thinking, *Yeah, right!*

Ossie sat up again, spewing a long black wad of tobacco juice off the porch, took the stained hanky from his overall pocket, and wiped his forehead and then his mouth. "I'd say ten thousand dolla's should be fair."

"I'd say that for something that doesn't rightfully belong to Miss Cora or you and you profiting from it, that's a little steep. Have you read through anything in the box to see if it's worth ten thousand dollars?" Phil asked.

"Oh, Ossie cain't read well. He's only got a six grade edya'cation," Cora advised.

"Shush, Missus!" Ossie snapped.

"Nothin' wrong wit' a six grade edya'cation, when ya' got bus'ness sense," Cora barked back.

"Well, Ossie, let me ask you one more thing. I know that farmers in particular are not having a good season this year. Some are saying they are down as much as—" Phil started saying.

Carrie could not take it anymore. "I'll pay you three thousand dollars right now for that entire box."

Sarge looked at her and grimaced.

"Shur—*OK*. Ya' kin' have it fer three thousand dolla's." Ossie reacted and spat off the porch again.

Reaching for her purse, she pulled out her purple leather checkbook. Taking out a pen, she opened it up.

"Wait a minute, lil' lady, we cain't be takin' no check," Ossie reacted quickly.

"Well, I don't carry three thousand dollars in cash with me on any given day," Carrie replied.

Phil sat up and said, "Ossie, is your bank nearby?"

"Well, shur it is. It's right close, won't take but jus' a quick minute."

Now Phil knew that neither quick, nor minute, runs together along the same road. Therefore, it could mean anything from five to thirty minutes away.

"What if you and I go to your bank and cash the check. Carrie can stay here with Cora to keep her company while we're gone."

"Good idea," Carrie said as she proceeded to write the check to Mr. Ossie Hall for three thousand dollars.

It wasn't long before Phil and Ossie were driving down the rocky driveway in the silver truck, leaving a cloud of gray dust trailing behind.

Looking at Cora, she asked, "How is your sister, Miss Agnes, doing?"

"Well, honey, she's been 'n a nursin' home fer 'while now. Her mind's goin'. It breaks my heart when Ossie takes me to visit her an' she don't rememb'r me no more. Aggie just sits there in a daze, like fog on a winda'. She still looks 'live on the outside, but seems like her brain battery is dyin' an' her clock is 'bout done tickin'. I don't reckon it'll be too long befo' she passes on," Cora said with tears in her voice.

"Hey, Miss Cora, did you know Howard McMurphy?" Carrie asked, trying to change the subject.

"Yeah, an' what a shame that whole mess was. Darn nice man he was. I think Miss Theodosia had her hand 'n that injus'ice too. Howard was an 'onerable man an' came from a good family. The McMurphys were church-goin' an' real good people. They'd do anythin' fer anyone, an' it made sense fer Howard to wanna brin' the lil' girl to a police station. He wann't no kidnappa', he jus' got caught up wit' the wrong family."

"I think Miss Theodosia had her hand in it too, just can't prove anything. But I'm going to work on that. Maybe after I find Camille, she can shed some light as to how Miss Theodosia may have been involved. You were married to Walter Holtz, were you not? How long were you two married?" Carrie asked.

"*Oh, Walta'*," Cora shook her head in disgust. "Yeah, I was married to *that man*. He's obsessed wit' Blackbeard's treasure, ya' know. He'd ratha' be out lookin' fer Blackbeard's gold than to be married an' home wit' me. Walta' neva' found one piece of treasure that I know of, but always swore his 'sources were right. There was one time when we were 'n school, Walta' was courtin' Lillie Eborn an' he read up on Blackbeard an' seemed to think that my bloodline was a relation. That's when he dropped Lillie an' pursued me. Gotta give it to him, he's dogged an' determined to win me ova'. It took him 'while befo' he did, but I gave him that one chance. I wish I neva' woud'ave. Our marriage dinn't end nice or anythin'. He started drinkin' an' threw me 'round one too many times. I left aft'r three years of marriage an' moved 'n wit' my parents, then filed fer a divorce."

"Oh, I'm sorry, I didn't mean to pry," Carrie said with empathy.

"I also found out that Walta' allegedly violated Miss Theodosia's oldest, Lydia, when she was a youngin'. Pro'bition was still goin' on an' Walta' was a drunk an' rum-runnin' fer Miss Theodosia's estab'ishment. He'd been havin' affairs wit' 'em ladies at the brothel, passed 'round like a bad cigar. But one day when Miss Theo was out to sum' parade or store showin' an' Aggie was watchin' the younga' girls, sum'how Walta' got 'nto Lydia's room."

"What?"

"Yeah, I saw it in Aggie's notes."

"Really? Did you read anything else?"

"I was too upset when I got that far. Maybe ya' should show that to yur' offica' friend, but I'd guess it'd be too late to do anythin' 'bout it now," Cora said in the most appalled voice. "Aggie did have sum' infermation 'bout the girl's school 'n her notes. So, ya' should be able to at least have a place to start yur' search fer Miss Theodosia's girl Camille. I do hope it helps ya' get clos'r," she said earnestly.

"I really am glad that you're selling Miss Agnes' box to me. Thank you. I'm sure it will provide a lot of information."

"No, darlin', *Thank you*! Yur' a godsend. We needed the money, otha'wise the bank was goin' to repossess our farm. *The Good Lord* heard my pray'rs an' brought ya' here to dry my tears. I'm glad that yur' friend, Phil, took my husband to the bank. I'm hopin' Ossie's smart 'nough to pay the mortgage when he's there."

Carrie felt bad for Cora.

To break the quiet between them Carrie asked, "So, how did you meet Ossie?"

"Aggie worked fer his olda' sista', Josie Magowne afta' she left Theodosia's employment. Ya' know Theodosia fired her afta' sum' big gov'na party she had thrown. Aggie was sup'osed to be watchin' Lydia that night, but Theodosia was short staff so she asked Aggie to uh-sist wit' the evenin' venue. How she could 'pect Aggie to be 'n two places at the same time was totally unreas'nable, but that's Miss Theodosia, always seekin' perfection 'til sumthin' goes wrong."

"Is that when Lydia took a shot at Walter?"

"Yeah, an' Lydia shoud've killed him. I'm sorry 'bout that, but God hisself woulnn't want that sonofabitch. Hate to say it, but Lydia was jus' a bad shot. Maybe I should give 'er sum' shootin' lessons. I can unnerstand why she wen' unhinged. Havin' a momma like that an' bein' violated by Walta', who knows how many times, that poor girl dinn't stan' a chance 'n that house if ya' ask me."

When the talk got quiet for a moment, they heard the truck coming up the rocky drive. They could see the billowing gray dust clouds through the firs that already wore a thick coat of dust before they actually saw the truck. The silver truck stopped out in front of the porch and Ossie lumbered out, spitting on the ground, adjusting his overall strap as he approached the porch.

"Go 'head an' giv' it to 'er, Missus. The check is good," he said, relieved, taking the white handkerchief out of his pocket and swiping his forehead dry.

"But Ossie, did ya' pay fer *thin's* when you were at the bank?" Cora asked him directly.

"Yeah, Missus, don't get ur' britches 'n a bunch. We's worked out an 'greement. Now, get to gettin' an' give 'er that there box. Now, get on." Ossie seemed to be in a hurry to get rid of them.

"Hey Carrie, are you ready to leave?" Sarge asked.

"Yes sir, I am."

Turning to Cora, Carrie took her hand. “Thank you for everything.”

With tears in her eyes, Cora replied, “Yur’ welcome, darlin’. Ya’ come ’round any time, ya’ hear.”

Carrie smiled at Cora and said, “Sure.”

Phil turned to Cora and took the box from her arms as Carrie thanked Ossie.

They retreated to the truck and as Sarge opened her door, Carrie felt a slight breeze up her legs as she climbed in. She straightened out the backside of her skirt in no hurry.

Sarge put the box on the back seat as they waved at Cora and Ossie sitting on the porch.

“So, how was your drive with Ossie?”

“Well, Ossie told me that the bank was about to foreclose on the property next week. So I bought a hog or two. He’s going to have them cut it up and package the meat. I just need to get it from the packaging company in a couple of weeks and buy a deep freeze in the meantime. I also told him that I knew a few barbecue places in and around Pheasant Mills that I may be able to persuade to buy fresh hog meat. There’s a Porky’s Cracked Rib Barbecue festival coming up, and I said I would see what I could do. Didn’t make any promises though.”

After loosening her seat belt, Carrie scooted over and kissed him on his cheek.

“How did your time with Cora go?”

“You wouldn’t believe what I found out. Miss Agnes is in a nursing home down state and can’t remember her sister Cora when she visits. That Walter dropped Lillie Eborn in school for Cora because he thought Cora was related to Blackbeard’s bloodline, and then he wrecked his marriage to Miss Cora after three years, being obsessed with Blackbeard’s treasure hunts. Also during the Prohibition era, Walter drank too much, was a rumrunner, and worked for Miss Theodosia’s establishment. Which I assume was a brothel. As Miss Cora stated, *Walta was havin' affairs with ladies there and was passed 'round like a bad cigar,*" Carrie said in Cora's slow drawl.

Sarge just smiled that gorgeous smile at her reenactment of Cora.

Carrie continued, "Walter also pushed Cora around one too many times when he was drunk. Miss Cora did say she knew Howard McMurphy and his family and said they were good people. Do anything for anyone, but the real kicker, ready for it—Miss Cora said that Walter violated Patty's oldest sister, Lydia, when she was young."

# Chapter 15

**"Really?** How did you go about getting that information?" Sarge said, intrigued.

"Miss Cora said that she read that information in Agnes' notes and Agnes' notes are in this beautiful box that I bought for three thousand dollars—What? Why are you grimacing like that at me?"

"I think if you would have let me handle it, I could have gotten it under a thousand dollars."

"Really? Do you have to be in control all the time? I think I did just fine on my own."

Surrendering, he asked, "Hey, would you like to go on a picnic at a winery really close by?"

"Sure." Carrie was pleased.

They drove for a short time before Sarge asked, "Carrie, what about your parents? Are they still alive?"

"You want to know about my parents? Well, my biological momma, Debra, had drug problems, and shortly before my grandfather died, went into a drug rehab program out of state. She had fallen on some ice during a heavy winter storm and developed an addiction to Percodan and Quaaludes. I was just a little one at that time. She was an egocentric, bitter human being and she stole from everyone she met to support her habit as it spiraled out of control. She used to leave me for days at Grandma Hattie's and no one knew where she was or what she was doing."

"That sounds like an addict."

"Debra also did a little dealing, but she wasn't too lucky. She was found guilty of felony possession with intent to distribute over in Raleigh. My Grandma Hattie was angry and exhausted with her by then. She cut her off and my Grandma Hattie died without ever mentioning Debra's name to me again."

"What about your father? What happened to him?"

"Tom Pyles, my biological father, is a sorry ass. He left Debra and me cold when I was born. Grandma told me that when Debra delivered me, the nurse put me into her arms and that is when Tom asked her for a divorce. Grandma was spitting bumblebees. When Tom saw the divorce granted, he then just up and disappeared. Debra tore up every picture of him in the house after he left. I never went looking for him. I didn't know what to look for honestly. All I can say is that Grandma Hattie loved me more than her own life, and with my parents out of reach, she became my legal guardian when I was six, and it was good for all of us."

Sarge was right. It wasn't long before they arrived at the winery on the river.

It was beautiful, a very peaceful place. It sat up high on a hill with the grapevines growing in blocks representing their own special community.

Going inside, they sampled some of the wines as they looked about the place. Sarge looked around to see if they might have beer and asked which wine she liked. The cabernet, with the unique, oak-wood flavors of vanilla and spice that complemented the natural Scuppernong grape with the flavors of red currant and tobacco, was what they chose. Sarge purchased the wine along with some cheese and crackers, and they sat outside under a pergola at a wood table in a beautiful and natural setting. It was like being in a Sung Kim Vineyard Terrace Painting.

"Carrie, I have to ask about what happened between you and Travis. Are you two dating? Do you still plan on seeing him?" Phil asked in earnest.

With the most sincere voice and looking directly into the Sarge's stupid-sunglass-covered eyes she said, "Sarge, I'm so sorry for what I allowed to happen that night with Travis. I am *truly sorry for hurting you.* Travis was a friend and I enjoyed his friendship. I am not interested in him other than as a friend. I would really like to—*just be with you,*" she said, looking down at her hands holding her wine glass, with her eyes tearing up and biting on her bottom lip.

Sarge reached over, took her hand, and brought it to his mouth, kissing it.

Looking up to his beautiful face, Carrie beheld his gorgeous smile.

"I just want to be with you, too," he confirmed it.

*He just wants me,* she thought. *OH, MY GOD!*

"So . . . you . . . forgive me?" she asked apprehensively.

"As far as I can see, there's nothing to forgive. We weren't exactly courting. Or were we?" he asked, baffled.

"Well, let's just start now, from this moment forward," she said with tears in her eyes that glistened in the sunshine.

He moved his hand to her right eye and caught the tear, just as it was falling. She moved her head to lean against his warm and gentle hand. Sarge leaned in and kissed her lips in the most adoring and sensual kiss he could apply.

*I love this man. I adore this man, but most important, I trust this man,* she declared to herself. Tears streamed down her face, and Sarge took out a white handkerchief and handed it to her. Wiping away at the drippage, she blew her leaky nose.

"I'll wash this before I give it back to you," Carrie said, choked up.

"Good."

They laughed, kissed—then kissed some more. The electricity between them could have lit up the vault of heaven.

Once they finished the food and wine, Sarge asked, "Ready to leave?"

"Yeah, about ten minutes ago," she replied as she got up quickly from the wooden picnic table.

The wind was blowing just right, a light warm breeze, as if angels' wings caressed the air, and she could feel her skirt gracefully flowing back and forth in the wind. Sarge was holding the small of her back as she walked slightly in front of him.

After Carrie climbed in, she allowed her skirt to rest a little higher on the thigh. She craved him. Carrie wasn't sure that she could hold off making love to him until they got home. It was going to be a long ride home otherwise.

As they were driving with the windows down, Carrie caught the breeze and her hair frenziedly moved about while the sunshine warmed her face. Phil hadn't reached the highway yet when he reached over, took her hand, kissed her palm, then kissed each finger and started sucking on her pinkie, biting at the tip. She was ready to explode when he released it.

Carrie reached over and stroked his thigh underneath his tight-fitting blue jeans. He let out a deep breath and pulled off onto a rocky cornfield road. Driving until they were surrounded securely by the cornfield on both sides of the truck, Sarge slowed down, stopped the truck—and that was it.

Not knowing if he was just getting out to take a piss, Carrie watched Sarge walk in front of the truck, open her door, move her legs through the door opening, and swiftly pull off her panties. He touched her face and kissed her mouth deeply, eagerly, while his other hand was already there.

As they were climaxing to the beat of "Don't Stop Believing" on the radio, Carrie's arm knocked the gearshift and put the truck in neutral. The truck started drifting.

Sarge looked up, "What the hell?"

"What?" and she saw the truck slowly moving away.

"Put it in park," yelled the Sarge.

"What—Oh, shit!"

Trying to get into a position to grab the gearshift, the truck's right front tire had already caught the ditch. She bounced about like a balloon in a hailstorm before the truck stopped abruptly when she was able to put it into park. The truck had moved about twenty feet before it hit the ditch and Sarge came up to her and asked, "Are you alright?"

"I'm so sorry."

"Are you alright?" he inquired again.

"Yeah, I'm fine. Did I hurt your truck?"

"It's a truck," he said, as he made certain she was okay and seated properly before closing her door. Sarge walked around the back and got into the driver's side door. He started the engine and reversed it out of the ditch without a problem.

"I'm sorry, Carrie, I never meant to put you in harm's way."

"What? *Are you kidding me?* I'm the one who put the truck in neutral. You were great. It's me who's sorry."

"Well, that sure did take the air out of our balloon so to speak," and she reached for her panties to put them back on.

"Carrie, if anything had happened to you, I—"

"Sarge, stop your worrying. My God, you're worse than an old lady," she said, rubbing her elbow.

He looked at her seriously and shook his head.

They drove in silence for a while, and she wrapped her arm around his bicep, kissing it and rubbing her face against it. She was wholly and without qualification falling deeply in love with this man.

Enjoying the moment, Sarge finally broke the silence. "Have you always had problems with cars?"

"What? Oh, I see, it took you awhile to think of something to give me shit about," and rolling her blue-gray eyes, she punched his arm. Carrie knew exactly what he was referring to, her speeding tickets, her car hitting the curb, and now this.

They both laughed out loud.

"Hey, Sarge."

"Yeah."

"I have to go to the restroom."

"OK, I'll see what I can do for you."

Seeing signs on the side of the road for both a gas station and a fast-food place, he pulled into the fast-food place.

Carrie got out and went into the eatery, and in the back, she found the ladies' room. When she finished up, she put water on her face, dried it, then took the perfume out of her purse and dabbed a little behind her ears and then onto her breasts.

Carrie readjusted her girls, fluffed her hair with the hand air-blower, reapplied a sexy shade of peach lip gloss with satisfaction, and she exited.

There was a commotion going on in the diner. People were standing up and kids were standing on their chairs, looking outside. Carrie was almost knocked over when a teenager brushed her aside as he tried to get a spot by the front door.

"What's going on?" she asked an older man who was looking between two other people.

"Looks like the gas station was bein' robbed 'cross the alleyway, ova' there."

"Really? What happened?" she asked, standing on her tiptoes to see if she could see anything.

"Heard a gunshot an' thought it might be a car backfirin' or sumthin'. Then I saw that there man wit' 'em sunglasses on, rushin' ova' to the robber wit' his pistol drawn."

"WHAT?" She pushed through the people and ran out the door.

"Don't go out there," she heard someone yell.

Carrie ran over to the gas station and saw the Sarge holding his left arm. He was shot, but he also had apprehended the robber.

Sarge, with the help of another big man who looked like a professional wrestler, handcuffed the dirty, thin, stringy-haired man. The wrestler guy kept watch on the robber as Carrie, breathless, ran over to Sarge.

The robber was wailing in pain.

"Are you alright?" Carrie started tearing up.

"Sugar, I'm fine. Go find out if anyone called the police," he said to distract her.

Someone heard Sarge say this and replied, "The police are on their way."

Carrie's nerves were jumping like water on hot oil.

"What in tarnation? I leave you for five minutes and look what happens to you."

Sarge smiled, but Carrie could see that he was in pain.

"Sarge, I want you to sit down on the curb, right here, while I go in and find something to wrap around your arm. *And you better not move*!" she declared.

Sarge sat down on the curb as directed while Carrie went into the gas station and asked the clerk for a towel or something. The young man behind the counter gave her a clean white rag.

Carrie told Sarge to let go of his arm and saw that it was a deep flesh wound. Her stomach turned forty going north, but she couldn't let him know. Tears were puddling in her eyes and she fought hard to hold them back.

She wrapped the white rag around his arm twice before tying it in a knot, but it didn't take long before it was filled with blood. Tears were streaming down her face like rain down a child's slide, as she could not hold them back any longer.

"Carrie, I'm alright. Take this money," he reached into his pocket, "and go get me something to drink, please."

"Only if you stay seated right here. Otherwise, I'm not leaving you." She wiped her tears with the white handkerchief Sarge had given her earlier and caught her runny nose.

"I'll stay right here until you get back."

Carrie left him reluctantly, and on the back wall, she found some white soda. She proceeded to the counter when the clerk asked if it was for the man with the sunglasses on who was shot. Carrie told him it was.

He said, "Take it."

When Carrie reached Sarge, the first police car arrived and then two more followed into the parking lot with lights and sirens a-blazing. One of the officers had come over to Phil and started asking him questions.

"Don't you drink anything," the police officer advised, as Carrie handed him the cold soda.

Phil identified himself as a sergeant of the Pheasant Mills police department. Carrie listened in and learned that he had seen something suspicious in his rearview mirror at the counter of the gas station, when a patron entering had left the door wide open. The patron was being distracted by his buddy, yelling at him about getting some things for their fishing trip while he filled up the small bass boat. Phil told the police officer that he had walked over behind one of the cars filling up with gas and told the owner to get into his car and stay low. Phil acted like he was the one filling up the car, and then, as the robber exited the store, he identified himself as the police with pistol drawn and told him to freeze.

Carrie heard Sarge continue saying, "Then that little sonofabitch pointed his weapon and took a shot, hitting me in the left arm."

Phil advised he was close enough to take a shot and hit the robber in the leg. He didn't want to kill him, as maiming was sufficient. With the assistance of the other guy, he was able to handcuff the robber when he fell to the ground.

The ambulance arrived promptly and the paramedics came straight over to Phil.

"I'm fine," Phil said, but the paramedics insisted that it would be best for them to take a look at it any way.

"It's either here or in the hospital and that's twenty miles away," Carrie heard one of the paramedics say.

Phil started unbuttoning his shirt. Carrie helped him take his good arm out of its sleeve and then the paramedic untied the blood-filled rag with his blue, gloved hands. Phil tenderly removed the other arm from the sleeve and grimaced the whole time he was doing this.

"Hey Carrie, why don't you sit down on the curb and let the paramedics do their thing," Sarge suggested.

"Oh, OK," and Carrie sat down putting her head in her hands.

There were two paramedics attending to Phil. As one checked his level of consciousness, alertness and awareness, asking him questions to determine his anxiety, the other was visually assessing his breathing, looking about his body, and checking his pulse rate and blood pressure.

Phil maintained his coolness and said, "I'm alright."

The paramedics continued doing their job, as they were more apprehensive about where the bullet might be. Taking Phil's good arm first, they started at the shoulder and finished at his fingers. Sarge squeezed his hand firmly and the paramedic attentively took the wounded arm, repeating the same process, only more cautiously.

The paramedics were trying to determine if it was just a flesh wound and whether the bullet had entered and exited cleanly. They checked the severity of the nerve damage affecting the functionality of the wounded arm and hand.

Carrie saw Sarge wince with pain. She didn't know if anyone else saw it, but she did.

The paramedics were busy talking to each other, assessing Phil's trauma and contemplating how serious the injury was.

A paramedic approached Carrie and advised that they were bringing him to the closest hospital and that she could follow behind them.

Phil was reluctant and suggested that they could get to a hospital quicker if they went down NC-264 and took him to Memorial Hospital on Eighth Street.

Looking sternly at the Sarge, Carrie's blue-gray eyes were slit like daggers as she was ready to growl out the words, "Let *them* take *you* to the closest hospital."

Then she heard one of the paramedics say, "You know that would probably be the closest hospital."

Carrie looked at Sarge, "I guess I'm going to have to drive your truck."

"Keys are in the ignition, sugar. Drive her safely, OK?"

She smiled a crooked smile at Sarge as the paramedics assisted him into the ambulance.

Starting the engine, Carrie was all out of kilter as she followed behind them.

Arriving at the hospital in less than twenty minutes, she parked the truck in a proper parking spot.

The paramedics took Phil in through the emergency room door and just like for Patty, Carrie was on her lonesome waiting for news.

The doctor scooted across the black-and-white tile floor, "Well, hello, again," he said as he recognized Carrie from her previous visit. "Sergeant Lament will be spending the night tonight. We want to run some more tests, CT scans and/or MRIs before a surgical treatment plan can be finalized. We still need to assess the tissue damage, control the bleeding, and prevent infections. We are not sure at this time as to the extent of the damage or if he will need skin grafts or not. His parents have been called and should be here shortly." Then he turned and left.

Carrie stayed until his parents arrived, recognizing them immediately as they approached the front desk. His mother was a tall, slender, very pretty woman. Her hair was black, shoulder-length, and she wore bangs. Her skin was perfect, and she noted that Sarge had her dark eyes. She was still in her nurse's uniform with her white nylons and white thick shoes. His dad, she would never have recognized. He was an inch taller than his Mom at best, with gray hair and a receding hairline, but Sarge had his mouth. He wore black-framed glasses and had on blue jeans and a black NC Tar Heel football T-shirt that displayed a protruding belly.

"Hi, Mr. and Mrs. Lament," she said, approaching them.

Mrs. Lament looked at Carrie first and said, "Hello."

"Hi, I'm Carrie Pyles, I was with Sarge—I mean, your son—when he was shot." She extended out her hand and gave them both a strong shake, receiving the same in return.

They identified themselves, Della and Gabe.

"Miss Carrie, can you tell us what happened?" asked his father.

They sat down as Carrie proceeded to tell them the story, starting from driving back from a Scuppernong winery. She didn't think they needed to know about Ossie and Cora.

His parents were holding one another tightly as Carrie told them the story. The ER nurse went to tell Dr. Orf that the Laments had arrived, and just as Carrie finished, he appeared.

"Hello, Miss Della," he said as he kissed her on the cheek and then addressed Gabe as they shook hands. "I'm sorry about seein' you under these circumstances. Your son is stable and we have him in a private room. We're goin' to keep him overnight for observation."

"Is he hurt bad?" Della asked with her voice quivering and tears in her eyes.

"Now, Miss Della, don't you go gettin' all blubbery on us. You know your son; he's complainin' 'bout takin' up space and insists on bein' released. We just want to run some more tests and scans before a surgical treatment plan can be finalized. We have the bleedin' under control and want to keep an eye out for infection. At this time, we're not sure of the damage or if he will need skin grafts or just stitches."

"Can we see him?" Della asked.

"Yes, I'll send a nurse to show you to his room."

"Thanks, David," said Della.

"Yeah, thanks David," said Sarge's dad, shaking the doctor's hand and patting him on the back.

Then Dr. Orf turned, hand-signaled to the ER nurse, and told her to show them to Phil's room.

"Well, it was nice meeting you," Carrie advised.

"What?" Gabe said. "Won't you be comin' along?"

"Um, well, I thought you two would like to have some time with him," Carrie said, trying not to intrude.

"Nonsense, I'm sure Phillie would want to see you too," said Della as she took Carrie by the arm.

"Now, don't let Phil hear you call him '*Phillie*', Momma. You know how he hates that."

They all chuckled as they walked behind the nurse.

Gabe was as polite as his son and opened the door for the ladies to enter first. Carrie saw him take out his handkerchief and wipe his forehead before he entered the room.

Della rushed to her son and hugged him hard, then kissed him on his forehead.

"How are you doin', my darlin'?" she said, and she kissed him again.

Phil was in a light blue nursing gown with an IV hooked into his good arm and his bad arm wrapped in gauze.

"Mom, I'm fine. I don't know why they just won't let me out of here. It's just a flesh wound."

"Honey, now, you listen to me and you let them do their business. They know what they're doin'."

Carrie stood back, watching his mom and dad fuss over Sarge. It was nice to see such a loving and caring family.

"Miss Carrie told us what happened," his father said.

Sarge looked directly at her when he said that.

"Yeah, I told them how we were coming back from a winery and I made you stop, so I could use a restroom," Carrie spoke up. *Good, now Sarge knows the start of the story.*

"Mom, Dad, you don't have to worry. I was just doing my job."

"Always on the job, no matter where you are," Gabe said.

"Well, you shouldn't have put your life on the line like that. You were off duty," Della said.

"Mom, now stop. If I hadn't have intervened, someone could have gotten hurt or killed."

"Yeah, like yourself," Della said, disheartened.

Taking Della's hand and bringing it to his mouth, Phil said, "Now Mom, you know what I do for a living."

"And I worry about you every day too," she said with tears in her eyes.

"Yeah, I know, Mom, and I love you too." With those words, her tears flowed without restraint.

"Hey, son, did you hear the Tar Heels beat Post 15–1 the other day? Barney played a good game, I'd say," Gabe said, trying to shift the ambiance the women brought into the room.

"Yeah, Dad, he had a good game."

"Oh honey, you look so tired," Della said.

"Yeah, I think the pain pills are starting to kick in."

"Well then, we're going to leave so you can get some sleep, but we'll be back tomorrow, bright and early."

"OK, Mom, Dad, thanks for coming by. Hey Carrie, can you stay for a minute?"

Miss Della gave her son another big hug and a few more kisses on his forehead. She was reluctant to leave. Gabe walked over to the door and waited for her. Slowly, Della eventually made it that way.

"If you need anything son . . ." Gabe said.

"Yeah, Dad, I'll let you know. Thanks," Sarge said, and they both left.

"You wanted me to stay? I can leave if you're tired."

"Carrie, I'm hoping to get out of here tomorrow. Will you please drive my truck back to your house . . . safely?" he said with a smile.

"Really? Worried about your truck? Really?" she teased.

"Well, I know how you drive," he said, slightly slurring his speech as his eyes grew heavy.

Rolling her eyes at him, Carrie said, "Those painkillers must be working because they're turning you into one big smartass."

He laughed, a tired laugh, but he laughed.

"Come here—Closer."

Carrie approached him as he tried to sit up to give her a kiss. Like a gentle wind, Carrie pressed him backwards and lightly kissed his lips. The drugs were really taking effect now. Sarge's eyes were too weighty to keep open.

"I'm going to go now and let you get some rest. I'll be back tomorrow."

"O…k," and just as Sarge was falling asleep, he said, "I…*you*."

***

Having slept like a buoy on a rocky ocean, after tossing and turning all night long, Carrie got up, washed up early, and went to the hospital. When she entered Sarge's room, he was not there. She looked in the bathroom but he wasn't there either. Leaving the room, Carrie approached a nurse and asked if she knew where Phil Lament was.

"I think they took him down to x-ray."

"Thanks," Carrie replied. She went back into his room just as his momma walked in. She looked the same as when Carrie had seen her yesterday, with the exception that Della now wore her black, shoulder-length hair pulled back in a bun today.

"Hi, Mrs. Lament, I just found out they took Phil to get an x-ray."

"Call me, Della, sweetie. Mrs. Lament is my husband's momma," and they both smiled at each other.

"I wonder how long that's going to take," Della said as she looked down at her watch. "I need to be at work in an hour."

"If you want, I can tell him you were here."

"Oh, I can wait a bit. They'll just have to understand. Family first. Right?"

"Yes, ma'am."

"Miss Della, may I ask you something?" Carrie was hesitant, but they were alone.

"Sure, Carrie, what do you need?"

"Well, you work at the nursing home with Miss Stacy Roosevelt, right?"

"Yes, Miss Stacy owns the place. She's 'bout ready to retire though. Why are ya' askin'?"

"I just wondered how long she's been in the business. It's been awhile, right?"

"Yeah, I'm thinkin' she took over the old business in the fifties? Do you know Miss Stacy?"

"No, ma'am, I do not. I know Miss Patty McMurphy and that Mr. Howard McMurphy, her husband, was arrested for kidnapping Miss Stacy's daughter, Lulu, back around 1940. I found some old newspaper articles on it, that's why I'm interested."

"I remember that. I was a youngin' when it happened."

"Really? Did you ever talk to Miss Roosevelt about it?"

"*No*, Miss Stacy is purely business. Sorry, sugar. Just to tell you one thing about Miss Stacy, you give her a dollar and she'd stretch it out to five dollars someway, somehow. Took me three years before I got a raise. She's pretty tightfisted with the money."

The door pressed open as a nurse pushed Sarge through in a wheelchair.

"Hey, Mom. Hey, Carrie. Been here long?"

Miss Della went over to her son and kissed his forehead as a good, caring mother would do.

"How are you feeling today, Phillie?" she asked very caringly.

"MOM—ughh."

"Oh, I'm sorry, sweetie. Are you still in pain?"

"No, Mom, I'm feeling better today. They took x-rays and determined there's no fragment of the bullet anywhere. They just want to make sure that an infection doesn't develop and may let me go home after they look at it again later this morning."

"What about a skin graft?"

"Mom, the plastic surgeon is coming by later this morning to take a look and decide."

"Do you want to come back to the house so I can take care of you?" Della asked.

"No, Mom, I'll be fine." Sarge replied as he turned his head towards Carrie and made a face.

"Sweetie, would you like a coffee or something to eat?" Sarge's mother, ever solicitous, persisted.

"Yeah, Mom, a black coffee would be great. Thanks."

"Can I get you one too, Carrie?"

"Oh no, that's OK. Thanks, Mrs. Lament . . . I mean *Della*."

Della smiled and said, "Well, OK, I'll be right back."

Carrie went over to Sarge's bedside and kissed him.

"Why don't you come home with me so I can take you care of you?" she said softly.

Without hesitation, Sarge agreed.

*Wow.* His quick response amazed her.

Carrie was determined to find out what she needed to do to take care of Sarge. When Della returned with the hot coffee,

Carrie excused herself and told them that she would be back in a bit. Carrie found a nurse at the station and asked her if she had a minute to talk about how to take care of Sarge's wound when he is released.

The nurse looked at his chart. "Oh, he should be out today, dependin' on what the plastic surgeon says. However, when he does get home, you'll need to change the bandages twice a day or more often, if they are wet with blood or fluid. He'll be on antibiotics for seven to fourteen days, so make sure that he takes all of his medicine. Keep his arm in a sling for a week *or two*. After that, he'll need to do physical therapy, with just light weight-liftin' exercises a couple times a day. He will probably be sore because that muscle needs to heal. That could take up to six months or more. If he's in pain at any time, just control it with ibuprofen, naproxen, or Tylenol. You'll have to watch out for infection though. Gunshot wounds are dirty and if there's goin' to be an infection, it would show within ten days of the injury, showin' up as a red, warm area 'round the wound, more painful too. It could possibly pus up and could cause your man a fever, where he may end up back here if not careful. So basically, sugar, keep your eye on him and make sure that he doesn't overdo it."

"Yes, ma'am, I'll take good care of him. Thank you."

Upon returning to the room, the plastic surgeon, a clean-shaven man in his late thirties, was there informing Sarge that the stitches looked good and he didn't feel that grafting was necessary unless he was vain and then he could work on him to make him look purty again.

"I'm not vain," he smirked at the surgeon. "I just want to leave. Can I go? Can I get out of here today?"

"I'll talk to your doctor, but I'd say you're good to go."

"Cool," Sarge said as he started to get out of bed, and before he could place one leg on the floor, the surgeon retorted.

"Now hold on, bucko, I didn't say you could leave right now. Let your doctor come in and do his once over. You know the procedures. There's paperwork that needs to get finished up first. I'll go find him and let him know."

"This one here's as anxious as a caught critter in a cage," the surgeon said to Carrie as he walked past her to the door, shaking his head and smiling.

It wasn't long before Sarge was released and driving back to Grandma Hattie's house, but not before walking all around the truck to make sure that it was still in good shape.

"You *dog*!" Carrie said, shaking her head as she watched Sarge inspect his truck.

He climbed into the driver's side and used his right arm to shut the door.

"I can drive," she said, knowing exactly what his response would be.

"I know how you drive," he said, starting the engine and smiling that beautiful smile.

"Well, OK, then let's go home."

# Chapter 16

"I need to go to my place to pick up some things, but I'll pick you up at the store around 5 p.m.," Sarge said as he signaled the left turn towards the yarn store. "If you need me sooner, all you have to do is call."

"But I thought I would take today off and help you . . . if you need it."

"Carrie, I'm fine. You have a business to run and you can't be taking more time off than you need to."

"Did the doctor give you some time off for being shot?"

"Yeah, they gave me a week or two off. Doc wants me to go back next week to see how it's healing."

*Oh good, I have him for at least a week,* Carrie thought to herself.

Phil went back to Carrie's house after picking up some bits and pieces from his place and stopping in at the Stop and Shop to buy food and beer. It was early afternoon when he reached the house and brought in the items. After putting the food away, he popped open a soda and sat at the kitchen table, slowly and scrupulously taking items one by one out of Agnes' box and examining each piece to identify the reasons that Agnes chose to hang onto them.

He found child drawings, hand-painted prints, little empty porcelain boxes, snuff box, comb and brush set, pieces of old jewelry, old vintage watch, old corsage flowers, and several journals. Upon taking out the first journal, the one that sat on top of the others, Phil opened it. Sitting back and sipping on his cold soda, he read:

*Aug. 11, 1939*
*Miss Theo visited the UNC College in Chapel Hill. The Dean and she are a little more than kissy and touchy if you ask me. She says she's interested in their law school and wants to contribute to the new law library. She can be generous when she wants to be. It's sad that I haven't seen a raise in some years.*

*Aug. 19, 1939*
*Lydia and Patty are up to something. I heard them talking together when I went into Patty's room and then they stopped. If Lydia wasn't so protective of Patty, I'd be knowing what's going on. I don't think Lydia trusts me. She's getting more troubled every day. I see her mind go on and off like some kitchen light switch with the bulb about ready to pop. She acts like one person and then another and it scares me when she acts like Miss Theodosia.*

*Aug. 27, 1939*
*Miss Theo is all worked up with the party. Responses to all the invites haven't been returned yet and responses were due yesterday. There she is . . . she's calling for me again.*

*Sept. 1, 1939*
*Getting ready for Miss Theo's 'End of Summer' party that she hosts every year for the important town folk. You'd think after 19 yrs. I'd get to have the day off. Isn't it called Labor Day?*

*Sept. 9, 1939*
*Miss Theo just learned that Patty eloped with Howard McMurphy, several towns over on Wednesday, Sept. 6. I remember this because it was a half-moon that night. She was fit to be tied. I stayed away as I heard her cussing, breaking things and having a conniption fit. Patty*

*was just out of school and Miss Theo thought her to be too young to be married, but to a Tar Heel worker made it even worse. When she called out to me, I just grabbed me a broom and started sweeping. I never looked up at her. I know what she was like when she got mad. The girls, Lydia and Patty, left on Tuesday to go somewhere and said they'd be back by the weekend. I heard whispers that Patty was thinking about marrying Howard and Lydia was excited as all get up. But I'd never tell Miss Theo. No Sir, I was smart enough to know better.*

*Sept. 14, 1939*
*Miss Theo is up in arms and is planning something. I can hear her talking to herself and swearing at Howard McMurphy, and saying "that no good piece of tar crap is going to get away with this." She paces a lot. I try to stay away but she keeps calling me. She says she has to get out of the house and ask me to drive her. I just start driving in no particular direction and I tell her we need to get gas. Miss Theo saw a little girl walking along the street. She's dirty and wearing old worn clothes with holes in the knees of her pants. I pull into the gas station to get the car filled up. Miss Theo gets out of the car, walks up to the little girl and hands her something.*

*Sept. 17, 1939*
*Something is up Miss Theo's crawl. She got up early to go to church—Church! Don't know last time that happened. I looked around when we entered, didn't know if the Good Lord was to strike us down or not. I see the Roosevelts and that little girl sitting at a bench. When church was over, Miss Theo told me to go get the car, but she stayed back and went on talking to the Roosevelts.*

*Sept. 21, 1939*
*Something strange going on here. Miss Theodosia never drives herself anywhere. Too dignified! But she had me to go get her the car*

*keys and said that she needed to drive herself. Where she needs to go by herself? Must be important. . . or she's hidin' somethin'.*

Phil kept reading the journal and looked around for paper and pen to make notes. Finding both, he proceeded to write down:

- Patty and Howard McMurphy eloped around 9/6/39
- Theo drove herself 9/21/39—alone—where?
- Has a relationship with the Dean at UNC in Chapel Hill—meeting 8/11/39—Did she contribute to the law library?

This tugged at Phil's curiosity due to the holes in Agnes' story, so he dug in even deeper and continued reading. He soon stumbled upon an interesting entry.

*Oct. 8, 1939*
*Mr. Wesley came home from the mills today. He and Miss Theo got into a huge spat. The mills weren't doing well and Miss Theo was still out spending money and doing this and that. Mr. Wesley told her that he was worried that he would have to close another plant. That, Mr. Wesley didn't like. He didn't want to put people out of work. The workers had families and Mr. Wesley was concerned for their well-being. Miss Theo said she didn't care about any of them. That's right, cause Miss Theo never cared about anyone but herself. Wonder what's going to happen to me if they close down another one of their plants?*

*Oct. 13, 1939*
*No sooner than Mr. Wesley left the house and went back to the mill, Miss Theo was in bed with Abraham Twiford. He comes round here a lot and Miss Theo ask me to go to the market or do some nonsense running for her. She acts like I don't know what's*

*going on. I don't say a word. It's none of my business, but I know what's going on.*

*Oct. 22, 1939*

*Miss Theo had me drive her to the college again. I stayed out in the hall while she was in the Dean's office talking. The door wasn't closed all the way and I heard them talk about a young man named Victor Abbott. The Dean says he's the best lawyer in school and made the best grades. Not sure why they're talking about him. I see the Dean escorting Miss Theo down the hall to show her how the library's coming along. She told me to sit and wait.*

*Oct. 29, 1939*

*Miss Theo had me take her to that gas station again. Why she like this gas station? It's not on our side of town. I pass a few other gas stations just to get to this one. Makes no sense. I see a young man and Miss Theo talking. What are they talkin' about? He's not someone that Miss Theo would ever talk to. They talk and he shakes her hand. Why does he shake Miss Theo's hand? I seen her wipe her hand on a handkerchief she took from her purse as she walked back to the car.*

*Nov. 1, 1939*

*The Good Lord himself has taken hold of Miss Theodosia. Unbeknownst to anyone, she had me call Patty up and extend an invitation to Howard and her to attend dinner. Miss Theo had asked me to make a special dinner for Howard and Patty, extending a kind offer to get to know Howard better. Miss Theo must have been taking Lydia's special drugs. She was paying special attention to Howard, but gave Patty the warm reception when they came over. Miss Lydia was so excited to see Patty and Howard and was still acting like their Matron of Honor. Miss Theo walked into the kitchen to check on dinner, when Lydia started talking about Patty's wedding. As they sat down to dinner, Miss Theo started asking*

*Patty about grandbabies and even about Howard's job. Lydia started to get so excited over Miss Patty having children, that Miss Theo had me take Miss Lydia back to her room. When I returned, Miss Theo was holding her own. She hated Tar Heel workers and thought they were the scum of the earth. I saw her look away one time when Howard was telling her about his work and she coughed as if disgusted by the taste of the conversation. She turned to Patty and started a conversation in the midst of Howard's conversation. Miss Theo was being very unreceptive to Howard but trying her best to be nice, which was impossible for her. Miss Patty said that she had an interview at a petroleum company in Bladen County, on Tuesday, Nov. 21. I hope she does well. She's such a good person, but not overly confident in herself. Miss Patty was so happy that her momma had invited her over for dinner and showed niceness to Howard. Miss Theo even asked Howard and Patty over for Thanksgiving dinner. Miss Patty hugged me on the way out and thanked me for calling.*

*Nov. 12, 1939*

*Miss Theodosia invited Miss Patty and Howard over for dinner again. She asked Howard what his family does for Thanksgiving. Howard said that he goes to his parent's house. Patty said that Howard makes the best mashed potatoes on this side of the river and that his aunt makes the absolute best pecan pie. Miss Theo said that we would have to invite her to dinner so she could get a taste of this pecan pie, but Howard said that his mother goes to her cousins in Raleigh every Thanksgiving. I don't know why Miss Theo wants to eat her pecan pie, mine is pretty darn good and I've been making it for Thanksgiving Day since I've been here. I haven't had any complaints.*

*Nov. 21, 1939*
*Mr. Howard was arrested today for kidnapping the little Roosevelt girl, Lulu, they call her. I know Mr. Howard and he's a good honest, honorable man. I don't believe that he would kidnap anyone. Why are the police saying that he kidnapped Lulu? I hear Miss Theo, she's happy today. Why is she so happy today? Patty is here and crying up a storm. She doesn't understand why her husband is being arrested for kidnapping. Miss Lydia is comforting Patty where Miss Theo should be. They say that Mr. Howard kidnapped the girl down the road from the gas station that we had went to on the other side of town that no one goes to. I wonder if something comes about when I brought Miss Theo there. Why was Howard in that area? I wonder if Miss Theo sent him there for something. Why would he kidnap Lulu?*

*Nov. 24, 1939*
*Patty came by the house yesterday for Thanksgiving, crying and all upset because Howard is in jail. She begs her mother to help her find a good lawyer. Miss Theo tried to comfort her but she's like a fish out of water. She can't even hug right, straight arm and stiff shoulder. But she did agree to find a lawyer for her. Maybe she's coming around.*

Phil pondered the dairy entries. *Sure does seem that Howard was set up. Why was Howard in that area? Why did he go there?* He continued writing on his list. First stop was going to be the gas station, second stop was going to be the Roosevelts, and the third was to talk to Victor Abbott.

He decided to take a drive to the infamous gas station where everything seemed to have started. The gas station was out of his jurisdiction as a police officer. The owner, Tommy Reeves, was not working that day, but a younger man named Donald was. Phil explained that he was a Pheasant Mills sergeant and was reinvestigating Howard McMurphy's case due to new evidence found.

Donald was several years younger than Tommy and didn't know too much about it, only what the rumors were 'round town.

"Well, what were the rumors that you heard?" Phil asked.

"Just what everybody knows, that Howard McMurphy kidnapped a little girl out in front of the gas station, and just down the street a few miles, the police caught him with the girl," said Donald.

"Did you ever hear anyone talking about what they may have seen, or heard, or anything strange that happened at that time?" Phil asked.

"Only thing strange was that sum'how Tommy got an inheritance an' bought this place from his parents when he was just twenny-one. He's had this place fer 'while now. Weird that he got an inheritance an' his olda' sista', Karyn, dinn't get much, if anythin'."

"Tommy has a sister, Karyn?" Phil asked. "Does she still live around here?"

"Naw, she's married an' moved out of state. Tommy's parents have pass' on too an' Karyn's the only kin he has left."

"Did Tommy ever marry?"

"Yeah, he'd married TerriLee, but they broke up 'long time 'go. Dinn't get married 'gain, but lives wit' Melissa Turner. Been livin' wit' her fer 'while down the road."

Phil continued taking several notes. He would investigate Tommy Reeves, TerriLee Reeves, and Melissa Turner. Then he asked, "What about the regular customers that are older in age that come in? Say around—sixty to eighty years of age?"

Donald only knew of a few in the area and gave out their names. Phil continued looking around the store and saw the old, black pay phone still hanging on the wall and made a note of the displayed phone number and telephone company name.

He called into the police station and got the address for Tommy Reeves and the older people within the area. When he called the telephone company, after hearing loud laughter and being asked if this was a joke, he was advised that the records were removed or deleted a long time ago.

Phil scrutinized the older people of the immediate area and no one really remembered the Roosevelt family except one, Jerry Richards.

Jerry lived in a house about two miles from the gas station. He was old, in his seventies perhaps, and raised his family there in the same house for over fifty years. His house was worn and in serious thirst for a new coat of paint, but the yard was kept up and the garden was free of weeds. Jerry was outside working in the yard and wiped his brow with a red bandana when Phil pulled into the driveway.

"Hey, ya'll, kin I help ya' wit' sumthin'?"

"Are you Jerry Richards?"

"Shur am. Who's askin'?"

"I'm Sergeant Phil Lament with Pheasant Mills police department. If you have the time, I just have a few questions about an old closed case regarding Howard McMurphy."

"Oh, I knew Howard . . . way back when."

"Oh, yeah? Can you tell me about him?" Phil asked and let Jerry converse.

"Howard's a good man. Wrongfully 'cused if ya' ask me. I met him at the gas station sev'ral years befo' the kidnappin'. He'd buy his smokes there too. Our first meet-up was when my brown, '38 Ford Woody Station Wagon radiata' was overheatin' an' Howard opened up the hood an' turned the cap by rollin' down his sleeve, coverin' his hand. The dang thin', heat an' steam was comin' off the engine an' blowin' all ova' the place like it was 'bout to ketch fire. Howard dinn't fear nothin' an' neva' wanted anythin' for his help. He did let me buy him a beer once." Jerry stopped to wipe his forehead with his red handkerchief. "I neva' thought he's a man that woud've kidnapped that lil' girl, Lulu, from the gas station down yonda'. I always ba'lieved he was innocen'. Why ya' comin' 'round now askin' 'bout him?"

"I found some old articles about him and things just don't make sense to me," Phil replied. "So, can you tell me what you do remember? What happened that day?"

"Well, if my mem'ry serves me right, Lulu used to walk these streets ev'n as a little girl an' I wonda' why she's neva' tak'n befo' then? Parents dinn't pay much 'tention to her an' Lulu was always dirty, in old worn-out clothes. My wife, Markita, when she was wit' the livin', bless her soul, used to brin' 'em food an' clothes that the kids grew out of down to where they's lived. The missus' was a kind heart, she was. Lulu's fatha', Percy, was a scrawny drunk that worked wit' the stills' 'n runnin' the shine." Jerry stopped for a moment and took a spit before he continued.

"The motha' Stacy was a nice lady. Heard she got a job as a nurse. Not shur where's they get the money to go to nursin' school, since they'd were so poor they'd have to borra' money to buy wata' to cry wit'. But it wann't much afta' Howard's trial that they comes 'nto money. Always thought that was strange, I did. Jus' like Tommy Reeves, right afta' Howard's sennencin' comes down, they'd both seem to be doin' betta' than theys' were befo' the trial. I'm not sayin' that it wann't 'onest or anythin'. I don't mean to be spreadin' no tales, but ev'ryone knows that Tommy was walkin' 'round wit' fists full of money an' sum'how Stacy Roosevelt got 'nough money to go to nursin' school. Why we's put our youngest dawta' Bonnie through nursin' school an' it cos' us a purty penny. Would'ave liked to knows how she done it, that's all."

"Did you know who Miss Theodosia Eden-Worth was? Did you happen to see her at the gas station?"

"Well, ya' know, now that ya' say it, yeah, I do rememba' seein' her there a few times. I thought she was promotin' sumthin' 'cause that's when ya' caught wind of her, when she's displayin' herself fer supportin' sumthin'. Ya' know fer parades and gran' openin's like at banks or stores. One time I ev'n saw that she had driv'n herself to the gas station. By an' large she'd been driv'n there, 'cause I see 'er lady driva' sittin' 'n the car. Neva' knew why she'd stop 'n there. Not on 'er side of town, ya' know."

"Did you go to that gas station often?"

"Yeah, when I's a smoka', I go fer smokes an' chew, jus' 'bout ev'ry day, but I quit when Markita, my wife, died. She'd get on me 'bout my's smokin' an' spittin', but I'd jus' goes outside to not o'fend 'er. Gotta keep the lil' woman happy, ya' know."

Phil nodded, then asked. "Did you know the Reeves family then?"

"Ya', I knew 'em *alright*. They's good people. They found a place 'n the mountains an' was talkin' 'bout movin' there befo' they'd let their son Tommy buy the place. He wann't a bad kid or anythin', jus' got a lil' of hisself when he got an 'heritance an' bought the store from 'em. I'd joke 'round wit' 'em that they'd miss all the action at their place when Howard was a'rested."

"Did Tommy have a sister?"

"Yeah, I knows Miss Karyn, she's his olda' sista'. She's the only kin Tommy's got left. Miss Karyn married my oldest son, Haas. Ya' know theys courted fer 'while 'n school. Then whens Haas got work at a mill ova' 'n Raleigh, theys got married an' left town. He's 'n St. Louis now workin' for sum' big comp'ny there. Doin' well fer thesselves an' ev'n have a couple of the gran'kids theres too. They's all grown up now an' doin' their own thin'. The kids, whens they first got married, use to come home 'round Thanksgivin' on the bus to visit. I'd picked them up right there at the bus stop jus' up from the gas station. Howard would drive his Aunt Jessica an' park on the side of the road an' sum'times we'd just sit there an' wait fer the bus to come."

Phil tried to regroup Jerry back into the conversation. "Hey Jerry, do you know if Miss Karyn got any of the inheritance that Tommy got?"

"Aw, um, I'd ask her once then she'd turned the talk on me. She dinn't say Yea or Nay, so I neva' asked 'gain. But'cha bet she dinn't get much if she did. Karyn did pay fer her bus'ness schoolin' though. She got 'nto a typin' pool, when they first got married, befo' the kids came 'long. Ya' wanna drink or sumthin'?" Jerry asked.

"No thanks, Jerry. Do you remember the time of day when the kidnapping happened?"

Jerry snorted, breathing noisily and forcefully, making a disturbing sound, before spitting on the ground and wiping his mouth off on his sleeve.

"Wells, I rememba' that it's gettin' dark, so it was 'bout dusk when it happened. As I was sayin', Lulu's fatha' was a drunk, an' when the missus was gone doin' whateva', Lulu ran 'round the streets. Ya' knows theys dinn't live fer from the gas station. Lulu ran 'round the woods an' streets a lot, always had a lil' doll 'n her arms. I'm surprise she dinn't get picked up soona', if the truth be known."

"So it happened around dusk," Phil replied. "The week of Thanksgiving, huh? Did any of your kids or grandkids come into town on the bus that Thanksgiving?"

"Oh, theys came 'n the Weds'day befo' Thanksgivin' that year, but Howard would brin' his Aunt Jessica there on Tuesday, *always* on the Tuesday befo' Thanksgivin'. She made the best pecan pie an' wanna get there early so she could make it fresh the day befo'. Jessie made me one once an' I do declare it was the *absolute best* pecan pie. I told my wife Markita that an'—"

Phil looked at his watch, "Hey Jerry, sorry for interrupting, but I've got some other things I have to do and I really need to leave. I really appreciate your time. It was nice meeting you.

Would you mind if I come by to visit you again?" Phil reached his hand out to shake Jerry's hand.

"Shur, stop on by any time. Got nuttin' else ta' do."

Phil had taken in a lot of information from Jerry. More than Jerry even realized he had given.

He recaptured, every Tuesday before Thanksgiving Howard brought his Aunt Jessica to the bus stop. That would have put him right there at the gas station on the day of his arrest. Lulu Roosevelt was unattended many times, walking the streets, dirty and in worn clothes. It placed the child in a dangerous situation. Jerry saw Theodosia at the store several times that could lead to a relationship with Tommy and Karyn. Tommy and Stacy Roosevelt came into money after Howard's trial, so Theodosia could have paid them off. But what about Eschammer? Was he in on it too? Phil wondered. Remembering when he did the tape interview with Eschammer, he was hesitant to go into a lot of detail about the incident, but he did state that the father just stayed at the car when the mother was going crazy.

Phil decided to visit his mom at the nursing home and see if she had heard talk or anything, ever, about the kidnapping.

Phil walked into the building and went to the front desk where nurses Devon and Julie were standing and talking. These were older women that Phil had known since his mom started working there.

"Hey, Phillie, how are ya' doin', sweetheart?" said Devon, the older but shorter of the two. She had dark black hair wrapped in a bun on top of her head and wore bright red lipstick that matched her red top and white polyester pants.

"Phil Lament, wha'cha doin' here? Ya' gave 'ur momma such a fright, when she caught wind you got shot. She was besides herself. Don't ya' put her through that ev'r again," Julie said.

Julie was taller, with cherry-red hair pulled in a ponytail. She wore pink scrubs and with no makeup on, was naturally pretty.

"Do either of you fine ladies know where my mom is?"

"I'll go find her for ya', sweetheart. Ya' don't go anywhere now," said Nurse Julie as she shook her right index finger at him.

Phil stood there and made conversation with Nurse Devon. She was asking about his gunshot wound and if he was taking time off work to heal, when he spotted Stacy Roosevelt talking to an older man in the middle of the hallway.

"Sorry, Devon, but who is Miss Stacy talking to over there?"

Devon stretched her neck, peering down the hallway, and saw Mrs. Roosevelt talking to a thin, scrawny old man wearing too-big blue jeans and an old white chambray button shirt. She said, "Oh sugar, that's her husband, Percy."

"Really? What do you know about Percy?"

"Not too much. Miss Stacy doesn't want us talkin' to him an' has reprimanded me fer just bein' nice to him. I offered him a donut one mornin' an' she berated me for doin' it. I don't unnerstand, but I need the job, so I do what I'm told. Why are ya' innerested 'n Mr. Percy, sugar?"

Phil saw that Percy was parting the conversation and Miss Stacy walked off in a different direction, so he took the opportunity to approach him.

"Excuse me, Devon," he said as he walked away.

"Mr. Percy Roosevelt?" he asked.

"Yeah."

"You got a minute? Can I have a word with you?"

"Um, does I knows ya'?" Percy asked exhaustedly, as if needing more sleep than he'd seen in many days.

He reached out his hand. "I'm Sergeant Phil Lament with the Pheasant Mills police department."

"Yeah," Percy shook his hand like a wet, dead fish, with no muscle vigor at all. "Wha'cha want?"

"How about if we go over here," Phil said as he walked him to a corner opposite the front desk. He did not want to be overhead. There was a fake tree in a light brown wicker basket in the corner and they stood next to that.

"Well, Mr. Roosevelt, I wanted to ask you about something that happened a while ago. It was about your daughter Lulu being kidnapped by Howard McMurphy."

"Ya' sorry, Serg'nt, but I's gotta get gettin'. Gots sumthin' I needs ta' do fer the missus," Percy said, nervously fidgeting with his hands in his pockets.

Percy turned to make a quick exit, but Phil stopped him in midstream by grabbing his arm.

"Mr. Percy, you're not leaving here until I get some answers about Howard McMurphy and that kidnapping. If you don't talk to me here, I'll find a reason to bring you into the department," Phil said tersely.

"Well, do's wha'cha have to, but I knows my rights an' I don't have to talk wit' ya'."

"What are you afraid of?" Phil's curiosity was piqued.

Percy grew more jumpy now, like a bitch in heat in a pen full of male dogs. "Why's ya' brin'in' up sumthin' that's done gone dead 'n the wata'? Howard's dead, inn't he? Cain't brin' him back now, can ya'?"

"No sir, we can't. But I know some things. I know that Miss Theodosia Eden-Worth and your family had several conversations. I know that you were dirt-poor before Howard's trial, and then, miraculously, afterwards you came into some money. How did your wife find the money to go into nursing school? I also know that you work the stills in the mountains and I can visit you there if you'd like. I think I have some friends that may have an interest in closing you down."

"Now, don't get'cha unnerwear 'n a bunch. I cain't talk here, ya' unnerstand," Percy said with breath that could melt cabbage.

"Fine, where you want to meet at? Don't even think about getting away from me, I know who you are," Phil said confidently.

Percy was visibly shaking by this time, like a drunk missing his drink.

"How 'bout at mile marka' 87.2. Take a left there an' then go down a rocky road 'bout a half mile 'nto the woods. I'll mee'cha there 'n fi'teen minutes."

"You better be there in fifteen minutes or I'll come looking for you," Phil said, watching Percy travel a minute in thirty seconds out the front door.

Della finally appeared, beating her feet toward her son. "Hey, honey, what are you doing here? Is everything OK? Are you feeling OK? You're not in any pain are you?" She gave her son a kiss on his cheek.

"Relax, Mom, I'm fine. I just came by to talk to you, but now I have to go. I just wanted to thank you for coming to the hospital." He had to think of something quick because he had not considered running into Percy Roosevelt here.

"Oh honey, you know we love you, and your dad and I will always be there for you. Are you sure you're alright?" she asked, concerned.

"Yeah Mom, I'm fine. Sorry I can't stay longer," and Phil gave her a hug and a kiss. "I really have to go now."

"Bye Phillie. Ya' take care of that arm now," Devon said as she watched Phil go for the door.

"It was good to see ya' again. Don't be a stranga'," Julie chimed in.

Phil wasn't that far behind Percy who drove like he talked, slow and tired. Making a left at mile marker 87.2 into the gray dust cloud that Percy had left behind, he pulled behind Percy's old 1981 black Monte Carlo and parked. Percy was already standing outside his car, pacing back and forth as he lit up a cigarette. His hands were trembling.

Phil approached Percy and asked, "OK, Mr. Percy, we're alone now. So what can you tell me about your daughter's kidnapping?"

# Chapter 17

**The** breeze was blowing cheerlessly and the leaves on the ground were rustling with the critters moving about in the woods. A threatening sky was in the distance, but it was not raining . . . yet.

Percy paced about, smoking his cigarette, and Phil displayed patience. He stood there before he broke the silence again.

"So Percy, what can you tell me about your daughter's kidnapping?"

"Are ya' recordin' this? Ya' wearin' a wire?" Percy asked with a quivering voice.

"No, I'm not recording this conversation. Percy how about if you start by telling me your relationship with Miss Theodosia Eden-Worth?"

"Oh, that bitch. Wells—did ya' know Miss Theodosia?"

"Can't say I had the privilege."

"Oh, it wounn't bin' no priv'lege, I a'sure ya'. Whens she gets 'er claws 'n ya', they stick an' she don't let go, like a red-headed turkey vulture." Percy made a claw-like motion with his hand, gritting his decaying teeth.

"So tell me how Theodosia got her claws into you then."

"Ya' giv' me 'ur word, ya' won't come afta' my family doin' anythin' lawful 'gainst us."

"I give you my word," Phil replied.

"Well, the missus an' I weres not wells off, if ya' knows wha' I mean, down on our luck an' purty much penniless. I kin

’onestly say I wann’t a good fatha’ wit’ Lulu growin’ up as a youngin’. The missus would leave durin’ the day to find sum’ work, an’ I’d lay down on the couch an’ Lulu’d kinda ’tend to herself. The child be outside playin’ an’ wonda’ off through ’em woods an’ head ova’ to the gas station. Then one day Miss Theo gives a note to our lil’ Lulu when she’s saw her walkin’ ’bout an’ said she’d like to meet wit’ us. Dunno how she finds out wheres we goes to church at, but she shows up one Sun’ay an’ in’duces ’erself. She’s all dress’ up real nice wit’ her jewels an’ all. Ev’ryone knows of ’er wealth an’ ev’rythin’. Made an ’mpression, if ya’ knows wha’ I mean. Missus was tak’n by Theo’s fanciness, so’s all the otha’s fer that matta’. When the church folks saws us talkin’ to her, we’s starts gettin’ food an’ clothin’ like we’s imporan’ or sumthin’. Theys mus’ve thought that if Miss Theodosia Ed’n-Worth was innerested ‘n us, maybe theys shou’ be too. That dinn’t last long; thin’s went back to the ways it was befo’. Anyways, Miss Theo ev’n drove herself to our place afta’ stoppin’ ‘n the gas station an’ met up wit’ Tommy, she said. She brawt us food, whiskey, an’ gave the missus a swanky red dress too that we’s could neva’ ’ford. She ev’n brought Lulu a bran’ new toy doll that she tooks ev’rywhere wit’ her. The child loved that doll, she did. She’d cry if you’d take it ’way from ’er.”

“So Miss Theodosia sounds like she treated you real nice.”

“Yea’, ’til she’s needin’ a fava’.”

“She asked you for a favor? When was that?”

“Well, if ya’ knows or ev’n if ya’ don’t, she dinn’t take to Howard McMurphy too much an’ dinn’t like him marryin’ her youngin’ dawta’, Miss Patty, eitha’. Ya’ know theys ran ’way’n got hitched three towns ova’, jus’ to do it wit’out ’er momma knowin’. I kin only says Theo’s spittin’ bullets when she found out. I knew Lydia—she’s a hoot, inn’t she,” Percy said, trying to change the conversation, moving about, and trying to light up another cigarette with a match that kept blowing with the shaking of his hand.

"Percy, right now I'm interested in your connection with Miss Theodosia and Howard's kidnapping of your daughter. What was the favor she asked you to do?" Phil's growing frustration started to show as he took the matches from Percy's hand and struck a good light on the first strike, lighting the cigarette and shoving the matches back into Percy's top pocket.

"Yea', OK, well, she'd come by our place a couple of times befo' askin' fer a fava'. Sup'ose she was butterin' our biscuit when's she brawt us more food, an' the missus a pair of fancy shoes that went wit' the dress she'd giv' her. Ev'n gave Lulu some new toys to play wit'. The missus was smit'n by all's her swankiness, an' she wanna be s'essful like her. That's *all* the missus would talk 'bout fer days afta' 'er visits."

"What was the favor Theodosia asked you for?" Phil tried to get Percy back on subject.

"Well, one day Miss Theo comes to the door an' she's all'n tears wit' her dawta' bein' unhappy wit' Howard's drinkin' an' beatin' Patty up. Says he's abusin' her an' ev'rythin'. Theo made a big fuss of it to the missus too. Theo said she had to get those two apart, but that whens she talked to her dawta', 'n that Patty just says they'd work thru' their prob'ems. The missus has a good heart 'n there sumwhere, an' she get cawt up wit' Miss Theo's ova'ly display of weepin' an' says she'd help Miss Theo out, entrustin' herself to wha'eva' Theo wanted. Now befo' I says an'more, ya' *gave me ya' word* that ya' won't go afta' my family fer an'thin' wit' wha's I's 'bout to say. I wan' that *'munity* thin', so's you cain't hurt my family. If ya' agree, I's tells ya' ev'rythin'," Percy said, dropping his shoulders as if a bag of rocks was about to be lifted.

Percy stood there waiting for Phil to respond.

He thought for a moment and guaranteed Percy that he wouldn't go after his family. The wind had picked up with the leaves energetically bouncing across the rocky path but all of a sudden, as if the trees told them to stop and listen, it grew quiet and still all around.

Percy lit another cigarette, spit on the ground and proceeded to tell the whole story.

"Well, wen's Miss Theo was there talkin' to the missus 'bout how to sep'rate Patty from Howard, I stays 'n the back drinkin' a cold beer she'd brawt ova'. They's doin' the talkin' at the kitch'n table. Miss Theo was cryin' an' blabberin' 'bout how Howard was beatin' her dawta'. Missus was clearly troubled ova' wha' Miss Theo was sayin' an' took Miss Theo's hands an' asked how she kin' help. Miss Theo seemed to calmed down a lil' afta' that, an' says that the only way, otha' than killin' Howard, which she counn't do as a *good Christian woman*, was to keep him 'way from Patty by puttin' him 'n jail. Missus says she'd call the police to report Howard was beatin' her dawta' Patty, but Miss Theodosia said that wounn't work 'cause Patty would deny it. Patty was takin' wit' him an' would stick by his side no matta' how many bruises he put on her body. It had to be sumthin' that Patty cain't be 'nvolved 'n, she says."

"And what were you doing when they were discussing this at the table?"

"I goes ou'side to have a smoke an' left Missus an' Theo 'lone. I dinn't want to be part of anythin' theys were plannin'. I knew not to trust Miss Theo. She was a snake 'n the grass waitin' to strike. I tried tellin' the missus that, but she won't list'n."

"Is that when they made their plan to kidnap your daughter at the gas station?"

"Yea', theys made a plan fer Missus to brin' Lulu to the gas station the Tuesday befo' Thanksgivin'. So, I's drive her ova' there an' she gives me sum' money to put gas inna' tank, so I get it goin'. It's 'bout gettin' dark an' I's rememba' the bus had jus' pulled up."

"So when the bus pulled up, what were you and the missus doing?"

"The missus told me to get 'nto the car an' we drove off as Howard pulled 'n, leavin' Lulu on the stoop cryin'."

"You and your wife just left your daughter crying outside by herself?"

"Uh-huh, shur did. I sees the missus's holdin' Lulu's doll that she wounn't go an'wheres wit'out. Lulu just sat there cryin' sittin' on that stoop. Missus told 'er to sit there, like she bein' punished fer sumthin'."

"Then what did you do? Where did you go?"

"We dinn't drive bu' a lil' ways befo' the missus started tearin' up fer doin' wha' she did to Lulu—leavin' her 'n all. I dinn't unnerstan' whys' she's doin' wha' she's done, nor whys we'rs leavin' Lulu there. I finds out that Howard lata' wens 'nto the gas station to report that the child was left out there by 'erself cryin' an' told Tommy to call the police. Tommy Reeves says the phone's brok'n an' that the police station was down the road a bit an' told Howard to brin' her there."

"Were you aware that the phone was in need of repair at that time?"

"Nah, the phone theres a'ways worked. I neva' knew it not to, but Tommy told Howard that the phone wann't workin', an' told him to brin' Lulu to the police station."

"Then what did Howard do?"

"I reckon he dinn't wanna leave her ou'side cryin', it's startin' to get cold ya' know. So he mus've put her 'n the truck an' brin' her to the police station where'd they'd help her there."

"How far did Howard get after leaving the gas station before being pulled over by the officer?"

"He dinn't get too fer wen's the police pulled him ova'. We's were sittin' off the side of the road, down a bit, afta' he'd tak'n off. Theys pass by us when Lulu was lookin' out the winda' an' saws her momma wit' her dollie 'n the winda'. I could see Lulu clim'in' all ova' the truck when theys pass up. That's when we see the police car wit' the sirens an' lights goes by."

"Then what did you do?"

"The missus told me to drive t'wards 'em. When the police car pulled Howard ova', that's whens Lulu got out of the truck, cryin' an' runnin' all 'round wen' she saw her momma carryin' her precious dollie. That's wen' the missus give Lulu her dollie back an' told the offica' that Howard kidnapped our dawta'. I jus' stayed back at the car. I dinn't wan' nuttin' to do wit' it. She clearly was good 'nough to have Howard 'rested by makin' the scene that she did. The missus continued beratin' Howard fer takin' Lulu an' 'nsisted that the cop . . . uh, I mean, offica', no dis'pect . . . 'rested him."

"So when did you end up joining your family?"

"I's goes up to both of 'em when's the missus waved me to get there. Then I's saw the offica' put the han'cuffs on Howard an' put him 'n the police car."

"Did the officer come back to talk to you and your wife?"

"Yea', the offica' did come back to both of us an' get 'r statements."

"Did you already know what you were going to say to the officer before he asked?"

"We's 'greed that Lulu wen' missin' from the house, 'n as we's drivin' t'wards the gas station we's saw that the offica' had pulled the truck ova' an' saw Lulu runnin' 'round cryin' an' scared. The missus makes' a big scene an' was ba'lievable 'nough to have him 'rested. Wen' Howard was inna' police car, his eyes were as big as silva' dolla's. *I counn't look at him.*" Percy said with his shoulders low on his butt. "He's jus' tryin' to help Lulu, an' wrongly 'cused bys alls we did. I have wann'ed to share this fer longa' than it took Moses to lead the Israelites out of Egypt. Then I find out that Howard was shot wen he's released from pris'n, I wen to his fun'ral to ask fer fergiveness, a lil' too late, fer wha' we's did to him I sup'osed."

"Did Miss Theodosia pay you for doing this?"

"Yea', Theo give the missus sum' money ons *if an' whens*, Howard's senn'ence to jail. If he's senn'ence an' woulds be 'mprison, fer ev'ry years he's 'n there, she give her sum' more money. The missus took it an' wen to nursin' school. Sum'tin' she's always wanna do, but we's would neva' be ables to 'fords it. At that time, she finds work only as a washa' woman an's barely made 'nough to put food on 'r table. I's 'n an' out of work, so the money came 'n handy an's 'nough to keep my mouth shut. Gotta say, Missus an' I's had many spats ova' this 'n wha' we did to Howard. I's wanna visit him 'n jail, but neva' did. Too 'shamed fer wha' we done to him. Ruinin' his life n' all."

"Is that how your wife bought the nursing home?"

"Naw, Missus bawt' that cut an' dry. She'd beens a nurse fer 'while an' saved sum' of's the money from Miss Theodosia ova' the years. She's worked hard to make that place run an' it runs good. The place was goin' unna'. She's saved it, she did. Look at all d'ose people she's helps ba'cause it's still opened, an' peoples gots a place to go."

"Relax, Percy. Did Tommy Reeves play a part in this too?"

"From wha's I knows, an's its only scuttlebutt, he mus've been. He tells the offica' that the gas station phone's a workin'." As Percy stopped and spat on the ground. "Tommy mus've done sum'tin' to's the phone that day or jus' told Howard that it dinn't work, 'cause when the reporta' drives by when we's talkin' to the offica', he goes inna' store an' uses the phone an's reports the story. So really, I dun'nos wha's wen on wit' that. Dinn't make no sense, but who's to say afta' doin' wha's we's did. I don't think Theo plan fer the reporta' to drive by an' makes a call's there, but it works 'n her fava', it shur did."

"Did Tommy tell the police he saw your daughter there by herself crying on the step?"

"Nah, Tommy ev'n says 'n court that he's neva' sees Lulu or us there befo' it happened. He lied 'n court too."

"Do you know if the police officer was involved in this thing, too?"

"Wells, I's reckon," Percy took his handkerchief out and wiped his balding head, "he'd had to be'n Miss Theo's purse too. She'd muss've paid him, likes she's did wit' ev'ryone else. Its jus' too co'ncidental that he's jus' happened to be 'n that spot at that perticulah time. Reckon it coud'ave happened likes it did, but doenn't it seems to be part of her plans too? Wounn't ya' 'gree?" Percy lit another cigarette, less shaky now and actually more relaxed.

Perhaps relieving his conscience after all these years did Percy some good.

"Not sure what I would agree to, but it does seem credible that if Miss Theodosia had Tommy in her pocket and your family in the thick of things, why not a cop too? Did you know the cop?"

"Naw, I's sees him 'round—drivin' an' stoppin' 'n the gas station buyin' his smokes."

"Did you ever see him with Miss Theodosia?"

"Naw, cain't says I did."

"I hear that Tommy Reeves was walking around with a lot of money after the trial. Do you know anything about that?"

"Well, Tommy get paid *fer shur*. Dun't knows hows much an' dun't wanna' know eitha'. He'ds bawt hisself a new car an' starts drinkin' a lot. Tell me, where's a youngin' like that comes up wit' 'nough monies to buys a bus'ness, if Theo dinn't pays him off?"

"Was Tommy married at that time?"

"Tommy got hitched to a real nice girl, TerriLee, not long afta'. She's a purty thin' an' ev'n helped run the store 'til she cawt' Tommy 'n back drinkin' wit' 'notha girl an' doin's wha'eva'. She dinn't stay 'round long afta' that. I's hears Tommy lives wit' a girl, Melissa, now. She's a nice one, but TerriLee's shur was a ketch."

"What about Miss Karyn, Tommy's sister? How was she involved?"

"Dinn't know she was. Why ya' think that? Karyn dinn't ev'n work there. She's the smart, skool's goer' likes the missus, an' I reckon she coud've bin home fer Thanksgivin' wen it happened. She's olda' than Tommy, ya' know. Maybe Tommy gives her a piece of the pie to keep 'er mouth shut?"

"Maybe, but I wonder if there really was an aunt that passed away that left them an inheritance?"

"I wounn't know, dinn't know the family that well. So, ar's we's good? I means yur not gonna charge my's family fer anythin', *right*?"

"I'm going to do whatever I can to exonerate Howard McMurphy. He's an innocent man and did nothing wrong. You can go, Mr. Percy. I'll be in touch if I need you."

Percy doubled back to his car, shuffling his feet in a hasty manner. He drove off just as fast, spewing dirt and rocks behind as he did.

Phil climbed slowly into his truck, shutting the door with his good arm, then drove back to the house thinking about everything. He was certain Theodosia was behind everything. *It made sense now. She paid all of them off. She was that proud that she would ruin her own daughter's marriage to Howard by having him incarcerated for a crime that she had staged. But what can I do with this information? It's my word against Percy's and I agreed that I wouldn't go against Percy and his family.*

Ring, ring . . .

"Hello."

"Sarge?"

"Hey Carrie, what's up?"

"Hey Sarge, where were you?"

"Oh, I did a little investigating today. Are you ready for me to come by and pick you up?"

"Yeah, I'm ready to go home. Can you come and get me?"

"Sure. I'll be there shortly."

***

Marla was in the store when Sarge walked in and she turned her attention to him. "Hey Phil, how ya' been? I heard you got shot. You doin' alright?"

"Yeah, I'm fine, Miss Marla. Carrie, you about ready?" He turned to Carrie. He was more interested in telling Carrie everything than in standing there talking to Marla. Carrie was just finishing sacking up Marla's purchases.

Marla picked up her package and turned to Phil before leaving. "Well, it was nice seein' you again. I'm glad that you're OK."

"Thanks, Miss Marla," Phil replied.

Carrie was getting her purse when Marla walked out the door. She looked at the Sarge and asked, "So, did you have a busy day or what?"

"Well, I found out some information that you may be interested in."

"Really? Like what?"

"After I dropped you off, I did some running around and when I went back to the house, I started reading Agnes' journal. I decided to make a run to the gas station and had a discussion with the store clerk, Donald, there. He gave me some information that I thought worthy of pursuing."

"Oh yeah? Like what?"

"Well, I asked him a few questions and he gave me some names of the older folks that come into the store on a regular basis. So I called into the department and got their addresses. I visited a few of them and no one remembered much of Howard's kidnapping charge except a man named Jerry Richards. So I took a visit to his house, and he told me that he knew the Roosevelts and that Tommy's sister, Karyn, married his son, Haas."

"So Tommy has a sister. Is she older or younger?"

"Older, but Jerry Richards also knew Howard."

"Really? How well?"

"Enough to know that he was a good man and didn't believe he could have kidnapped Lulu."

"How did he know Howard?"

"They actually met at the gas station when Jerry's car overheated and Howard helped him with it. They became friends. He even knew that Howard would drop his aunt off at the bus station the Tuesday before Thanksgiving, the exact day that Howard was arrested for the kidnapping."

"Oh, do tell me more, but start from the beginning," Carrie said as she put her purse down on the counter to listen as Sarge told her the whole story.

He took out the notes from his top pocket that he had written down while reading Agnes' journal and handed them to Carrie. He proceeded to tell her the story, starting with meeting Jerry Richards at his house and how Jerry's wife, Markita, had befriended Stacy and Percy Roosevelt by bringing them food and clothing.

"What about Stacy Roosevelt? What did she do before she owned the nursing home?"

"Stacy was just a washer woman and picked up work here and there. Apparently, she supported the family. Percy didn't work much, and when Stacy wasn't home, Lulu would run around the streets dirty and in worn-out clothes. He admits he didn't keep a good watch on her."

"So did Mr. Richards know Tommy at the gas station?"

"Yes, and Jerry knew that Tommy was married to TerriLee at the time, but they're divorced now, and he presently lives with a Melissa Turner. Jerry even knows that the Roosevelts suddenly came into money right after Howard's sentencing. He asked his daughter-in-law, Karyn, if she got any inheritance and she never really answered him, so he dropped the question, but she did put herself through a tech school and learned typing skills."

"Does Karyn still live in town? Can we visit her?"

"No. His son, Haas, and Karyn live in St. Louis, so they're not available to visit. Jerry, as well as Agnes' journal, did say something about Howard bringing his aunt to the bus station every Tuesday before Thanksgiving and that Theodosia was aware of this."

"So Theodosia knew about the bus station, which would have put Howard in that area."

"Yes, she sure did. So I took the information that Jerry gave me and thought I would visit my mom at the nursing home that Stacy Roosevelt runs and guess who I met up with there?"

"Who?"

"Percy Roosevelt was there talking to his wife."

"Get out. Really? Did you get a chance to talk to him?"

"Well, he didn't want to talk there, so we met up down the road a ways and had a nice discussion."

"A discussion, you say? Oh please, tell me what that was about." Carrie was wide-eyed and intrigued.

"Well, Percy was real nervous, shaking like a leaf in a windstorm. I told Percy that I'd keep the conversation in confidence and what I learned was most interesting."

"OK, so do I have to tie you up and beat it out of you? What did he tell you?"

"He told me that Theo was behind it all and paid them off. I'll have to look at the court records. You still have them, right?"

"Yeah, at the house. Will you tell me what he said, puullleeeease?"

"He said that Theo endeared herself to them on several occasions by actually bringing food, whiskey, and drink to their house for the family. She gave Stacy a fancy new dress and shoes to match, and even bought Lulu a brand new doll and toys. Stacy was so enamored by Theo's generosity and wealth, she would have done anything for her. When Theo felt secure enough with Stacy's allegiance, that's when she told a story about how

Howard was beating up Patty and really did a great performance, as Percy described it, crying and going on about it. She advised that Patty wouldn't divorce Howard, so being a good, concerned, Christian mother, she devised a plan to put him in jail and Stacy agreed to help her.

"Right, if she was such a good, Christian mother, Theo would have never went to such extremes to keep her daughter away from a man just because she didn't like him."

"I agree, but Theo and Stacy came up with an arrangement and used Lulu to carry it out. See, Percy said that Lulu never went anywhere without that doll Theodosia had given her. So knowing that the Tuesday before Thanksgiving would put Howard in the area after he dropped his Aunt Jessica off at the bus station, they devised a plan to leave Lulu at the gas station and Stacy would take the doll away from her knowing that she would have a crying fit when she did."

"So Stacy Roosevelt left Lulu outside the gas station and took her doll away, just to get Lulu to cry? What kind of person does that?"

"A destitute one."

"Then what? Howard just pulled up to the gas station and saw her outside crying? How could Theo even plan on that?"

"Well, Howard normally went into the gas station at the same time on that Tuesday. The Roosevelts left the station as the bus pulled up. But before leaving, Miss Stacy sat Lulu on the gas station step and took the doll away and Lulu had the fit she expected."

"Then where did Percy drive to?"

"Percy drove Stacy down the street a bit, pulling off the road to watch and see if Howard would play into the plan."

"Seriously? They just drove off and watched? Did Percy know if the cop was involved?"

"No, Percy can't say for sure, but he must have been. First Howard passed them, and Stacy lifted the doll up when Lulu was looking out the window. Then Lulu was climbing all over the truck and crying. That's when they saw the cop's car pass with the sirens on and pull Howard's truck over."

"And that's when they drove up and saw Lulu running around crying."

"Miss Stacy took Lulu's doll away when she left her at the gas station and that's how her momma settled Lulu down when she got out of Howard's truck. Then Stacy got all upset and said that Howard had kidnapped their daughter. Percy stayed back at the car like Eschammer had described in the recording I played you, remember?"

"Yeah, I remember the recording," Carrie said.

"It wasn't until Miss Stacy had started shouting and accusing Howard of kidnapping Lulu that Percy got involved."

"So was the cop involved in this too?"

"Can't say, but I would gather a guess that he would have had to be involved to have been in that spot at that particular time."

"Yeah, me too. So what do we do now?" Carrie asked.

"I think the next step is to take this up with Victor Abbott. I don't know if he was in on Miss Theodosia's plan, but I think it's time we find out."

Carrie didn't hesitate, reached for the phone, and dialed Victor's phone number. The phone rang and rang until the recorder came on. Carrie left a message and asked Victor to return her call as soon as possible.

"Wow, you had a busy day," Carrie said. "What do you want to do now?"

"Well, I went to the grocery store. Do you care if we go back to the house and I'll cook you some dinner? I would like to review the court records again."

"Oh, you don't have to cook. I can make us some dinner."

"I know how you cook. Besides, I like cooking. Been doing it for a while now," he replied.

"So you don't like my driving and now you don't like my cooking, either?"

"Well, they both need a little improvement," he said with a snicker.

Rolling her eyes, she asked, "Are you ready to leave now?"

"Sure, sugar."

When Sarge was driving, Carrie asked, "How could a mother put her daughter in a situation like that? What type of mother would have done that?"

"A dirt-poor one. They didn't have any money; Stacy was enamored with Theo's wealth, and she wanted to have that lifestyle. Theo did do a fine job of convincing Stacy that Howard was beating Patty, and taking advantage of Howard's decency, she played Stacy and just used Howard as a cat's paw. I guess it helped that Theo paid them for their service when Howard was put in jail. Percy said that for every year Howard was in jail they were paid accordingly."

"Durn, Theodosia was such a bitch. She had it all planned out, didn't she?"

"It worked. Don't think she planned on the reporter driving by at that time, but when he went into the gas station to report the story, it all fell into place."

"I guess Tommy got paid too. Why did you bring up his sister Karyn? What did she have to do with this?"

"Well, Jerry Richards said that Karyn put herself through typing school and my guess is Tommy had to give her something when he said that he got an inheritance to make the story more conformable. Tommy's parents were staying at their home in the mountains when this all took place. They were even thinking about putting the business up for sale right around then, and with both his parents passed, we can't go around asking them now."

"No, I guess we can't do that. Wow, Jerry Richards provided you with a lot of information. So, did you meet with Stacy Roosevelt when you were at the nursing home?"

"No, I saw Percy talking to her in a hallway while I was waiting on my mom, and when they had finished talking, I stopped Percy and started asking him questions. He was very nervous when I brought up Howard's case and said he couldn't talk to me there. He gave me a place to meet up with him, and when he left, my mom found me. I told her that I had to leave, so I didn't get to talk to her."

"So you went to talk to your mom about Stacy Roosevelt, but you didn't get the chance to talk to her?"

"Yeah, didn't know Percy was going to be there."

"So did she ask you why you were there?"

"Yeah, she asked if I was OK and if I needed anything. I told her I was OK and that I just wanted to thank Dad and her for coming to the hospital, but that I really couldn't stay and talk to her. She understood."

"Does she know that you will be staying with me for a while?"

"No, I didn't go there. She'd be asking me too many questions if I told her that."

"Oh, really? So you don't think she'll be calling you to see how you're doing?"

"When she does and if it comes up in the conversation, I'll tell her then. I just wanted to meet up with Percy and I had to leave."

When they reached the house, Carrie was surprised by the beautiful array of flowers on the table and a bottle of wine with two crystal wine glasses set out, romantically displayed.

"Well, aren't you nice? The flowers are lovely. Would you like some wine?"

"No, I think I'll have a beer," and he went into the icebox and took out a bottle. "You want one?"

"Sure, I'll save the wine for dinner."

Sarge started the barbecue pit to grill up the steaks he had bought earlier. He asked if Carrie would make the salad for dinner while he prepared the steaks for grilling. After making the salad, Carrie went to the pile of articles on Howard and looked for the court records. Finding them, she opened them up and started reading. She hadn't read these thoroughly before and with the knowledge that she obtained from Sarge today, she pored over them, scrutinizing every detail. Not actually knowing what the legal jargon meant, she laid them out for Sarge to read.

# Chapter 18

**The** steaks were grilling to perfection. The aroma of the sizzling meat tantalized the taste buds as if the Good Lord himself had consecrated the food. Bringing out another cold beer and a platter of vegetables, she noticed Sarge was deep in thought.

"Hey, what'cha thinking about?"

"Well, I know I told Percy Roosevelt that I wouldn't use his statement and go against his family. I'm pretty sure the statutes would have run out by this time. I just need to find that one hitch that I can use to exonerate Howard McMurphy. I'm really close, I can feel it."

"Do you think that Victor was involved in this too?" Carrie said as she put her arms around his waist, kissing his neck while standing on her tiptoes.

"You know, I really don't. He was fresh out of college and I think Theo used him as her lackey. He had everything set up against him and she knew that. I just wondered how she interfered in Victor's case, because you know she did."

"Well, when Victor calls, we can set up a meeting to discuss the case. I found the court records and have them on the table when you get the time."

"OK, thanks. I think Theo had this so tightly wrapped that the court records would prove a solid case against Howard. I just need to get someone to sign an affidavit recanting their story. Maybe I need to visit TerriLee, Tommy's ex-wife, and ask her some questions about Tommy before I talk to Tommy himself. Or revisit Eschammer and advise him of what I found out and see how he reacts. If I can get one of them to recant and sign an affidavit, I can bring it to the prosecutor and see what we can do to exonerate Howard. I just have to make this happen."

"Sarge, I think the steaks are done," Carrie said as the thickening smoke swirled all about.

"Oh, shit!" Regaining his focus, he flipped the steaks one more time and took the vegetables off the platter, placing them on the grill. The steaks were picture perfect.

"Hey, I'm really happy that you're helping me to exonerate Howard. I really appreciate everything you are doing. When I went to see Tommy that one time, he wanted nothing to do with me. He avoided eye contact and got real nervous when I mentioned Howard McMurphy. I definitely felt like he was hiding something. I think you may be right by visiting TerriLee first. She would have known him at that time or shortly thereafter. Maybe with them being divorced, she can tell you something that will help before you go talking to Tommy."

Phil removed the vegetables from the grill, and they went inside to eat. It was a delicious meal. No doubt about it, he was the better cook.

Sarge did look at the court records and saw Cora Holtz was a juror, which Carrie already knew.

"Did you know Cora Holtz was on Howard's jury?"

"Yeah, didn't I tell you that?"

"I don't remember. I think talking to Victor might shed some light on how the jury was positioned."

"Do you think Cora was caught up in this too?"

"She didn't get paid if she was, or at least it doesn't appear that way."

"Do you think Theo paid the jury off?"

"No, but only because everything else she did seemed so perfectly carried out. Why spend extra money when it was executed flawlessly. I think the reporter sealed the deal by using the store phone to report the story. I'm sure at the time it was all over the news and papers. A high-profile crime with the prominent Worth family versus a Tar Heel worker—the town would have wanted to see it to the end."

"Yeah, I have to agree with you on that."

Carrie took the dishes to the sink and ran the water to clean them. When she was finished, she asked the Sarge what he would like to do next.

Sarge got up from the table, reached his arms around Carrie's waist and pulled her in tight, kissing her passionately as if they had spent many a days apart from each other. He picked her up, and she wrapped her legs around him and the sparks were flying. The olive oil was still on the counter that Sarge had put on the vegetables before grilling. He placed Carrie on the counter top, undoing her shirt as she unsnapped her pants. He kissed her breast, biting at her nipples. He found the olive oil and poured some on his hands. Carrie had already unfastened her green lacy bra and was unbuttoning his shirt, kissing his neck and his shoulders before she knew there was oil being spread all over her breasts. When he unbuttoned his pants, dropping them down below his chiseled buttocks, his erection could not be contained any more. She found the olive oil and warmed it with her hands. She wanted him now, and Sarge was on the fast track.

They went at it and exhausted themselves thoroughly. When their heavy breathing was contained and their passion relinquished to one another, they decided the only way to get the oil off was to take a bath.

They went up into Hattie's immaculate, large bathroom to the old-fashioned, stone-colored bathtub with the lion legs. Carrie poured some bubbles in and ran the hot water. The aroma was jasmine, rose, and coconut, a special blend that Hattie herself had made for special occasions.

Sarge climbed in, slowly descending into the hot water. His naked body was such a spectacular sight that Carrie wished it was not hidden beneath the bubbles. With his left arm wrapped in white gauze, he stretched it out alongside the rim of the tub. He leaned his head against the backside, and Carrie thought the blessings were all hers.

"Get in here," she heard Sarge say.

She climbed in as lady-like as possible. As the water rose, Sarge sat up, wrapped his arms around her, and pulled her in close to his chest. He wrapped his long, firm, muscular legs over hers. They lay together, and when Carrie placed her head on his solid chest, for the first time in a very long time, she surrendered to the calm. Sarge moved his good arm slowly across her breasts, encompassing them. He started gently kneading them as he relaxed and inhaled slowly. Carrie stroked her hand on his big, strong thighs, lightly stroking them up and down in slow motion. They lay there for a while with no worries in the world . . . then the phone rang.

Startled from their calm by the unwelcome interruption, Carrie decided without a thought to let it go to the recorder.

After rising from the now-cool bath water, Carrie assisted Sarge with toweling off and they both decided to call it an early night. Replacing the gauze on Phil's arm, she made sure he took his pain pill, albeit having to fight his reluctance to do so.

Carrie checked the recorder. It was Victor Abbott returning the call from earlier and she decided that it would have to wait until tomorrow.

As the night evolved into a new day, Sarge rolled back and forth in his sleep. He was dreaming about the robbery at the gas station and it was clear as day to him. He envisaged that he had finished putting gas in his truck, when he looked into the store as the door was open, and a man was yelling at his friend to buy some chips. He saw a robbery stirring and as the robber left hastily, pointing his gun at the clerk, Sarge stood firm. Reaching for his gun strapped to the back of his waistline under his shirt, he shouted, "**POLICE! Drop Your Weapon**," and hearing a gunshot, he awoke and sat straight up.

Carrie was lying there frozen, staring at him. "Are you OK?" she asked.

"Yeah, go back to sleep," he mumbled and laid back down, rolling on his side opposite to where she lay. It seemed so real to him. He was at that place again, hands wrapped around the gun and pointed at the perpetrator. He wondered if there was something else he could have done.

Carrie could not go back to sleep. She was worried that when Sarge shot at the robber, it might have caused some post-traumatic stress or something. She knew she would have to keep her eye on him to see if this affected him in the daytime.

***

Carrie called Victor Abbott first thing the following morning and a meeting was set up for 11 a.m. They met at the yarn store, and this time Phil went to the store with her. Victor arrived shortly after Phil and Carrie.

"Mr. Abbott," Phil said with his hand out.

"Sergeant Lament," replied Victor, shaking Phil's hand.

"Hey, Victor," said Carrie.

"Miss Pyles, you called?"

Phil stepped in and took over the conversation, "Yeah, Victor, I'd like to talk to you about Howard McMurphy's case."

"Well, that's a closed case from a long time ago," he said as he put his briefcase down on the floor next to him. "What do you want to know?"

"Miss Theodosia Eden-Worth hired you fresh out of college, right? What college was that?"

"Yes, she did. I graduated from UNC in Chapel Hill."

"Do you remember her giving you access to Howard's investigation, or did she just dictate what you could and couldn't do?"

"Why are you asking me that kind of question?"

"I have information for you, but please, answer me first."

"Well, Miss Theodosia, as everyone knows, was a proud woman. She hired me to defend Howard for her daughter, Miss Patty, but yes, she had her fingers in everything I did and since she was paying me, her *conditions* were that I show her everything I found and tell her about people I took testimonies from."

"Can I ask you about your investigation into Howard's case? Where did you start and where did you end up at?"

"Well, I interviewed the Roosevelts and they, without a doubt, caught Howard McMurphy red-handed with their daughter, as well as the police being there at that exact time pulling Howard over for reckless driving. Then when the child came screaming and crying out of Howard's truck, that seemed proof enough that Howard had abducted her, or at least, she was in his possession. Then in the Roosevelts' statement, they advised that Lulu wasn't at the house. Therefore, they started driving, looking for her and they, too, just happened to see Lulu climbing out of Howard's truck, in a distressed state, after his truck had already been pulled over by the police. The whole thing was perfectly executed."

"Yes, it was. Did you happen to interview anyone at the gas station?"

"Well, yes, I went to the gas station and talked to a young man, about twenty, and he said he never saw Howard or Lulu there. I picked up the pay phone in the gas station, and it was working. I talked with the phone company and their records showed it was in good working condition too. So, nothing was out of the ordinary."

"Did you happen to talk to any of the local folks in that area?"

"I did think about visiting the people of the area, but Theodosia told me she wouldn't pay for me trying to bid her out of more money when the facts were all there. Everything seemed to be in order."

"Did you happen to interview Sgt. Eschammer? What was his response to the incident?"

"The officer said he was just driving around when he passed the gas station and spotted Howard McMurphy's truck driving recklessly. He was just going to pull him over and see what the problem was. Then, as he pulled the truck over, Howard started explaining that he was bringing the child to the police station. By then, Lulu had climbed out of the truck screaming and crying. When the officer saw her hysterics, that was when her parents pulled up and said that Howard kidnapped their daughter. Howard tried explaining to the officer and the Roosevelts that he was bringing Lulu to the police station. By that time, Mrs. Roosevelt gave Lulu a doll to stop crying. Then the mother started screaming at Howard for kidnapping their daughter and told the police officer to arrest him. The officer had no other recourse but to bring Howard to the station and take his and the Roosevelts' statement. I take it you read the police report."

"Yes, I did, but I have some additional information for you."

"Really? Other than what I just told you?"

"Yes. I went the gas station today…," and Phil proceeded to tell Victor about Donald at the gas station and meeting up with Jerry Richards.

"Jerry knew Howard personally, and lives about two miles from the gas station. He also knew Howard would drive his Aunt Jessica to the bus stop by the gas station every Tuesday before Thanksgiving. Anyone that knew Howard would have known this, which puts him there that day. Did you ever ask Howard why he was there?" Phil asked.

"Yes, and I do remember Howard telling me, but it just proves that he was in the area."

"Did you talk to his Aunt Jessica to see if she saw anything?" Phil asked.

"The bus had already stopped and picked up the people before the incident happened," Victor replied.

"Did you know that Karyn, Tommy's sister, is married to Jerry's son, Haas? They live in St. Louis, and Jerry even asked her if she received an inheritance like Tommy did. Karyn didn't say too much, but she did put herself through typing school. If she did get some, she didn't get much."

"What does that prove?" asked Victor.

"It would suggest that if Tommy got paid by Miss Theodosia and was telling everyone that he got an inheritance, to keep up with the appearance, his sister should have to have gotten something too. Maybe he paid her to keep her mouth shut."

"That's quite a stretch. What else you got?"

"Well, Jerry did see Miss Theodosia on several occasions at the gas station prior to the kidnapping."

"Really? Now that puts an interesting spin on things. So you're saying that there is a witness that saw Miss Theodosia there at the gas station. Was she alone or with someone else?"

"Both. Her nanny, Agnes Weeden, had driven her there, but Theo was also seen driving herself there, too, on more than one occasion, and it was right before the incident occurred."

"Can you get Jerry Richards to sign an affidavit stating that fact?"

"I can only try, but I don't know why he wouldn't. I got something else."

"What?"

"I got Percy Roosevelt to tell me the whole story of what happened that day."

"You talked with Percy Roosevelt? What did he make you do? Did he ask you for protection from prosecution?"

"Yes, and I agreed to it. However, he did tell me that Theodosia endeared herself to his wife Miss Stacy. You knew they were destitute and living in poor means."

"Sure, but how did Miss Theodosia endear herself?"

Phil proceeded to tell Victor the story of how Agnes had taken Theodosia for a drive one day and Theodosia saw the little girl walking around the street by the gas station. Then Theodosia wrote a note and gave it to Lulu that she wanted to meet her parents. He continued with how Theodosia drove herself after that, and visits the Roosevelts on several occasions, bringing nice things for the family, and even brought little Lulu a doll that she carried around with her everywhere. Miss Theodosia played them like a fiddle and knew that Miss Stacy was taken with her lifestyle. Miss Theodosia just reeled her in after that."

Carrie interrupted the conversation when she sneezed and Phil turned to her and said, "Bless you," then continued the discussion with Victor.

"Once Theodosia knew instinctively that Stacy was in her trust, she proceeded to tell Stacy a story about Howard mistreating her daughter, Patty, and carried on, making a big scene about it. Percy heard her say that as a good, Christian lady she couldn't kill Howard and that the only way she could get Howard away from her daughter was to put him in jail. Percy said it was clearly evident that Theodosia loathed Howard for marrying Patty."

"And Theodosia took it upon herself to do something about it," Victor interjected.

"That's when Theodosia formulated a plan after she had Stacy wrapped around her finger. They planned to put Lulu on the gas station step crying and leave her there for Howard to pick her up. Even in her journal, Agnes wrote how Miss Theodosia hated Howard."

"What? Miss Agnes kept a journal?" Victor asked. "I was wondering how you knew Agnes had stopped and got gas there."

"Well, Jerry Richards saw Agnes with Theodosia there too. But yes, Agnes has several journals. I was reading the one written after Miss Patty had married Howard, and Agnes stated that Theodosia was trying to be nice to Howard right before

Thanksgiving that year. It had to be a ploy. It read that Theodosia was in a snit right after Patty and Howard got married. Agnes had brought her to the church the Roosevelts attended, and then had Agnes get the car while she stayed back to talk with the Roosevelts. She wrote that Theodosia was planning something but Agnes never knew just what it was."

"So Miss Agnes wasn't involved in Miss Theodosia's plot?"

"I don't think so, but Percy confirmed everything. When Stacy left Lulu at the gas station, she took away the doll that Lulu loved and carried around all the time, knowing that Lulu would have a conniption fit. Stacy told her to stay seated on the step as if she was being punished."

"So with Howard driving his aunt to the bus station, that would put him in the area, but how did anyone know that Howard would go into the gas station?"

"Jerry said that it was a normal thing that Howard did every year. But yeah, if he didn't, the whole thing would never have happened. Maybe he saw Lulu crying or something."

"Well—continue, please," Victor urged.

"The Roosevelts drove off when they saw the bus pull up, leaving Lulu crying, and drove down the road a bit. They pulled off onto a rocky road and waited. When they saw Howard's truck drive past them, Lulu looked out the truck window and saw her momma holding her doll. Percy said he saw Lulu climbing all over the truck crying and that is what caused Howard to drive recklessly. I don't believe the Roosevelts knew if the cop was in on it or not, but when they saw the cop turn on the siren as it drove past them, they waited until Howard pulled over and that's when they pulled up. Then Lulu came climbing out of the truck screaming and crying and Stacy gave her the doll back. After Stacy calmed Lulu down, that's when she started screaming at Howard for kidnapping their daughter."

"So *the doll* was the key for Lulu," Victor said. "Always wondered how the parents lost sight of their daughter and she ended up at the gas station crying, as Howard told the story."

"The cop wasn't lying when he said that Percy stayed at the car when Stacy ran over toLulu. Percy said he didn't want to get involved, but Stacy made him drive her and Lulu that day to the gas station and executed everything. When Stacy was yelling at the cop, she signaled to Percy, and that's when Percy came over and got involved," Phil reported.

"So Miss Theodosia endeared herself to the Roosevelts, then tried to buy them with her influence and through monetary means, which paved the way for her to execute the plan to incarcerate Howard," Victor confirmed. "My gut told me Howard was innocent, but Miss Theodosia was always in my face when I was reviewing the information I had at hand. I just thought she was tightfisted with her money and wanted to make sure that I wasn't ripping her off. She took control of the investigation . . . and apparently the results."

"With the information that I gave you here, what do we need to do to exonerate Howard? I think it is long overdue, and we should do everything we can to absolve Howard from a crime he didn't commit," Phil said.

Carrie stood in the background when the two men were talking, but took the first opportunity to speak. "Victor, if we got an affidavit signed by Jerry Richards about Miss Theodosia being at the gas station by herself and Percy Roosevelt recanting his statement, is there a chance to get Howard absolved from this crime?"

"Well, in reality, there's no crime with Miss Theodosia being at the gas station as it doesn't really prove anything. Maybe it gives a reasonable doubt for the case, but Theodosia was not a person of interest in the case. However, if you get a signed affidavit from Percy, recanting his story and stating his involvement in the kidnapping, that might hold some water. I'm sure the prosecutor will want to know why Percy is recanting his story. If he lied then, what's not to say he's lying now?"

Phil spoke up. "Would Miss Agnes' journal help identify Theodosia's involvement or her character in this? If we can prove that Miss Theodosia undermined the entire action of events, could the information be taken to a judge to consider exonerating Howard?"

"Possibly, but if we can prove somehow that Miss Theodosia orchestrated the entire thing, we will need more than a journal or a signed affidavit by Percy Roosevelt. If you could get the cop and Tommy to recant their story, then I think you may have a better chance of exonerating Howard. You get that, and I'm in. I'll bring it to the prosecutor and the judge and do my best to help."

"OK, good to know," Phil said as he reached out and shook Victor's hand.

"Well, I can actually say that I'm relieved that this is what this meeting was about. I wasn't sure what you wanted to discuss today."

Phil looked a little uneasy at that and asked, "Were you thinking it was going to be about something else?"

"Oh, no worries, I only meant I had no idea what we were meeting about, that's all," he said as he turned away and bent down to pick up his briefcase. "You get the signed affidavits or other proof of Miss Theodosia's involvement, and I'll discuss it with the prosecutor and see if we can propose it to a judge."

"Thanks. Hey, Victor, can I ask you something else?" asked the Phil.

"Sure," he said a little hesitantly.

"How well do you know Walter Holtz?"

Victor took a deep swallow and adjusted the snap on his briefcase before he answered.

"Yes, I know Walter. Everyone knows Walter. He's the postman for the town."

Carrie said, "Yeah, I saw you talking to Walter a couple of weeks ago on the street, remember?"

"Yes, I was talking to him. Why are you asking about Walter Holtz? Does he have something to do with this case?"

"No, but it does have something to do with Miss Lydia Eden-Worth."

"Oh, really?" Victor said as he looked at his watch. "Perhaps we can discuss this at another time. You see, I have another appointment I'm late for. If you would like to make an appointment, just call my office and Hope will schedule a time," he said and turned to Carrie.

"Miss Carrie, Phil," he nodded, "I really must leave now."

"Oh, OK. Hey, thanks for coming over," Carrie said, unconcerned over Sarge's question about Walter or Victor's answer or his lack of a response.

When Victor left the store, she turned to Sarge and asked, "Why did you ask Victor about Walter?"

"Well, I read in Agnes' journal that Walter may have had relations with young Lydia."

"Didn't I tell you that Cora Holtz or Hall told me that when we were up there?" Carrie pointed out.

"Yeah, I think you did. What did she say again?" Sarge was trying to keep all the stories connected to the correct synapses in his brain.

"That she was disappointed with Miss Lydia's shooting skills when Lydia missed when she took the shot at Walter at Miss Theodosia's party for Governor Cronkright."

"OK, start from the beginning."

"Well, when you went to the bank with Ossie, Cora and I were talking on the porch. She said that Theodosia was throwing a big party for the future-Governor Cronkright. Gary's gramma was even there. Didn't I tell you this?"

"Not sure. Tell me again."

"OK, I was looking through the library articles I printed off and found the one about Theodosia throwing the future-Governor Cronkright a fundraiser to help him get elected. So I talked with Gramma when I went to her house, and she said during the festivities, Miss Lydia came down the steps all made up in her momma's clothing. According to Gramma, she was acting and talking just like Miss Theodosia. When she met up with the men there, she took their hands and when they went to kiss her hand, she placed it down her dress and had them touch her breasts. Very strange behavior."

"Yeah, I would say."

"But when more guests had arrived, she looked out the door and saw Walter's car waiting in line for the valet. Gramma said she saw Lydia run, get a gun from a table drawer, and then Lydia knocked into her as she went back to the door and took a shot at Walter. The governor's security team seized the gun and escorted her from the area. I remember Gramma saying that Lydia mumbled something like, *You sonofabitch. I'm not going to let you get away with it.*"

"Did Gramma know why she took a shot at Walter?"

"No, she just thought she was loony or something, but it would make sense if Lydia was after Walter for the harm that he'd done to her at a younger age."

"Do you know what year that party was?"

"Well, I still have the article at the house. Theodosia sure does know how to make friends in high places, doesn't she?"

"If it works in her favor," Sarge said, shrugging his left shoulder.

"So . . . what's next? Do we visit Percy and get him to sign an affidavit? How do we get an affidavit? —*What is an affidavit?*"

"Well, an affidavit is a legal document containing a written statement that something is true. We just need to get Percy's written declaration, made on oath before Hope or Victor, and use the statement to present to the prosecutor, who hopefully will be influenced enough to present it to a judge. We can't absolve Howard without it and even that may not be enough. Victor had mentioned to get one from Tommy Reeves and Officer Eschammer, which may be a little tougher to do."

"Do you think I should visit TerriLee and maybe Melissa to see if they can tell me anything?"

"Maybe, but I think I should come with you when we do."

"Why? I can take care of them while you're working on Percy and Eschammer. Kill two birds at one time, so to speak—or even four birds for that matter."

"I have a little more experience than you do with interrogating a person."

"Yes, you do, but I think I can get information from the ladies without you."

"Possibly—I'm not being disrespectful, sugar, but I just would like to go with you when we visit them. Plus, do you have any idea where they live or how to get ahold of either of them?"

"No."

"Well, I have the resources to get that information, so the decision is made."

"Always in charge, huh?"

"Carrie, if we're trying to exonerate Howard, we have to get the information that will help us. It has to be performed correctly. You understand that, right? We have to make certain what we do is legal and truthful."

"Yeah, you're right. I'm glad you're determined to help me not only vindicate Howard, but also help me find Patty's missing sister Camille."

Right when she had said those words, loud banging sounds came from the cellar downstairs.

"What in Sam's hell was that?" Sarge exclaimed.

# Chapter 19

**"Oh,** I guess I didn't tell you about that either," Carrie advised.

"About what?" Sarge said as he walked to where he heard the noises come from.

"Well, the day Miss Patty died, a moth had flown into my eye and I bumped into some wooden shelving. Then the shelving fell like dominoes and that tapestry fell from one of its hangers behind it. That's when I saw the wall had moved and I found a strangely constructed door that led down to a cellar."

"What? Show me."

Carrie approached the door to the cellar and pushed on the wooden case she put in front of it. Sarge jumped in to assist her.

"It's behind the tapestry."

She slowly pushed in the door and as it moved inward, the stinky smells came up once again.

He was intrigued.

"Before we go down there, let me get us a couple flashlights. The lighting isn't too good down there." She went into the other room to get a couple of flashlights.

When she returned, Sarge was already looking around the door, checking out how it was put together.

"This is like something Thomas Edison would have built," he said, astonished at the design. "It's a pretty old but ingenious contraption on pulleys." He took a flashlight from her and proceeded to go down the stairs first. Flashing the light all around, like a big, moving spotlight going back and forth on the ceiling, walls, and floor, he made his way down the wooden stairs.

"How many times have you come down here?"

"Not too many."

"Who else knows about it?"

"No one that I know of."

He flashed the light around slowly when he reached the cellar floor as Carrie pulled the damp string attached to the bulb light.

Carrie felt a lot more secure and protected with him there. The biting cold feeling she had felt before was not so strong today.

"This cellar is like a large watertight chamber . . . but, why? What was its purpose?" he asked in amazement. "Looks like heart pine and oakum was used." He saw the 'Worth Manufacturing Company' stamped on the crate and saw that it was slightly pried open. "Did you try to pry this open?"

"Yeah, but I could only get it loose."

He looked around for a pry bar, when he spotted something on the floor. Looked like oil or grease . . . or spit.

He shone the light on the small area, and as he bent down, he placed a finger in it. He brought it to his nose. "Smells like chewed tobacco."

"Chewed tobacco? How could that have gotten here? The only person I know that chews tobacco is Walter, but how—?"

"Carrie, there's a lot of people who chew tobacco in this town. Travis chews."

"But how could someone get in here? I have the store locked up when I leave, and I put the tapestry and the wood cupboard in front of it to hide the door from sight."

"Then there has to be another way in."

Sarge continued to walk around. The fact that it was a dark, cloudy day outside didn't help. He was determined to find out how someone could have gotten into the cellar and why.

*What would they be after?* He wondered.

Shining the light onto the heart pine and tarred walls, he saw the reflection that had frightened Carrie during her first visit and approached the portrait. Brushing the cobwebs away, he saw that it was an oil painting of a red-haired lady, very well dressed. He asked, "Is that the infamous Miss Theodosia? She doesn't look like she's more than twenty years old here."

"Yeah, I think so."

There was more creaking and moving sounds in the distance—sounds that were moving away from them. It caught Sarge's ear, and he looked in the direction of the sound, moving the flashlight on the walls, floor, ceiling, looking for something—a clue—*anything.*

Not seeing anything out of place, he looked for more tobacco spit, moved cobwebs, but found nothing. He touched the heart pine walls and found only moistness and more spider webs. He kept moving along the wall but still found nothing.

Carrie moved slowly behind him, trying to copy his actions, but feeling the ickiness of the walls, she didn't try too hard.

When Sarge was ready to give up and turn back, Carrie went to his left side and caught her heel on the floor. She stumbled into the wall, hitting her elbow.

"Durn it," she said aloud as she rubbed her elbow.

Sarge turned and spoke quietly but firmly, "Don't move, Carrie." Sarge shone his light carefully in her direction and saw that there was a little lift of mud from the dirty cellar floor. He moved the dirt away and as he brushed found a small circular clasp. He pulled up on the grip and the sounds that Carrie had heard many times before came clearly from the hinges. Sarge told Carrie to hold the flashlight while he pulled open the trap door.Carrie could see that the door was made of heavy metal with a heart pine covering. Taking the flashlight back, he bathed the area in light before he climbed down into the vast darkness.

She stood back, but before Sarge's head was under the floor, he looked back and said, "Carrie, are you coming?"

She wasn't sure what she was going to do, but decided to be brave knowing that Sarge wouldn't let anything happen to her. She apprehensively approached the trap door, bent down, and shone her light to see beyond Sarge. She slowly descended the oakgum and heart pine steps immediately aware of the familiar scent of rotten eggs and humidity flooding her senses. Uneasily, she continued her descent to meet up with him.

"What is that sound?" Carrie asked.

"It sounds like water."

Who built it and who used it? Sarge was intrigued.

Sarge continued to walk toward the sound, and Carrie followed closely behind him. There were a few turns, nooks, and crannies that they climbed over and these continued downward until they reached the water. It was a subterranean vault. Geologically, it was very interesting with a small-mouth opening where the water and some light entered, and they could see eroded formations displayed along the walls. Outside, the purple marsh grasses hid the river mouth. From the inside, the cave opening was a beautiful moving piece of abstract art. It was obvious from the watermarks on the wall that when the tide was in, this entrance would be hidden from the outside.

"Feel like going for a swim?" Carrie asked Sarge childishly.

"Why yes, I do," and he bent down to take his boots off.

"I was just kidding!" Carrie exclaimed.

"Sugar, keep it down a little. If someone was just in here, they couldn't have gotten too far."

"Oh yeah, I guess that would be true. So you really are going for a swim? What about your arm?"

He shrugged his shoulders at her. "Don't you swim?"

"Yeah—but I don't know."

"You don't know, what? If you want to go swimming?" Sarge said, dropping his pants down his muscular thighs. "Then you stay and watch my clothes." He took off his shirt and jumped in the water with the gauze wrapped around his arm.

It was cold and Sarge reappeared with a "WHOOOOO!"

When he made that sound, she heard rustling, flashed her light on the wood and tarred fortification, and saw hundreds, maybe thousands, of bats. The bats were slowly rustling around and poking their heads about. They looked like they were being disturbed from a restful nap.

Seeing this, she gasped and then panicked.

Carrie took off her shoes and clothing as fast as she could and jumped right in with only her purple-and-pink bra and matching panties on. Sarge looked back when Carrie's head reappeared on top of the water.

"Oh shit! It's so cold!" she exclaimed loudly without thinking, and the bats took flight, fully awake and aware that their alarm clock had gone off a little too early.

Both of them dove under the water as fast as they could, only just missing the flight of the disturbed bats by milliseconds. They were both good swimmers and they swam toward the entrance underwater. They surfaced for a breath and went back under again, away from the swirling black cloud of bats, until they reached the opening and swam out behind the marsh grasses, toward the river's edge.

Phil looked around, searching for anyone that may have been in the cellar, but found no one. He listened and thought he heard a single, outboard engine in the distance, but the sound quickly faded away. Treading water while he waited for Carrie to swim up to him, Sarge watched a few bat stragglers still exiting the cave, reluctant to give up their slumberous nap.

The sun tried to push through the skies, but the dark, blue, ominous clouds still crowded the heavens. The accompanying breeze was invigoratingly brisk today and Sarge stayed in the water after reaching a place to stand by swimming up a ways.

Carrie swam vigorously up to him and safely stood up. She breathed a little heavier than Sarge.

"I didn't think you wanted to go swimming today."

"Are you crazy? Did you see all those bats? I wasn't going to stay in that grotto alone with all them critters."

"Are you afraid of a few bats?"

"A few? Did you see them fly out? There must have been hundreds, if not thousands of them. I didn't see you staying around to wish them a Merry Christmas."

They laughed as Carrie started a splash fight. Sarge wrapped his arms around her and kissed her intensely, moving a stray hair from her eyelash.

"Where are we?" Carrie asked as she looked around. "Do you recognize anything?"

He stood with Carrie in his arms and looked around the river's edge to see if he recognized anything. "I think we're by the bend near River Road," he said as he continued to scan the area.

"Well, I don't see any more bats coming out. Do you want to go back?"

"I don't know. It's kind of nice out here. Something different," Carrie replied.

"Yeah, but we need to go and talk to Percy and try to find TerriLee and Melissa, before we talk to Tommy Reeves."

"All work and no play makes Phillie a dull boy," Carrie said as she splashed Sarge in the face, pulled down his light blue boxers, then swam away quickly.

He caught up to her in no time and grabbed her by the ankle, then dunked her head under the water. She came up coughing as if choking on a huge swallow of water. It clearly bothered him enough to take her into his arms and say, "I'm so sorry."

She laughed and said, "Gotcha! Just kidding."

They eventually swam back through the hollow space on the side of a crag, uncommon for North Carolina.

It appeared hidden by the marsh grasses but was big enough for an offshore boat to enter, Sarge thought.

They picked up their clothes and walked through the passageways with Sarge leading the way back.

When they were safely back in the yarn store, clothed, Carrie told Sarge she wanted to go over to Patty's house. As they did, he scrupulously paid attention to anything lying around that could be used to help vindicate Howard or learn more about Camille's whereabouts.

"Did this house belong to Theodosia's family or the Worth's?"

"I'm not sure. I just assumed it belonged to Theodosia's family because of the textile crates in the cellar, I guess it could have belonged to the Worths. Patty's been here since I've known her."

"Have you looked around here? Have you ever seen or found anything on Camille?"

"I found pictures of the girls that Gramma took a look at and identified them. I thought I showed them to you. I still have them in my purse. I actually found them in a box from Patty's closet."

"Were there more?"

"Yes, a whole box of old black and whites."

"Show them to me."

"Sure, they're in her bedroom. Follow me," Carrie said as she led the way.

There were some pictures still spread across Patty's bed.

Sarge walked into the room with his police instincts in full gear. He walked around the room, looking at the pictures on the table and at the items on the dresser and the bed. Sarge saw the large jewelry armoire, asked, "May I?" and pointed to it.

Carrie had retrieved them both a towel to use to dry off. As Carrie sat on the bed, she towel-dried her hair and watched him move about. She raised her hand, "Feel free," giving Sarge permission to investigate.

His eyes enlarged when he saw the extent of the jewelry on display. He sat on the other side of the bed and touched the pearl necklaces that were hanging on the inside door. He then proceeded meticulously as he opened the small drawers inside the cabinet. He noticed the parrot drawer, pulled, and found the safe-deposit keys. "What are all these for?"

"Oh yeah, I think they must be safedeposit keys. I went to a bank and looked through one. You wouldn't believe what was in it!"

"Yeah? Try me. What did you find?" He asked as he continued looking around.

Carrie tried to remember everything. "Well, there were several boxes containing gems, silver and gold bars, a diamond necklace like what a queen would wear, and a tiara with rubies, diamonds and various gems on it. There were also some stock certificates from old textile mills in the area. But yeah, near the bottom I found an old folded paper, the ink had faded and it was barely legible, but it was something that looked like a birth certificate."

"Do you still have it?"

"Yeah, but it's at the house. I couldn't read it. Maybe you can tell me what's on it or get one of your forensic crime-solving buddies to see what it says."

He continued looking through the armoire and found and examined an old skeleton key. When finished, Sarge stood up and pointed at the closets as if asking Carrie for permission to open them and look.

"Be my guest," she said as she continued looking at the pictures on the bed.

He opened the double door and saw clothes, then looked underneath them and pulled out the box of hanging folders containing monthly receipts, check stubs, invoices, and other miscellaneous bits of paper. He sat on the floor and leaned against the wall next to the closet with the towel wrapped around his neck and proceeded to rummage through them. Finding mostly receipts from vendors or stores, Sarge stumbled on bank receipts and saw that Patty had a lot of money in her account. He saw several bank copies of certified checks from the Henderson's Bank and Trust attached to transaction invoices of their handling and marketing of gems.

"I see that Patty had some gems sold by Henderson's Bank and Trust. Did Patty ever say anything about selling off gems or anything?"

"Not that I know of, but I did go there and talk with Mr. Twiford about those transactions."

"What did he say?"

"He told me that Patty inherited everything when her momma died. Then she selected a few gems and other items and asked the bank to send them to auction for her. Twiford said the jewelry appeared to be more in the category of artifacts, and they even made inquiries—I guess to make sure they weren't stolen. They didn't find anything to dispute the ownership, so they sold them for her and she deposited the money in their bank."

"I wonder where Miss Theodosia got all that jewelry from."

"Maybe they're part of Blackbeard's treasures," Carrie jested.

"If they were, I'm sure Walter would have been all over it."

"Then I'm guessing from her family. When Miss Theodosia and Miss Lydia died, I guess Patty inherited everything. Camille had already gone to who knows where. Oh yeah, we're supposed to be looking for things that could tell us the whereabouts of Camille, aren't we? I don't know anyone in these pictures anyway," Carrie said as she climbed off the bed.

Sarge stood up and went into the guest bedroom, slowly opened the door, and saw the closet full of shoes. "Wow, she really liked shoes. Who buys this many shoes?" he laughed and shook his head. Turning to Carrie he asked, "Are they your size?"

"Yes, I have my own shoe store now."

He looked around some more and said, "I think we can only solve one thing at a time. Let's work on exonerating Howard and see where that takes us."

"I remember Thelma, the waitress at SamiJo's, saying that the Roosevelts lived down by the river? It was supposed to be somewhere near Heart Strings cemetery."

"Let me make a few calls," he said. "Stay put."

Carrie took the opportunity to pick up the pictures and put them back in the box. She looked around Patty's room and sat down at the stunning vintage Baroque dressing table. Carrie opened a drawer and found Patty's makeup and perfume selections. Opening another drawer, she found Patty's brushes, combs, and hairpieces. In the middle, she saw what looked like an ornamental claw. Carrie reached under the claw and pulled it open. There was a picture of Patty and Howard and another one of Lydia, Camille, and Patty.

This was the only color photograph of the three sisters that Carrie had ever found.

Carrie studied the picture and noticed how similar Camille and Patty looked, although one of them was not looking directly at the camera. Same height, weight, hair color, not a lot of difference—they could actually be twins.

Sarge reappeared. "I got some information on—" and he saw Carrie studying the picture intently. "What did you find?"

"Look," Carrie said, handing him the picture.

"Is this a picture of the three girls?"

"Yeah, I think so. That one looks like Patty but notice how the two girls look so much alike."

"Yeah, I see that."

"When I was younger and worked over at the shop, I didn't even know that Patty had a family. I always thought she was an orphan. You were saying that you got some information."

"Yeah, I got the Roosevelts', TerriLee's and Melissa's information, and you're right, the Roosevelts aren't too far from Heart Strings at all. It's just a walk up the river's edge. Feel like making an unexpected visit?"

"We're not swimming over there are we?"

"No, I think we can drive there from here," Sarge said, flashing that gorgeous smile.

When they arrived at the Roosevelts' house, they approached via the porch and knocked at the door. The house was a very nice waterfront home nestled in a partially wooded lot. It had several decks and a dock with majestic views of the Pamlico Sound to complete the picture. No one answered the door, so they decided to walk around back.

There, sleeping on the deck, was Percy in an old white T-shirt and a tattered pair of jeans with a jar of shine by his side.

Phil walked up to him and kicked his feet.

"Wake up!" he barked at Percy.

"Hmm—wha'?" Percy said, inebriated and almost falling out of his wooden rocker.

"Percy, I said wake up!" Sarge bellowed again.

Tardily, Percy opened his eyes and tried to focus.

"Who? Wha'? Ohs' is ya' 'gain. Wha'cha wan' now?"

"I want to talk to you. Get up."

Percy moved slowly in the rocker.

"Who 'r ya'?" Percy said, looking at Carrie.

"Don't worry about who she is. We have something to discuss with you," Phil replied, taking control of the situation.

"Wha'? Wha'cha wan' now?"

Carrie chimed in. "Percy, we're trying to exonerate Howard McMurphy, and we need you to sign an affidavit recanting your story about what happened the day Howard kidnapped your daughter."

Sarge scrunched his lips tightly and looked at her as if to say, *Will you be quiet and let me deal with this?*

"Sorry," was all Carrie could say as she looked at Sarge sheepishly.

"Percy, you told me the story yesterday about how Theodosia had planned the kidnapping of your daughter and how you participated in it. I can keep your family safe, as I agreed to, and not prosecute your family with this information. However, I need you to help us clear Howard's good name. He may be dead, but he doesn't have to go down as a kidnapper, and you can help us to exonerate him."

"I tells ya' ev'rythin'. I don't needs to do anythin' else," Percy replied groggily.

"Percy, I can make your life a living hell. If you want to make sure that your family is protected and I don't have you arrested for running shine, I think it best you assist us here with what we want from you."

"An' wha' issit? Wha'cha wan' me ta' do?"

"We need you to give your statement under oath to an attorney and sign an affidavit to the fact."

"Wha' makes ya' think they'd ba'lieve me or anythin' that I's says now?"

"Is the information you told me the other day true, or were you lying to me?"

"Nah, it's the truth."

"Then why would you be afraid to tell an attorney the same information that you told me?"

"Fine, I'll do it. Will's it get'cha off my back?" replied a disgruntled Percy.

"I'll set up a meeting with the attorney, and I'll personally take you to the meeting. Do you understand?"

"Yessir," Percy slurred and saluted Sarge as if he was in the army.

Phil motioned to Carrie that it was time to leave.

Carrie climbed into the truck and perceived that he wasn't too happy with her. She realized that he was better trained in interrogating people, and she apologized.

They drove to TerriLee's place on the other side of town, about ten miles away from the gas station. Pulling onto a rocky driveway, they saw not far off the road a small red-brick, ranch-style house.

Phil knocked steadily on the door and an aged, but pretty, fair-skinned lady opened the door.

"Hello?"

"Hello, I'm Sergeant Phil Lament from Pheasant Mills PD, and this is Miss Carrie Pyles. Are you Miss TerriLee Reeves?"

"Yea, I'm TerriLee Reeves," she admitted.

"Do you have a minute that we could talk to you?" asked Phil as he reached out his hand to shake hers.

"Is something wrong?"

"No, ma'am, we would just like to ask you a few questions about your ex-husband, Tommy Reeves."

"Oh yea? What's he done now?" she asked as if it wasn't the first time someone had inquired. "Why don'cha come on in," she said politely and pointed to the sofa for them to take a seat.

"Thank you, ma'am," he responded, taking a seat after Carrie sat down.

"As I said, we just want to ask a few questions about Tommy. Do you happen to remember Howard McMurphy and the incident that happened at his parents' gas station?"

"Oh, you're talkin' 'bout the kidnappin'. Why are ya' bringin' that up now? Hasn't Howard McMurphy been passed fer 'while?"

"Yes, but we're trying to clear his name. We believe that he was innocent," Carrie said anxiously.

"He was," TerriLee replied.

"Say again?" Carrie asked and looked at the Sarge in wonderment.

"Yes, I said Howard McMurphy was an innocent man. See I was courtin' Tommy at the time the thing happened. Tommy was a good guy befo' this all comes 'bout an' ev'ryone liked him."

"Miss TerriLee, do you mind starting from the beginning?" Phil asked.

"Well, Tommy and I were sweethearts in school and were still courtin' after we graduated. But then Miss Theodosia Eden-Worth changed ev'rythin'."

"So you saw Miss Theodosia with Tommy?" Phil asked.

"Yeah, I saw 'em together talkin' an' Tommy was smitten by her bein' famous, an' rich an' ev'rythin'."

"What did Theodosia Eden-Worth have to do with Tommy Reeves?" Phil inquired.

"Well, Theodosia came into the store an' asked Tommy if he knew the lil' girl that was outside an' walkin' the street in dirty clothes. Tommy told her ev'rythin' she needed to know an' was more than willin' to do it too. Nevertheless, lil' Lulu was at the store quite of'en. She come in sumtimes through the woods. I'd feel sorry fer the poor lil' thin' an' give her a piece of candy, an' even brawt her back home few times."

"Where were her parents when Lulu would go off like that?" Carrie asked.

"Her daddy was usually drunk and sleepin' on a couch. I neva' saw her momma at home."

"Did you ever see Miss Theodosia at the store?"

"I was there at the store when Theodosia came in a couple of times. I ev'n took a picture of her wit' Tommy when she wann't lookin'. I could tell she's not the trustin' type, had a bad aura 'bout her, she did."

Phil asked three quick questions. "You took a picture of them together? Could I see it? What made you think you could not trust her?"

"Well, if ya' think 'bout it, she wann't there to promote anythin' an' her only inn'erest was in lil' Lulu. I guess she could've been tryin' to be polite, but it was her manna' wit' the way she went 'bout it."

"Why would you think that? With Miss Theodosia having the resources, why didn't you think she wasn't just trying to be charitable?" Phil asked.

"Call it a sixth sense. It wann't like she was actin' like she wanna offa' a'sistance to the family, more like an inquisition."

"Well, do you know if she ever visited the Roosevelt's family and provided them with food, clothing or any kind of assistance?"

"Yeah, I heard that she did, but that type of woman made no sense in bein' in this neck of the woods. The news always disposed her as bein' proud. I saw her once in a parade an' wen' up to meet her, an' she snubbed me like no tomorra'. She had no time of day fer the small people. So when Theodosia was at the store an' acted all concerned fer lil' Lulu, I just had a feelin' that she was up to no good. I ev'n told Tommy to stay 'way from her, but he was smitten and dinn't listen to anythin' I had to say. I'm sorry. Where's my manna's? Can I get you two sumthin' cold to drink?"

"No, thank you," they both replied in harmony.

"But could I take a look at that picture of them, if you still have it?" Phil asked.

TerriLee got up, found the photo in a photo album in the hall closet, and handed it to him with Carrie looking over his shoulder.

"Miss TerriLee, can you continue, please? Why do you think Howard McMurphy was innocent?"

"Oh, I know he was. Miss Theodosia 'proached Tommy one day when I was at the store, but I don't think she knew I was there. I was in the back room organizin' a new shipment, an' Tommy was cleanin' up the lot from trash an' stuff. I heard a car drive up an' a car door shut, so I looked 'round the corna' an' saw that Miss Theodosia had driv'n herself there. She had Tommy go back into the store, 'cause she wanna talk in private. When they came into the store, I heard her talkin', so I lissen in on their conversation, wit'out her knowin' that I was 'round the corna'."

"So what were they talking about?" Carrie asked, scooting to the end of the couch, paying special attention now.

"Well, I heard her ask Tommy if he worked on the Tuesday befo' Thanksgivin'. Tommy said that he usually works durin' the week, an' I looked 'round the corna' and saw that Theodosia was lookin' at the pay phone in the store."

"Did she ask about the pay phone?" Phil questioned.

"Yeah, Theodosia asked Tommy if that phone was in workin' order. He said yeah, the phone people kep' it in good repair. She asked Tommy if he was innerested in makin' some extra money."

"Then what did Tommy say?" Carrie asked.

"Tommy looked 'round, but he dinn't see me, an' asked her wha' she needed him to do. Then she asked him if he knew who Mr. Howard McMurphy was. Tommy told her that he knew Howard. She asked him if he was 'ware if Howard comes into the store afta' he drops his aunt off at the bus stop right near the station. Tommy told her that Howard would normally come in an' buys cigarettes an' a soda afta'wards, but there's no guarantee that he would."

"So Theodosia confirmed that Tommy knew Howard, and then she checked to make sure that Howard would come into the store after the bus left. Then what did Theodosia ask him?"

"She asked Tommy, on that Tuesday befo' Thanksgivin', if he could disconnect the pay phone so that no one could make a call just when the bus came, and afta' Howard drove off, if he could connect it again."

"What did Tommy tell her when she asked him that?" Carrie asked.

"He asked her why, an' she told him that there may be an 'ncident happenin' that day an' that she needed to make sure that the phone wann't workin' at the time Howard would come into the store."

"Didn't Tommy question Theodosia about this?" Carrie asked.

"He asked what type of 'ncident, an' she said that if he cooperated, she could make his life a little richa' an' pay him well fer his cooperation. She told him that if lil' Lulu was there that he had to say he dinn't see her."

"So, Tommy did it for the money then?" Phil asked.

"Tommy did ask her, 'What's in it fer me?' an' she said that she would pay him well for his lookin' the otha' way."

"Do you remember when that was? Was it the week before the kidnapping happened?" Phil inquired.

"Miss Theodosia was there sever'l times befo' the 'ncident, but that wann't her last visit. She came in on the Monday befo' an' made shur that Tommy was still obligin', an' paid him two hun'red dolla's cash an' said that there will be more if ev'rythin' goes as planned."

"How do you know she paid him two hundred dollars? Did you see Theodosia actually give Tommy the money?" Phil questioned.

"Yes, I knew that she's plannin' on comin back in. So I parked down the road, an' came in through the back door. I stayed in the back room when I saw her arrive. That's when I saw her pay Tommy the money."

"Did you say anything to Tommy?" Phil asked.

"When Miss Theodosia drove off, I came 'nto the store from the back. He asked when I got there, an' I told him I saw Miss Theodosia give him sum money an' asked wha' that was 'bout. He said that he was workin' on a project fer Miss Theodosia an' she paid him fer it. I said wha' type of project, an' he told me not to mind it, an' got mad at me fer askin'. It caused us a big fight, but wit' that money, he bought me a nice engagement ring an' 'pologized fer his bad behavior. Tommy started bein' really nice an' ev'rythin' to me afta' that."

"Did anyone ever talk to you about Tommy or anything that happened at the gas station?" Phil asked.

"Nope, not until now."

"So you actually saw Miss Theodosia hand Tommy money, and heard her ask Tommy to mess with the pay phone in the store on the day that Howard was to drop his aunt off at the bus station, that being the same day that Howard was arrested for kidnapping, am I correct?"

"Yeah, why?" TerriLee asked.

"With what you saw and heard, it will prove without a doubt that Howard McMurphy was set up and Miss Theodosia was behind everything. Miss TerriLee, we need you to sign an affidavit stating what you just told us under oath so Howard can be vindicated," Phil stated.

"Miss Theodosia *was* ba'hind ev'rythin'," TerriLee said, looking at the both of them.

"Yes, and with your statement, under sworn testimony, we may be able to exonerate Howard McMurphy," Carrie stated.

"Miss TerriLee, with everything you told us, it will help our cause considerably. May I set up an appointment with an attorney to take your statement?" Phil said thoughtfully.

"Wha' if I don't wanna get 'nvolved? Wha' will ya' do then?" TerriLee asked.

"Can't make you do anything you don't want to," Phil responded.

"But Miss TerriLee, if Howard was your father or uncle and he was wrongfully accused and you knew someone who could vindicate him, wouldn't you try to convince them to do the right thing? That's all we're trying to do. You are right, Howard has passed, but his name is still linked to a crime that he didn't commit. You may have the proof that will acquit him. Don't you want to correct a wrong?" Carrie said emphatically.

"I'm not shur I wanna get 'nvolved in sumthin' that happened so long ago."

"You were married to Tommy Reeves, right? May I ask why you divorced Tommy?" Phil asked.

"Tommy was a good man 'til Miss Theodosia undid him. When Tommy got paid befo' an' afta' Howard's senn'encin', his whole at'tude change."

"You said Tommy got paid before and after the sentencing. Miss Theodosia paid Tommy money after Howard received his sentence?" Phil queried. "You didn't say that before."

"Oh, dinn't I? Yeah, Miss Theodosia gave Tommy two hunnerd dolla's befo' it happened, then five hunnerd dolla's befo' the trial. If Tommy had to testify 'n court, Miss Theodosia told Tommy to just say that he dinn't see anythin'. If he helped 'n gettin' Howard jail time, fer ev'ry year Howard was senn'enced, she would make it very rewardin' fer him."

"So, you said that if and when Howard received jail time, Miss Theodosia would pay Tommy every year that Howard was sentenced?"

"Yeah," then TerriLee paused for a moment. "OK, I'll do it. It's time to right this wrong. I always felt bad that I kept this to myself. An' when I found Tommy drunk an' cheatin' on me 'n the back room at the gas station—well, all I can say is yea, I'll do it. Ya' set up the meetin' an' let me know when. I'll be there," TerriLee replied.

"Miss TerriLee, if you wouldn't mind, when the appointment is made, I'll call and let you know. Then I'll come by to bring you there, if that's alright with you?" Phil requested.

"Shur—OK," TerriLee responded.

"I can't say how much I—we—appreciate your helping us to pardon Howard McMurphy from this wrong," Carrie advised.

"Can I ask ya' one thin'?" TerriLee said, looking quizzically at Carrie.

"Sure, what would you like to know?" Carrie asked.

"What's 'n it fer ya'?"

"Pardon?"

"Well, it seems that 'ur tryin' to do right by Howard an' gettin' his name cleared an' ev'rythin', but watcha gettin' out of this? Why do ya' care?"

"I was friends with Miss Patty, his wife. She was my godmother and my grandmother's best friend and passed just a short while ago. I thought I would do her a favor, that's all," Carrie replied.

"Miss TerriLee, we won't keep you from your day any longer. I'll be calling you to let you know about the appointment. Do you have a preference on time or day of the week?"

"Well, I keep my mornin's busy, so any time afta' 3:30 durin' the week should work out fine."

"As soon as I know, I'll call," said Phil as he stood up. It was time to leave.

Carrie stood up and shook TerriLee's hand. "I can't thank you enough for everything you're about to do."

"It's been a long time comin', my dear."

"Thank you for your time." Phil shook TerriLee's hand and opened the door for Carrie to exit. Carrie looked back with tears in her eyes and smiled at TerriLee as she left the premises.

As they were driving, Carrie asked, "Now, what? Do we call Victor and set up an appointment for Percy and TerriLee to give their statement?"

"You're forgetting one thing."

"What?"

"We haven't talked to Eschammer yet."

"Really? Do you think he will help us?"

"Don't know. It's worth a try. I'm just wondering about something."

"What?"

"There are not too many cops who would admit they took a payoff," Sarge said, and he considered how to approach Eschammer when they did meet up.

# Chapter 20

**The** shadows of the night were starting their dance under the streetlights, and Sarge asked Carrie if she wanted to get something to eat. She was starving and thought Sarge had heard her stomach rumbling.

"Yes, please. I'm famished."

"I am too. Where do you want to go?"

"Anywhere close."

Finding a street-side diner, they went in and ordered food. Sarge was quiet during dinner and chewed over Sgt. Eschammer, wondering how Theodosia could have got him in her purse. He knew they really weren't too far from Eschammer's place, and after dinner they could stop in to talk with him, but on the last visit with Eschammer, he wasn't too forthcoming. Eschammer was agitated, but he also did share an important fact: Percy had stayed in the car when Stacy rushed to Lulu.

*Maybe he'd be like Percy and want to get this off his chest as well. Too hopeful,* thought Sarge. *Never known a good cop gone bad to later cooperate and admit their wrongdoing.*

Sarge had a gut feeling. He knew Eschammer when he was in training and tried to remember something about him. Sarge recollected that Eschammer was a widower and that his wife died of breast cancer back in the '60s. Aside from that, he was a real dickhead.

Sarge wondered what Miss Theodosia may have had on Eschammer that would have put him in the spot and made him assist in her plan. It had to be something important. Seeing a black pay phone on a wall nearby, he reached in his pocket for a dime.

"Hello, Mom."

Carrie sat and listened, wondering what he was up to.

"Yeah—OK," and he turned to Carrie. "Are you interested in going to dinner at my parents' place next weekend?"

"Sure."

"Yeah, I think we can make it," Sarge spoke into the phone. "Hey Mom, can I ask you something?"

"Sure, honey, what do you need?" Della replied.

"Mom, did you ever know a cop by the name of Sgt. Edward Eschammer from the Bellefontaine PD? He's a widower. I think his wife died of breast cancer a long time ago."

"Eschammer? Let me think. Can I ask you why you want to know?"

"Mom, I'm working on a case and just wanted to know if you know anything about Eschammer or his wife?"

"Well, sugar, I remember a Verdi Eschammer who had breast cancer and was one of the first at the hospital to start a trial of some new cancer therapy. Way back then, it was real costly too. I did a paper on it when I was in nursin' school."

"Do you remember when the hospital started using chemotherapy?"

"Oh sugar, that was befo' my time. It could have been in the late forties to early fifties. It was a brand new medicine at that time, an' only a few patients were given it. Do you want me to see if I still have my paper? I may have kept it an' put it in a box with my nursin' books."

"No, not yet, but thanks for the information, Mom. Carrie and I look forward to dinner next weekend. Thanks, Mom."

"You're welcome, sugar. Did I help you with your investigation?"

"Yes, you did. Thanks, Mom."

When Sarge hung up he said, "Well, I guess we're going to my parents' next weekend."

"Cool, I like your mom and dad. But why were you asking her about Sgt. Eschammer's wife?"

"I remember that he was a widower and since Mom's a nurse and worked at the local hospital when she started out, I just wondered if she'd heard of Eschammer's wife and knew what she died of. Mom told me it was breast cancer and that the medicine at that time was a new and an expensive therapy. Maybe that's something we can use when we talk to Eschammer."

"Do you think Miss Theodosia was involved somehow?"

"All we can do is ask some questions and see where that takes us."

After dinner, Sarge pulled onto the street Eschammer lived on.

"Now Carrie, you're going to have to let me ask the questions. We will have a better chance of getting the information we need to acquit Howard. That's if I can get Eschammer to open up and come clean."

Sarge knocked on the door and Eschammer answered in an old white T-shirt and blue jean pants. Carrie looked into his dark, careworn eyes and noticed that he looked lonely and sad.

"What do you want, Sergeant Lament, and who is your friend? — *Come on in*," he said reluctantly.

Sarge held the door and allowed Carrie to enter before him.

"Hi, my name is Carrie Pyles. It's very nice to meet you, sir." She went to Edward and shook his hand with a firm shake.

"Nice grip," he said to Carrie with a grin, and she could tell there was something kind but lonely inside this man.

"Ed, I guess you know that I'm here to discuss Howard McMurphy's case again."

"Dinn't ya' get ev'rythin' from me the last time ya' were here? Ya' recorded it fer chrissake."

"Just have a few more questions, if you don't mind. This time it's about Miss Theodosia Eden-Worth and if you knew her."

"Ev'ryone knew who Miss Theodosia was. Why are ya' askin'?"

"Not to bring up a personal matter, but your wife died of cancer, right?"

"Yeah, she passed 'way twenny-four years tomorra'. She had a good run of it, though. What's that got to do wit' anythin'?"

"Did Miss Theodosia know your wife?"

"Yeah, the Edens were a contribut'r to the hospital an' helped 'stablish the cansa' wing there. Theodosia met my wife when she was first di'nosed back 'n the late forties. Wha' does this have to do wit' anythin'?"

Carrie chimed in, "Oh, I'm so sorry to hear about your wife's passing. My Grandma Hattie died of cancer too. Did you know my grandparents, Hattie or Scott Jennings?"

"Yeah, I did. Good people they were."

"Thanks. I think so too. Cancer is such a harsh disease. Did the cancer medication help your wife?"

"Well, she had a radical mastectomy back then an' stayed 'n remission fer 'while. Then, 'n the early sixties, it metastasized an' got 'nto her bones. Dinn't have a chance afta' that," he said rather solemnly.

"Oh, I know. It's very sad, isn't it?" Carrie respectfully played on his vulnerabilities. "Mr. Eschammer, did Miss Theodosia help you out with her bills?"

Phil looked at her and then looked at Eschammer to see his expression.

Edward looked rather weighed down, but he responded to Carrie's question.

"Yeah, she did. As ya' know, Lament, our health insurance wann't exactly the best, an' the operation an' cansa' medication was new an' expensive."

Phil chimed in. "So how did Miss Theodosia help you out exactly?"

"Ya' know how."

"Sir, I need you to tell me, please."

"Miss Theodosia an' the missus ba'came friends afta' her mastectomy. Despite wha'cha think of Miss Theodosia, she did have a kind heart t'wards people wit' cansa'. Think it was 'n her family or sumthin', don't really rememba', but she took to my wife. . .Ya' wanna know 'bout Howard McMurphy, don'cha."

"Yes sir, we do."

"Well, one day wit' the missus at the hospital, the docta' had talked to us 'bout usin' a trial med'cation fer her breast cansa'. When they told me the cost of the new med'cine, I told them to do what they could to save my wife. I had no idea where I'd get that kind of money from. I rememba' the nurse brought my wife sumwhere, to draw blood or sumthin', an' left me 'n the hallway while they did it. Miss Theodosia sat down next to me an' we strummed up a conversation 'bout cansa' an' the cost of the new med'cation."

"Were you in uniform at that time?" Carrie asked.

"Yeah, I was 'n my uniform, an' Miss Theodosia asked me what police station I worked fer. I told her Bellefontaine PD. That's when Miss Theodosia said that she may be able to help me wit' some money if I would provide a service fer her."

"Did she explain what that service would be?" Phil asked.

"I asked her wha' she meant. Miss Theodosia asked me fer my person'l phone numba' an' said she would call me wit' the details. We shook hands, but at that time I dinn't know wha' she was up to. My wife returned wit' the nurse right afta' that."

"Do you remember when she called you?" Sarge inquired.

"Yeah, it was the Monday befo' the day that I a'rested Howard."

"What did she say when she called you?"

"She gave me a time to be 'n a position by the Double D gas station. So that when the bus came by, an' picked up the people at the bus stop, I should wait fer Howard's pickup to pull out of the gas station. She told me that I was to follow Howard an' pull him ova' fer wha'ever reason I thought nes'sary. I dinn't ask why, seemed credible. I dinn't know wha' she was conspirin' to do—I really dinn't. She had already paid fer my wife's docta's visit, so I just did wha' she asked. It wann't 'til I pulled ova' Howard's truck an' the lil' girl came jumpin' out, screamin' an' cryin', that I knew wha' she was up to. Then, when the Roosevelts drove up, ev'rythin' ba'came clear. Miss Theodosia had set up Howard fer a kidnappin'. I dun'no how she got the Roosevelts or the kid at the gas station entwined wit' her plan, but I had to a'rest Howard fer the kidnappin'."

"So she just told you where to drive to and what to watch out for, that's all?" Phil questioned.

"That's all I knew befo' ev'rythin' happened."

"Then what happened after you arrested Howard?"

"I did wha' I had to do, an' got statements from the Roosevelts an' the boy at the gas station."

"Did the lawyer, Victor Abbott, talk to you too?" Phil asked.

"Yeah, but he's jus' a young punk out of law school, an' it was his first case. Victor was as green as a gourd, an' unner constant direction of Miss Theodosia. He tried to figure out wha's goin' on, I'll give him that, but Miss Theodosia kept him unner her thumb."

"Did you have to testify in court?" Carrie asked.

"Yeah, but I told 'em ev'rythin' as I knew how it happened. I dinn't lie. I was neva' asked if Miss Theodosia was ba'hind anythin'—'til now."

"Did Miss Theodosia do anything for you after you gave your statement in court?"

"Yeah, she told me that if Howard was a'rested, she'd continue to pay fer my wife's treatment, an' she kept to her word."

"Mr. Eschammer, can we get you to give your statement of how Theodosia was behind Howard's kidnapping and how he was set up? We're trying to pardon Howard from this and clear his name," Carrie implored.

"Shur, but why now? Miss Theodosia an' Howard McMurphy's passed on, so why are ya' innerested 'n a closed case?"

"We're just trying to right a wrong. When I set up an appointment to have your statement drawn, I'm going to call you," Sarge advised.

"Shur." Eschammer found a piece of paper and wrote down his phone number.

"I'll come by and pick you up to take you to the office. OK?"

"Mr. Eschammer, I really am sorry to hear about your wife," Carrie said as she and Phil stood up to leave. Carrie reached out her hand, but decided that Edward needed a hug. "Thank you for talking with us today."

"Ya'r welcome, Miss Carrie," he said as they drew apart.

Phil shook his hand. "Thanks for the information, Ed."

"No prob'em, glad it's ova'. I'm shur the missus will rest 'n peace now."

As they drove off, the picture was drawn and everything was known. Now it was time to call Victor as soon as possible and tell him everything they had learned.

Phil pulled into a gas station and made a call to Victor. Luckily, Victor had given him his personal line and Phil reached him on the second ring.

"Hello, Victor Abbott."

"Hello, Victor, Phil Lament. I have some information that you may be interested in." He proceeded to tell Victor everything that had transpired today.

"Victor, we need to set up appointments for these people to come in and give their statements under oath. I'm going to bring each of them in by themselves. I want you to setup Percy first, then Edward Eschammer, and around 4:15 p.m. for TerriLee Reeves."

"Ok, I'll have my secretary, Hope, call you with the details."

"This can't wait. It has to be done first thing Monday morning. Do you understand?"

"Yes, we'll be in contact with you. I have your phone number."

"Thanks," Phil said, and they ended the conversation.

Sarge turned to Carrie in the truck, "Didn't I say I would handle the discussion with Mr. Eschammer?"

"Yeah, but being that I knew personally about what a person goes through when their loved one has cancer, I knew I could take that and use the emotions to open him up. Did I do bad?"

"No, you were great. Not sure he would have opened up if you didn't take that route."

"We make a pretty good team, eh?"

"Eh!" Sarge said with that gorgeous smile of his. "Interested in shooting some pool? I feel like doing something other than going back to the house now."

"Yeah, sure, if you feel like getting your butt kicked again," Carrie replied playfully.

They pulled up to the pool hall and saw several guys, Travis included, spitting tobacco and shooting the bull along the side of the building.

Sarge walked by Travis.

"Hey, Carrie," Travis nodded, "Phil." Then Travis spat some tobacco on the ground.

Carrie said, "Hey," and entered the pool hall feeling uneasy. She saw only one pool table open and told Sarge that she would claim the table. He nodded his head and went to get them some beer. Travis didn't bother them that evening and they had a really nice time together as Carrie whipped Sarge four games to two. Sarge didn't complain as Carrie displayed her sexuality playfully while measuring her shot, shaking her butt, and then rubbing the stick up and down in an attempt to distract him as he took a shot. It was late now, so they decided to go back to the house and call it an evening.

The sex was amazing that evening. It left them exhausted and naked in the bed until morning arrived.

"Are we going to Gramma's today?"

"Have to. Can't miss her fried chicken," he said.

They both took a shower, and Carrie replaced the gauze on his arm. Carrie noticed that it looked a little red, but thought maybe the gauze he had on was too tight. She made him take his medicine, as they split a biscuit with some strawberry jam.

"Oh Carrie, do you have a bottle of wine I can bring to Gramma's?" Sarge asked as he buttoned up his shirt.

"I think I only have red."

"Then she'll be happy with a red wine. Thanks."

They went to Gramma's and had a nice time. Gramma went at handsome about him getting shot. She was all over him like white on rice.

"Just doing my job, Gramma."

Gramma turned to Carrie, "Got any more old pictures?"

"Nothing this time," Carrie replied.

Phil advised Gramma that he had a few things to discuss with her. Gramma was sitting at the head of the table when he asked, "Hey Gramma, what do you know about Walter and Lydia?"

"Wha' do ya' mean, handsome?"

"Carrie told me that you were at a party that Miss Theodosia had for a governor when Lydia took a shot at Walter. What was that about?" Phil asked as he took a drink of his beer.

"Oh yeah. We did have that talk. Well, Miss Theodosia always had parties like that. Wha'ever she could do to endear

’erself wit’ important people, she did it. She had the resources ya’ know.”

“Yeah, but tell me in detail about that particular party, starting with Miss Lydia at the party.”

“Well, I told Carric that I saw Lydia make a gran’ entrance . . .,” and Gramma proceeded to tell Phil as everyone else listened. The story ended with Miss Lydia taking a shot at Walter and then afterward she was escorted to her room for the rest of the evening.

“Do you have any idea why Lydia took a shot at Walter?” Phil asked.

“No tellin’, I jus’ heard ’er mumble to ’erself, that he wann’t goin’ to get away wit’ it. Dun’no why she said that, though. Wha’cha askin’ ’bout Lydia fer?”

“Just interested, that’s all. Hey, Carrie, you need another beer?” Phil pushed his chair back as Carrie nodded yes.

Gary and Sadie started up a new conversation at the table and everyone proceeded to make their way through the fried chicken, fish stew, steamed shrimp, and the smorgasbord of food in front of them.

When the meal was over, Carrie helped with the cleanup and dished out the desserts. After that, they left and went back to the house. Taking a beer out of the icebox and opening one up for her, Sarge proceeded to read more of Agnes’ journal, as Carrie looked for clues of Camille’s whereabouts in Agnes’ box. Giving up, Carrie said she wanted to finish her project on the loom.

The next day, Victor called early and notified Phil that Percy’s appointment was at 10 a.m., Sgt. Edward Eschammer was at 12:30 p.m., and TerriLee’s at 4 p.m.

Phil called all of them up and informed them of the times. They were all still receptive.

Carrie had the weaving class at the shop, so Sarge dropped her off on his way to Percy’s.

When all of them had finally sworn under oath and had their statements recorded, with affidavits signed and witnessed, Phil felt some relief.

Driving everyone back and forth, Phil had informed Victor that he would return to the office and that he was to stay put.

Phil picked up Carrie and drove back to Victor's office. They found Hope still there and asked that their statements be recorded too. They signed a testimonial that they did not coerce anyone into making statements and that everything was legitimate. Victor was quite pleased and relief was evident on his aged and lined face.

"I don't know how you both did it—how you got everyone to agree to sign affidavits, but I am certainly most pleased that this has been resolved. I will speak to Prosecutor Storr and set up a meeting to discuss this and let you know if and when he will bring this to a judge. It may take a while to get into his office. He's a busy man."

"No, it won't take that long to get into his office," Phil advised sternly. "It will happen tomorrow."

"I'm sorry, Phil, you have to understand, you can't just walk into Prosecutor Storr's office. There are processes and procedures that one must set up before a meeting can be made."

"I have worked with Prosecutor Storr before on many cases. I'll set up the meeting if you won't."

"I didn't say that I wouldn't set up a meeting, I'm just inferring that I have to follow procedures."

"**Bullshit.** ***This will not be delayed***. We will get into his office tomorrow. You better be at your phone when I make the arrangements. Or would you prefer that I pick you up on my way there?" Phil was clearly incensed.

"If you think you can get into the prosecutor's office tomorrow, pick me up on your way. I'll be more than happy to go with you."

"Fine. I'll pick you up at 9:30 tomorrow morning and we'll be in his office by 10 a.m. You will have to bring all the affidavits and anything else you need to give to him. We're getting this thing done this week," Phil said confidently.

Carrie was impressed with Sarge's ability to get things done. *When he puts his mind to something, there is no stopping him*, she thought.

Before he left Victor's office, he had placed a call to the prosecutor's office and advised that he would be visiting him tomorrow at 10 a.m. He apparently knew the person he was talking to and it just so happened that the prosecutor would be in the office tomorrow at that time. As Sarge moved with Carrie toward the office door, he reminded Victor that he would pick him up promptly at 9:30.

When they got into the truck, Carrie turned to him and asked, "How in the world did you get an appointment with the prosecutor?"

"He's Gary's cousin."

"Oh sure, that explains everything. When were you going to tell Victor you were good friends with the prosecuting attorney?"

"I wasn't going to tell him anything at all. I wanted to see what he could do and he proved me right in my assumption of him as a lawyer. I don't doubt that he would have followed the proper protocol, but I'm not a patient man. Howard was served a wrong-doing and it needs to be corrected."

"Wow! You're such an honorable man. I'm very impressed."

"Did you think I was just going to allow him to sit on his hands while following the correct protocol to bring this to the prosecutor's attention?" Sarge said rather indignantly.

"No, sir. *I meant no offense.* I'm just very proud of you and admire your tenacity to get Howard absolved from this crime that we know now he evidently didn't commit."

"Sugar, it's getting late. You want to get something to eat?"

"Yes, please, and perhaps we need to get to bed early tonight for the big day tomorrow," she said smiling.

***

Later that evening, lying in bed, Carrie could not sleep. She was thinking about how tomorrow would go and if Prosecutor Storr would be able to clear Howard's name.

Sarge fell asleep rather quickly, but it wasn't long before Sarge was again dreaming of the gun going off as he shot at the gas station robber. Tossing, turning, and suddenly sitting upright, Sarge seemed so disturbed that Carrie asked again if he was alright.

"Yeah," he said, and he laid back down, putting his arm underneath his head.

"Sarge, this isn't the first time that you've had that dream, is it?"

"No."

"You were dreaming about the gas station robbery again, weren't you?"

"Yeah."

"Was that the first time you ever shot at anyone?"

"No, but it was the first time that I injured anyone. I could have killed him."

"But you didn't. You were only serving and protecting. You were a hero, Sarge. Don't be sorry for what you did."

"I'm not sorry for what I did," he said candidly.

"Then why the nightmares?"

"I don't know."

"Were you worried that someone could have gotten hurt if you didn't shoot him? Like me?"

"If anything ever happened to you, Carrie, I don't know what I would do—" He reached over and hugged her tight.

"Sarge, nothing is going to happen to me. I wasn't even there when it happened. I was still in the restroom when people heard the shots."

"Anything could have happened, Carrie. We don't know where the bullet went when he shot at me. What if—"

"Oh, hush now. I'm safe and right here in your arms. No place in the world that I would rather be," she said as she kissed him on his neck and cheek.

"I love you, Carrie."

"I love you too, Sarge," Carrie replied as tears appeared in her eyes.

"Are you crying?"

"No," she said rather quickly. "I just feel so lucky. You're such a good man, Mr. Lament, and to have you say you love me, it's just—"

Sarge turned to her and kissed her as the tears flooded down Carrie's face. They made sweet, tender love after that and both slept with ease the rest of the night.

Phil did as he said and was there to pick up Victor ten minutes early. Victor was on the phone and promptly got off when he walked into the office.

"Ready to go?" Phil asked Victor.

"Yes, let me just wash up. It won't be a minute." When Victor returned, he picked up his briefcase and said, "Let's do this."

Driving to the prosecutor's office, Sarge did bring up Miss Theodosia and asked him questions about her demeanor when he was working on Howard's case. Victor told Sarge of the position that she put him in and how she needed to know everything about the case. She even went with him on several occasions when he talked to Percy and the gas station clerk. She was always—there.

They arrived at the tallest building in town and approached the front desk of the building, where Phil advised the security guard that he had an appointment with the prosecutor. The security guard called to confirm the appointment and issued them a visitor's pass.

Upon reaching the office, the secretary said, "Hi, Phil, how ya' doin'? I see you have an appointment with the prosecutor. First time you made an appointment," and she laughed. "Go on in. He's expectin' you."

Victor looked at the both of them and wondered what Phil's relationship with the prosecutor was, but he didn't ask.

"Hey, Tony, didn't see Christy or you at Gramma's yesterday."

"Yeah, I had a case I was working on. What's up, Phil? Hello, Victor."

"Mr. Prosecutor," Victor nodded.

"Yeah, Tony, got something that you might be interested in, I'll let Victor tell you what's going on."

Victor proceeded to open his briefcase and took out the signed affidavits. He told the prosecutor everything that had transpired and that they were interested in exonerating Howard McMurphy from the kidnapping charge.

The prosecutor took the signed affidavits and individually reviewed every one of them.

"Well, with Percy Roosevelt's affidavit, how do we know for sure he isn't lying again? If Percy lied the first time, why would a judge believe him now? Even if he signed an affidavit recanting the facts."

Phil stepped in. "Tony, I personally talked to Percy and everything that he has in the statement is true and confirmed. Take a look at Miss TerriLee's statement and Sgt. Edward Eschammer's. They took part in it too. They all corroborate that Miss Theodosia was behind everything. She paid them before the incident and continued paying them after Howard was convicted. Theodosia executed her plan effortlessly, and until the day she died, she thought she got away with it, and she did . . . until now."

Phil took the picture of Miss Theodosia with Tommy Reeves at the gas station and handed it to the prosecutor. Victor asked to look at it after the prosecutor appraised it.

"Well, OK, I think I have enough here to bring to a judge. Now Phil, I know how anxious you are. I'll let you know when I get an appointment with the judge, but I know that you will be callin' me every five minutes to find out. Don't you do that, as I give you my word that I'll call you first . . . and Victor, I'll call you too."

"You better," Phil said as he got up and shook Tony's hand firmly.

"Mr. Prosecutor," Victor nodded politely.

"Victor, good to see you again. Don't let this guy get under your skin. He's a very determined man when he sets his mind on something."

"Yes, I believe I found that out already. Good day, Mr. Prosecutor," Victor replied.

As Phil drove Victor back to his office, he inquired again about Walter. "I'm not done with the conversation on Walter. I want to know your relationship with Walter and what you know about Miss Lydia and him."

"Why do you think I know anything about Walter and Miss Lydia?"

"I know you do," Phil replied earnestly.

As he drove, he looked over at Victor, who swallowed hard and looked out the window.

"When I get more information, and I will, with the happenings behind Walter and Miss Lydia, I'm coming back to do some investigation on it. So be prepared for questions."

"What do you think happened between Walter and Miss Lydia?"

"I'm only assuming at this time, and I have some hearsay, but there's something there and I'm going to find out what it is."

Phil pulled up to Victor's office and Victor swiftly exited.

*He may not have been involved, but he knows something,* Phil surmised.

Reaching the yarn store, Sarge told Carrie about the events of the day. How Tony would take all of the information to a judge and see what he could do to pardon Howard.

"Tony Storr? Tony and Christy?"

"Yes."

"You didn't tell me that."

"Oh, I didn't?" and he smiled that gorgeous smile at Carrie, "Oops."

"Oops, my butt," Carrie exclaimed, hitting Sarge on the arm.

"Hey, watch it. I'm still a wounded man."

"It's your other arm that was wounded, you silly man."

"Hey, did you hear any of the noises from the cellar today?"

"No, not a sound." She knew Sarge was changing the subject on her. "So, what's going to happen now?"

"We have to wait to hear from Tony about the judge's decision."

"Oh, so you don't know the judge, huh? You can't get him to get this resolved quickly?"

"I may have a connection or two to make the process go a little quicker."

"Oh, I have no doubt. You're a mystery, Mr. Lament."

"What does that mean?"

"Meaning that you have connections that no one else has. You get things done expediently."

"Not all things, my love," Sarge replied as he kissed her hand and gave her a wink.

"Well, if you don't mind, may I go into Miss Patty's house and continue looking around some?"

"Sure. You still looking for something on Camille?"

"That, and Walter, and anything else I can uncover."

"When do you have to report back into work?"

"Well, I was planning on going to the office on Wednesday."

"So I don't have you to myself too much longer then," she said sadly and pushed out her lip to pout.

"Carrie, you have me now."

"I'll take whatever I can get," and she kissed him. "Go ahead, get on over there, I have business I need to tend to here," and she kissed him again. "I'll let you know if I hear some cellar noise again, OK?"

"OK," he replied as he retreated to the house.

Carrie looked at her magnificent man, the man who took charge and had taken control of her heart.

Sarge walked through the living room, sat down at the kitchen table, reached for the rotary-dial phone, and made some calls. Eventually, he called Tony.

"Hey, Tony, Phil here. I made a few calls and got you a meeting with Judge Alfred Ecklestine on Wednesday morning at 8:30. Can you make it?"

"Well, Phil, it took you all of about an hour—you're gettin' slow!" He could hear Tony snicker in the background.

"Can you check your schedule and see if you can make it, please?"

"Shur, I'll rearrange my schedule for you, Phil."

"I just want to get this thing resolved, that's all."

"I know, Phil. Well, I'll do my best to talk to the judge and see if I can convince him to vindicate Howard."

"Do you want me to come with you?" Phil inquired.

"Phil, as the county prosecutor, I think I can do this by myself. You gave me plenty of information to give to the judge."

"Yeah, but what do you think our chances are?"

"Really, you're worried about this? I think you have all the bases covered. Don't think Percy Roosevelt's statement will prove worthy of anything, so I'll show him that first. You know he lied before. He could be lying again. The picture you gave me of Theodosia and Tommy Reeves together? I'm not sure about that. Doesn't really prove anything other than that she was a customer at the gas station. It doesn't help that the little girl, Lulu Roosevelt, was found in Howard's truck when Eschammer pulled him over, either."

"I'm going to have Victor Abbott join you in the judge's chambers. He was the lawyer for Howard and he can also testify how Miss Theodosia conducted his investigation," Phil advised.

"Sure, Phil, anything else you want to help me with?"

"No, Tony. I do appreciate your help in this. If I don't hear something back on Wednesday—"

Tony interrupted Phil in mid-sentence. "Phil, I'll *let you know* as soon as I find out."

"OK, Tony. Thanks."

While Phil was calling Victor to let him know about the meeting on Wednesday, he saw Patty's Bible on the table.

"Hello, Victor Abbott's office. Hope speaking."

"Hi, Hope, is Victor in?"

"May I ask who's calling?"

"It's Phil Lament, and he better take my call."

"Hello, Victor Abbott," Phil heard before he could say anything else.

"Hey, Victor, I made some calls and you'll be meeting Prosecutor Tony Storr at Judge Alfred Ecklestine's chambers on Wednesday morning at 8:30. I expect you to be there. Your testimony to the judge about how Miss Theodosia conducted your investigation is crucial to absolving Howard."

"Phil, I—"

"I don't want to hear any excuses. If you have a meeting that day, you're just going to have to reschedule. You understand me?" Phil said sternly.

"Yes sir. I'll be there promptly at 8:30 a.m. at Judge Alfred Ecklestine's chambers. Is there anything else you wish me to do?"

"No. Just make sure that Howard gets cleared of all wrongdoing."

"I'll do my best."

"I'm sure you will," said Phil as he hung up the phone.

Taking the Bible and opening it to the family tree, he saw the name Jakayla Hicks.

*That has to be a relative of Travis. Small town,* he thought.

Phil proceeded to look around for other items in drawers and closets. While in the kitchen, he found some crackers and bit into one. It was stale and soft. He spit it out in the kitchen sink. He went up the stairs and back to the box that had the hanging folders. He was intrigued by the source of Miss Patty's wealth.

Carrie came over after the weaving session had ended and found him upstairs. "Have you eaten?" she asked

"Only a stale cracker," he said. "You want to go get some lunch?"

"Yeah, I'm hungry. Did you find anything you were looking for?"

"Only that Jakayla Hicks was named on Howard's side of the family tree."

"Yeah, I saw that, too," Carrie said as she retreated toward the steps to go downstairs. "Does that mean anything?"

"Do you know if she's a relative of Travis Hicks?"

*Oh shit!* Carrie thought remembering that she had showed that to Travis the day that he came over and they had sex. "Yeah, I think she is," and she left it at that. "Man, I'm hungry. What do you feel like having for lunch?"

"There's a good Chinese place a little ways from here," Sarge suggested.

"Oh, that sounds wonderful."

***

The rest of the day and the next were the longest ever. Sarge studied Agnes' journal while Carrie went to the yarn store. He went through the boxes and saw that there were missing journals—the years didn't match up.

*Now why would Miss Cora and Ossie keep some of Agnes' journals?* That didn't make sense, unless they did it for more money, thinking that Carrie might pay more for the rest of them. Phil grew angry considering this possibility. In fact, it really pissed him off. Carrie paid way too much for the box in the first place. Now, finding that they had ripped her off, he wasn't going to just sit by and let that happen.

Sarge called Carrie at the store and asked her if she was busy. She had customers and couldn't really talk.

"Carrie, I'm going on a road trip. I'll call you when I get back. I don't know if I'll be late picking you up from the store, but I'll let you know when I'm on my way back."

"OK, that's fine. Thanks," she said and then hung up suddenly.

Phil took a drive to Ossie and Cora's house. As he pulled in, he saw Cora outside hanging up laundry. He got out and approached her.

"Hey, Mr. Phil, wha' brings ya' here 'gain so soon?" she said sweetly.

"I'm here for the rest of Miss Agnes' journals."

"Wha'? Theys were all 'n the box I gave to Carrie."

"No, ma'am, they were not all there. I'm here to collect the rest of them."

"I don't unnerstand. I'm shur theys were all there—**OSSEEEEE!**"

Ossie appeared on the front porch. "Wha'cha wan', woman?"

"Ossie, Mr. Phil's here an' he says that all of Aggie's books were *not* 'n the box."

"Wha'? I dunno wha'cha talkin' 'bout," Ossie said, spitting off the porch, then swiping his brow with his white handkerchief.

"Ossie, did ya' take some of Aggie's books out of that box?"

"Dunno wha'cha talkin' 'bout, woman. Ya' knows I cain't read."

"*OSSEE*—I know I dinn't take 'em books out of that box. Wha'cha do wit' 'em? Ya' betta' ***GO GET 'EM RIGHT NOW!***" Cora growled at Ossie.

Miss Cora followed Ossie into the house leaving Phil in her dust.

Phil could hear her bitching up a storm and heard Ossie tell Cora to stop hitting him with the broom. When Cora reappeared, she had several journals in her hands.

"I'm sorry fer my husband's doin's. Miss Carrie 'n ya' are the nicest couple we met 'n a long time. We're not thieves or anythin'. I neva' meant to cheat ya' out of anythin'. Ya' two were's a godsend, ya' were. We woud've los' our farm if Miss Carrie wounn't have giv'n us the money an' all. Here, take these. If I fin' anythin' else of Aggie's, I'll call ya'. *I promise*," she said most sincerely.

"Ossie, ya' betta' get 'ur butt out here an' 'pologize to Mr. Phil fer wha'cha did. **Now!**" she said, screaming with a red face and gritted teeth.

Ossie reappeared on the front porch and slowly came down the steps. Spitting on the ground and wiping his brow again, he said, "Yeah, sorry 'bout that, guess theys fell out of the box 'r sumtin'."

Phil stood there and looked at the both of them, then he said, "You can't cheat people like that. Carrie paid you a fair wage for that box."

"Yeah—says I's sorry," Ossie said, looking down at the ground.

"Well, I hope I don't have to come back here for anything else," Phil said sternly.

"No, sir. I do's ba'lieve that's to be ev'rythin' of Miss Aggie's."

"Well, OK then, I'll be leaving now. Miss Cora, if you do happen to stumble on anything of Miss Agnes', please call me anytime."

"Oh, I will. *I promise.*"

Phil got into his truck and when he was driving down the rocky road, he could still hear Cora yelling at Ossie.

*Man, am I glad I'm not Ossie. Cora seemed like such a sweet lady, but I'll be sure never to cross her. What a temper!*

When Phil reached the interstate, he decided to face the fear that had been bothering his sleep every night. He drove to the gas station where he shot the robber. He filled up his truck and went inside. The clerk recognized him at once. "Hey, aren't you the cop that shot the robber in the leg?"

"Yeah, how's it going?"

"Great. The owna' wanna thank ya' an' told me to call him if ya' eva' came 'n 'gain. Can ya' stay fer a minute? He just wen' ova' to the fast-food joint to get sum suppa'."

"No, that's OK."

"No, really. Jus' wait fer a minute," the clerk said, and he told a customer to run over and get Yadi.

Yadi shuffled over as quickly as he could. He was an older, full-bellied man, tugging on his pants as he entered the door.

"Are ya' Sergeant Phil Lament, who shot the robba'?"

"Yes, sir."

"I cain't thank ya' 'nough." He shook Phil's hand vigorously. "Yar' a real hero, ya' are. Did'cha fill yar truck up wit' gas?"

"Yeah. The silver truck."

"Oh, Johnny don'cha' charge him fer that. It's on me."

"No, you don't have to go and do that."

"Ya' don't unnerstand. There have been sever'l robb'ries 'n the area an' they stopped afta' ya' shot the guy. Ya' saved a lot of bus'nesses from bein' robbed. Yar' a real hero."

"Sir, I'm no hero. I just saw what was going down and did what any police officer would have done."

"Nah, yar' a real hero, ya' are."

"Well, I'm more than happy to pay for my gas," Phil said as he went into his pocket to get his wallet.

"Naw ya' don't—Not ta'day. I jus' cain't thank ya' 'nough fer ev'rythin' tha'cha done."

"Well, I got to go now. Thanks for the gas. You really didn't have to do that."

"Oh yea' I did. I'm jus' thankful no one got hurt, otha' than the sonofabitch tha'cha shot. Oh shoot! Ya' got shot 'n the arm, dinn't 'cha? How're you doin' wit' that?"

"I'm good—real good."

Phil started walking toward the door.

"Did that bullet hurt? Neva' been shot."

"Well, it was just a graze, no worries. Thanks again." He retreated quickly out the door.

"Ya' come back any time. It's bin real nice ta' meet ya'." The owner said, standing at the door.

Phil looked back and waved, "Yeah, nice meeting you too."

He got into the truck and drove off as politely as he could.

He drove to the shop and asked Carrie if she was ready to leave.

"So, tomorrow's the day. What time are you going into work?"

"I was thinking that I may take a few more days off."

"Really, why?"

"I won't be any good at work not knowing what's going on with the judge. I just wish I could be there."

"I'm sure you would like that. You controlled everything up to this point. Let them do their job. I'm sure Tony will call you as soon as he knows something." She tried to sound reassuring.

"Yeah, but I'm not the most patient man."

"Yeah, I sort of noticed that."

***

The next morning came and went without a call. Phil was trying to act cool and calm, but he was really a nervous wreck. His stomach was churning, his neck was aching and palms were sweating.

Phil thought over everything that they would present to the judge and remembered what Tony had told him. He had hoped the picture of Theodosia in the store and Percy's statement wouldn't prove to be damaging to the presentation. Phil felt certain that TerriLee's and Eschammer's signed affidavits would prove that Theodosia was behind everything. Then again, the child had been found in Howard's car, proving that he had her in his possession.

Phil went to the grocery store while he waited for the call. He had to do something with his time. He bought beer, wine, steaks, ice cream, and other items that he wouldn't normally have picked up. After checking out, he brought them back to the house. He was about to put them away when the phone rang.

"Hello?"

"Hey, Phil," Tony said.

"Hey, Tony, what's taking so long?"

"Well, Victor and I talked to the judge and presented everything."

"Yeah, so, what is he going to do? Do you have to set up another meeting to present it to the courts?"

"No, he didn't want to go that route."

"What?" Phil said as his voice tuned up an octave on the diatonic scale. He could hear Tony laughing.

"What so funny?"

"I'm just toyin' with you, that's all."

"What do you mean?"

"The judge signed the paper pardonin' Howard of the crime."

"WHAT? Really? Are you playing me?"

"No, Phil, I'm serious now. We had a hard time in the beginnin' convincin' him that Miss Theodosia was behind everythin'. As I predicted, Percy and the picture didn't help matters. But when he read the signed affidavits from TerriLee and Sgt. Edward Eschammer, that helped a lot. However, when he talked to Victor, that's what convinced him. They talked for a long time and he convinced Judge Ecklestine that Miss Theodosia had her hands in everything. It was Victor who got the judge to sign the exoneration papers and pardon Howard. You should thank him."

"I'll do just that. Thanks, Tony. I owe you one."

"You owe Victor, not me. Hey, Phil, the judge will be holding a press conference outside the courthouse in about an hour. He would like you to be there. Can you make it?"

"Yes. See you then."

*Wow! Howard's name is cleared and it didn't even go to court*, Phil thought as he wiped his brow and drove over to the shop without calling Carrie first.

When he entered, Carrie was with a customer but saw that Sarge looked happy—and slightly feverish.

After the customer made her purchase and left, Sarge approached Carrie and gave her a big hug and kiss.

"We did it! Howard was pardoned from the charges."

"What? WOW! That is great! I'm so proud of you," Carrie said excitedly.

"You played a big part in all of this," Sarge said with a huge embrace.

"Oh, how humble thou art."

"We need to call Victor. Tony said that it was his help that closed the deal."

"Sarge, are you sure you're feeling alright? You look a little flushed," Carrie said as she picked up the phone to call Victor.

"I'm fine," was all Sarge would say.

They called Victor and thanked him for what he did to get the judge to free Howard from the kidnapping charge.

Victor was happy too, as it meant that he actually *won* his first case out of law school. Then Victor asked if they were planning to attend the press conference at the courthouse.

After the discussion with Victor, Carrie asked Sarge again, "Are you sure you're feeling alright?" She then put her hand to his head and said that he felt feverish.

"I'm fine. We need to get going to the courthouse. The judge requested us there," Sarge said, trying to distract Carrie.

Carrie picked up her purse and locked the door.

She was all excited. This was big news for a small town.

"Now that Howard has been cleared of this crime, how do we go about finding his killer? I can't help but think that they still may be out there—somewhere. Could Theodosia have been behind that too?" Carrie wondered aloud as she looked out the window.

"I wouldn't put anything past Theodosia and what she would do to keep Howard away from her daughter."

"Yeah, that's true. Do you think Theodosia would have done away with Camille too?"

"That's still a mystery to me. Sure would be nice to find someone who knows Camille's whereabouts."

"Poor Patty, to have such a wicked bitch for a mother."

"True, but she did pretty well with the inheritance from her momma. Maybe that was Theodosia's way to repent for what she did to her. Can't help but wonder where all those gems came from, and how Patty got all that money in her account."

"Maybe Theodosia found a pirates' chest or something, and told Patty about it before she died. If we could find Camille, maybe she would be able to share some insight into that family."

Sarge drove up to the courthouse where the streets were filled with cars, vans, and people walking from every direction.

"Wow! Can you believe it? Look at all this press waiting on news about Howard McMurphy and his name being cleared from a crime that happened so long ago. It's like a different ending to a story that everyone knows by heart. Who would have thought that you *can* rewrite history?"

Carrie wasn't paying much attention to Sarge as she watched several television stations set up and raise the antennas on top of their vans.

Tony came out of the courthouse. When he caught sight of Phil, he waved to him to come into the building.

"Miss Carrie, do you have a minute?" Virginia chirped out.

Sarge whispered in Carrie's ear that he would be right back.

Carrie turned and saw that it was Virginia Firth bidding for her attention.

"Hey, Virginia, what's up?"

"I don't mean to pry, well . . . actually, that's a lie—yes, I do." Virginia laughed frankly and swept her shiny, black hair back, took note of how the sun hit it, and continued.

"Did I hear correctly that the very diligent Offica' Phil had cleared Howard McMurphy's name? That's an old, sad story, but folks 'round here rememba' it and it's not small change. By the way," Virginia continued as she watched Phil walk away, "Phil's a fine-lookin' man."

Carrie blushed, but was pleased to get the verbal thumbs up and decided to humor Virginia, especially as Phil definitely *was* a fine-lookin' man.

"Yes, Virginia, I'm happy to say. It came too late for Howard, but he has been declared an innocent man," Carrie replied happily.

"How on earth did that happen?" asked Virginia, willing to be amazed.

"Phil came across some new information in a bunch of old papers written by Patty McMurphy's nanny, or *governess* if you're Miss Theodosia Eden-Worth. Phil pursued several people involved, in one way or another, and learned some new interesting facts. With that new information, affidavits were taken and they provided enough reason for doubt that it encouraged the judge to take another look at the evidence. Victor Abbott had a hand in presenting the new evidence and the discussion with the judge too. If you remember, Victor was straight out of college when Theodosia employed him to defend Howard and he lost the case. Not many people get a chance for a do-over that lets them right a serious wrong. So not only was Howard vindicated, Victor was too."

"What type of infermation?" Virginia said as she clung on to that part of the conversation.

"It's a long story, Virginia," said Carrie, politely cutting off the conversation.

Carrie stood on her toes trying to see where Phil had gotten off to. The crowd was growing fast, like a herd of animals at feeding time. Carrie knew that regardless of what she told Virginia, within an hour Virginia would know how the whole business went down. An hour after that, the rest of Pheasant Mill would too. Carrie was okay with that. The young weaver was proud of the part she had played.

"But when did this all happen?" asked Virginia.

"Just found out, so it's hot off the press," Carrie replied. "Now go on, Virginia, get it going. Disseminate. Time's a'wastin' and the whole town's waiting on you," Carrie laughed, knowing that Virginia was shameless, and if she was the first to get hold of a smoking gun, she served it up hot. Virginia tossed her hair and sailed about.

Carrie just smiled, then looked around some more and saw Phil standing on the platform next to Victor and Tony. The judge's secretary made a short announcement that the Honorable Judge Ecklestine would be out shortly.

The photographers and news media were thick as bees making honey, setting up and making ready to capture the first images of the judge. It was nothing in comparison to when Billy Graham came back to Charlotte. Nevertheless, this event was an important moment for the sleepy town of Pheasant Mills.

As Carrie tried to make her way to the side of the platform, the Honorable Judge Ecklestine was announced. Carrie stopped short to listen to his announcement.

"I want to thank you all for comin' out today for this important announcement. We don't get too many of these in Pheasant Mills, so since I do have some breakin' news on current events, I thought it only right to share with everyone. Let me first introduce Prosecutor Tony Storr and Attorney Victor Abbott along with Sergeant Phil Lament from the Pheasant Mills Police Department. Without these three, this event would neva' be takin' place today."

Phil leaned in and whispered something to the judge.

"What's that? *Oh—OK.* Is there a Miss Carrie Pyles out there somewhere? Miss Pyles?" the judge asked as he looked all around for her, "Would you please come up here and join us?"

Carrie tried to get around the reporters as Phil came down the steps and escorted her up to join them.

"Miss Pyles," the judge acknowledged her.

"Judge Ecklestine . . . sir . . . thank you." Carrie had no idea how to address him and was as nervous as a billy goat in a hot pepper patch.

The judge proceeded to address the findings that these three, he meant four, individuals had put together to exonerate Howard McMurphy from an unjust blame in a crime.

"While Howard McMurphy has long been passed now," the judge advised, "it is neva' too late to right a wrong 'n this county."

The judge even went so far as to say, "Since Howard McMurphy's murder is still an unsolved cold case, perhaps these three . . . excuse me, these four fine people of our community, may learn some new information to end that quandary."

Just as any politician in a grand spotlight situation loved and desired all the attention on them, he made sure to remind the fine people of Pheasant Mills, "To get out an' vote this election year," before he left the platform.

As Tony followed the judge into the courthouse and Victor turned to walk away, the media hurriedly packed up their story. Sarge turned to Carrie and asked, "Are you ready to leave?"

Then he fainted.

**The end of Book 1**

Thank you for reading the first book of the Threads of the Departed Trilogy - Strands.

If you enjoyed this book, I really hope you will do me the favor of leaving a review. You can connect with me at:

www.mabonuso.com
**www.facebook.com/mabonuso**

On the website you will find a list of unique vernacular used in the book along with their descriptions.

For fun, which actors would you imagine to portray characters in the story? (Read my selection)

For your further enjoyment, post pictures and play along:
**Guess the Location of this Cemetery**

There's also a ***Come Ta' Dinner Recipe*** section to include your recipes for good southern cooking. I got the page started with my favorite recipes for:

Sausage with Red-Eye Gravy & Biscuits
Shrimp & Grits

Thank you again for reading Strands the first book in Threads of the Departed Trilogy and please sign into the website to learn about the future release of Unraveled and Frayed.